SHARPENING THE BLADE

BY

FRANK ROCKLAND

A Canadian Expeditionary Force Novel

1916

Other Books by Frank Rockland

Forging the Weapon
A Canadian Expeditionary Force Novel
1914

Who knew? In the fall of 1914, Canadians had earned a reputation as hard-drinking and poorly disciplined troops. No one expected much from them. Certainly not the British! All they wanted was a sharp salute as the men did what they were told.

Prime Minister Sir Robert Borden and his Minister of Militia and Defence, Colonel Sam Hughes, had different ideas. Borden had no choice! When England declared war, Canada was automatically at war too. Hughes, however, was eager to get his boys bloodied before the war was over. He would do anything in his power to get the Canadians into the fight.

As the guns sounded in August, the first contingent gathered at Valcartier. Corps of Guide Captain James Llewellyn had trained for this moment, and he was not about to miss out. Gunner Paul Ryan had volunteered to escape his family and to impress a girl. Nursing Sister Samantha Lonsdale had answered the call because she needed a job, and going to war was an adventure.

As the months rolled by, it was at Valcartier and Salisbury Plain that they helped forge the Canadian Expeditionary Force into one of the most formidable weapons of the First World War.

Hammering the Blade
A Canadian Expeditionary Force Novel
1915

The Canadians are being hammered on two fronts.

On the home front, Sir Robert Borden's government is being rocked by scandals. First it was the soldiers' bad boots, then charges of graft and corruption in the militia department's contracts, followed by the shell crisis. With an election in the air and the opposition pounding his minister of Militia and Defence, Major-General Sam Hughes, Borden is fighting desperately to save his government.

On the western front, after six months of constant harsh training, the CEF finally enter the trenches in France. Infantry Captain Llewellyn struggles to keep his men alive as snipers take their toll, and the Ross rifle fails its first combat test. Nothing prepares him for the chlorine gas attack at Ypres. A frustrated Gunner Paul Ryan watches helplessly as his comrades-in-arms suffer. He can't help, since artillery shells are in short supply. As the battles rage, nursing sister Samantha Lonsdale is nearly overwhelmed as she cares for the sick, the wounded, and the dying.

As the hammer blows fall, the blade is being tempered into cold steel.

Fire on the Hill

What really happened on the night of February 3, 1916, when a fire destroyed the Centre Block of the Canadian Parliament buildings?

Inspector Andrew MacNutt of the Dominion Police's Secret Service, his wife Katherine, and Count Jaggi know, since they were there in the reading room when the fire started.

Ever since the war began, MacNutt has been struggling to secure Canada's borders against acts of sabotage organized by German military attachés based in New York City. The good news is that the Americans have finally ordered them back to Germany. The bad news is that Berlin has sent one of their best operatives, Count Jaggi, to replace them.

Using his cover as a Belgian Relief representative, Count Jaggi visits Ottawa, where he meets and is attracted to Katherine, who is helping him organize a local fundraiser.

Unaware that Inspector MacNutt has intercepted his secret messages and is hot on his trail, Count Jaggi takes a final trip to Ottawa to see Katherine, with tragic consequences.

Author's Note

Sharpening the Blade is a work of fiction. All incidents, dialogue, and characters, with the exception of historical and public figures, are products of the author's imagination and are not to be construed as real.

Where real-life historical or public figures appear, the situations, incidents, and dialogue concerning the person are fictional.

In all aspects, any resemblance to the living or the dead is entirely coincidental.

CHAPTER 1

"Don't bring me any work for the next few days," groaned Sir Robert Borden.

"Yes, Prime Minister," Austin Blount replied as he stood in Borden's bedroom. Borden did not look well. He was lying in his bed with his back propped up by a couple of pillows.

"Lean forward," said the nurse as she slipped a hot water bottle underneath Borden's lower back. Borden moaned and tensed when a back spasm struck. The tension began to ease when the heat from the bottle started taking effect. Since New Year's Eve, Borden had been confined to his bed, unable to move.

"Is your back improving?" Blount asked. He had known Borden for nearly twenty years. First, as Sir Charles Tupper's private secretary, he had dealings with Borden as a freshman MP. Later, when Tupper handed the leadership of the Conservative Party to Borden, he had helped in the transition. He had been with the new leader ever since. Blount felt a moment of regret when he thought of Sir Charles. He had passed away last October and lain in state in Halifax. Tupper had been a great man and was the last Father of Confederation.

"The pain has lessened somewhat. I just can't seem to concentrate. I can barely read more than a few minutes. And after which I can't remember what I was reading."

"What does Dr. Laidlaw have to say?"

Borden pulled his blanket higher before he answered. "He indicated that it was the sciatic nerve giving me trouble. It seems that my liver and kidneys are not functioning properly. The poisons are running through my system. They've been applying hot water bottles and linseed poultices every hour, unceasingly."

"It's what the doctor ordered," stated the nurse, catching Blount's attention. From her bedside manner, she seemed to be efficient. "The doctor also gave me a hypodermic injection for you, which you refused to take."

"It was four in the morning," Borden snapped.

The nurse didn't appear to be fazed by the prime minister's temper. "I'll check on Lady Borden," she said as she sailed out of the room.

"How is Lady Borden?" Blount inquired. The Bordens had vacationed in Atlantic City over the Christmas holidays. It was on their return, when they had a layover in New York City, that Lady Borden was taken ill.

Borden replied with a concerned sigh, "She seems to be better today. Yesterday, she was running a bit of a fever. She's still pretty weak."

"I'm sorry to hear that. Please give Lady Borden my best wishes. I'm sure that her health will improve."

"Thank you, Austin," replied Borden. "How was the New Year's levee?"

Blount hoped Borden didn't notice his expression of dismay. "There was the usual line-up. It ran from his office in the East Block to the gate entrance. Every one of note was in attendance. They all wanted a brief word with the governor general."

"I assume he was in his usual field marshal's uniform."

"Of course," replied Blount. He then reached into his leather satchel and withdrew a note with the governor general's seal on it.

"What's that?"

"It's a note from Colonel Stanton."

Borden grimaced and groaned. Colonel Stanton was the governor general's military secretary. Borden had experienced several unpleasant run-ins with the colonel. "And Doctor Laidlaw has advised me to avoid mental strain. What's he complaining about now?"

"It's about your New Year's message," Blount replied.

Borden blinked at Blount. "As far as I'm aware, my message was well received." It had been published in the newspapers, and he had George Perley, the Canadian high commissioner in London, convey it to the troops. In the message, he had conveyed his sentiments that Canada had been inspired by their bravery, their splendid gallantry, and his confidence that their cause was just and victory was assured.

"It seems that he has been informed the message had not been cleared with the O.C.," Blount said as he handed him the note.

Blount saw the annoyance appear on his leader's face as he read it. He looked up at Blount as he handed the note back to him. "Can you take a message for me?"

"Of course, Prime Minister," he replied as he took one of his note-books out of his briefcase.

"Write down exactly what I'm about to say," Borden ordered, and dictated his response.

Blount winced as he took down what Borden said. He wondered if there was any way that he could clean it up before he delivered the terse message to the governor general's military secretary.

JANUARY 8, 1916
RICHMOND FUSILIERS HEADQUARTERS,
SAINT-JANS-CAPPEL

Major Llewellyn was smoking his pipe outside the Fusiliers' HQ when a staff car drove up. He watched as it parked near Lieutenant-Colonel Tennison's vehicle in the farmhouse's courtyard. A couple of armed NCOs got out of the front while a major, a captain, and a French officer clambered out of the back.

He wasn't particularly happy to see Major Wallace, the paymaster for the Canadian 1st Division, especially since Llewellyn was in a particularly foul mood. That was why he had decided to take a five-minute break. He had spent most of the morning arguing with one of his captains concerning his rank. The Corps, fortunately or unfortunately, had an abundance of senior officers. The problem was that there weren't sufficient slots in the combat regiments for all the captains, majors, and colonels that were available. Llewellyn would gladly have offered the captain a lieutenant's slot. He had a desperate need for lieutenants. That was why he was sending NCOs to the Corps officer training program. The stubborn captain's refusal didn't give him any option but to inform the man that he would be transferring him back to Shorncliffe, the Canadian training depot.

"Looking for me, Major?" Llewellyn asked. Major Wallace was rather young for a paymaster. He was in his late twenties early thirties, with a thin moustache and angular features. Prior to the war, he would have been a lowly lieutenant at his age.

"Yes, I am," he answered. "Do you have a moment?"

"Sure," Llewellyn said. "Come inside."

The Fusiliers had been set up in an old farmhouse about a kilometre from the Saint-Jans-Cappel village. He could see the church steeple above the tree line in the distance. The village was a small one, about nineteen hundred souls. The Fusiliers had been billeted here ever since they were relieved from trench duty the week before.

Llewellyn led them through the main reporting centre, where the NCOs were answering the phones and reading messages, to the small bedroom they had converted into a conference room. There was a battered table in the middle surrounded by six mismatched chairs.

"This isn't about one of my officers' pay, is it?" Llewellyn demanded. He and the major had been going back and forth concerning the pay of one of his officers. One of his other captains was supposed to have been paid as a lieutenant, and they had demanded he repay the difference, nearly eight hundred dollars. They had finally tracked it down to a clerical error that had been made at Valcartier.

"No, not that," the major replied. "I would like to introduce you to Captain Tyrrell. He's replacing Captain Grant, who is being transferred to London. I'm helping familiarize him with his duties. And this is Lieutenant Francois Goulet, our French interpreter."

"Captain, Lieutenant," Llewellyn replied. The captain appeared to be the same age as the major, with a thin frame and sandy brown hair. He had the same pale complexion as Wallace that indicated that he spent most of his time indoors. The French officer was a bit old to be a lieutenant. He was dressed in the standard French uniform. His badge was the image of an Egyptian sphinx that told Llewellyn he was an officer in the French Army's interpreter unit. The unit dated from Napoleon's invasion of Egypt, where he needed interpreters to deal with the locals. The unit had continued this role ever since. Now, it was providing liaison between the Corps and the locals. They interviewed captured German prisoners and translated captured German documents. Llewellyn thought it rather ironic that Hughes's discouragement of French-Canadian recruitment meant they were reliant on the French to supply them with interpreters.

"First, I have received a request from a French farmer who claimed that one of your men damaged his house."

"Yeah." Llewellyn snorted. "It's a bit of a nuisance. It's a case of he said/he said. I had no choice but to forward it to you."

"I'm afraid that Lieutenant Goulet and I could not locate the farmer. Would you happen to know where we may locate him?"

Llewellyn shrugged. "I have no idea. But I'm not surprised. I got the impression he just wanted some quick cash."

Wallace pursed his lips. "We'll leave it in the accounts as a liability. If he doesn't make a subsequent claim, we'll retire it."

"Sounds fine."

"The other matter I need to discuss is that some of your officers have been coming to us for requisitions. I would greatly appreciate it if they would give us an advance warning. When they show up, we don't have the appropriate funds waiting for them. It's been causing delays in dispersing the monies, and it has been difficult keeping our accounts in order."

Llewellyn raised an eyebrow. Captain Tyrell interjected, "We're the ones getting the complaints from the men when they don't get their money on time."

"Well, we can't have that. I'll pass that along in the daily orders," replied Llewellyn with a hint of a smile. "I like to keep the men happy if I can."

"And I would like any of the cheques you currently have returned to us," Wallace stated.

"Why?" asked Llewellyn. "Is there a problem with them?"

"No, no," Wallace said as he waved his hands to reassure him. "We're replacing the current cheques with these new ones." He pulled out a chequebook from his leather satchel and handed it to the major. Llewellyn flipped the book, and judging by the sequence numbers, there appeared to be about a hundred cheques in it. On each cheque, near the blank amount field, was printed *Not to exceed 20 pounds*.

Tyrell said, "These will be more efficient, since your pay people will not have to maintain multiple cheque books." Llewellyn nodded in agreement. The previous leave cheques had preprinted amounts on them from 1 to 20 pounds. It had been a nuisance, since they frequently ran out of the lower-denomination ones.

"What about cash?" Llewellyn asked as he handed the book back to the major.

"We will continue to supply cash. In fact, I have here your weekly allotment," Wallace said as he pulled out several large bundles of French francs from his briefcase and placed it on the desk.

"They are all five francs?" Llewellyn asked as he examined the bundles. The one thing he noticed was the lack of a Colt .45 in Wallace's satchel. He remembered the paymaster major at Valcartier

Camp who had taken one out just before the bank notes came out of his case.

"The men seem to prefer them," remarked Wallace. "We do have a few bundles of fifty francs for the requisition officers. They need them for paying the locals for the supplies they ordered."

"Good, I'll pass them along to my pay people," said Llewellyn. "I was going to ask. Our men have been complaining that they can't seem to exchange their paper francs for silver."

"We have noticed the same thing. We could not find the reasons for the scarcity of silver. I've spoken with the French authorities, but they don't have any ideas why it is happening."

"Are the locals hoarding them?" asked Llewellyn as he turned to the French lieutenant. "What do you think?"

The lieutenant frowned as all three officers turned their heads toward him. He said, "We are a practical people. Some do not trust paper."

"So, if the Germans break through they could use silver rather than paper," stated Llewellyn.

"*Oui, c'est possible*," the lieutenant reluctantly agreed.

"Do they know something that we don't?" asked Wallace with a touch of concern.

"I certainly hope not," replied Llewellyn.

JANUARY 8, 1916
OBSTACLE COURSE, SAINT-JANS-CAPPEL

"Present smoke helmets!" ordered Lieutenant Morley, who was standing in front of the obstacle course. Behind the lieutenant, straw-filled dummies were swaying slightly as they hung from wooden frames.

Sergeant Duval clamped down on a smile that tried to escape. The brigade-major was standing beside the young lieutenant. Neither one would have missed it if he had. Both of them would have wondered why, for different reasons, he was smiling.

Morley was relatively new to the Fusiliers. He had arrived shortly before the New Year from the Bramshott Training Depot. For a change, the young officer knew what the pointy thing at the end of the rifle was used for. In fact, he was a product of the Canadian Officers Training Corps the Department of Militia and Defence had established at McGill

University in 1912. Duval didn't hold it against the twenty-two-year old when he found out the lieutenant was in the Arts program, with a major in History, before he volunteered.

Duval had been pleasantly surprised when he suggested to Morley that it might be a good idea to have the smoke helmets inspected. The lieutenant had been rather hesitant about his suggestion. Morley had taken command of the platoon just a couple of days after it was pulled out of the trenches. He had wanted to get the men to the ranges to sharpen their musketry skills first. Before he dismissed it out of hand, he had actually asked why he made it.

"Well," Duval had said, "The brigade-major is rather fond of snap inspections. What I've heard was that he wasn't very happy with the state of the smoke helmets that he saw with the other sections?"

"I see," said Lieutenant Morley. "You think our section is next?" Duval had answered with a shrug.

"Hmm," the lieutenant had murmured and given him a thoughtful look. He had heard about what had happened with the last officer who displeased the major. Morley had been quite diligent with the trench foot inspections.

It was a good thing they had. Some of the men's tube helmets had cracked or had foggy lenses. Others had dried out to the point that the chemicals the canvas had been dipped in to protect the men from chlorine, sulphur dioxide, nitrous oxide, and other noxious gases were no longer effective. The ones with the problematic lenses had been returned to stores for replacement, while the dried-out ones had been sent to the regiment's chemical officer to get them rebathed with the appropriate protective agents.

The situation wasn't as bad as it seemed, since the men had been issued with two smoke helmets. All thirty men in the platoon had pulled out the ones from the waterproof canvas pouches attached to their webbing, which they were wearing overtop their overcoats. It was January. While not as cold as the Canadian winters that they were used to it, was still cold enough for them to see their breath. They all wore wool caps under their steel helmets, since the metal didn't provide much insulation against the cold.

"And the second one as well, please," the lieutenant instructed.

Sergeant Duval unbuttoned his overcoat and reached into his service jacket. When the first smoke helmets were issued, a problem arose. How could the men carry them so they would be easily accessible during a gas attack alert? The Second Army's solution was a rather obvious one: they simply issued to every man a ten-by-seven-inch cloth patch with two buttons. The patch was to be sewn inside their jackets, on the left side, to create a pocket. The right side already had one; it held their field dressing. The men had gotten busy with their housewives, with a variety of results. For some, the pricked, bleeding fingers from the sewing needles were too much, so they simply hired some of the local women to do the work for a few centimes.

Last October, a new smoke helmet, designated P, had been issued to replace the hypo helmet. The new ones had a goggle-like lens replacing the single rectangular plastic window of the hypos. It also had a mouthpiece to reduce lens fogging when the men breathed. That was one of the reasons the men hated wearing them during bayonet drills. They had been ordered to keep the current hypos as a backup in case there were failures with the new Ps. The latest rumours were that an updated version, the PH helmet, would be issued soon. This meant that the hypos would be permanently removed from service.

When the lieutenant and the major disappeared from the corner of his eye, he could hear the crunching of their footsteps on the frozen ground as they continued their inspection. Major Llewellyn asked someone, "What's the first thing that you do when you hear the gas alarm?"

Duval glanced at the Klaxon horn located on a post near the hanging straw dummies. It was painted grey, and its wood handle crank was much polished from use. There were two other types the Corps used to give the alert of an impending gas attack: the Norwegian foghorn, which was a large box with a crank handle on the side, and the Strombus air horn, which used compressed air to drive the horn. The horns had been strategically placed every four to five hundred feet to ensure once the alarm was sounded, everyone could hear them.

"Put on my tube helmet, sir," replied the private behind him.

Duval tried hard not to laugh, but a chuckle escaped. He could hear a few of the men in the review trying to cough to cover their guffaws.

"Private Simmons, that is not what the major meant," Morley replied angrily. Llewellyn must have waved his objections away, because the lieutenant stopped berating the boy.

"And after you put on your tube helmet?" the major asked. Duval could hear amusement in his tone.

"We empty our rifles toward the enemy trenches," Private Simmons replied.

"The purpose of firing at the enemy trenches?"

"To minimize the impact that the gas will have on our rifles and to discourage the enemy from launching an attack."

"Very good," the major said as his footsteps continued for a few more steps. "Private Reid, is it? I see that you're the telephone operator."

"Yes, sir."

"What are your instructions?"

"Once I've put on my tube helmet, I'm to inform HQ and the sections on my left and right of the attack. Also, I'm to provide the artillery with the coordinates of the trenches that the Germans are using to launch their gas attack so they can bombard them."

"Good, very good," replied Major Llewellyn.

"May I ask a question, sir?" Duval heard the private ask.

Duval could hear Morley suck in his breath before the major said, "You may."

"How do we know when it's safe to remove our tube helmets, sir? My telephone receiver will be under my helmet. The only way to find out if it is safe is to take my helmet off," Reid pointed out.

Duval heard the major's sigh. "I'm afraid that it's the only thing we can do right now. The Second Army has its chemical officers looking at providing some kind of means to determine if the air is clean. Something that will change colour, perhaps. Until they do…" Duval could hear the major's shrug.

He grimaced at the news. It meant that someone would have to be the canary to determine when it was safe for the other men to remove their gas helmets.

JANUARY 9, 1916
DUCHESS OF CONNAUGHT RED CROSS HOSPITAL,
TAPLOW

"Okay, take him to surgery immediately," said Samantha Lonsdale after she had read the tag on the man's left breast. The administration entrance was filling rapidly with the incoming patients. The alert they had received was to expect a hundred and sixty wounded coming in from the Dardanelles.

She felt somewhat out of her element, though not because of the number of patients or the injuries she was seeing. Sadly, that she was quite familiar with. No, the reason for her discomfort was that she had arrived at the hospital only two days earlier. She had received orders from the Nursing Service in London transferring her to Taplow from the Moore Barracks Military Hospital at Shorncliffe.

When she arrived, she had reported to the hospital's CO, Lieutenant-Colonel Correll, and Matron Campbell, to whom she had been assigned. She had been given a brief orientation and a history of the hospital before she started her assignment. She barely had time to send a letter to James to let him know that she had been transferred. She was afraid that his letters would continue to go to Shorncliffe and wondered how long it would be until his correspondence found its way to her.

The hospital itself was located in Cliveden, at the Astor estate. The Astors had offered their home to the War Office as a hospital. The War Office had agreed and asked the Canadian Army to provide the medical staff while the Canadian Red Cross provided equipment and medical supplies. Maintenance was to be paid by the War Office.

She had actually met Lady Astor, briefly, in October 1914 when the first contingent arrived in England. When she and the other nurses had disembarked at Plymouth, Lady Astor was on hand with pans of Devonshire cream for them. She shook her head. It seemed such a long time ago. She had known that they were wealthy, but she didn't realize how wealthy they were until she saw their four-storey mansion with its tennis courts, manicured lawns, and gardens.

The first wards had been built on the tennis courts. Since then, the hospital had expanded to a thousand-bed facility. The building she was standing in was just south of the courts. Its five wards had been built in a butterfly configuration. The walls were half of wood and half glass. The windows ran the full length of the building, giving the patients plenty of light and air.

"Miss! Can I have something for the pain?" asked the corporal she was examining. According to the tag, he had been shot in the chest. He had received medical care at Gibraltar and aboard the medical ship that had transported him. From the tension she could see on his face, he was in great pain. She turned to the tray next to the nurse's station and saw that the morphine supply was rather low. They had a couple of doses left in the small green bottle. She glanced around the room to call an orderly or nursing sister when she spotted two VADs standing near the window, looking rather lost. She beckoned them over. She had met them briefly when the Honourable Clifford Shifton and Lady Minto had come to inspect the hospital.

She had forgotten their names. They hadn't impressed her much. They were the latest crop of upper-class young ladies who had been inspired to volunteer when British nurse Edith Cavell was executed by the Germans last October, to worldwide outrage. Cavell had been a matron at the St. Gilles hospital in Brussels when the war broke out. She had been famous for treating the wounded, Allied and German, equally. The Germans had her arrested for helping British soldiers escape German-occupied Belgium. She was found guilty and sentenced to death by a firing squad.

The brunette Samantha thought might have potential, but she felt the girl with chestnut hair liked the idea of being a VAD but didn't want to do the work. Both of them had the dazed look of being overwhelmed by the hectic activity that swirled in the admitting ward. Normally, Samantha would be tolerant with the trainees. However, the Nursing Service frowned on using the VADs for nursing duties. With one hundred and sixty men coming in and being short-staffed, she didn't have the time or the inclination to coddle them.

"Run to the infirmary and get me more morphine," Samantha ordered. She shifted her attention to the next patient that the stretcher bearers had wheeled in to her left. "Take him to the fifth ward," she stated after reading the medical tag. She turned right to see how the corporal was doing when she bumped into the brunette. "You're still here? What's the problem?"

"We don't know where the dispensary is, ma'am," replied the brunette with a flushed face. In truth, neither did Samantha, but she wasn't about to admit it. Besides, it would be good to test her initiative. "I would suggest you ask someone and be quick about it."

"Yes, Matron," she replied as she curtsied and headed toward the main building. Samantha saw her stop an orderly to ask where the dispensary was. She then walked briskly in the general direction the man had indicated. Samantha then returned to the chestnut girl to figure out what to do with her.

"Have you ever given an injection before?"

"No, ma'am," the girl replied.

"It's about time you learned."

"Now!" she gulped.

"Good a time as any," replied Samantha. She hoped that the girl didn't faint at the sight of blood. That would be all she needed. She lifted a syringe and a green morphine bottle from the tray. She handed it to the VAD, who took it gingerly.

"The standard dosage is ten milligrams. Plunge the needle into the bottle and draw the medicine out until it reaches the mark on the glass." Samantha watched as she complied. "Not too much. Good. Push on the plunger so one or two drops appear on the needle. We want to make sure that there aren't any air bubbles in the syringe."

"If there is?" asked the VAD.

"That would not be a good thing. Now find the vein," Samantha instructed as she took the corporal's arm. She gave him a smile and winked. When he returned her wink, she knew he understood that sometimes you had to throw the raw recruits into the deep end. Despite that, she could feel his arm tense. "Do you see the vein?"

"Yes, Matron."

"Now gently push the needle in and then the plunger."

The man's arm became stiffer when he saw the VAD's hands shaking as she tried to administer the injection. She had to take a couple of pokes before she got the vein. Just as she pushed the plunger, a pan dropped. The loud clang caused her to spasm. The VAD stared in horror when she saw that the needle had snapped in half. The half in the arm was slowly beading drops of blood. "Oh my God! Oh my God!" she yelled in a panic.

"Quit that!" Samantha ordered. It didn't inspire their patient's confidence having attendants panicking over a simple broken needle. Now, if an artery had been severed that would be a different story. To calm the VAD, Samantha ordered, "Go get some forceps."

When she returned, she attempted to hand them to the matron. Samantha shook her head. "You broke it, you fix it."

Samantha watched as the needle was extracted. "Now clean it with antiseptic and put a plaster on it."

"Yes, Matron."

"No more hysterics," Samantha said sternly.

"Yes, ma'am."

With luck, both VADs would be gone by the end of the day, Samantha thought as she watched the girl put a plaster on the corporal's arm. If not, she might find some use for them cleaning bed pans.

CHAPTER 2

"What the hell are you using?" demanded Sergeant Duval. Major Llewellyn turned his head to his left to see a private lying in a prone shooting position nearby. The private was looking up at Sergeant Duval as he was crouching beside him. His binoculars were bouncing gently against the sergeant's chest as he leaned down.

"Why?" asked the private. Llewellyn knew the private's name, Toby Rose, from Innisfil, Ontario. He didn't know much about him since he was new.

"You're missing the fucking target," retorted Duval. "Let me see your ammo."

Rose lifted up slightly as he pulled out a charger from his ammo pouch and handed it to the sergeant.

"Mark sixes," Duval said when he saw the bullets' round shapes. "That figures. Did you zero your rifle for the mark six or the seven?"

"No, Sergeant. I didn't know that I was supposed to do that," Rose said.

Duval's head dipped slightly in disgust. "The six will drop nearly ten inches at two hundred yards. The seven will only drop half that."

"It does?"

"Yes, it does. Didn't you listen during my instructions?" Duval replied curtly. "Never mind! It makes a difference between a miss and a kill."

"I didn't know that. How do I zero my rifle?" the private asked as he looked at the sights on his rifle.

Llewellyn could see Duval clench his jaw for thirty seconds. His face was reddening. "Wait!" Duval went over to a table on which several rifles were laid. He picked up a Lee-Enfield then returned to the prone soldier. "Try this one," Duval said as they exchanged weapons. "Tomorrow's fucking lesson will be on how to fucking zero your rifle."

"Yes, Sergeant," Rose replied as he pushed a charger in the Lee-Enfield's open breech. He then fired five slow rounds.

Peering through the binoculars, Duval grunted, "That's a little bit better. And I mean a little bit." Rose accepted the faint praise stoically.

Duval then moved the lens slightly and examined the major's paper target. He smiled. "Good shooting, Major."

"Thanks," replied the major as he affectionately patted his Ross.

"I told you it makes a great sniper rifle," Duval said.

Major Llewellyn chuckled. The Canadian Corps was slowly, too slowly for some, phasing out the Ross. One advantage the Ross had over the Lee-Enfield was its long-range accuracy. A competent shooter could hit a target at six hundred yards.

"Do you want to try one with a scope?"

"Sure," replied the major. He pulled the bolt back and locked it into place, indicating that it was empty and safe. He then rose to his feet and followed Duval back to the table.

He felt the wind pick up. He glanced at the tops of the surrounding poplar trees to gauge how strong it was, since it would affect a bullet's long-range trajectory. The trees that normally hid the small hamlets that surrounded the five-hundred-foot-tall hill they called Mont des Cats were denuded. The wind buffeted what remained of an old windmill. Above the frozen broken fan blades was a medieval abbey perched on the summit. It was currently being used as a military hospital.

"The wind is pushing towards the southwest," remarked Duval.

"Yeah," replied the major. "What do you have for me?"

"Take your pick," Duval said, pointing to two Rosses with attached telescopic sights.

"Nice," said Llewellyn as he picked up the first one with a long, thin blackened steel tube.

"That one has the Winchester A5 scope," said Duval.

Llewellyn raised the rifle, pointing it downrange. The sight was mounted on the left side. That allowed him to use the Ross's standard sights and chargers. When he peered through the lens, the target jumped out at him. When he made an adjustment, the image sharpened.

"What's the magnification?"

"Five."

"And this one?" Llewellyn said as he replaced the rifle on the table and picked up the second one. The sight was a black, boxy affair with two knobs and a rubber eyepiece.

"This has a prismatic Warner & Swasey sight. It has a slightly better magnification, nearly six."

"It's heavy," said Llewellyn as he raised it to his eye.

"It adds two pounds to the rifle. It also has wind and elevation knobs. The shooter will need to rest it on sandbags for accuracy."

Llewellyn hefted it for a moment then said, "I see you have some Lee-Enfields."

"Yeah," Duval replied in a noncommittal tone.

"How's the instruction coming along?" Llewellyn asked, changing the subject.

"Major, that was a dirty trick."

"What dirty trick?"

"Volunteering me for the job."

"You were pretty handy with that Ross of yours."

"Thanks for the babysitting job."

"Ah." Llewellyn nodded in understanding. "The students?"

"Yeah, the students."

"The same old."

"Yeah! Half the students can't pass the basic target shooting test, since most of their rifles and sights aren't set correctly. And they don't even know how to do it."

"I see," replied Llewellyn. The Canadian Corps had set up the sniper school to help train men to counter the effectiveness of the German snipers. The corps had some excellent sharpshooters, but the quality varied from unit to unit. The intent of the course was to standardize a basic syllabus, identify the best skilled men, and train them with the skills that corps desperately needed.

"We're not getting the more experienced men volunteering," Duval pointed out.

"I can fix that," replied Llewellyn. "At least with the Richmond Fusiliers." The more experienced men didn't feel they needed additional training, since they already knew how to shoot. There was more to being a sniper than that — a lot more.

"What's the syllabus for the next few days?"

"Most of tomorrow will be teaching them to zero their rifles. After that, compensating for windage and elevation, concealment, stalking, map reading, and observation."

"Sounds good," replied the major.

"Well, then you better get your butt back down to it," Duval ordered. He then added, "Sir."

"Yes, Sergeant," Llewellyn replied with a grin.

"Ryan! Paul Ryan!" yelled the burly MP as he jangled a set of iron keys set in a large ring.

"Yeah," Paul replied from the back of the crowded cell.

"You're being released," the MP said as he turned the key and opened the cell door. A second guard, just as large but older, with white hair, had taken a wary position near the door. He was slapping a wooden truncheon into his hand, signalling to the rest of the inmates if they tried something it would make his day.

"It's about bloody time," Paul muttered as he pushed his way to the door.

The cell was overcrowded with Brits, Australians, and Canadians who had run afoul of the military police while on leave in London. Most of them were being held on minor charges such as breaches of the uniform regulations, AWOL, brawling, and public drunkenness. Those who were charged with serious crimes were held in different cells.

"When the hell am I getting out?" slurred a British Tommy who still hadn't slept off the previous night's bingeing.

"When you're sober or hell freezes over!" retorted the MP as he relocked the cell door.

The MP led Paul down the corridor to the release desk. The Metropolitan London Police were sharing the station with the British Army's Military Police. The station's cells temporarily held the men until they were, depending on the charges, transported to their units for trial and punishment.

At the front desk sat a Metropolitan Police staff sergeant who looked like he wanted to go home to rest his tired posterior.

"Lieutenant Paul Ryan, Canadian Corps?" he said as he stared at him with flat eyes. "You're free to go." He indicated the exit with one of his hands.

Paul stared at the sergeant, the MPs, and the door. He was warring inside as to whether he should lodge a complaint about his treatment. After all, he hadn't done anything wrong, and they had ruined the ten-day leave Major Masterley had finally managed to get for him. It had been a reward for the hard work he had been putting in before he was to report to the new mortar units the Canadian Corps was forming.

When the major had handed him the pass, he said with a grin, "It might be time to get your ashes hauled."

After that, he didn't have much time to get ready, since he needed to contact the paymaster to request leave pay. He had an anxious two days until it was authorized and he got his hands on the fifty francs, the maximum they were allowed to hand over in cash. He also got a cheque for twenty pounds, which he could take to the Bank of Montreal in London. Once he had gotten the money, he hustled to the G.S. wagon that was making its weekly run to the train station at Abeele. The cobblestone road rattled his tailbone, although he had set his ass on his kit bag. He had taken the afternoon train to Le Havre and made the ferry to Folkestone in plenty of time, but he had to sit anxiously at the train station for several hours as they loaded the wounded onto the ambulance trains. The casualties took priority over all other traffic.

It was dark when he got to Waterloo Station in central London. The station had an eerie feel, since London was blacked out because of the Zeppelin raids. Light was provided by the luggage handlers and railway personnel using lanterns and torches to show the disembarking troops their way to the exits. Most were like him, on leave, anxious to enjoy what London had to offer to men with cash in their pockets. He had passed troops going the other way. From what he could tell, most of them had looked exhausted from having too much of a good time. Some of them looked tense and sombre, since they knew what they were facing when they returned to the front.

He had been concerned when he discovered how large the train station was. It was actually three stations: North, Central, and South. He had asked Maggie to meet him at the front entrance so they could spend the week together. It was nearly a year since he had last seen her at her family's farm near Salisbury Plain. He had been pleased that she accepted when he sent her a gram asking her if she would join him. He remembered from their talks that she wanted to visit London to see the sights and visit her aunt.

He had an itinerary planned for the week, with visits to London's tourist attractions and theatres. It hadn't taken long at the train station for the MPs to start giving him the eye. He didn't know how long he would have had before he would be asked to move it along. He was concerned about the discolouration from where his sergeant stripes used to be on his sleeves, but in the poor light he hoped no one would notice.

18

Paul had become really concerned when an MP stationed himself directly in front of him but was relieved when in the early morning light he finally spotted Maggie enter the train station from the street. She was dressed in a tweed jacket and ankle-length skirt. Her outfit had been topped by a beige hat trimmed with cloth flowers. He should have known that his leave would not go well, since it had started on the wrong foot.

"Where have you been?" she exclaimed when she finally spotted him.

"I'm sorry," he answered in chagrin. "I didn't realize how big the station was."

"Humph," she said. Paul could see that she was about to continue a complaint when she decided to put on a happy face.

"Did you find your aunt's place?" he asked.

"I did. She's in East London. She has a small flat with my uncle and my two cousins."

"I see," Paul said. He had hoped he could have stayed with her, but it didn't sound like there would be room. He had noticed she didn't offer to put him up. He then put on a brave face. "So, what do you want to do today?"

On the first day, they saw Buckingham Palace, Westminster, and the House of Commons. They lunched, which was expensive and not very tasty, at one of the eateries they found nearby. It was late afternoon when he finally dropped her off at the Tube station so she could get to her aunt's place before curfew. He tried several hotels in Central London, but they were all booked up.

He had heard of the Maple Leaf Room, which offered Canadian soldiers a place to eat and sleep at reasonable prices. He was heading in that direction when he spotted a London Bobby salute a Rolls-Royce Silver Ghost. As he admired the car's lines, he recognized the badge that was bolted to the grill.

When he caught up to the Bobby, he asked, "Excuse me, Officer, can you direct me to the Royal Automobile Club?"

The Bobby had looked him up and down and finally told him with an amused smile, "Of course, sir." Paul had him repeat the directions several times before he memorized it.

When he arrived at the club, they were starting to turn off the street lamps on Pall Mall. He estimated the building's frontage was nearly two hundred and thirty feet and three storeys high. It occupied most of the block. From what he could tell of the club's exterior, it was built using a late French Renaissance style and the brick work seemed to be quite fresh. He would later find out the edifice had been completed five years earlier.

He was anxious when he approached the doorman with his kit bag, but once he had given his name, he was allowed to enter. He tried to appear confident as he made his way to the rotunda. He had to salute a colonel, two brigadier-generals, and a major-general as he took the wide steps that were flanked by smooth stone columns protected by potted plants. Once in the rotunda, he had to stand on the plush rug to gaze up to the glass ceiling that the Grecian columns were holding up. He was impressed. He was a bit nervous when the club steward approached him. For once, he was thankful that his father had insisted he attend the meetings and social gatherings at the St. James Club in Montreal, so he knew the appropriate way to behave. From what he knew of the Royal Automobile Club's history, it had been formed in 1897 by members interested in the new-fangled automobile. In 1907, King Edward VII, who also had a keen interest in motoring, decreed that the club could use the "Royal" prefix. When Paul's father visited London, he had stayed at the club and informed him he had been impressed by the facilities. He had told Paul about the building's 107 bedrooms, its Turkish bath, its swimming pool, its billiards room, its library, and its gymnasium. It even had a rifle range. Plus, it also had amenities such as committee rooms, reading rooms, and several restaurants.

"Can I be of assistance, sir?" the steward asked with a raised eyebrow.

"Of course, sir," he answered. "I'm in London on a ten-day leave, and I was hopeful the club could accommodate me?"

The steward's eyes hadn't moved, but Paul was certain that he was examining his uniform and had not failed to notice the lieutenant's stars on his collar and the discolouration on his sleeves. Paul had heard the club extended its membership to the senior officers of the Canadian Corps.

"My father, Mike Ryan, is a member of the St. James Club in Montreal," Paul said. When the steward's eyes flickered, he continued, "I believe he has made arrangements for me. He said that I could find accommodations here when I'm in London."

"Of course, sir. If you would give a moment, I will see what I can do."

"Sure," Paul replied. He knew that the steward would be verifying his story. When he had left Quebec in October of 1914, his father had told him of the arrangements that he made for Paul with the Royal Automobile Club. If he were in London, he would have a place to stay, and his father would take care of his bills, if they were reasonable.

A few moments later, the steward reappeared. It was difficult to tell, but he seemed somewhat warmer. "We are fortunate that a room is available. One of our staff will take you to your quarters."

"If I may, can you recommend a tailor? I have need of a new uniform."

"Of course," the man replied with a slight cock of his head. "There are several that we would be glad to recommend."

The room he was shown was rather small, but didn't notice, since he was mesmerized by the bed. It was so soft and clean. He would have been lying if he said that he had fallen asleep as soon as his head hit the pillow. After he had taken a bath, he slid naked into the sheets. The bed was so comfortable that he spent a half-hour luxuriating in the sheets before he fell asleep.

He awakened late the next morning, but he was grateful that the club's staff had already washed and ironed his uniform. He barely had time to eat breakfast at one of the restaurants before he headed out to catch the Tube to Maggie's aunt's place in the East End.

It was nearly noon when he knocked on the flat's door. The building was old, but the owner and the tenants seemed to be maintaining the building well. It had a respectable air. He knew right away that the woman who opened the door was related to Maggie's mom. She had the same crinkled hair and suspicious look in her eyes. "So you're Maggie's young man?" she said dryly.

"Yes, ma'am," he replied as he handed her a kraft bag. "For you, ma'am."

Ryan had purchased several small items as house gifts. In the sack, there was a tin of Earl Grey, but most importantly, there was a box of sugar. As the result of food shortages, the British government was beginning to impose rationing. To buy sugar, you had to also buy tea. For the working class, it was a dilemma. They had the cash to buy one or the other, but not both at the same time. When he saw her smile, he knew that he was in.

Maggie looked lovely when she finally entered the small kitchen with her hair down. Her aunt shook her head when she saw them staring at each other. "What are your plans for the day?"

Paul pulled out a London guidebook from his pocket and put it on the table. "I was thinking of starting on page one."

That was what he and Maggie did for the next few days as they crossed off as many sights as they could during the day such as Trafalgar Square, the Tower, the British Museum, and Kew Gardens. He managed to find time to browse the local bookstores, where he snagged several Sherlock Holmes novels. Inspired, he tried to find 221B Baker Street, but the street numbers didn't seem to run that high. He never did find the time to go to the tailor, which he would regret. In between, he managed to steal a few kisses from Maggie.

On the fifth night, he took her to the Hippodrome to see the musical review *Joyland*. Maggie appeared to be enjoying the show. She didn't seem to mind when he put his arm around her. She snuggled closer. He was hopeful that they would progress to the next level. They were holding hands when they tried to leave the theatre.

Paul was wondering why the lines were so slow until he saw the MPs stationed at the exits. They were checking all the soldiers' passes. He had been warned when he left France that he needed to keep his pass on his person at all times. When he reached the young MP, he handed his over before being asked. The MP glanced at the pass then at his uniform.

"Canadian?" the MP stated.

"Yes."

He grabbed Paul's arm and rotated it so he could examine the cloth. "Promotion from sergeant to lieutenant has been rather quick," he said with a bit of derision.

Paul was at a loss as what to say. "If you say so." What else could he have said? He had been promoted because a lot of officers got themselves killed? Paul glanced at Maggie. She was wringing her handbag nervously.

"Where are you staying?"

Paul didn't want to say, but he felt he didn't have a choice. "The Royal Automobile Club."

That raised the MP's eyebrows. He then glanced at Maggie and asked, "Who's she?"

"Maggie O'Brian. She's my girlfriend."

"She's staying with you?"

22

Paul shook his head. "No, with her aunt. In the East End."

He eyed her up and down and then dismissed her. "Right. We're taking you in."

"What for?" demanded Ryan.

"First for being an imposter," the MP replied. "We're getting a lot of men impersonating officers. And I think this is a fake pass."

"But I'm not an imposter," he protested. "Maggie can vouch for me. And my pass is good."

"A trollop's word," he sneered. "We've arrested a bunch of you Canadians with fake passes. Some of them were pretty good. Now, let's go! If you're a civilian, the Metropolitan Police will take care of you. If you're military, we'll send you back to your unit for court martial and sentencing."

"How's my girlfriend going to get home?" he demanded.

"I'm sure that she'll manage," the MP said dismissively.

Now, Paul gritted his teeth as he stared at the desk sergeant and held back a sharp remark. He didn't want to say something that could cause him to be tossed back into the hoosegow. He turned and headed for the door. He hoped that Maggie was still in town, but then he only had about a day's leave left before he had to head back to France.

JANUARY 22, 1916
BOMBER TRAINING SCHOOL, SAINT-JANS-CAPPEL

"Holy shit!" someone yelled as a lieutenant-colonel fumbled the sputtering grenade from which he had just pulled the pin. It finally fell to the bottom of the trench with a loud thunk. Major Llewellyn caught a glimpse of the man's horror as he scrambled out of the trench to get away from the hapless lieutenant-colonel. He was being hampered by his canvas waistcoat loaded with twelve Mills grenades. Since each one weighed one pound, eleven ounces, it meant he was carrying an extra twenty pounds. Once out of the trench, he threw himself into the slushy snow piled behind the parados. He grunted when he slammed into the ground. For a moment he thought the Mills bombs had crushed the ribs he had previously cracked. He held his head down, waiting for the expected explosion. He counted to seven and then seven again before he slowly raised his helmet to peer into the trench.

There were only two men left in the trench. The lieutenant-colonel appeared to be frozen in the cricket-style grenade-throwing stance they were being taught. His left arm was shoulder-height, pointing at the parapet. He had placed his left foot forward with his weight on his back right foot. His fumbling right hand was at his waist, pointing down. Beside him, bending down to pick up the grenade, was the instructor Sergeant McConnell. He was younger by two decades.

"Do you think what you're doing is wise, Sergeant?" asked the major. "There are proper procedures for unexploded ordnance."

The sergeant snorted through his walrus moustache. "It's a dummy grenade. The ammonal has been removed." Without the ammonal, the grenade's fuse would not be enough to shatter the bomb's iron pineapple casing to turn it into deadly shrapnel.

"What!" demanded the lieutenant-colonel with bulging brown eyes.

The sergeant said matter-of-factly, "It's standard procedure before giving you a live one. We don't want you to drop a live Mills." He then added, "Safety first!"

The major doubted much of that statement. Even without the ammonal, the grenade's fuse could cost someone a hand or a finger. It was true, however, that the lieutenant-colonel had nervously dropped it after he pulled the pin.

"Okay, everyone get back down here and let's try it again," the sergeant said crisply. The nine officers scrambled gingerly back into the trench. Llewellyn felt his knees buckle slightly when he landed because of the additional weight.

The sergeant didn't seem to be fazed that the lowest-ranked officer in his class was a captain, while the highest ranked was the aforementioned lieutenant-colonel. It was the sergeant's job to run them through the ten-day bomber training course that Corps HQ had ordered all senior officers must attend. The classroom classes were run by the bomber school's CO, a Major Tye.

Since November, the Corps had been creating a specialized bomber company in each battalion. A lieutenant led the company, and he had a sergeant and four corporals under him. The company was then divided into four seven-man platoons. Two men in each one had two bayonet men to protect the two bombers. The other three men were carriers who kept the bombers supplied with Mills grenades.

They had been training in the basic attack and defence tactics. The attack was actually very simple. Each man carried waistcoats loaded with twelve Mills bombs. The only ones carrying rifles were the bayonet men and the NCOs. Since he was currently assigned as a carrier, he was only armed with a knobkerrie that he had slipped into his bayonet holder. The knobkerrie was essentially a wooden club with a metal cup with studs. It was quite effective in bashing enemy heads. His job was to keep the bomb throwers supplied with grenades. He would have preferred to use the canvas buckets to carry them. It was easier and a lot less painful simply dropping the bucket if he needed to hit the dirt.

What was more complex was in the defence. The bombers were usually stationed in the second line instead of the frontline. If the frontline trenches were ever overrun by the Huns, the bombers would use their grenades to clear the enemy from them. To do this, he needed to create bomb dumps of fifteen hundred grenades to keep them sufficiently supplied. A further two thousand were kept in reserve at battalion HQ.

He knew when he got back to the Fusiliers, the fatigue parties weren't going to be happy with him. It seemed humidity caused the bombs to deteriorate. He shouldn't have been surprised. Water was a blessing and a curse. Ideally, the grenades were to be stored in a building, but at the front, buildings were frequently artillery targets. Hence, dumps had to be dug underground with wooden floors and walls to keep the grenades dry. Oh, the joy.

"Now gentlemen," said the sergeant as he took a Mills bomb from the live grenade box. "Who'll be first to try it?"

Llewellyn waited a couple of moments before he raised his hand, since no one else had. He didn't mind. He actually enjoyed things that went boom.

JANUARY 26, 1916
RICHMOND FUSILIERS HEADQUARTERS, SAINT-JANS-CAPPEL

Major Llewellyn found Lieutenant-Colonel Tennison sitting outside the Richmond Fusiliers' HQ smoking his pipe. He was reading reports as he leaned back against the farmhouse's whitewashed wall that showed shrapnel scarring. They had set up their headquarters there while they were in the rear rest area. The locals considered the building relatively new, since it was only forty years old. The nice thing about it was its modern amenities.

When Tennison saw Llewellyn, he used his pipe to point in the general direction of the billets. "Anything I should know about?"

"I'm afraid so," the major replied after he saluted his CO. "We lost two men to carbon monoxide poisoning this morning."

A hint of pain flickered across lieutenant-colonel's face. "Add that to the two men we lost last week to the fire, and we're losing more men to accidents and sickness than we are to enemy action."

"I know," replied Llewellyn. The two men had died when they neglected to open the windows while using a coal heater. He was the one who had to compile the weekly returns on the number of Fusiliers available for operations. He also had to prepare the reports on the men's cause of death and what corrective measures were being taken. He then had to notify the division's paymasters. The government had this thing about keeping dead men on the payroll. The men's belongings were then collected, packed, and shipped to their families, along with a condolence letter explaining the circumstances of their deaths. They were becoming quite standard now, but he liked to add a couple of personal touches if he could.

"General Currie at the morning conference asked what steps were being taken to prevent such future incidents. We're not the only ones, I'm afraid."

"There isn't much we can do if the men don't have any common sense," Llewellyn said in exasperation.

Tennison gave him a thin smile. "Well, at least the general was pleased with us for a day or so."

"What was he happy about?"

"We have the lowest rate of trench foot in the Corps."

"Well, that's a bit of good news. Last December he tore a strip off me," replied the major. He still remembered the phone call from Major-General Currie when he found out about the regiment's first cases of trench foot.

Tennison chuckled. "Let the men know but stay on top of them. I don't want it to go to their heads."

"I'll pass the word along."

"Good. Also, Currie asked me to attend the senior officer's course next week at Bailleul."

"Oh?"

"It seems that too many junior officers are being sent on course. They feel that the senior officers could benefit from the lectures and the discussions," Tennison said. From his tone, Llewellyn suspected Tennison thought it was a good idea.

"Who do you want to take off the list?" Llewellyn asked. He was trying to recall the names of the lieutenants he had submitted to Corps HQ.

Tennison waved his hand. "Leave them for now. One more officer will not do any harm. Besides, it will give the subalterns a good impression that old dogs can learn new tricks."

"That they can," Llewellyn agreed.

"I'm putting Major Dawson in charge while I'm gone."

"Yes, Colonel," the major replied. Dawson wasn't his favourite officer, but the lieutenant-colonel was rotating the senior officers through so they could get a taste of command.

"Now, what do you think about the replacements that we are getting from Shorncliffe?" When Llewellyn made a face, that was all he needed to hear. "That bad?"

"We'll have to run them through at least a week, if not two, of basic training before we even consider introducing them to the trench training course. Most of them haven't even fired the Lee-Enfield they've been issued with. They went through training with the Ross."

"I thought that would be the case," said Tennison. For the last several months, the 1st Division had been reequipped with the Lee-Enfield. The problem was that the troops at Shorncliffe were still being trained on the Ross until the Canadian Army's standard rifle was officially replaced. The 3rd Division was just now being converted to the standard Imperial weapon.

"I'm putting them through the range course. It's a good thing we built the damn thing," stated Llewellyn. Near the billeting area, they had built a thirty-yard rifle range where the Fusiliers could practice their musketry, train the replacements, and where the sniper teams could zero their rifles before they relieved the other sniper teams out in No Man's Land.

"Do what you can for them."

"Yes, Colonel."

"Also, Currie mentioned he was happy that we captured those two Germans before we were relieved last week."

"We got the translation back from the documents they were carrying?"

"Yes, the German XV Corps has been replaced between the Ypres–Comines Canal and Hooge by the XIII Corps. It seems most of the regiments of the XIII Corps are from Wurttemberg. They have been transferred in from the eastern front."

"Well, it's good to know whom we're up against when we go back into the line."

"There's that."

"I guess we'll be giving them a warm welcome shortly."

"We'll have to see that we do," the lieutenant-colonel said with a predatory smile.

CHAPTER 3

B orden watched as firemen pulled back from the Victoria Tower. He could see a fire captain arguing with one of the officers of the 77th Battalion. From the arm-waving, he suspected the fire captain needed the officer to move his troops back to safety.

When he lifted his eyes, he saw flames engulfing the Victoria Tower's iron crown. Behind the tower, he could see more flames and black smoke billowing from where the glass roofs of the House of Commons and Senate chambers had already collapsed. It was obvious the fire was eating the tower's support beams, and it looked to him it would soon fall. When it did, it would bury the main entrance to the Centre Block under tons of rubble.

The evening had started off rather uneventful, dull, actually, since he had been in the Green Chamber listening to the debates on the fisheries. The House of Commons was nicknamed the Green Chamber because of its green carpeting. For the same reason, the Senate was called the Red Chamber because it was carpeted in red. Seeing it was rather quiet, he had left the House and gone to his office in the New Wing of the Centre Block to catch up on his correspondence. He used the nearby office when the House was in session in case he was needed on the floor. He had barely started when Phil, one of the House of Commons messengers, burst into his office yelling, "Fire! Prime Minister, there's a fire in the Reading Room."

When he followed Phil into the corridor, he saw smoke pouring out of the Reading Room. Its glass doors were in flames. The Dominion Police and men who had volunteered to help were struggling to get the fire hoses out in an attempt to douse the flames. The spray from the hoses the coughing men held seemed to have little effect. He was quite familiar with the room, since he had used it frequently when he was an MP to read his local papers from his riding. They usually arrived daily, and the most recent ones were hanging on racks ready to be pulled and read on the room's oak tables. He suspected that all the paper in there was fuelling the fire.

"We have to leave, Prime Minister!" his secretary, Boyce, exclaimed, pulling on his arm.

Borden reluctantly agreed. As he turned to go back to his office to get his coat, they stopped him. "We have to go now! There's no time!" they yelled.

The smoke had become so bad that he had no choice. He had to follow Phil into the Centre Block's basement. The route the messenger had taken led them to the Centre Block foyer. The foyer was packed with MPs, staff, pressmen, and visitors. They had been milling about, hoping the fire would be contained. No one wanted to go out into the frigid February temperatures. It wasn't until a series of explosions rattled the windows that the Dominion Police and the firemen's exhortations forced them to get out of the building.

He had been grateful that several men in the crowd were kind enough to lend him a hat and an overcoat to protect him as he made his way across the icy ground to the East Block. One of the first things he did when he entered his office was call Laura to tell her he was okay. She still hadn't recovered fully from the illness that had struck her when they vacationed at Atlantic City last December. He also told her that he needed his spare overcoat and boots. Boyce, he told her, would be along shortly to pick them up.

As he waited for Boyce's return, Commissioner Sherwood had briefed him. His Dominion Police constables were still gathering information, but he was confident the fire was the result of a tragic accident. There was no evidence of German sabotage at this point. Borden knew, despite the lack of evidence, that everyone would be blaming the fire on the Germans.

After Boyce came back with his overcoat and boots, Borden walked out to the central lawn to show the crowd that had come to watch the fire that he was all right. He was pleased Sam had called out the 77th Battalion and had personally led them onto Parliament Hill to help fight the fire and for crowd control.

When he was informed that some of the injured had been taken to the Château Laurier, he went there to visit the survivors. Afterward, he went up to Hazen's room and with Rogers and Reid spent several hours deciding what to do next and what messages they were going to release to the press. They were all in agreement that Parliament had to open as soon as possible.

After his meetings, he went back to the East Block for a final look before he headed home. He knew that he wouldn't get much sleep tonight. He had been hoping that at least the library would be saved, but someone had told him it was now gone.

When the Victoria Tower shifted, he saw the firemen move back hurriedly. Then the unmusical tones were heard as the clock tower's bell crashed through several floors. When it broke through the last floor, it landed in front of the Centre Block's entrance. If anyone had been still in the building, their escape route was now blocked. The bell continued to ring as the debris from the tower fell on it. As the iron crown collapsed inward, the tower clock's hands were frozen at 12:20.

As the smoke cleared, he was grateful there were no bodies to be seen.

FEBRUARY 7, 1916
VICTORIA MEMORIAL MUSEUM, OTTAWA

"I'm amazed," exclaimed the governor general as he stood at the brass railing that was blocking his entrance into the auditorium. By tradition, the Crown was not allowed to step onto the floor of the House of Commons. The Duke of Connaught had come to see how the Public Works Department had transformed the Victoria Memorial Museum, named after his mother, into the new temporary home for the Senate and the House of Commons.

"Deputy-Minister Hunter has done a superb job," Robert Rogers said as he stood beside the khaki-clad governor general.

"Thank you, Minister," Hunter acknowledged with a tired smile. From what the duke could see, the man looked so tired that even his bow tie was drooping.

"You managed to do all this over the weekend?" the duke asked.

"On Friday morning, the priority was to get the auditorium set up for the House of Commons' afternoon session, as requested by the prime minister. We didn't have to worry about getting the Senate ready, since it was suspended for the day. Also, there was still much discussion as to whether or not the new Custom Building on Sussex Street would be more suitable. Once it was settled that we were to use the Victoria Museum, we converted the gallery in the southwest wing into the Senate Chamber. As you have already seen, it's ready for today's afternoon session." They had already visited the new Red Chamber. He was impressed that it had been quickly red carpeted and furnished with thrones for him and his consort. Not only that, they also found a speaker's chair, tables for the Hansard reporters, and chairs for the senators. On the room's walls, they had hung paintings of King George and his consort. "By Friday afternoon, the auditorium was ready for the House," Hunter continued.

"The session was quite brief. Only forty minutes," Rogers added.

The governor general nodded. He had been briefed on the session. It had focused on paying tribute to the victims of the fire. Deputy Speaker Laplante, who also had been a victim that night, had been honoured by having his chair sit empty.

"As you can see, we removed the totem poles from the auditorium. And we also removed all the meteor and fossil exhibits, like we did in the Senate." Some wag had joked that the Senate had replaced one fossil with another. "We then brought in 213 chairs for the House members, tables for the Hansard reporters, and the chair from the Privy Council Chamber for the speaker that you were so kind to provide."

When the duke spotted the three tiers of benches built behind the speaker's chair, he said with a hint of amusement, "I see that the press gallery is ready."

"Yes, Your Excellency," replied Hunger with a sardonic grin.

"If you will come this way, you will be able to view one of the offices that we have constructed for the members," Hunter suggested.

The governor general followed the minister and the deputy minister down the Beaux-Arts style corridor. The building's interior had been intended to complement the interior of the Centre Block that now lay in ruins. Nicknamed the Castle, the museum was at the south end of Metcalfe Street. The exterior was a Scottish Baronial style with Tudor and Gothic influences. It had been constructed as an end piece to the buildings on the Hill. The duke had officially opened the museum in 1911, the same year Borden won his majority. After the opening, a minor problem was discovered when the entrance tower started to list. It was found that the clay under the building was unstable, so they had to reduce the tower by eighty feet to avoid it collapsing. It all could have been averted if the architects had consulted with one of the building's future tenants, the Geological Society of Canada.

As they were passing one of the rooms, the duke asked, "The Post Office is already functioning?"

"Yes, Your Excellency. We managed to salvage some of the equipment from the Centre Block. The Post Office is already directing mail to this address. The staffs have been sorting it and have started delivering mail to the MPs and senators," replied Hunter as he led the governor general to the stairs.

After they had climbed to the second floor, Hunter opened one of the doors. "This is one of the newly constructed MPs' offices. We used Beaver Board for the walls then furnished them with desks and chairs that we have salvaged from the Centre Block. And we've ordered additional furniture from the local firms."

Hunter then pointed to the black candlestick phone on the desk and continued, "All the offices have been equipped with telephones, and all of them are working. As well, we've installed the division bell to call the members to the House for Question Period and for voting."

"All of the members have offices?" asked the duke.

"Yes, we also managed to find space for the Hansard reporters, the speakers, and their staff, and even a press room. We're setting up a reading room as well." When Hunter saw the look on the governor general's face, he quickly added, "We'll make sure that it will be fireproof.

"A barbershop and the Parliamentary Restaurant will be constructed at the old Ashbury College across the street."

"This is most impressive to accomplish this in less than three days," the governor general stated.

"Thank you, Your Excellency," answered Hunter with a pleased look on his face. "We still have a fair amount of work to do."

"Of course; of course," replied the governor general. "If there is anything that my office can do, do not hesitate. We are at your service."

"Thank you, Your Excellency," both Rogers and Hunter replied.

"We do have a problem concerning the Mace," stated Rogers. "I'm sure the speakers of the Senate and the House of Commons have consulted with you concerning the matter. The House used the Senate's Mace for the Friday session. Both the House and the Senate have scheduled their sessions for three o'clock today."

The duke understood the problem. By tradition, the House and the Senate could not conduct business without the Mace being present. The House of Commons Mace had been destroyed during the fire.

Rogers continued, "We have requested a temporary loan of the Ontario legislature's Mace until we can acquire a new one for the House. But it will not be arriving until tomorrow."

"I'm sure we can find a solution," stated the governor general confidently.

"Of course," replied Rogers as he turned and headed down the corridor with the governor general and Hunter trailing him. "Now, I would like to show you what we have done to the third floor of the museum."

CHAPTER 4

Major Llewellyn slammed the phone down so hard that several clerks in the Richmond Fusiliers HQ jerked their heads in his direction, despite their best efforts to studiously avoid looking at him. He had been yelling into the mouthpiece.

"I hope that wasn't Divisional HQ?" asked Lieutenant-Colonel Tennison as he entered the hut.

"Nope, Corps HQ," replied Llewellyn with a touch of chagrin.

"Well, that's different then," Tennison said sarcastically.

"I lost my temper. Stupid staff officers."

Lieutenant-Colonel Tennison raised an eyebrow. Both Tennison and Llewellyn had been attached to Major-General Currie's Divisional HQ as staff officers before being assigned to the Richmond Fusiliers. As Tennison sat on the corner of Llewellyn's desk, he asked, "What did they want?"

"They can't seem to make up their bloody minds," Llewellyn ranted.

"About what?"

"They asked us to send an officer to the officer's course at Bailleul they're running next week. When I got the orders, I sent a reply back saying that all our officers had already gone through it. There's no point in putting our men through the same thing again," Llewellyn said as he waved his hands. "If they were willing, I wanted to send some of our senior NCOs with officer potential to it."

"And?" prompted Tennison.

"I got a phone call from Corps HQ last Friday. I can't remember who it was who wanted to talk to me. When we finished, I was under the impression that everything had been cleared up. I cut orders for Sergeants Ellis, Graham, Bryce, and Kealey to go." Tennison nodded in approval after each man's name.

"Today, I got a gram from Corps demanding we send them officers for the course forthwith." Llewellyn pointed at the phone. "I've spent the last half hour arguing with a jackass colonel at Ballieul."

Tennison winced at the mention that it was a colonel on the other line, then he chuckled. "I suspect I'm going to get a call from HQ about this."

"Colonel sir," a clerk shouted to get Tennison's attention. He held up a telephone receiver. "Corps is on the line."

"I bow to your predictive powers," Llewellyn said with a slight bow.

"I'll be there in a minute," Tennison informed the clerk. The clerk nodded then relayed the info in the receiver.

"What about the meeting?" asked Llewellyn.

"Get it started. I'll be there shortly," Tennison answered.

"Yes, sir," Llewellyn replied as he rose from his chair. He picked up his greatcoat and his forge cap from the coat rack near his desk, and his swagger stick, then exited the Richmond Fusiliers HQ. Their HQ had been set up in a clapboard hut built at Kortepyp Camp. The camp was two miles south of Neuve-Église and was located on a plateau on the south side of the Neuve-Église Hill. Most of the weathered clapboard huts were well-built and spacious.

As he passed the YMCA hut, he saluted several squads who were going out on work parties. Several other squads were heading out to the large grass field nearby. According to the schedule he had prepared, it would be bayonet training. Half the men were replacements from Shorn-cliffe and needed to be retrained. His hand tightened on his swagger stick as he watched the drill line up the men. He hadn't been impressed with the quality he had been receiving. All he could do was complain to Corps HQ and hope they would sort it out.

The guard in front of the meeting hut was saluting the officers as they entered the building. In between, he was chatting with a man in his forties. The man was hunched over as if he had a bad back. There were a number of locals that worked in the camp. They mainly sold locally produced fruits and vegetables to supplement the men's rations and did maintenance services such as laundry and building repairs. They were vetted and given ID cards to allow them entry to conduct business. Normally, someone was supposed to accompany them while they were in the camp.

When the man heard the major's feet crunching on the gravel, he swivelled his head toward him.

"Monsieur Dupont," the major said.

"Major," he replied. The major didn't like the way the man looked at him.

"Here early today?" Llewellyn asked. Normally, he arrived in the morning with hay for the horses.

"*C'est une belle journée,*" he said.

"*Oui,*" the major replied.

"I was looking for Captain Gavin. I was informed he was in a meeting," Dupont said, pointing to the hut.

"Yes, he is," Llewellyn replied tersely. He didn't like the fact that Dupont was curious about the captain.

"*Je comprend.* I'll talk with him *plus tard.*"

"Of course. Private Huff will accompany you back to your wagon," Llewellyn said, pointing to it with his swagger stick.

The private's eyes flicked back and forth between the two men. "Yes, sir."

"*Il n'est pas nécessaire,*" the man protested.

"It's for your safety," the major insisted. "We have a lot of things that go boom."

Realizing that Llewellyn was insistent, he turned away with Private Huff escorting back to his wagon.

Llewellyn watched them for a few moments before he turned to the hut. When he entered it, he found Captain Peter Gavin seated at the far end of the table, flanked by his four lieutenants, Machie, Longfellow, Draws, and Kellogg. Seated behind them in the cramped space were the platoons senior NCOs. When he spotted Sergeant Ellis, he indicated the door with his head. The sergeant knew what he wanted, so he exited the hut to stand guard outside.

The major took one of the empty canvas chairs, leaving the chair at the head of the table empty for Lieutenant-Colonel Tennison. "The colonel will be arriving shortly. Let's begin."

The captain, who was from Charlottetown, PEI, cleared his throat as he ran his hand through his blond brush-cut hair. Gavin was in his early thirties, and his broad shoulders stretched the khaki uniform. He was the 2nd Company's new CO.

The 2nd seemed to have bad luck with its COs. First, Captain Lamb was killed by a sniper when the 1st Division entered the front lines last February. Then his replacement, Captain Jordan, had died at Ypres after being run over by an ambulance. Just before Llewellyn's arrival last November, Captain Gavin became the 2nd Company's CO when the previous captain was killed when a farm building collapsed on him.

Gavin shuffled some of his handwritten notes with stubby fingers then said, "We planned our scheme along the lines that you and the colonel suggested. We have set the tentative day for our minor enterprise for February 15th. My company will raid one hundred yards of German trenches on the night of." Llewellyn nodded in agreement. The rule of thumb was that for every one hundred yards, fifty men were needed. "The main objective of our raid is to knock out their strong point across from the trench at U.2.D.1.4. There are machine guns there we want to take out. The second objective is to grab as many prisoners and documents as we can and get out."

Llewellyn knew the German strong point 450 yards in front of their trench was a pain in the neck. At least knocking it out would give them a bit of reprieve until the Germans rebuilt it.

Gavin looked up at Llewellyn and said, "We decided on the 15th because there will be a full moon. It will give us some light, so we will be able to see what we are doing. We considered the 14th, but since it was Valentine's Day, we didn't want to stop spreading any love beforehand." The captain waited until the men stopped chuckling before continuing. "We've just been rotated out of the trenches, so that will give us a week to train for the raid."

"Where will we be setting up the training?"

"We?" asked Captain Gavin in surprise.

"I'll be joining you on the raid," replied the major with a grin.

"Of course," replied the captain after a pause. "There is an area near the training field that is blocked off from view. It will be suitable for our needs. I've gotten the quartermaster to supply us with stakes and tape so we can mimic the German trenches we will be attacking. We will be coordinating with the artillery so they can pound the trenches to keep the Huns' heads down while we get out."

"What's the current intelligence about the Huns in the trenches? Are they being relieved?" asked the major.

"We believe so. The new units won't be used to their new trench routine. They should be slow to react, and it will be difficult for them to coordinate a defence when we attack."

"Sounds good," replied the major. "We'll keep the company separated from the other men. We don't want word going around. Also, I don't want this operation discussed over the telephone lines or the tele-graph wires. Use the runners or the cyclists to transmit details of our plans," he ordered just as the door to the hut opened.

Lieutenant-Colonel Tennison stepped into the hut and scanned the room. "What did I miss?"

"Just the preliminaries. We are about to go into the details," replied Llewellyn.

"Good," Tennison said as he rubbed his hands. "Let's get to it."

FEBRUARY 15, 1916
DUCHESS OF CONNAUGHT RED CROSS HOSPITAL, TAPLOW

"Damn!" Samantha yelped as the glass plate slid from her fingers. She could hear it shatter on the second bounce on the concrete floor.

"What the hell do you think you're doing?" demanded Woolsworth. "Those plates are expensive!"

"I'm aware of that, Lieutenant!" Samantha said as she glared at the officer. Woolsworth peered at her from around the X-ray stand that he had parked near the wall to make room for the next patient.

She had put an emphasis on the lieutenant's rank. For most of the morning, he had been in a foul mood. He had always been difficult to deal with ever since he arrived from Canada about a month and a half ago. Her mood wasn't any better, since ten nurses had been struck off strength yesterday.

The lieutenant opened his mouth and closed it when he thought better of it. When he finally spoke, it was in a slightly more respectful tone. "Yes, ma'am."

It had taken a moment for him to realize that she outranked him. Also, she suspected her influence with the hospital's CO was part of his calculation. Woolsworth's arrogance was being tolerated, barely, because the surgeons depended more and more on his valuable techni-cal knowledge and skills in the new science of X-ray photography when they operated. But there was a limit.

She crouched to pick up the kraft envelope. She could feel the broken pieces of glass through the two layers of paper that protected the plate from exposure. She had been taking it to the camera so that she could insert it into the cassette for the next patient's X-ray. Thank God it hadn't been one that was already exposed.

"I'll take the box into the darkroom," the lieutenant grunted as he lifted a box of new plates from the nearby bookcase. "I can't wait until we use these up and get a supply of the Eastman dry plates. They are lot lighter, and they don't break when people drop them," he remarked, giving Samantha a cutting glance before he crossed the hall to the next room that had been converted into a darkroom.

Samantha glared at his back. She had been expecting reinforcements for the nurses that had been transferred out, but they weren't scheduled to arrive until tomorrow. So she had agreed to spend the day in radiology because she thought it was a good idea to learn more about the new medical tool. It might have been useful if he bothered to give her proper instructions besides "fetch this" or "fetch that." From the rumours she had heard, the CAMC was looking to create a school of instruction for radiology in the Shorncliffe area. Since it was so new, finding well trained and experienced men was difficult.

X-rays had been discovered about twenty years before, ironically, by a German physicist, Wilhelm Conrad Röntgen. At first, X-rays had been a novelty. Samantha remembered as a child taking a trip to Toronto where some of the photographers were offering X-ray photographs, along with your family portraits. It had taken a while for the medical profession to start using the new technology. The potential was first seen by the military medical officers. They recognized how X-rays would be invaluable in dealing with foreign objects in men's bodies.

"Okay, Gary, we're all set up," she said as she glanced at the orderly who stood ready with the next patient. Gary nodded as he pushed the stretcher into the room. She helped move it into position next to the X-ray couch, although Gary didn't need much help. He was a big man. His size proved to be quite useful.

She glanced at the patient's chart then looked at the burly, bandaged chest covered by a thin white cotton sheet. "Doctor Hasting says he needs a chest photo," she said when the lieutenant returned with a heavy box of cassettes loaded with plates. He grunted as he placed them on the nearby bookshelf.

He snapped his hand out, demanding the chart. Woolsworth studied it to confirm what she said. He took a cassette from the shelf and locked it into place with the sensitive side up.

"This ain't going to hurt?" the patient asked as he looked around the thirty-by twenty-five-foot windowless room. Light came from the fixtures ten feet above them. In the corner sat a transformer with black cables that ran to a switch table that regulated the power and the timing of the X-rays. Down the wall there was a stand housing an array of cathode tubes ready to be used. The tubes were delicate, and spares were constantly needed. Samantha could see he thought he had entered a modern torture chamber.

When Woolsworth grunted a derisive dismissal, the man turned his shorn head to him.

"You'll be fine," Samantha said soothingly.

"Okay, let's get him on the table," ordered Woolsworth. When Gary and Samantha were in position, he said. "One, two, three."

The man groaned and grimaced in pain as they lifted him.

"Are you okay?" Gary asked.

"It couldn't be any worse, I guess," he muttered.

Samantha tapped him gently on the shoulder. "You'll be fine."

As the lieutenant put the cathode tube into position, Gary asked, "Did you hear about your request to be transferred to the front?"

"I don't want to talk about it," growled the lieutenant.

Samantha raised an eyebrow at Gary. He simply shrugged. The lieutenant had been talking enthusiastically about the new mobile X-ray units that the CAMC was acquiring for the front. The plan was to provide two-ton trucks equipped with X-ray machines and darkrooms to the front-line field hospitals and casualty stations. He said a Madame Curie had developed a fleet of X-ray trucks for the French Army. She had no idea who Madame Curie was. Some French aristocrat, she assumed. What was important, Samantha knew from first-hand experience, was that the wounded needed to get the best care as soon possible.

But it also explained why Woolsworth had been short-tempered for most of the morning. Samantha felt another sigh coming. It meant that she and the rest of the hospital staff would have to put up with him until the CO decided it would be best to send him to the front and let the Corps deal with him.

FEBRUARY 15, 1916
MOCK NO MAN'S LAND, SAINT-JANS-CAPPEL

"Shit!" said Major Llewellyn when he heard the loud rattle of tin cans from the barbed wire in front of him. Then he was lit up by electric torches.

"Bang! Bang! You're dead!" said a voice from the trench behind the wire.

"Shit!" said the major again.

"You really should stop getting yourself killed, Major," said the voice again from the trench in front of him. "It's getting to be a bad habit."

Once Llewellyn's night vision returned, he spotted the flash of his CO's grin. Tennison's steel helmet was looking at him from above the trench's sandbags. Beside his CO, there was a soldier wearing a similar grin. The soldier's Lee-Enfield had a torch attached to its underside.

"Yeah, yeah, I know," replied the major as he rose to his feet. He was encased in mud. He had been crawling in the last fifty yards of mud to the barbed wire defence they had built to replicate the German trenches. In actual fact, there was only one strand of barbed wire; the rest of the four lines were rope cords.

The tin cans had surprised him. He hadn't ordered them attached to the fence as an early warning system. He should have thought of it. It was realistic, and it would have had a devastating effect on his attack. It would have resulted in a machine gun cutting him and his men to pieces. He looked to his left and to his right and saw that the raid had collapsed into chaos. One platoon was caught in the middle of the barbed wire with nowhere to go. Another hadn't even made it to the wire.

Lieutenant-Colonel Tennison pulled out a whistle from the loop on his Sam Browne and blew it. A few moments later, the platoon leaders had also blown the signal to halt the attack and gather around.

"That didn't go particularly well," Tennison remarked. The men stared at him rather grimly in response to his understatement. "What happened with the wire cutting?"

"It's these damn wire cutters," groused Private Olsen, who waved a long wooden tool. The man was in his mid-twenties, and his Brodie helmet was pushed back so everyone could see his mud-smeared face. "The wire takes too long to cut. Slows us down, and some tricky bastard added cans to the wire to boot." He gave the major a pointed glance. Major Llewellyn knew he had developed a reputation of being tricky. In this particular case, it wasn't him.

Lieutenant-Colonel Tennison spoke up. "I'm the tricky bastard. You can't depend on the Huns to do what you want when you want them to. The 1st battalion had to cancel a raid the other night because the Huns put out a patrol. The Boche in the trenches were on a high alert, ready for them. I want it clearly understood. I'll postpone the raid if I feel we don't have a good chance of success."

"Yes, Colonel," the men replied.

"Does anyone have any ideas as to how better cut the wire?" asked the lieutenant-colonel.

"We can try ammonal," suggested Major Llewellyn. Ammonal was an explosive made from ammonium nitrate and aluminum powder. The engineers were starting to use it for their mines. When Llewellyn saw the frown on the lieutenant-colonel's face, he continued, "I just finished reading a report from the 2nd and 3rd Field Companies. Their engineers claim that ammonal is quite stable. They've been experimenting with it in cotton tubing, steel, and wrought iron pipes to clear barbed wire. One-inch wrought iron pipes they said work the best. Sixteen feet of pipe can cut ten feet of wire. They also said that the shrapnel from the pipes neatly cut the fencing's wooden support posts."

"That sounds promising," said Tennison with an approving nod. "Let's talk with our engineers and see what they can come up with. I would like to see a test before we put it into effect."

"Yes, Colonel," replied Llewellyn.

Tennison glanced at the men standing around. "Take a ten-minute break. Smoke them if you have them. I would like to have a word with Captain Gavin and the platoon leaders."

"Captain Gavin. Before I ask that the men try it again, I want to make sure that they all know their assigned tasks. I don't want to see such a muddle again."

"Yes, Colonel," replied the captain, who looked chagrined. "I've been pounding CUPS into them. With tonight's foul-up, I'm sure that they will be taking it more seriously."

"I'm glad to hear that," replied the lieutenant-colonel.

The major nodded. CUPS was an acronym for: consolidation, unearthing, protection, and supplies. Once the teams breached the wire and entered the trenches, they were to consolidate their position and establish a temporary supply dump. The unearthing was to check for ammunition caches, dugouts, and wires connected to hidden grenades or mines. The squads had orders to clear the dugouts with grenades. The protection part was to ensure their flanks and rear were covered. They were going to have two potato diggers placed on each flank to provide them with covering machine gun fire.

The signalling for the raid was going to be simple enough. They would be stringing telephone cables to the wire to provide communications to the mortar and artillery teams. They would supplement the cables by runners. Also being drummed into the men were the basic hand signals to indicate when they needed more supplies. All the men had to do was to raise a rifle when they needed ammo or wave a sandbag when they needed more sandbags.

"We still have a timing issue," said Lieutenant Longfellow, the CO of the 3rd Platoon. He was lanky and in his early thirties.

"Yes?" asked the lieutenant-colonel.

"My platoon has an extra fifty yards from our starting point to the German trenches. And we have shell holes that we either have to crawl through or around." Llewellyn nodded in agreement. He knew timing was critical for the raid to be successful. If a platoon was not in the right position at the right time, it could spell disaster.

"What do you suggest?" asked the lieutenant-colonel.

"Give us an extra half hour to get from our trenches to the start line."

"What do you think?" Tennison asked Captain Gavin.

"I agree. We'll need to synchronize our watches. And the flanks can signal me when everyone is ready to go," said Gavin.

"Good." Tennison glanced at the dial on his wristwatch. "We have four more hours before sunrise. Let's see if we can get one more in, shall we?" The lieutenant-colonel's tone indicated that they better get it right this time.

FEBRUARY 18, 1916
PRIME MINISTER'S EAST BLOCK, PARLIAMENT HILL, OTTAWA

"Prime Minister Borden, Prime Minister Hughes has arrived," Blount informed him by telephone. Borden had to admit that it took getting used to hearing the words 'Prime Minister' and 'Hughes' in the same breath. The Hughes Blount was referring to was William Morris Hughes, the prime minister of Australia.

The Australian prime minister had arrived in Vancouver four days earlier, and Borden had a train car waiting for him. The newspapers had been providing him with updates of the speeches Hughes had been making as he travelled across the western part of the Dominion. Upon Hughes's arrival in Ottawa, Borden had sent a card inviting him for an interview in his office.

Borden rose from his desk to greet him when the Australian was ushered in. He was surprised to see that Hughes was a short man; he couldn't be more than five feet five or six, and thin. He was fifty-four years old, with blue eyes, and his hair and moustache were silver grey. Borden knew Hughes had been born in Wales and had emigrated to Australia when he was twenty-two. There, he had spent his first few years living hand-to-mouth before he got involved in the labour movement. He had risen up the ranks to become the president of the Waterside Workers Union. After that, he had entered politics as a member of the Australian Labour Party. He became prime minister last October when Andrew Fisher resigned due to ill health.

"Prime Minister," Borden said as he shook Hughes's hand.

"Prime Minister," replied Hughes.

"My, we're being formal. Why don't I call you Robert, and you can call me Billy," Hughes said with a grin.

"Please have a seat, Billy," Borden said with a smile as he indicated the comfortable red and gold floral couch in his office. "Were your travels comfortable?"

"Quite comfortable. Thank you, Robert, for the rail car you provided. It was much appreciated," replied Hughes as he adjusted his hearing aid. The black four-inch Acousticon microphone was clipped to the outside of Hughes's breast pocket. Two wires ran down to his jacket's waist pocket where Borden assumed the battery was. Two thin wires ran up to a black earpiece being held in place by a thin metal headband. Borden had been informed that the Australian was going deaf. He also had been told that if Hughes didn't like what he was hearing, he would turn the device off.

"First, I would like to apologize that our meeting will be brief. I, unfortunately, have to be in the House for Question Period."

"I understand perfectly," replied Hughes. "My train isn't due to leave for New York until the 22nd, so I'm sure we'll have plenty of time for further discussions." Billy Hughes was travelling to Great Britain for a six-month stay to meet with the Imperial government and to visit the Anzac Corps in France.

"Normally, it would have been a few minutes walk to the Centre Block. With the House set up in temporary quarters at the Victoria Museum, it takes a bit longer."

"I've seen the remains of your Centre Block when I came on to the Hill. I would have liked to have seen it before it was so severely damaged by the fire. I've been informed it was once a magnificent building," Hughes said in a sympathetic tone. "Has the cause of the fire been determined?"

"We've appointed a Royal Commission to examine the matter. Commissioner Sherwood, the head of our Dominion Police, believes it was a tragic accident. Others believe it was German sabotage," Borden replied.

"That is unfortunate. I was looking forward to viewing your legislature. So what are your plans now?"

"We're hoping we can reconstruct the old building. I've been told we can, since most of the building's materials are salvageable. Our public works department is looking after it," Borden replied. "I've been told you have plans to build a new legislature building in your new capital, Canberra?" Borden knew Canberra had been chosen as Australia's new capital as a political compromise, since no one could decide between Sydney or Melbourne. Hughes had broken ground for the new city three years ago.

"That's true," replied Hughes. "But we had to cancel the project when the war started. When I get back to Australia, I'll have to see that it gets started again."

"From the preliminary estimates, it will take us four to five years to complete," Borden stated.

"The same for us, I suspect," replied Hughes.

Borden nodded. "One of the reasons I wanted to talk with you briefly today was … would you do me the honour of accepting an appointment to my Privy Council?"

Hughes's eyes widened in surprise. "I would be honoured."

Borden beamed. He had been fairly certain Hughes would accept, but one could never be certain. He had wanted to treat Billy Hughes as a visiting head of state and to honour him. More important for him, though, was that he wanted the Australian prime minister to address his Privy Council. To do so, Hughes needed to be sworn in, since all Privy Council meetings were secret, and no records were kept of its discussions. "A Privy Council meeting is being held tomorrow at ten thirty. If you're agreeable, I would like you to attend after being sworn in by the governor general."

"I would be honoured," Hughes said. "We have much to discuss. I would like to brief your cabinet on my country's war efforts. And I have some thoughts concerning our relationship with the Imperial government and trade policy. I think we have much in common. I also want to touch on our concerns about the future of Japan and its navy after the war has been concluded."

"That is agreeable. I believe we have many of the same concerns," replied Borden. He was beginning to like the Australian.

"I have to warn you. I'm going to do my best to convince you to attend the Paris Economic conference," Hughes said with a grin, confirming his reputation as a wily politician and debater.

Borden leaned back into the couch and laid his hands on his lap. He had wanted to attend the conference that was being held in June. All the Allied countries had been invited to discuss economic sanctions against Germany and Austria. "I'm afraid that it's not currently feasible." He paused then said with an airy wave of his right hand, "I have to warn you, I'm quite a debater myself."

FEBRUARY 22, 1916
GERMAN TRENCH, SAINT-JANS-CAPPEL

It felt rather unsportsmanlike when Major Llewellyn put a knife into the German's back. The feeling didn't last long. He had a hand clamped on the man's mouth to muffle any cries that might alert his companions. Llewellyn grimaced when he felt the knife grate along the ribs until it finally entered the man's heart. The man stopped struggling beneath him. He gave the shadowy moonlit German trench about twenty to thirty yards away a glance. So far, there was no indication that anyone in the trench had heard the death throes of the patrol he and his men had just wiped out.

He returned his gaze to the man underneath him. It had been his first kill. Rather, it had been his first kill with a trench knife. He had killed Germans before, using the Ross, the Lee-Enfield, like the one strapped to his back, jam tins, and Mills grenades. This was different. It had been up close and personal. He had no choice, since his team had the bad luck to run into a Hun patrol just minutes before the Richmond Fusiliers were ready to launch their raid.

He had been surprised that the Germans sent out a patrol. He guessed the new Hun unit that had been rotated in hadn't believed or

47

weren't intimidated by the reputation the Canadians were making in No Man's Land. The reports from the listening posts (Llewellyn had insisted they were staffed with men who spoke or understood German) had indicated that their "Silent Death" tactic was making the Huns rather nervous and jumpy. The lowly German *Jägers* were starting to speak of the Canadians with a touch of fear and awe. With good reason. The Fusiliers had become adept at eliminating the Boche patrols quietly and without leaving a trace.

Well, thought Llewellyn, *after tonight they'll be taught another lesson.*

He eyed Sergeant Ellis, whose mud-smeared face was broken by a white, toothy grin of approval. Not everyone had the stomach to get up close and personal. Sure, there were plenty who had no qualms about putting a bullet into a man, at a distance. But a knife at close quarters was different. Many couldn't do it.

A slight movement to his left caught his attention. He saw a shadow reach up near one of the fence posts that supported the barbed wire. There was no coiled wire in this section; that was why it was chosen. The shadow paused, then pushed the wire aside and crawled a few feet, and then paused. Llewellyn knew the wire cutter was listening for activity in the German trench. Llewellyn was trying to decide whether or not to call off the attack. Contingencies had been planned if the Germans were on high alert or if they ran into something unexpected. The shadow got to the second line of wire, and several others appeared behind him. They followed him through the gap that the wire cutter had created. He knew that the rest of the company was getting into position. He couldn't see far in the moonlight; the craters and dips in the terrain provided excellent cover.

He signalled to the sergeant to move forward. He acknowledged and passed the order to the rest of the ten-man squad assigned to protect the assault's right flank. The major had wanted to be with the teams going into the trenches, but Lieutenant-Colonel Tennison vetoed that. It was bad enough he had his brigade-major on the raid. There was no point adding more risk than absolutely necessary. Let Captain Gavin and his men do the jobs that Llewellyn had trained them to do.

It took Llewellyn ten minutes to get to the assigned spot about twenty yards south of the suspected machine gun nest. The squad was setting up the Colt. They were quietly digging a small hole under the gun to allow room for the potato digger to operate. If mud got caught in the mechanism, the gun would jam. Beside him was Signaller Private Thompson with his telegrapher and a nearly empty wooden spool. Black telephone wire trailed back to the Fusiliers' trenches.

They had barely set up when they heard the familiar crack of Lee-Enfields on the north side of the strong point. He could hear yelling, screaming, and cursing in English and German. The bright flash of a grenade going off in the trench nearly blinded the major, since he was caught off guard. It took several minutes for his night vision to return. Even after it had, there was a blurry spot in the centre of his vision. He hoped the rest of the men hadn't suffered the same fate.

He turned his wrist and had to stare around the blurry spot to see the luminous dial of his watch. The raid had started on time. The Fusiliers would be in the German trenches for twenty minutes. The signal that they were on their way out was a green flare just after they destroyed the strong point where the machine guns were supposed to be. He tried to follow the battle. The muffled grenade sounds, he suspected, were the ones being tossed into the dugouts to clear them.

It was at the fifteen-minute mark that he put his hand on the signaller's shoulder. The private readied the telegrapher to transmit the GO code to Lieutenant Ryan and his 18-pounders. It was on the twenty-minute mark that the top of the machine post got raised by a couple feet by explosive force. It settled slightly, with dust and smoke coming out of the gun slits.

When he spotted the green Very flare Captain Gavin fired to indicate they were out, he tapped the signaller's shoulder twice. Llewellyn heard telegraph clicks as he sent the message. The wait for the incoming shells seemed long, but in less than a minute they started to drop on the enemy trenches.

He then motioned to Sergeant Ellis that it was time to get the team out of Dodge.

★ ★ ★

"What the hell is it?" asked Major Llewellyn as he stared at the black, pitted and scarred one-foot-tall steel cylinder. It had three protruding feet that were keeping it upright on the plank table in the dugout.

"That, sir," replied Captain Gavin, "is a flamethrower. A *Kleinflammenwerfer*, to be exact. No. 1 Platoon found it."

Llewellyn glanced at the captain. Gavin's khaki uniform was stained with mud that was starting to dry. His helmet strap was undone and dangled as he spoke. It had a couple of scratches. Just above his left ear, there was a ding in the brim. The lines on his face showed his exhaustion, and there was a shadow in his eyes. Gavin had lost some good men tonight in the raid. Llewellyn knew how the captain felt. The men who had made it back were resting in the trenches and dugouts. A couple of squads had been tasked to gather the documents, the weapons, and the prisoners they had captured.

Llewellyn returned his attention back to the black cylinder. He lifted the bell cover and saw that there was a brass valve, a pressure gauge, and what he assumed was the filling port. A short metal hose was attached to the valve. He tried lifting the flamethrower. There were shoulder straps attached to a metal plate soldered to the front of the cylinder. Black felt covered the plate to make it more comfortable when a soldier strapped it on. He grunted, surprised by the weight. The waist belt dangled for a moment before he put it back down on the table. "It's a heavy bugger."

"Yeah, when it's filled it weighs nearly seventy pounds," replied the captain as he patted it. "It has two chambers inside, one for the pressurized gas and the other for the oil. This one has a four-gallon capacity." Llewellyn raised a questioning eyebrow. "You did send me on to that First Army demonstration several weeks ago."

Llewellyn returned a smile. "I did, didn't I. I'm glad that you learned something."

"What can I say? You *can* teach an old dog new tricks."

"You attach this metal wand to the hose, which is then attached to this port," continued the captain as he picked up the steel wand lying on the table near the bottle. There was a flexible five-foot hose attached to it. He handed the wand to the captain. "This swivel valve controls the amount of oil it shoots out, and this is the igniter which detonates the flame."

"What's the range of this damn thing?"

"About 70 to 120 feet, depending on the pressure."

"Jesus!"

"What they told us during the demonstration was that they weren't particularly effective, since the flame shoots out in a straight line. It's fairly easy to avoid."

"Not if you're standing in a trench, you're not. The first thing that you're going to do is get out right quick."

"That's what they are counting on. When the men jump out, they'll be mowed down by a machine gun."

The major paused to think. "That means we'll have to kill the operators before they can get into range."

"Yes, sir."

"Get a sketch of this and have a copy sent to all of our snipers. I want them to keep an eye out for these flamethrowers."

"Yes, Major. What I was thinking was since we have one here, we can have a demonstration to show how effective it is."

Llewellyn cocked an eyebrow. "If the engineers okay it, I'm fine with it. Just make sure that the damn thing doesn't explode."

"Of course, Major."

"Did we capture the operators of this thing?"

Gavin replied flatly. "No, they killed Private Saunders. After that…" Llewellyn grimaced then nodded in understanding. Gavin added, "They had death's-head badges that identify them as belonging to the Garde-Reserve-Pionier Regiment."

"Well, if it couldn't be helped, it couldn't be helped," the major said with a sigh. "Where are we at with the documents, the prisoners, and the other souvenirs we brought back?"

"The French translator is taking a look at them to see if there isn't anything of immediate interest. He'll be interrogating the prisoners to find out if they know anything."

"Good, keep a guard on them and we'll send them down the line as soon as we can. They'll be spending the rest of the war in a prison camp."

"Yes, Major."

"How did the new men do?"

"The corporals reported that they did good, all things considered. When do you think we'll be getting more replacements? We're under-strength as it is. With three of my men killed and ten wounded, we're spread pretty thin."

"I know," replied Llewellyn. "We've put in a request, but we're all in the same boat. Getting proper replacements from Shorncliffe has been a real pain in the ass." When the major was assigned to Shorncliffe last summer, he had seen firsthand how the camp was turning into a boondoggle. From the grapevine, things haven't improved much.

"Get some rest, Captain. I'll be calling all the men together in an hour to go over the raid while it is still fresh in our minds."

"I want to write those condolence letters to the men's next of kin first," replied the captain.

"Understood," the major replied with a tired sigh.

CHAPTER 5

Sir Sam Hughes was royally pissed. He attacked the three-page letter he was reviewing with a vengeance. He drew an arc where he wanted a paragraph moved to. He changed a word here and there to make his point more forcefully. He stroked through an offending sentence with such force that the ink bled through the paper, tearing it.

What had brought him to a boil was the letter that Major-General Gwatkin, the Canadian's army's chief of staff, had shown him. It had been written by Lieutenant-General Alderson criticizing the Ross. It had irritated him to no end. He thought he had made his position quite clear, but obviously it hadn't stopped the criticism or, despite his orders, the slow replacement of the Ross by the Lee-Enfield. By God, he wasn't about to waste the last fifteen years he had spent on the rifle, from its initial development as a member of the Standing Small Arms Committee to when he became the minister of militia and defence.

No one had a clue of the amount of testing, as well as comparison testing with the Lee-Enfield, they had done. So far, none of the results from Europe and Quebec City had shaken his faith in the Ross. All indications were that the fault was with the British ammunition. So, once again, he had to make his views known, in the strongest possible language, to the commander of his Canadian Corps.

"It's time, General," said the staff captain as he entered his office. Hughes glanced at the wall clock, which read 8:40.

"Yes, it is." He rose with the three sheets of paper in hand and carried them to his secretary in his outer office. The secretary was a balding man in his forties.

"Mr. Keith, have this retyped with the indicated revisions. Have it ready for my signature on my return from the caucus meeting."

"Yes, Minister," he replied.

"Anything urgent?"

"I have the latest reports concerning the situation at Verdun," Mr. Keith replied. "The news is somewhat encouraging. The French have stopped the Germans at Corbeaux Woods." On the 21st of February, the Germans had launched a massive attack against the French Second

Army in northern France at Verdun. The fighting had been fierce for two weeks, with heavy losses, but it seemed it might start to stabilize. He flipped through the classified reports from the War Office then said, "Include them in my box. I'll read them on the train."

"Yes, Minister," Mr. Keith replied.

"Thank you, Captain," Hughes said when the captain helped him with his overcoat. He then accepted the forge cap the staff officer handed him. Then he ordered, "Walk with me, we have matters to discuss."

It was only a five-minute walk from the Woods Building on Slater Street to the East Block on Parliament Hill. The weather was mild, and some of the snow on the lawn was beginning to melt. He paused for a moment before entering the East Block to watch workmen starting to dismantle the blackened remains of the Centre Block. It hadn't been decided as of yet whether to repair or replace the building. He could still recall vividly the night he had led the 77th Battalion onto the Hill to help the fire department fight the blaze.

The Dominion Police constable on duty snapped a salute when he marched through the main entrance. Hughes barely glanced at the parolees sitting in the main corridor who had come to make their weekly reports to the Dominion Police. Their offices were on the main floor of the East Block. He took the stairs two at a time to the second floor. The constable guarding the Privy Council chamber doors saluted him and held it open for him. The staff captain remained outside, since only ministers were allowed into the Privy Council Chamber.

He noticed when he stepped into the room that he was among the last of the ministers to have arrived. A couple greeted him warmly, but most of the eighteen ministers seated at the table were giving him cold stares or silence. He ignored their hostility. He rose to his feet, as did the others, when Borden entered with his private secretary Blount in tow. Borden gave him an icy stare himself when he took his seat.

Hughes wasn't surprised, but he had hoped that the prime minister would have mellowed somewhat. Borden hadn't been too pleased with him since last Thursday, when he stood in the House and presented his department's accomplishments for the past year. During his speech, he had defended his good friend, Colonel Allison. Borden had made it very clear his disapproval of his relationship with Allison. The Liberals had spent the bulk of the Thursday session attacking him and his friend. Most of the attacks were on his patronage list for defence contracts and

Allison's involvement in the Shell Committee. He thought he had done a good job, but the newspapers had not been impressed with his oratory.

"Everyone's here, I see. Let's begin. The first item on the agenda is deciding our policy on prohibition," Borden stated. That was the main reason he was attending today's meeting. He wanted to his make his views on prohibition quite clear.

Hughes watched as Justice Minister Charles Doherty adjusted his glasses as he peered down at his papers then said, "I had my department's staff prepare a report on prohibition. As you're aware, the regulation of wines and spirits is a provincial jurisdiction. In peacetime, we would not even consider being involved. We would leave it to the provinces. Now, alcohol is viewed as a detriment to the war effort. We have been placed under great pressure to make our position clear on the issue."

Hughes glanced at the draft in front of him. He had always been a strong temperance supporter. When he became the minister of militia and defence, he had ordered all the military canteens to be dry. His decision had been particularly popular with the temperance movement. It annoyed him that Alderson had overridden him in England and France by allowing wet canteens and rum to be served to the men in the front lines.

"What we are proposing is to make it illegal to send intoxicating beverages into a province that has enacted prohibition," said Doherty.

"If a province does not have prohibition?" Hughes asked.

Doherty looked at Hughes over his glasses. "If they haven't, there is very little that we can do, since it is up to each province to enact legislation concerning the production, distribution, and sale of alcohol." He tapped the paper in front of him. "What this legislation is proposing is it is up to each province to decide, and we will abide by their decision."

Hughes grunted a reluctant agreement. "It doesn't go far enough, but it's a start. To some extent, the temperance people will be pleased. And it will be popular with the voters."

Hughes saw Borden acknowledged his statement with a polite nod.

"Very well," Doherty said. "Please review the current draft that has been provided to you. And send your comments to me by the middle of next week."

"Thank you, Minister Doherty," Borden said. "Now, we will need to discuss the bilingual question. I've spoken with Premier Hearst this morning concerning Regulation 17." The Ontario government's legislation demanded English be taught in French-language schools.

Casgrain injected, "We're gravely concerned about the situation in Quebec. We believe that the hostility in the province against us will be quite grave. Especially if an election is called." Casgrain was the postmaster general, but, more importantly, the man represented the country riding that surrounded Quebec City on the north shore of the St. Lawrence.

"Blast Quebec," muttered Hughes. Casgrain turned his bald head to him and gave him a baleful glare. Borden fixed his eyes on him as well. Hughes broke his gaze away from Borden. As a prominent member of the Orange Lodge, he had been fighting the Catholics for years, and he strongly supported the Ontario legislation.

"I am well aware of the issues. I just wish that a compromise could be achieved that would satisfy everyone," Borden said with a tired sigh.

For the rest of the meeting, Hughes's fingers drummed impatiently on the table, waiting for the meeting to end, when Thomas White mentioned Laurier's attempt to get a resolution passed to investigate the Shell Committee. He sat up and was about to interject when Borden cut him off by saying, "He was rather weak and ineffective when he proposed that. I think I have put an effective end to it. I put on the record the various investigations that have already taken place and our efforts to improve the Shell Committee's efficiency. I don't think it will be any more than an irritant."

"They will continue to come after us this afternoon in the House," White said.

"I know," replied Borden. "Let them."

White turned to Hughes. "I hope that you will be prepared for this afternoon's session."

Hughes shrugged. "I'm afraid that I will not be in the House this afternoon."

"Why not?" demanded White with a touch of heat.

"I'm taking the train to Montreal this afternoon, and then I will be sailing to England for meetings with the War Office."

"Now! You're leaving now!" White snapped at him as he turned to Borden for support.

Borden glared at Hughes. "You may go."

The room had fallen into an angry silence as he rose from the table. Once the door was closed, he could hear a burst of angry voices that penetrated the padded door. He didn't have time to go back to defend himself. He needed to catch a train.

MARCH 10, 1916
RICHMOND FUSILIERS BILLETS, NIEPPE

Major Llewellyn stared at the chessboard, trying to figure out what his next move would be. The boxwood board was a folding type with a brass clasp and hinges. It became a storage box for the chess pieces when not in use. When unfolded, it expanded to an eight-and-a-half-inch square. Some of the varnished white and brown squares showed chip marks from use. On both ends of the board were the letters A to H. Running up the sides, the rows were numbered 1 to 8. The white and black pieces had seen much use since the green felt on their bottoms had fallen away.

He was sitting in a canvas chair in Lieutenant-Colonel Tennison's spartan billet. An oil lamp was on a shelf beside a black and white photo of the lieutenant-colonel's wife. Photos of two children, who appeared to be five and seven, were arranged on each side of the thirty-year-old woman with a handsome face. The shelves were set between two neatly made cots. On the nearby walls where the batman had hung them were his CO's pressed uniforms. A single naked bulb hung above the small folding oak table that supported the chessboard.

"It's still your move," said Tennison with a grin as a trail of smoke escaped from the left corner of his mouth from his pipe.

"Yeah, yeah," replied Llewellyn as he continued to study the board. The position on the board was the result of the classical Sicilian Defence. Tennison enjoyed a good game to relax from the day's work. Llewellyn was a so-so player at best, but he had gotten better as he played against Tennison. He had been forced to get every chess book he could get his hands on so he could improve his skills. It had been embarrassing losing games after ten or so moves. He still lost more than he won, but at least he was starting to give his CO a decent fight.

"So how was the meeting at Division HQ?" he asked. If you can't beat the board, beat the man.

The corner of Tennison's mouth quirked. He knew what Llewellyn was doing. "The usual discussion about strategy," he said as he watched Llewellyn move a knight from C1 square to the D3 square.

"Ah," said Llewellyn when he saw Tennison look satisfied after he made his move. That was one thing he struggled with when he played chess, developing a strategy. His tactics were improving, though. Supposedly, chess was ninety percent tactics. "Anything new?"

"Nothing much," Tennison replied. "Everyone is trying to figure out how to break the stalemate we are currently in. No one likes it, but we're stuck with it. The problem is exactly like our game here. We're fighting on a flat board where everyone can see your moves.

"For example," he said as he pointed to the squares in the centre of the board. "I'm controlling the centre. You have two strategies; you can try to wrestle control of the centre from me or you can attack along the wings.

"Basically," Tennison continued as he castled on the queen side. "We are trying to figure out how to get a decisive victory that will convince the Boche to surrender or at least come to the negotiating table. That is different from what's happening at Verdun. There, the French and the Germans seem to be in a war of attrition where whoever gets exhausted first loses."

"Shit," said Llewellyn as he looked up at Tennison. "I prefer the decisive victory rather than the war of attrition. There is no way we can sustain severe losses, especially since we're having a tough time getting reinforcements."

"I know," replied Tennison with a nod. "But getting a decisive victory might be a fool's mate." Llewellyn cringed when he remembered the four-move mate that had cost him his first game. "I don't think the Huns are going to make that kind of blunder. In the long run, we'll have to rely on tactics like pins to lock pieces in place and forks that allow you to attack two pieces at the same time. Don't forget skewers, otherwise you'll have to decide which piece will hurt less to lose."

When Llewellyn placed a pawn attacking a white pawn and knight, Tennison said, "Or the Zugzwang." In chess, the Zugzwang was a move that caused the opponent's position to worsen. Tennison took the black pawn opening the H file, otherwise he would have lost the knight. "Or the Zwischenzug." The Zwischenzug was a setup move to which the other chess player had to respond; otherwise, he would eventually be checkmated.

Llewellyn stared at the board, trying to figure out if he had left himself open to a discovered attack on his queen or king. He couldn't see an immediate threat. He said, "So where we are then is us trying to place our men in the best possible position to maximize the damage on the Germans and minimize our own losses."

"Yes," replied Tennison. "And it ain't going to be easy with the resources that we currently have. When we actually breach the German lines and get sufficient cavalry and troops through, we will then have to start thinking about a war of movement. That will bring another set of problems."

Llewellyn nodded. "In the meantime, we're stuck doing what we have been doing."

"I'm afraid so."

"Lovely," the major muttered as he stared at the board. He wondered if he were winning or not.

MARCH 15, 1916
TRENCH MORTAR SCHOOL, NIEPPE

"Not bad, not great but not bad," Lieutenant Ryan said as he tried to keep the nervousness out of his voice. It was his first course of instruction that he was leading. He wanted to project confidence to the mortar teams that were crouching beside him, particularly since it was only last week that he attended the Second Army's Trench Mortar School's instructor course at Berthen as a representative of the 65th Artillery. It was where he had been introduced to the new weapon that was being added to the Canadian Corps' inventory. Now, he was tasked with passing on what he had learned to the new mortar companies the Corps was forming.

"We'll have to do better than that," remarked Major Llewellyn who was standing beside him. Near them, there was a stack of open wooden boxes. A mortar crewman was removing a bomb painted dark blue with 'PRACTICE' stenciled in white. Only one remained of the three mortars that the crate had contained.

"Practice, practice, and more practice," replied Paul.

Llewellyn chuckled. "I've heard that somewhere before."

Ryan chuckled in agreement.

"How are the men getting along?" asked the major.

"It's still early, but they seem to be getting the hang of it," Ryan replied as he glanced to his left at the trench mortar section. They were manning four brand-new three-inch Stokes mortars. He had concerns when he learned that new companies would be created within both the 65th and the Richmond Fusiliers. Major Masterly had informed him there were heated discussions as to whether the new mortars were considered artillery pieces. As a compromise it had been decided, for now, that artillery men would handle the actual firing while the infantry would provide a protective screen and be pack mules for the eleven-pound bombs the Stokes launched. So far, the teams had coalesced along regimental lines.

"Time will take care of that," the major stated.

"Of course," replied Paul. He recognized a fair number of the Fusiliers. He had fought with them in the trenches of Ypres. Also, a fair number of the 65th had fought there as well. He recognized the handiwork of both majors. They wanted this to work, so they had hand-picked the men for the new mortar teams.

"I must admit that I'm beginning to like the Stokes."

"It's a hell of a weapon," Ryan answered. Since the major had expressed an interest, Ryan began spurting information about the Stokes mortar. "That Commander Stokes is a real genius to come up with such a simple design. And it's light. It weighs only 105 pounds, and it's easy to disassemble into three parts, the firing tube, the base plate, and the legs. The heaviest piece is the firing tube. It weights 42 pounds and is 51 inches long. One man can easily carry it. The base plate is 26 pounds, while the legs come in at 37 pounds."

"What's the maximum range you've managed so far?" asked the major. He was amused by Ryan's enthusiasm.

"It's rated for eight hundred yards max. I managed seven-fifty with three rings. If I can get the wind right, I should be able to get eight hundred yards, if not more." The mortars came with three propellant rings. For safety reasons, they were only using one ring, which meant that the mortars were landing about a hundred yards downrange. The discarded rings were visible in the empty mortar box nearby.

"Lieutenant," Llewellyn said formally. "I think you will need to deal with that."

Paul's eyes followed the direction that the major indicated with his head. What he saw was a private peering down the barrel of a mortar. It took him a moment to recall the man's name. "Private Cresswell, what the hell do you think you're doing?"

The platoon sergeant jerked the private away from the mortar's muzzle then began berating him. He then ordered the private to give him fifty. The private dropped immediately to the ground and started doing pushups.

"That's all I need," muttered Ryan. "Someone getting his fool head blown off."

"He'll learn," replied Llewellyn. "I think he has potential."

"If you say so?" said Ryan dubiously.

"I do."

"Okay. I'll keep an eye on him."

"What's the syllabus for the rest of the week?"

"The usual physical drill, building emplacements, mortar maintenance, range finding, and tactical schemes."

"Sounds good," Llewellyn replied, pleased. "I'll have a talk with the colonel as to how we will deploy the company when they're ready."

"Yes, sir."

"Once you get to the tactical schemes, let me know. I want to be here to take a look."

"Of course, Major."

They paused as one of the nearby mortars coughed. They saw a white cloud appear fifty yards left of the target that was one hundred and fifty yards distant. The second one that followed a few seconds later landed right on top of the flag.

Llewellyn said with a glint in his eyes, "I wish I had them at Ypres."

"Damn right, sir," replied Ryan.

CHAPTER 6

"I'm open!" Samantha yelled, trying to get Cecilia's attention as she tapped her stick on the ice.

Cecilia gave her a quick glance then passed the puck down the ice to her. Samantha was too busy to see whether the forward who was rushing Cecilia had knocked her down. She caught the puck on her stick then slid it between the skates of the defenceman who had been trying to intercept Cecilia's pass. Her blue skirt brushed Orderly Macpherson as she skated around him with two quick strides. As she picked up the loose puck behind him, she could hear the blades of the burly orderly's skates digging into the ice and then starting to chase her. She caught the tip of his stick from the corner of her eye; he was trying to hook her. But it was too late. Samantha flicked her wrist, sending the puck hurtling to the empty net.

She yelped in glee when it slid in. A moment later, Cecilia hugged her, then the rest of her team piled on. As Macpherson retrieved the puck, he said grudgingly, "Nice goal."

"Thanks," Samantha replied. The orderly was usually a nice man until he stepped onto the ice. She lifted her stick to acknowledge the cheering crowd that had gathered to watch the exhibition game at the Maidenhead rink between the CAMC hockey team and the nursing sisters. Most were curious locals. Maidenhead wasn't a particularly large village. It only contained about twelve hundred souls. The rest of the crowd's members were ambulatory patients from Taplow who had come out for an evening's entertainment. The two squads were quite a sight. The nurses were dressed in their standard uniforms while the CAMC's team of doctors and orderlies were dressed in khaki.

The rink they were playing on was one of the ponds frozen over by the subzero temperature. There were no artificial ice surfaces in the Berkshire. Actually, there was a skating rink in Reading, thirteen miles away, but it was a roller rink with a maple hardwood floor. It was doubtful the rink's owners would have allowed it to be flooded for ice hockey.

Their game was the latest in a series of hockey games the CAMC had arranged to foster relations with the locals. In fact, there was an interunit league with the other Canadian units in the area. Samantha had attended some of the previous games that the Taplow squad had played. She, like most of the hockey team, hadn't been happy with the opposing team's rough play.

Their game tonight was being played according to pond hockey rules, which meant there was no contact, no raising the puck more than six inches off the ice, and no goal minders. Also, they were playing seven-man hockey, since there were still some traditionalists among the CAMC.

As for skates, those weren't much of a problem since skating was a popular activity during the winter months in England. There were plenty of blades they could borrow and were easily attached to their army boots with leather straps. The blades were slightly different from those she was used to in Canada, but they were serviceable. She knew her legs were going to be sore in the morning. As for the hockey sticks, they were easy enough to make.

Samantha was pleasantly surprise by how many of her nurses actually knew how to play hockey. Most of them had played on the streets or ponds back home. She had found enough nurses to put together a team after the CO of Taplow had approached her about putting on an exhibition match. So far, they were giving the men a run for their money.

When Samantha first saw the pond, she had expressed her concern about the ice's thickness and the pond's depth. One of the elderly men who maintained it had chuckled. "Don't fret, missus," he had assured her. "Since the great London disaster, we're a mite careful with the ponds."

"London disaster?"

"Yes, missus," said the old man as he scratched his head. "It was 1868 or 1867, or thereabouts. Two hundred people fell into the pond in Regent Park when the ice broke. Lots drowned. We drain the pond. If it breaks, there's only three or four feet of water in it." Samantha was surprised. When she grew up skating on Ramsey Lake in Sudbury, someone always fell through the ice at least once a season, but never two hundred at the same time.

It felt great being on skates again and getting away from the hospital for some recreation. It almost felt like home. And, more important, they were winning. They were up 3–2. The first period was nearly over, and they only had one more ten-minute period to protect their lead.

Samantha glanced at Cecilia on her right and Tess on her left. Since they had scored the last goal, they had to give their opponents half-ice. She glanced behind her and saw the four nurses who made up the rest of her team take up their defensive positions. She returned her attention back to the CAMC squad in front of her and watched as they set up for their attack. She knew the men were embarrassed and were determined not to lose, especially to women.

"Watch it! Watch it!" she yelled as they started passing the puck. "Here they come!"

MARCH 22, 1916
RITZ HOTEL, LONDON

"What did Lord Kitchener say when you spoke with him about the Ypres Salient?" asked Sir Max Aitken. He was sitting at the corner table in the Palm Court dressed in a khaki uniform with lieutenant-colonel stars on his shoulder boards. His stars were honorary, given to him by the man sitting across from him. They allowed him to visit the front to get stories for his *Canadian Eye-Witness* news reports.

"I told him point blank that the Ypres Salient was indefensible. To keep our boys there is a great and unnecessary sacrifice," Sir Sam Hughes replied as he sipped his tea. "Our men should be withdrawn and the Salient mined to prevent the Germans occupying it."

"What did he say in reply?" asked portly Major-General Carson, who was sitting near Aitken.

"I could tell he was deeply affected by what I said. His eyes were teary when I spoke of what our boys are enduring in the Ypres trenches."

Aitken kept the disbelief off his face. It was unlikely that Lord Kitchener would have shed a tear for the Canadians' plight, especially since his own Imperial units had suffered far more and had greater losses than the Canadians. As an elected Liberal member of the British Parliament for the constituency of Ashton-under-Lyne, he had dealings with the secretary of state for war. The fact that Aiken had been relatively young, thirty-four when he was elected six years ago, and was a wealthy Canadian businessman didn't seem to bother the electorate.

One of the first things Sam Hughes did when his ship docked at Falmouth the day before was to head to London to meet Kitchener. Colonel Murphy, Major-General Carson, and he had greeted Hughes when he stepped off his ship. The local city council had been on hand to grant him the freedom of the city. Hughes had been immensely pleased when one of the local officials called him the "Lord Kitchener of Canada."

Aitken noticed, in the bronze-framed mirrored panel beside him, a flicker cross Carson's face. Ever since Carson's ill-fated meeting with Lord Kitchener in the fall of 1914 to complain about the wet conditions at Salisbury Plain, the secretary of war had denied all the former Montreal businessman's requests for meetings. Aitken knew that Carson still resented Lieutenant-General Alderson over the episode. Alderson had turned down Lord Kitchener's offer to move Imperial troops to accommodate the Canadian Contingent.

He frowned slightly when he scanned the Palm Court in the mirror. Afternoon tea at the Ritz Hotel in Piccadilly had grown in popularity ever since the hotel was built ten years before. With the war, patronage had dropped. Most of the current patrons in the room were military officers. Since accommodation in London was tight, the hotel's one hundred and eleven rooms were booked solid. Hughes was staying in one of the hotel's twenty-three suites while he was in London.

He saw a waiter, dressed in black tails and a red vest covering a starched white shirt, heading toward them with a silver teapot. Following him was another waiter pushing a cart with pastries and dessert items. The Palm Court's tearoom was famous for its scones and Cornish clotted cream.

"Did he indicate the Corps would be redeployed?" asked Carson when the waiters were out of earshot after filling their cups and dessert plates.

"He told me to put my scheme in writing, and he'll forward it to General Haig," Hughes replied as he took another sip of tea from the flower-patterned porcelain cup.

Aiken suspected Lord Kitchener had told him that to placate and to get him out of his office. He knew quite well what British officials thought of Sir Sam Hughes. It was not flattering. From his sources in Canada, he had learned Borden had warned Hughes not to irritate the Imperials.

"That sounds promising," Carson replied, sounding encouraged. Carson was Hughes's personal representative to the United Kingdom, and so was Aitken. Aiken knew that while Carson's authority was rather vague, he had managed to expand his role to become de facto head of the Canadian Overseas Force in England.

When Aitken offered his services to the Canadian government, Hughes had made him, besides an honorary colonel, one of his personal representatives in England as well. As the head of the Canadian Records Office here in London, he reported directly to Hughes, not to Carson. Hughes was quite happy with his *Eye-Witness* reports on the exploits of the Canadian Corps in the front line being published in the British, American, and Canadian newspapers regularly. This meant, though, that both of them were rivals for Hughes's attention. The rivalry became sharper when, at Falmouth, he had announced yesterday that he "was here to perfect the reorganization of the Canadian forces."

"At the rate of the current wastage, I don't know if we can sustain four divisions in the field," Carson said. The Imperial government had recently announced the acceptance of the Canadian government's offer for a fourth division. Carson had expressed his doubts to Hughes about adding another division to the Corps. They could barely support and supply the current three Canadian divisions in France. "We had nearly 22,000 casualties in the past year. That is a third of the Canadian Corps." Currently the Corps' strength in France was 62,000. "And General Alderson has been complaining about the lack of replacements for his losses."

Hughes said testily, "Recruitment is doing fine. In the last two months, we had over 50,000 volunteers. This month we should be on track for another 25,000 men. We currently have 132,000 men undergoing training in Canada. As you know, we have authorized increasing the size of the force to 500,000 men.

"As for General Alderson," he said with a sour note, "beside the Ross, what the hell else is he complaining about now?"

Aiken couldn't help giving Major-General Carson a glance. Both men were on the same page concerning Alderson. The way things were going, it was only a matter of time before the commanding general of the Canadian Corps would do something that would trigger his dismissal. Alderson passing over qualified Canadian officers for promotion, which he had to speak with the War Office about, was one strike against the lieutenant-general. Hughes was pushing to replace as many British officers as possible with Canadians. And Alderson's letter to Gwatkin concerning the Ross rifle's deficiencies was another large black mark.

"He has been complaining he can't get adequate reinforcements when he needs them, even though we have 44,000 men here in England," answered Carson with pique in his tone. He didn't need to remind the minister that only about half were actual combat troops. The other half were medical, communications, ordnance, and pay and administrative personnel needed to support the Canadian Corps in the field. "He also has been claiming the training of the reinforcements is not up to standard. When the men arrive, he is forced to retrain them."

"Isn't that why we have General Steele commanding at Shorncliffe and General Lord Brooke at Bramshott?" Hughes demanded.

Major-General Sam Steele, of the North West Mounted Police fame, had been made the GOC of the 2nd Division when it arrived in England last summer. Aitken knew the War Office had concerns about Sam Steele's age. They felt the sixty-six-year old officer was too old to command a division in the field. When the 2nd Division had been given to Major-General Turner, instead of being sent home, Steele was given command of the Canadians at Shorncliffe, which included the Canadian training base commanded by Brigadier-General MacDougall, as compensation.

What complicated matters was the second training base at Bramshott. Carson and Aitken had worked together to have the command of the camp given to Brigadier-General Lord Brooke. They had to. It was a delicate political problem, since it was Sam Hughes who had given the command of the 2nd Division's 4th Brigade to Lord Brooke. Problem was that Turner was less than impressed with the man and didn't want him. Lord Brooke, who had been posted to Ottawa in 1913, was one of the few British officers Hughes liked. The War Office wasn't pleased when they discovered a second training camp.

"It seems that the friction between generals Steele, Lord Brooke, and MacDougall is causing issues," replied Carson.

"General MacDougall is causing problems?" asked Hughes sharply.

"Yes," replied Carson. Aitken knew what Carson was doing. Hughes was prejudiced against the members of the permanent force, and Brigadier-General MacDougall was one.

"Didn't I make myself clear that General MacDougall was responsible for training at Shorncliffe and Bramshott and that General Lord Brooke was to report to him?"

"Yes, Minister," replied Carson. "I've been doing my best to calm the waters, so to speak. As I've indicated in my previous correspondence to you, we need to create a central authority. There seems to be some confusion with the War Office and with the Canadian Corps over who is responsible for what. And with the confusion, there is duplication of effort. Recently, I discovered that when the Corps requested a cavalry unit both Shorncliffe and Bramshott prepared a unit to be sent to France. There was some disagreement which unit should be sent. They requested only one."

The dismay on Hughes's face deepened. When Hughes turned to Aiken, there was a brief flicker of irritation in Carson's eyes. "What do you think?"

"I agree with General Carson," he replied. "I think we need to reorganize the apparatus here in England to become more efficient and to avoid the issues General Carson has just mentioned."

"As I indicated yesterday in my speech, the main reason I have come to England is to perfect a reorganization. To that end, I would like both of you to provide me with your ideas."

"Of course, Minister," replied Aitken as Carson acknowledged with a nod. Aitken knew that both he and Carson were competing as to who would head the reorganization of the Canadian Overseas Force in England. Whether Hughes was willing to concede any control was a real question mark.

Hughes then switched subjects. "I understand *Canada in Flanders* has done very well." Aitken permitted himself a small smile. He had written and recently published *Canada in Flanders*. The book detailed the Canadian Expeditionary Force's valour and exploits during the battle at the Ypres Salient last April.

Aitken beamed. "Since its release in January, it's in its thirteenth printing."

"Excellent," replied a pleased Hughes.

"I just want to mention," Aitken said. "If we want to continue to tell the story of our boys in France, we require the unit commanders to prepare and send to us at the Canadian Records Office copies of their war diaries and reports regularly. When the war is finally over, they will be extremely useful for us and for historians when they sit down and write the histories of our boys."

"I agree. Let's do it," Hughes ordered without hesitation.

MARCH 22, 1916
PRIME MINISTER'S OFFICE, EAST BLOCK, PARLIAMENT HILL,
OTTAWA

"Ah, General Gwatkin," said Sir Robert Borden when he arrived at his office on the second floor of the East Block. The major-general was waiting for him in the southwest corner of the building just a few doors from the governor general's office. He shed his gloves and coat and handed them to one of the pages. "I apologize for being late, but my lunch with the Russian trade delegation took longer than I had anticipated."

He and R.B. Bennett had a pleasant meal with two members of the delegation. Richard Bedford Bennett was the Conservative MP for the Calgary riding and was James Lougheed's partner. He couldn't recall the Russians' names, and if he did, he doubted he could have pronounced them correctly. It had been politic to meet with them, since they had just deposited $40 million in gold bars in the basement vaults of the East Block. The gold had been shipped on two Japanese cruisers to Vancouver and from there via train to Ottawa. There had been a bit of a kerfuffle when news of the gold shipment had been leaked. The gold was collateral for British loans to the Russian government to buy military equipment and supplies. He had been hesitant meeting with them. Last month, Flavelle had told him a story about an American businessman looking for contracts from the Russian government in Petrograd. He had been told that for $50,000 he could get a private meeting with the Russian war minister. After the meeting, he discovered it had been a con, and the man he had met was an imposter. Also, he was getting reports from Sherwood that there was another case of graft, this time between a Canadian businessman and one of the Russian delegations in New York. He wasn't pleased with the news.

He still ended up having a pleasant lunch at the Château Laurier. He had spent most of it trying to convince them that Canadian industry was well suited to supply the Russians with much of what they needed. The two Russians had been interesting and spoke excellent English. He had been surprised that one had learned his English on his trip to Canada. They had asked questions about the conditions in the United States, which he had answered the best he could.

When he had asked about the conditions in Petrograd, they had mentioned the Anglo-Russian Hospital and how grateful they were for the care it was providing the Russian soldiers. He had been pleased and had informed them that he had personally authorized ten thousand pounds sterling, nearly twenty thousand dollars, for the hospital for last December. One of the Russians said he had actually met Matron Cotton, a Canadian nurse that had been assigned there.

"Not a problem, Prime Minister. You had a question concerning the standing orders for ammunition?" he asked as he followed the prime minister into his office. Borden indicated the chair in front of him.

"I'm afraid that I will need to be brief, as I am required to be in the House for Question Period." The one thing he was glad about was that Hughes had left for England. It was simpler and easier dealing with such questions when he wasn't in the capital. The telegram he had received that morning concerning the current friction between Hughes and the governor general was not satisfactory. Both seemed to be at fault, but it seemed to put a strain on everyone's relationships. Borden was afraid that questions would be raised in the House that afternoon.

"It's about this two-million-dollar sale of ammunition to Vickers and the Dominion Arsenal's request for one hundred and sixty thousand dollars for new equipment."

"Of course, Prime Minister. I brought the details with me so you can take a look at them," he replied as he took several folders from his briefcases.

MARCH 27, 1916
CONSERVATIVE CAUCUS ROOM, VICTORIA MEMORIAL MUSEUM,
OTTAWA

"I don't think we have much of a choice," said Arthur Meighen with barely contained fury when Sir Robert Borden entered the Conservative caucus room. It was nearly midnight, but the room was full of angry, shell-shocked MPs.

Borden's face was grim when he acknowledged, "I know."

"Was this what you were expecting?" asked his finance minister, White, who was seated beside the solicitor general.

Borden grimaced. "I had heard rumours Kyte was going to spring a mine under Sam, but nothing like this." He was referring to John William Kyte, the Liberal MP for the Richmond riding in his beloved Nova Scotia.

"Do you think Sam knew it was coming? Was this why he left a few weeks ago in such a hurry?" asked White. Sam had angered most of his caucus members three weeks ago when he defended his good friend, Colonel Allison, in the House of Commons. He did himself no favours when he disappeared to England shortly after.

Borden sighed. "I doubt that. You know how much Sam loves a good scrap." Which was true. Sam had a reputation, since he was young, for getting into fisticuffs with his political opponents. Hughes hadn't changed much since then. He and White nearly got into a brawl in the Privy Council chamber, of all places.

"The question is are Kyte's allegations concerning Yoakum and Allison true? Did they earn nearly two million dollars in commissions on the shell, fuse, and rifle contracts?" Meighen paused then asked, "The more important question is, did Sam know about it?"

That was the heart of the matter. Since six o'clock, Kyte and his fellow Liberals from eastern Canada, William Pugsley from the St. John's New Brunswick riding, and Frank Carvell, from the Carleton Nova Scotia riding, had been raking his government over the coals. That was why Meighen was so angry. He was the one who had stood in the House and defended the government, saying there was no need to have an inquiry into the Shell Committee. First, the committee had been an agent of the British government. Second, it was British money, not Canadian taxpayer money, that had been spent.

Then Kyte's mine exploded.

Kyte had directly contradicted Hughes's statement in the House, where Sam claimed his friend of thirty years was so patriotic, he hadn't asked for any compensation. In fact, Allison had helped the Canadian government save fifty million dollars.

Kyte had informed the House that Yoakum and Allison had profited from the Colt machine gun and rifle contracts award in the United States to the tune of six hundred thousand dollars. But the most damning of the accusations was the fuse contracts.

"What were Bertram and Carnegie thinking when they advanced 1.2 million dollars to an American firm when Canadian firms like the Russell Motor Car Company were begging for contracts?" White demanded. General Bertram had been the Shell Committee's chairman, while Colonel Carnegie had been the committee's technical advisor.

Borden replied, "What I was told was the fuses they needed were very complex, as many as fifty-two separate parts that needed to be built to strict tolerances. They didn't feel that Canadian companies had the technical expertise to manufacture artillery fuses. The Shell Committee said they needed two types, time fuse Models 80 and 85 and graze fuse model 100."

"What's a graze fuse?" asked White.

"It detonates the shell only when it lands."

"An American firm with no experience did?" White blurted in disgust.

"They admitted they were wrong. Firms such as the Russell Company have been meeting, even exceeding the War Office specifications," replied Borden. The company had finally started shipping the fuses in February. That the company was also employing thousands of workers, mostly women, didn't hurt the Conservative Party. "And the committee stopped giving advances to companies on the contracts to help them set up their factories."

"I wonder why," White said sarcastically.

"Be that as it may, what's the most damning is the fact that Sam authorized the contract. It was a fixed price contract at $4.35 per fuse. Our companies have been producing them for a dollar cheaper. It makes it look as if Sam directed it toward Allison and his cronies," said Meighen.

"I know," replied Borden.

"So what do you want to do?" asked Meighen.

"I don't like it, but I think we have to call an inquiry into the fuse contracts," Borden said. From the look on Meighen's face, Borden knew that he didn't like that idea at all.

"That would be dangerous. We don't know what we shall find once we start turning over rocks," replied Meighen.

"Damned if do, we damned if we don't," replied Borden.

"Sam is definitely not going to like it," White pointed out.

"I really don't care," replied Borden.

"You want me to make the announcement?" Meighen asked.

"Yes," Borden said as he watched Meighen wrinkle his face in disgust.

"Okay, so what are we going to do with Sam?" asked White.

"I'm ordering him back here on the next available ship from England."

"Do you think that he'll come?" asked Meighen.

"He'd better," was Borden's firm reply.

CHAPTER 7

"What's the latest from the front lines?" asked Lieutenant-Colonel Tennison as he made room for his batman, Corporal Higgins, to pour hot coffee into two white enamel mugs on the plank desk. The weather outside was cool and showery, and that added to the dugout's gloomy interior. Some of the water could be seen coming up through the duckboards when weight was placed on them. Higgins gave them a brief nod before he set the pot on a sideboard so they could help themselves. It was relatively quiet at this hour of the late morning, or at least in this sector it was.

"So far the Huns' retaliation has been very light. Very little damage has been reported to our forward trenches. No one's been killed. Some have been wounded from shrapnel, but nothing serious. They'll recover," Llewellyn replied. "It was kind of them to wake me up this morning with the big bangs."

At five forty-five this morning, the 1st Division's artillery, the 9.2s, the 4.5s and the 18-pounders, plus the Stokes mortars, had fired a combined seven hundred shells at the German positions for forty-five minutes. The Fusiliers' observers had reported extensive damage to the Boche's trenches at Factory Farm.

"Dreaming of Samantha?" Tennison teased. He grinned wider when Llewellyn gave a disgusted look.

"A nice thick steak, actually," Llewellyn replied.

Tennison chuckled as he sipped his coffee. "They were supposed to blow the mines under the mound at St. Eloi at four forty-five this morning. The British 3rd Division have been tasked to capture it."

Llewellyn knew from the maps that St. Eloi was about five miles south of Ypres. The Germans had captured the village, the trenches, and the thirty-foot mound just south of the village last March. The British had recaptured the village and the trenches, but they were unable to take back the mound. It was a source of irritation, since it gave the Germans an excellent view of the British trenches. Llewellyn nodded to himself and glanced at the showery weather. The 3rd Division was going to have a tough go. The Hun trenches there were six hundred yards wide and a hundred yards in front of the mound.

"If we waited for the weather, we'd never get anything done," Tennison remarked.

"From the sound of things, the 2nd Division must've done a good job. The Germans have been pounding their lines for most of the morning," Llewellyn said as he took a sip of his black coffee. The 2nd Division's artillery had targeted Piccadilly Farms, and the 2nd Division's brigades were to use Bangalore torpedoes to blow gaps in the wire in front of the German trenches. One of their other jobs was to prevent the Boche sending troops across the Diependaal Beck valley to support their units being attacked by the 3rd Division.

"Yes, they have," agreed Tennison as he leaned back in his chair. He had both hands on his coffee cup to keep them warm. "When General Loomis came from the brigadier's conference at Division HQ yesterday, he phoned me. We're still on schedule to be relieved on the thirtieth by the 17th Brigade's A and B battalions. We'll be transferred to the reserve at Grand Nunque and Bulford. Divisional HQ will be transferred to Flêtre."

"Not a problem, everything should be ready by then," Llewellyn said.

"Good, it'll give us a chance to send Lieutenant Morley and four of his men on that grenade course they are starting next week. Plus, we're going to be the alert brigade on the first and second. We may need to man the Kennel Defence if we have to support the 2nd Division."

"Do you think we're going to have to support General Turner?" asked Llewellyn.

"I don't know," replied Tennison with a shrug. "I hope not. General Turner and his men are to relieve the 3rd Division once they have consolidated their positions. He is slated to do that by the end of next week. While he is doing that, we're to exchange places with the 5th Corps. The 2nd will then be responsible for the trenches from F1 to the canal."

Llewellyn glanced at the map pinned to the wall. "What about us?"

"We'll be south of the canal."

"Okay," Llewellyn replied.

Tennison must have caught something in Llewellyn's tone. "Something bothering you?"

"Oh nothing, just that some of Turner's men are still green," he answered.

"He's had six months to whip them into shape," Tennison pointed out. Major-General Turner had been given command of the 2nd Division when the Canadian Corps was formed last September. "We were just as green last year at Ypres."

"Don't remind me," Llewellyn said with a shake of his head. He stared at his black coffee. "I hope they have an easier time than we had."

MARCH 29, 1916
2ND DIVISION HEADQUARTERS, WESTOUTRE

"General, I think you will be pleased with this note forwarded to us from Corps HQ," said Captain Furry Ferguson Montague as he entered Major-General Turner's office. Along with the note, he was bringing in the daily intelligence summary for Turner's review and comments before he distributed it to the Division's brigade commanders and to Corps HQ. The captain was in his early thirties, average height, with a dark complexion, brown hair, and grey eyes. Before the war, he had been a prominent Winnipeg lawyer.

"Oh," Turner said as he raised his head from the document he was reading. Grey light filtered through the office window. The sky above the Roman Catholic Sint-Eligiuskerk church dominating the small Flemish farming community was cloudy. It had rained hard the previous evening, but it was starting to clear and be fine for the rest of the day. They could hear men cursing as they moved furniture onto wagons one storey below them.

"It's from General Haldane. He sent his thanks to the Corps for our help that we've been providing him for the last several days. He appreciated how effective we've been in drawing the Huns' fire on our positions and that we did everything possible to distract them while the 3rd Division launched their attack. He says they suffered a thousand casualties, but it would have been worse without our demonstration. He goes on to say they captured nearly two hundred and five Hun officers." When Montague glanced from the note at the general, he saw that Turner was pleased. "He also informs us that because of the heavy rains and the damage done by the mine explosions, the ground is pretty bad. But he's hoping to get it consolidated and cleared before he transfers St. Eloi to us."

"That's good to hear," Turner said as he adjusted his glasses. "The last reports indicated that his right battalion had reached their objectives, but his left had been held up."

"I think that is what General Haldane is referring to. The 3rd Division requested our artillery shell the German positions for forty-five minutes," Montague pointed out.

"Have you received any reports from our observers assessing the damage?" Turner asked.

Montague replied with a touch of frustration, "I've haven't yet, but I'm expecting them shortly."

"Good, at least thinning our lines during our demonstration reduced our casualties," Turner remarked. "Anything I should know from last night?"

"Nothing much, I'm afraid. The Huns are continuing to shell all three of our sectors. We had patrols out in No Man's Land last night, and they didn't find any signs of German patrols. The Boche are continuing to make repairs to the damage we have caused.

"They spotted a German officer examining our lines with binoculars. Our snipers tried to get him, but they missed," Montague added with a shrug. "They did notice a considerable amount of train traffic between Roulers and Menin, Courtrai and Tourcoing, Geluwe, and Menin. According to the reports, trains were moving to and from them every ten minutes."

"I don't like the sound of that," Turner said with a frown. They could be moving their reserves and ammunition. They have been using a lot of them."

"Could be, but until we capture some prisoners and interrogate them, we won't know," Montague replied.

"Mention that to the 50th when they relieve us," Turner stated.

"Yes, sir," replied the captain.

"Okay. Send a copy of General Haldane's note to the brigade commanders. I want them to know that the hard work they and their men have done was appreciated," ordered Turner.

"Of course."

"How are we coming along with the move?"

Montague knew Turner was referring to the 2nd Canadian Division HQ's move from Westoutre to Reningelst scheduled for April 3rd. "Pretty well. We've been here since September, so we've accumulated a lot of paperwork. We're going through it and discarding what we don't need," he said with some discomfort. It went against his lawyer's training throwing out documents, but it couldn't be helped. Transport was limited to the essentials.

"Good," Turner said. "I've been looking over the tables for our relief of the 3rd Division. There are some changes that I would like to make. I want you at the meeting this afternoon to go over the plans and…"

APRIL 3, 1916
3RD BRITISH DIVISION HEADQUARTERS, RENINGELST

"My men were less than fresh when we launched our attack on St. Eloi," said Major-General Haldane, "and now they are exhausted." The fifty-four-year-old general's tiredness extended to the tips of his moustache. Haldane was a career soldier with nearly thirty-five years' experience. While he outranked Major-General Turner, he had saluted first when the Canadian general entered his office. It was the standard protocol for those who wore the miniature Victoria Cross on their ribbon bar.

"I understand," replied Turner. Both men were sitting in Haldane's office, which was technically now Turner's. Until the transfer of the 2nd Division's HQ from Westoutre to Reningelst was completed, they were sharing the same office.

"My boys have done their best. The German counterattacks and the artillery haven't given them any rest, and they're just worn out," Haldane stated grimly. "This is why I asked we accelerate your relief of my division."

"I'm pleased to help," replied Major-General Turner. He understood well the feeling of exhaustion. He had been there before. "I've ordered Brigadier Ketchen's 6th Brigade to start relieving your men this evening."

"Good," replied Haldane as he rose to his feet and motioned Turner to come over to his desk. He pointed to the sketch map that showed four craters numbered two to five from left to right with a line drawn above them. "And last night, we established this new line in front of the craters the mine detonations created." The acronyms jotted near the line indicated that the 7th King's Shropshire Light Infantry was on the left near the Canal, the 8th East Yorks and the 12th West Yorks were in the centre, and the 1st Gordon Highlanders were on the far right.

"Wouldn't it have been better to use the craters as the new line?" asked Turner as he studied the map carefully.

Haldane's lips thinned. "We tried that at Hooge. We discovered the German artillery would shell our positions without putting themselves in danger. What I would recommend is making the new line good, building a new support trench directly in front of the craters, and digging three new CTs as there's only two at present. You'll have to do a fair amount of revetting and draining since they're full of water. The mine explosions and the recent rain have turned the ground soft. So soft that men have been sinking up to their armpits when they've attempted to cross the mound."

"I'll have my engineers and the 4th Pioneer Battalion make plans for improvements once we have completed the reliefs. I'll be joining Brigadier Ketchen for a reconnaissance to get a better picture of the situation," replied Turner as he lifted his head to look at Haldane.

"I'll loan you my GSO1. He's quite acquainted with our operations and the enemy dispositions. You can have him as long as you need him."

"I appreciate that, General Haldane," replied Major-General Turner as he straightened and tugged at his khaki jacket. "I'd best get on with it."

APRIL 4, 1916
COMMUNICATIONS TRENCHES, ST. ELOI

Major-General Turner sloshed through the narrow, water-filled communications trench. It was high enough that his socks in his rubber gumboots squished as he made his way to Brigadier-General Ketchen. Mud from the trench wall streaked his uniform when he pressed against it, making room for the stretcher bearers who were struggling with a wounded soldier. Through the dirty haze of his wire-rimmed glasses, he could see the strain on the faces as they lifted heavy, mud-covered boots out of the water, moving to the rear.

He felt the same strain as he moved forward to inspect the trenches being taken over by the 27th Battalion from the 3rd Division's units in the line. So far, what he had seen confirmed the conditions his men were facing that Captain Jukes, the 6th Brigade's brigade-major, had reported earlier that morning.

"Are you sure we want to make the line good?" asked Brigadier-General Ketchen, the GOC of the 6th Brigade, when Turner finally stood beside him. The 6th Brigade was made up of the 27th (City of

Winnipeg), the 28th (Northwest), the 29th (Vancouver), and the 31st (Alberta) battalions. Ketchen was two inches short of six feet and wore the standard military moustache. He hadn't been in the relief's initial planning. He had only arrived back to his command, on April 1st, after a two-week leave in England. "It isn't much of a line. It's broken in places so badly it isn't even a trench, and there are no traverses. I think it would be better to defend the craters instead."

Turner pursed his lips. "General Haldane recommended we make the current line good. It's been his experience that craters are vulnerable to artillery fire."

"It's going to be difficult. We're still clearing the dead. Both ours and the Germans, out of the trenches," Ketchen replied as he indicated the communication trench with his hand. "We only have two CTs, one on each side of the mound. They're getting congested with traffic from the men going in and coming out. We're behind schedule with the relief." Ketchen then stated the obvious. "The water is slowing us down, and the men are getting exhausted just getting into position. I'm hoping we can drain them as fast as possible, but the mines destroyed much of the drainage system here. Unless the weather improves, though…" Both men glanced up at the grey-black clouds overhead. The crackling of rifle fire and the dull thud of German mortars landing nearby didn't cause them to blink.

"The CRE has dumped ten thousand sandbags at battalion headquarters at Dickenbush. Also, they've dumped ten thousand more at SP 8. At Shelling Farm, they dropped off with three hundred iron picks and same number of wire coils. Start getting the trenches wired and have the pioneers start digging new CTs. I know General Haldane said to have the CTs go through the craters, but from what I've seen, there isn't much room between them. Draw on the reserves for the work parties."

"Yes, sir," replied Ketchen. He didn't look happy about the orders, but he had voiced his suggestions. There wasn't much else he could do. "I've made arrangements with the 8th and 76th Brigades to lend us their Lewis guns. They'll be useful for enfilade fire when the Germans counterattack."

"Good," stated Turner as he tried to clean the haze from his glasses with a dirty handkerchief. At that moment, a German barrage opened up on the newly occupied Canadian trench line.

APRIL 5, 1916
SUPPORT TRENCHES, SAINT-JANS-CAPPEL

"What's this?" asked Major Llewellyn as he stared at the contraption lying on top of a stack of grenade crates marked *12 Mills Bombs #5*. There were twenty-three other boxes stacked in the Bomber Company's supply dump. He was inspecting the Richmond Fusiliers' support positions in the second trench line, verifying the bombers' readiness. So far, the reports from the company's CO, Lieutenant Markham, had been good. Not that he didn't like the lieutenant, but it didn't hurt to keep the twenty-seven-year-old from Portage la Prairie, Manitoba, on his toes. Llewellyn was pleased he had found the requisite five hundred Mills bombs in the dugout.

The contraption he was staring at was a piece of wood one-foot square. Attached to it was a coil of copper wire wrapped around a cardboard tube. A wire ran from it to a screw in the wood. An old, battered telephone receiver was attached to the screw. A second wire from the tube ran on the other side of the board. It too was connected to a screw from which ran a coil of copper wire ten feet long. A third wire connected the two screws with a metal post in the middle. A wire from the post touched the copper-covered tube.

"It's a radio, sir," explained Private Damien Leggatt nervously as his brown eyes bounced between the major and the lieutenant. The major had spotted the copper wires when he was inspecting the two grenade catapults that were placed along the wooden slate walls in the dugout. The larger of the two was the wooden Leach catapult. It was seven feet long and two feet wide, and it weighed nearly fifty pounds. It looked like a giant slingshot, and it worked on the same principles. A hand crank pulled a wire clipped to a leather sling. The sling was connected to the two 'Y'-shaped arms by thick red-coloured rubber bands. Once the crank wound the rubber bands to the proper tension, a grenade was placed into the sling, the pin was pulled, and the trigger was released, slinging the Mills bomb toward the enemy. It had a range of about one hundred and fifty yards. Beside it was the newer French-made *Arbalète sauterelle type-A* catapult. No one called it that. The *Sauterelle* resembled a crossbow. Since it had been made of steel and wire, it was lighter and more reliable than the Leach. Its steel arms didn't degrade like the Leach's rubber bands. While it didn't have the same range as the Leach — it was thirty yards shorter — the men liked it better. Most of the bombers were happy they were getting rid of them, with good reason. The Stokes mortar's arrival had rendered them obsolete. The mortars could deliver a heavier punch, more accurately, and with a greater rate of fire than the catapults were capable of.

The major had been ready to chastise the private. The Corps had strict orders not to play with the telephone cables. He suspected that was where the copper wires came from.

"It is?" Llewellyn asked in surprise. He stared at the supposed radio. "Does it work?"

"Yes, sir," replied Leggatt. The major raised an eyebrow at the lieutenant, who acknowledged with a nod.

"The concept is really simple, sir. All you need is copper wire, a capacitor, a crystal detector, and an earphone," the private said as he eagerly pointed to each component on the board.

"But does it work?" the major interrupted. He was certain if he allowed the private to continue, they would be here for quite a while. He was always amazed by the various skills he found among the Fusiliers.

"Oh." There was a hint of chagrin in the private's voice. "If you'll put the telephone receiver to your ear…"

The major had to remove his steel helmet to make room. He listened for a moment. "Are you sure that this thing is working? All I hear is static."

"May I, sir?" Leggatt asked, holding out his hand. The private took the receiver and concentrated as he fiddled with one of the components on the board. He started nodding when he was happy with the adjustment he had made.

"Here, sir," he said as he handed it back to Llewellyn. When the major put the receiver to his ear again, this time he could hear a voice speaking in French over the static. It wasn't particularly loud, but his French was good enough that he understood what they were saying. "Someone is reporting the news in French!" he exclaimed.

"Yes, sir, that is the broadcast from the Eiffel Tower." Leggatt beamed.

"That far?" asked Llewellyn.

"Oh yes, sir, that station has a three-thousand-mile range."

"What else can you pick up?" Llewellyn asked curiously.

Leggatt glanced at his CO and then back to the major. "I can get some of the London stations, and occasionally I'll pick up one of the German radio stations."

"You have?"

"Yes, sir, but I don't understand German, sir," he replied in an apologetic tone.

"I see," replied the major. "How do you know all this stuff?"

"I've been making radios at home for years. I applied and got accepted to U of T's engineering program. Before I started my classes, I had volunteered," he said with a shrug. "When I saw all of the scrap copper wire, I couldn't help myself."

"And you ended up here?" the major said in surprise.

"Yes, sir."

"Well, I think that your talents are wasted here."

"Oh no, sir, I like throwing bombs," Leggatt answered.

"He has a good arm," replied Lieutenant Markham. "He's also the pitcher for our baseball squad." Llewellyn guessed throwing grenades was excellent practice.

The major grunted. "Well, I've received orders from Corps HQ to submit names for wireless training. We're supposed to get something called a Tuner Wave something or other…"

"The Tuner Short Wave Trench Set MKII," the private said, correcting Llewellyn. "I would love to get my hands on that. It's a beauty."

"So you heard about it then?"

Private Leggatt nodded eagerly. "It needs a three-volt battery to run. You can use either a Person or a carborundum crystal." Llewellyn had no clue what that meant. "It's a receiver only, so you'll need to pair it with a transmitter. They'll probably have one of the Wilsons. The Wilson is 120 watts with a range of nine thousand yards." When he finished, he had a dreamy smile on his face.

The major turned to the lieutenant and said, "I need to transfer him immediately."

"Sirs?" Leggatt asked hesitantly when he stared at both officers.

"I'm afraid that you know too much. We can't risk losing you now," replied the lieutenant with a touch of annoyance. It left the lieutenant short-handed.

From the look on the private's face, he wasn't particularly happy about it.

★ ★ ★

Lieutenant Sean looked concerned when Major Llewellyn came in through the communication trench to the section he was responsible for. Sean was in his early twenties, of medium height and build, with straw-blond hair barely visible under his helmet. The officer from Berlin, Ontario, for which he was mercilessly teased, wished he could grow a proper moustache. The best he could do was a peach fuzz that didn't impress anyone.

It was early morning, and the trench walls had a watery gleam from the slow melting of the previous night's frost. The sun was out, but its rays hadn't yet touched the interior of the trench. He was relatively new to the Richmond Fusiliers; he had transferred in from Bramshott about a month earlier. After two weeks of orientation, he was put in charge of the 4th section of the Fusiliers' 3rd Company. The real reason why the major was inspecting his trench was confirmed when Llewellyn asked, "I hear that you're having a spot of bother?"

"Yes, sir," replied Sean with some reluctance.

"Let's take a look, shall we?" the major said. When he spotted Sergeant Ellis coming up the trench, he greeted him. "Good to see you again, Sergeant."

"And you, sir," replied the sergeant with a grin. Sean knew that Sergeant Ellis had been assigned to him to keep an eye on the newbie.

"If you come this way, sir, I'll show you the section that has been giving us trouble," the lieutenant said as he led the major, with the sergeant bringing up the rear, down the trench that Ellis had just come from.

The major's visit had not been totally unexpected. He had made sure the men's appearance was up to the Canadian army standards. They were all shaved and their uniforms relatively clean; they were in a trench, after all. More important, the Lee-Enfields had been cleaned and well oiled.

The lieutenant had tidied up the trench as best he could. He had arranged that their reserve ammunition and grenades were neatly stored in niches in the walls. When the major paused at a sandbag hanging from one of the wooden posts supporting a retaining wall of corrugated steel, he had been a touch concerned. He was relieved when the brigade-major grunted. He had seen that it was one of the garbage bags that the sanitation men would remove later in the day. The lieutenant knew garbage generated by his men would be sorted for metal and other recyclables before what was left over was burned.

When the major spotted a corporal looking over the trench with a pair of telescopic binoculars, he stopped and asked, "May I?"

"Of course, sir," replied the corporal as he handed them to Llewellyn. The major peered at No Man's Land for a moment then gave them back to the corporal. "Thanks, carry on."

When they had reached the first traverse, Lieutenant Sean cautioned Llewellyn, "This is the area where we lost the three men. It's not particularly deep, so you need to keep your head down." The major was a tall man, and his helmet was nearly the same height as the top of the sandbags. It was obvious the lieutenant didn't want to lose the battalion's brigade-major on his watch.

"Understood," replied the major. He had taken just a few steps when the lieutenant heard a thud in the sandbag near the major's head.

"Good God," exclaimed the lieutenant.

The major looked at the fingertip of wet mud protruding from the ragged hole the 7.92 Mauser bullet had made in the wet sandbag. From under his Brodie helmet the major flashed him a grin. He then turned his head as he examined the sandbags at the top of the trench. "Hmm," he muttered as he took two more steps then paused. A moment later a second bullet struck the wooden stake, supporting the corrugated steel wall in front of Llewellyn.

"Just as I thought. Did you have the top of the trench done recently?" Llewellyn asked him.

Lieutenant Sean glanced at Sergeant Ellis who had a blank face, then he examined the top layer of sandbags that had been laid bricklayer straight. "Yes, sir. When I arrived here, I noticed that the top of the trench here needed repair. A lot of the sandbags were split, messy, and needed replacement."

"Didn't your NCO's have any suggestions and comments?" the major asked.

Sean glanced again at the sergeant, who still gave him a blank face. He wondered if Ellis had complained to the major. He still didn't understand what the big deal was about the sandbags.

"They did make comments and suggestions how the sandbags had to be laid, but I ordered them to be relaid as I was instructed at Bramshott," he replied. "Neat and tidy."

"Well, they are that. Per the training manual," the major replied. Sean winced at the training manual comment. "Sadly, that is the reason we lost three men this week."

The lieutenant's mouth dropped slightly. "I don't understand?"

"I don't know what they are teaching at Bramshott but this…" The major pointed to the top of the trench. "Did you notice that the second shot was fired after I took two steps?"

"Yes."

"The sniper saw my helmet over the sandbags as I was walking. Since most men walk with a slight up-and-down movement, the sniper spotted it and tried to get me. When I had taken two more steps and stopped, he fired where he thought I would be." The lieutenant finally understood. "That is the reason that the top layer of sandbags needed to be messy and broken up. It makes it more difficult for them spot movement."

"Major. I didn't know!" replied Sean.

"Well, now you do," the major answered. The lieutenant was grateful that Llewellyn hadn't added that he had learned a lesson. He knew it was a very expensive one with three men dead.

CHAPTER 8

APRIL 6, 1916
TRENCHES, ST. ELOI

"Where the hell is the fucking trench?" swore Lieutenant Maurice Bédard to Sergeant Ian Baker. The sergeant was crouching beside him on the lip of what they thought was Crater 2. It was pitch black. Only the flashes of exploding shells provided them with some light. The lieutenant had to look away from time to time. The sudden light caused his vision to ghost, and it took several minutes for his eyes to clear. Along the crater's rim, his squad lay waiting. There were four bombers, their vests loaded with Mills bombs, the four bayonet men to protect them, and four scouts. They had been tasked to relieve the men in the trenches at point 33.

"I have no fucking idea," replied Sergeant Baker. The two men from Vancouver had been together for several months, so the lieutenant was used to his language. They couldn't find any landmarks to match the ones they had been given. That shouldn't have been a surprise, since both the Germans and the British were continuing to create shell holes. One shell hole looked pretty much like another. From the feel of the shells landing nearby, they were from the 6-inch guns. It explained why the trenches the pioneers and the work parties had worked so hard to dig were now gone. The work of a thousand men had disappeared in less than forty-five minutes.

"Let's head that way," the lieutenant ordered, pointing down the crater's slope, where the shells were landing. He figured the Germans knew where the trench was, since they were obviously trying to destroy it.

About fifteen minutes later, he fell into it and was nearly bayoneted for his effort. Luckily, it was a weak thrust, and it slid off his helmet. "Hey, I'm a fucking Canadian!" he yelled.

"Bugger me, why didn't you say so!" a voice swore. From a shell flash, he saw the private was wounded. He had a bloody bandage covering his left arm. A moment later, he had to dodge the rest of his squad as they slid in. "Welcome to the party, such as it is," the wounded soldier said.

"I'm looking for Lieutenant Wainright. I'm here to relieve you."

"Yeah, right," the private said sourly. He turned his head and yelled, "Get the lieutenant." The sound of the message being passed down the line got drowned out as the shells continued to land in front of the trench.

Hot shrapnel pelted the trench. He yelled at the private, "Where are the dugouts?"

"What dugouts?"

Bédard winced when several of his men yelped in pain after being struck by hot metal fragments.

"Medic!" Sergeant Baker yelled.

"There ain't no medic," said the lieutenant, who suddenly appeared. Even in the dark, Bédard could tell that the man had a thousand-yard stare. He probably hadn't slept since he entered the trench three days ago. "You'll have to bandage them yourselves," he said to Baker. He then turned to Lieutenant Bédard. "I'm Wainright. You're here to relieve me?"

"Yes, so what's the situation?"

"Not good," the lieutenant replied. "Half my men are wounded. Three seriously. Half the trench is gone. There's a forty-yard gap between here and the other trench. I can't get in touch with them."

"Do you have a Lewis gun covering it?"

"Yeah, but fat lot of good it's doing us. The stupid thing jams after every three rounds. Mud is getting into the breech."

"What about your bombers?"

"They're gone. They were out front in a shell hole when a mortar landed on top of them," Wainright replied hoarsely. "I need to get my wounded out."

Lieutenant Bédard indicated with his head the trenches behind him and said, "The CTs and the support trenches are gone."

"Shit!"

"Shit is right," agreed Bédard.

"I sent a runner to Battalion HQ. The wire's out, and we used all of the pigeons the first day. So I guess he didn't make it."

"It looks like it. We'll have to hold out 'til morning."

"Lieutenant!" yelled a sentry who was trying to keep an eye on No Man's Land.

"What?" asked Wainright tiredly.

"I think that they are fucking coming now," he yelled back.

Both lieutenants looked over the top of the trench line. Through the single row of barbed wire, they could see ghostly shapes moving.

"Better get your men in the firing line," Wainright ordered just as the barrage ended.

The shapes became clearer as they rushed the trench. The cocking of the Lee-Enfields couldn't be heard over the sounds of the Germans shouting as they lunged toward them.

"Fire!" yelled Wainright. Bédard's bombers tossed their grenades at the Germans as fast as they could pull the pins. They then opened up with their rifles. Germans tumbled as they were hit. A whole German section moved to their right. Bédard could see their rifle flashes flow through the gap and head up the slope to the crater behind him.

A squad of Germans dropped into the trench behind him. Sergeant Baker went down first. Bédard speared the Hun who killed Baker in the throat with his bayoneted rifle. It enraged the German behind the Hun he had killed. The Boche slammed his Mauser's rifle butt into Bédard's head. Bédard's steel helmet didn't protect him.

APRIL 8, 1916
SECOND ARMY HEADQUARTERS, CASINO, CASSEL

Major-General Turner barely glanced out of the office window. The meeting Lieutenant-General Plumer had called was too important for the view to distract him. Today, the dull grey clouds disguised the picturesque town of Cassel that was spread out below the headquarters of the British Second Army in the Casino-Hotel complex. The village, with its narrow streets and windmills, was built on a five-hundred-foot hill. It was once home to General Foch, until he was promoted to command the French Army Group of the North. When he had driven in, he had noticed there was not a large contingent of British soldiers in the town. He knew that some of the Canadians had taken their leave here, but they hadn't been pleased. It had been too quiet for them, and the village liked it that way.

Turner hoped his meeting with Lieutenant-General Plumer would be the same. The last few days at St. Eloi had not gone as planned. He rose to his feet, as did his senior brigade commanders, when Plumer entered the room.

"Please be seated, gentlemen," he said as he gave Turner a quick nod. Turner wasn't sure if the general remembered his actions last year at Ypres, and he wasn't about to bring it up.

"I would like to discuss first the latest intelligence reports on the current situation at St. Eloi, then our plans for the next few days," Turner said as he adjusted his wire-rimmed glasses.

"Very well, please begin," Plumer ordered.

"We had patrols out to reconnoitre the craters. The 21st Battalion had taken a look at Crater Number 2. They couldn't approach the crater directly, since it was constantly being shelled. They did report the trenches from 73 to 96 were being well manned and they could hear the Germans working hard making improvements. At Crater 3, which appears to be one hundred yards long and seventy-five yards wide, they found the crater's parapets had been destroyed by shell fire. Our patrols were fired upon as they approached it, and they reported Boche SOS flares being launched from inside the crater. The 28th Battalion reported that Crater 5 was being garrisoned by our men. They have a trench dug, and they have suffered very few casualties," Turner stated. "Unfortunately, we have not been able to obtain aerial photos to confirm, since the aeroplanes cannot fly in this weather," he added.

"I see," Lieutenant-General Plumer replied. Turner knew that Plumer was well aware of the price that his 3rd Division had paid taking St. Eloi. The lieutenant-general studied the large detailed map of St. Eloi that lay on the table.

Turner continued his report. "The Huns have been pounding our trenches continually with their 12-cm, 15-cm, and 77-mm guns. Our CTs and our support trenches are constantly being shelled with shrapnel. It's hampering our ability to move men, ammunition, and rations to our forward lines.

"We have captured a number of German prisoners and deserters. During our interrogations, we have learned we're facing the 26 MG Trupp, the 215 Rifle Regiment, the 46th Division, and the XXIII Corps. Based on other intelligence we have obtained, it appears that the Germans have allocated nine battalions to take back St. Eloi."

Lieutenant-General Plumer grimaced at the news. "What are you proposing?"

"The trenches in front of the craters are exposed to the German artillery on three sides. We would like to pull them back and occupy the craters," stated Major-General Turner.

Lieutenant-General Plumer stared at the map. "Very well. I would suggest you link the craters' south edges with trenches. During the day, have the men withdraw to the north side of the crater. You'll need deep dugouts to protect the men from shell fire. I don't think the Hughes Trench is tenable during daylight, so it shouldn't be occupied. I would suggest your 4.5-inch howitzers bombard the Germans this afternoon and use shrapnel shells for Crater 2 and 3."

"Yes, sir," replied Major-General Turner. He was pleased that Plumer had accepted his plan.

"Good," Plumer said. He gave Turner a brief smile. "I would like to mention that General Joffre and I have spoken on the phone earlier. He wanted to thank us for our efforts here at St. Eloi. We seemed to have relieved some of the German pressure on his forces at Verdun."

"Thank you, General Plumer," Major-General Turner replied with a brief acknowledging nod.

APRIL 10, 1916
CRATER 2, ST. ELOI

"Is that the right crater?" asked Captain Carter as he peered over the trench.

"I think so," replied the mud-smeared scout standing beside him. It was dusk, and it was difficult to see what colour the man's face and hair was. When he spoke, his yellowed teeth were a sharp contrast. "The damn mound changes every time we and the Boche shell it."

Captain Carter examined the ridge line of the crater that his orders had instructed him to capture. "Well, is it or isn't it?" he demanded.

"Yeah, it's the crater," replied the scout. The captain could still sense some doubt in the man's voice. If this was Crater 2, then Crater 3 was supposed to be on his left. But all that he could see from his position was a thin ridge line about a hundred yards in front of him. Since it was on an incline, he couldn't see what was behind it. Supposedly, Crater 2 was occupied by the Huns. The garrisons at craters 4 and 5 had attempted to raid the crater but were forced to fall back with heavy losses.

The captain grimaced when he took a second look at the ridge. He had too many men for his assault. The frontage was smaller than he had been informed. He would need to reduce the first wave by at least a third or to half, otherwise they would be crowded during their attack and would be in each other's way. If there were machine guns, which was likely, his men would be mincemeat.

He grunted, then told the scout, "Inform lieutenants Cramer and Hoskins I'm putting them in the reserve. Tell lieutenants Moore and Butcher they will be leading the assault, and I want to talk with them first."

The scout acknowledged then disappeared down the trench. He then turned to his signaller and asked, "Is the line good?"

The man removed the receiver from his ear and replied, "It's been cut again."

"Shit!" muttered the captain as lieutenants Moore and Butcher arrived. "Get your men ready. The plan is basically the same as we discussed. The bombers will lead, and the bayonet men will protect them and clean up. It looks from the frontage that it's pretty crowded, that's why the 3rd and 4th will be our reserve. We'll go in fifteen. Any questions?"

Both men shook their heads before they headed back to their positions.

When Carter had climbed out of the trench, he was satisfied that his two sections were slowly making their way toward the crater. When the bombers had reached their designated positions, he took his whistle out of the pouch on his webbing and blow into it hard. At the sound of the sharp whistle blast, the bombers started tossing their grenades into the crater. Some of the grenades sounded muffled when they detonated. Spurts of water told him they had fallen in the water in the crater's bottom.

Once the initial wave of bombs had detonated, the bayonet men jumped in. What surprised the captain was he heard no yelling or screaming in German. The only language he heard was English. When he finally slid over the top, he saw scattered bodies wearing German and English uniforms. From the smell that hit his nostrils, they had been there for several days.

"Sir, there's no one here," said Lieutenant Moore. "Alive, that is."

"They are supposed to be here. Where the hell are they?"

"Damned if I know. At least the crater is ours now."

CHAPTER 9

When Samantha opened her eyes, she croaked, "What the hell are you doing here?"

The man who was slouched in a white chair next to her bed hadn't heard her. His forge cap was pulled down over his familiar face, and she could see part of his left eyelid fluttering. She knew he was dreaming. He snorted then abruptly shifted in his chair. As he did, he adjusted the dark grey CAMC blanket covering him. He raised a hand, rubbed his nose, then he finally opened his eyes. When he saw she was awake, Major Llewellyn chuckled warmly. "I see you're going to make it after all."

"How did you get here?" she rasped. Her tongue seemed to be stuck to the roof of her mouth, and her throat was sore. Her blankets felt damp. No surprise, she had been running a fever for the last few days.

"You shouldn't be here," she whispered. "I'm still contagious."

Llewellyn cocked his head. Even though he was smiling, she could see worry lines etched on his face. Her fever had been so bad, she had been given last rites. "I've spoken with the doctor. You're no longer contagious," he said with a grin. "I think they like me around here. Otherwise, they would have let me in to see you sooner. Besides, I had it when I was a kid, so I'm immune."

"I must look awful," she said as she pulled her blanket up to her neck.

"Like a strawberry," he replied.

Samantha groaned. She should have known what it was when the first symptoms appeared. She had been getting headaches, and her throat had been feeling scratchy. It wasn't until the rash on her neck and tongue had taken on a strawberry appearance that she realized she had contracted scarlet fever. The hospital's CO, Major Kingsworth, had immediately quarantined her and any patients she may have had contact with.

How she had contracted it, she didn't know. She was usually quite diligent with her hygiene, washing her hands frequently and not touching her mouth or eyes. Scarlet fever was usually a childhood disease and a deadly one. In Sudbury, where she grew up, she had been to a number of funerals of classmates who didn't survive after being infected.

"How did you get here?" she then got a worried look. "You're not AWOL? Are you?"

A look of surprise crossed Llewellyn's face. "What kind of example would I be if, I, the brigade-major, went AWOL?" he demanded. When she managed a look of chagrin, he said, "Colonel Tennison gave me a pass when I received a telegram informing me you weren't feeling well."

Samantha gave him a startled look. She wondered who had sent him word. She asked puzzled, "Your CO gave you a pass?"

"Don't look so surprised. He's married. Besides, he likes you."

"He does?"

"Oh yes, he said you had a nice bottom," Llewellyn replied.

Samantha was sure she was blushing. She doubted he would have noticed with the red rash running down her neck to her breasts. She knew that in the next few days her skin would start to peel as if she had been sunburned.

"How many days leave do you have?"

"Why? Do you want to go dancing?" he teased. When she glared at him, he quickly said, "It's only for five days."

"How many days do you have left?"

"Two," he replied sadly. "But, I need a travelling day to get back to my post. The colonel might be sentimental, but he'll still court martial me if I don't report for duty on time."

"Well, next time we'll go out dancing," she replied.

"It's a date," he replied. It was a promise that both knew that in the circumstances might never be kept. "All teasing aside, how are you really feeling?"

"I'm tired, but my head is clearing. I think I will be up and about in a few days. It's embarrassing getting sick like this," she replied. She started to reach out to him but stopped when she realized what the consequences were if she still were infected. "Thank you, James, for coming. It means a lot to me."

Llewellyn gave her an understanding smile, but he didn't hesitate reaching out and moving a lock of hair from her eyes.

"By the way, where are you sleeping?" she asked.

"Why right here."

"Oh my God! I'm ruined! I'm ruined!" she exclaimed hoarsely.

"Really? Haven't I done that already?" he jested just as a young VAD entered Samantha's room with fresh blankets.

APRIL 14, 1916
PIER, NEW YORK CITY

"My friends need not worry. My enemies will be dealt with. There is no doubt as to the outcome," Sir Sam Hughes said to the reporter with a broad smile.

Normally, he enjoyed exchanging barbs with pressmen. Despite the pouring rain, there had been a large crowd of newspapermen waiting for him on the New York City pier. It was no secret he would be arriving this afternoon; it had been published in yesterday's papers that he would be on the American Line's SS *Saint Paul*.

When he glanced at Wallace Nesbitt, his lawyer, standing near his elbow under the umbrella being held by his aide Captain Bassett, he couldn't help seeing his deep frown. Wallace, a former Canadian Supreme Court justice, was well known in Conservative circles. Hughes had been surprised when Wallace took a cutter out, the first thing this morning, to board his liner farther down the Hudson to brief him on the charges the lying scoundrel Liberal MP Kyte had put before the House. Wallace had warned him to say as little as possible to the press.

"I have no further comments," Hughes informed the reporters as he headed for the pier's exit. "I'll be issuing a statement later."

As he reached the exit, he glanced back at the ship that he had boarded in Southampton. When he had dinner with the ship's captain, he had learned that the vessel was one of the US Navy's auxiliary cruisers. This meant that in time of war the 553-foot steamer would be armed with six 5-inch, six 6-pounder, and six 3-pounder guns on her decks. The berths, 320 first-class, 200 second-class, and 900 steerage, would be used to transport troops.

He frowned when he spotted Major-General Lessard on the gangplank. He hadn't spoken with him much during the voyage besides pleasantries. He didn't particularly care for the man, but he was still annoyed Lessard had been offered a position with the Imperials by the War Office. During the Boer War, Lessard had served with Field-Marshal French and Major-General Smith Dorrian, so he was well known to them. To accept the post, they had offered he would have to resign from the Canadian Permanent Force. He had already sent his resignation to Borden, but the prime minister had asked him to reconsider. That was one of the reasons why he too was on his way back to Ottawa.

Hughes wasn't looking forward to sitting in the House on Monday. It wasn't because of the false charges being laid against him by the Liberals. What annoyed him was he thought he had an agreement with them not to attack him while he was gone, and they had broken it. It was because of that broken promise that the prime minister had ordered him to come back to Ottawa immediately.

He had left much work undone in England and France. His personal investigation, following his meeting with Major-General Carson and Colonel Aitken, had confirmed his suspicions that it was Major-General MacDougall who was causing the problems. There was considerable friction between him and generals Carson and Steele. Also, there was a great deal of animosity among the members of the generals' staff. He had called a town hall meeting in Shorncliffe to lay down the law to his senior officers to get along. Also, he had ordered Brigadier-General Paul Watson to report to him in London from France. It had been his intention to make him, the former commander of the 2nd Division's 5th Brigade, the inspector-general in charge of reorganizing the Canadian Army's operations in England. He had plans to promote him to major-general and make him his supreme commander in England. They were placed on hold when Borden demanded Hughes's return.

He had thought of ignoring Borden's order and staying in England to complete his task of perfecting the machinery supporting his boys in France. But when Nesbitt had boarded his ship, before it could dock at its pier in the New York harbour, he then realized how seriously Borden was taking the charges. If he had ignored Borden and stayed in England, it would have been the wrong decision.

He had planned to take the evening train to Ottawa, but Nesbitt had told him that some of the men Kyte had named in the House were in New York and wanted to discuss the matter with him to clear up misunderstandings. Unfortunately, his good friend Allison wasn't among them, the one person he wanted to talk to. A day's delay would give him more time to prepare. Without a doubt, when he got to Ottawa his days were going to be long and trying ones.

CHAPTER 10

APRIL 16, 1916
2ND DIVISION HEADQUARTERS, RENINGELST

Captain Montagne waited tensely, as he stood in front of Major-General Turner's desk, for the bad news he had just delivered to set in.

"What do you mean the Germans are occupying the craters?" he demanded, stabbing at the aerial photos the captain had just given to him. "All of them?"

"I'm afraid so, sir. Captain Ross, from the 24th Battalion, late last night sent me a report after his personal reconnaissance of the craters. He said 2, 3, 4, and 5 were all occupied by the Germans. And from the look of their dispositions, for some time. With the weather clearing, the Air Corps finally sent up scout planes to get aerial photos of St. Eloi for us," he said, pointing to the photos Turner had been stabbing. "Our staff has taken a close look at them. They clearly show the Huns occupying all the craters."

"When did we lose Craters 4 and 5? All the reports we've been receiving have indicated we have garrisons at those two craters."

"I agree that's the information we've received. However, it has come in sporadically, and our communications lines have been constantly disrupted. The artillery barrages have destroyed many of the landmarks on the mound. Without accurate landmarks, our men might have reported they were garrisoning Crater 2 when in fact they were in Crater 7."

Turner turned grey at the news. "We have an assault planned this evening from the craters we were supposed to be occupying. They were to take back those craters that the Germans had taken from us?"

"Yes, sir," acknowledged Montagne uncomfortably. "This is why I brought it to your attention as soon as the picture became clear to me."

Turner's mouth thinned under his moustache. "We'll have to cancel the operation. No point wasting more men until we determine exactly what we are facing."

"Yes, sir," replied Montagne.

"Now, I have to figure out what to tell General Alderson and General Plumer," Turner said as he removed his reading glasses and cleaned them vigorously with a handkerchief from his uniform pocket. Montagne understood Turner's dilemma perfectly. He was the one who had been providing the information for the status reports flowing to his CO, to the Canadian Corps, and to the Second Army. He had a strong feeling what their reaction would be once they have been informed the picture the 2nd Division had been painting was not entirely accurate.

APRIL 16, 1916
TRENCH MORTAR SCHOOL, NIEPPE

Major Llewellyn watched as a mortar landed just short of the barbed wire. The entanglement disappeared in a cloud of exploding dirt. It took a few moments for the sand cloud to dissipate. When it cleared, the major could see what remained. He lowered his binoculars then said to Lieutenant Ryan standing beside him, "That looks good. Very good."

Ryan smiled. "Like I said, 'practice, practice, practice.'"

"Where have I heard that before?" said Llewellyn with a snort.

"I have no idea, sir."

"Let's take a look see," said the major.

"Yes, Major." Ryan turned to the sergeant leading the closest mortar team and ordered, "Secure the mortars."

"Secure the mortars!" the sergeant yelled. The order was repeated to the remaining three mortar teams.

Major Llewellyn climbed out of the trench built on the range to acclimatize the mortar teams with trench duty. With Ryan in tow, he marched to the wire entanglement built at the 400-yard marker. The ground was uneven, pockmarked with shell holes from earlier mortar rounds. Both men kept a wary eye for unexploded ordnance as they walked. Not all the shells that had been launched had exploded. A certain percentage of them were duds. After each session, the engineers would come out and police the misfires. Usually, they would detonate them where they were found. A few were carefully disarmed then sent for analysis to determine why they hadn't exploded. The shell serial numbers were recorded to determine which manufacturers and batches had production problems. A dud, at the inopportune time, could spell disaster.

When they finally reached the barbed wire, Llewellyn stopped and cranked his neck to examine what remained of the entanglement. They had built a fence fifty-six yards wide, thirty-three deep, and four-and-half feet high. The wire had been in four loose strands at one-foot increments. "It looks even better here," Llewellyn finally said. "The gap looks about thirty to forty feet."

"Thereabout," replied Ryan after he had made a similar calculation.

"We should be able to get a company through right quick," Llewellyn pointed out.

"Yeah, that's what the Third Army said in their report when they had run this experiment."

"I read the report. But they used the 2-inch mortar," Llewellyn said.

"That's why we ran the same test using the Stokes," answered Ryan.

"How many rounds did you fire?"

"Forty. Four short and six long. The rest you can see landed right on the target," Ryan answered with a sweep of his arm.

"Well, I like this better than the ammonal experiments the CRE ran two months ago."

When Ryan gave him a puzzled look, Llewellyn cocked an eyebrow. "Obviously, you didn't get the report. They fill a metal pipe with ammonal then slid it under the wire and detonated it."

"How did it do?"

"It worked pretty well. Ammonal isn't particularly affected by water. You need only six ounces per foot. The pipe needs to be capped at both ends to increase the force needed to cut the wire and the supports."

Ryan looked at the wire fence again and did another calculation. "You'll need thirty feet of pipe and men to get to the wire to slide it underneath it."

"There's that," the major acknowledged. "It might prove useful during our raids. Sending the scouts to the wire first before the assault teams go in."

"I'd rather pound them from afar," said Ryan.

"So would I," agreed Llewellyn. "The problem with the mortars is the timing. If the company goes in to soon, they'll get cut to shreds."

"I know," Ryan acknowledged. "It's a problem."

"We'll have to figure it out. Also, I'm sorry to see you go."

"What can I say? I'm being recalled back to the 65th."

"No more mortar teams?"

"The 18-pounders. I heard we might be attached to the 2nd Division"

"They are having a tough time at St. Eloi, based on the rumours I've been hearing."

Ryan cocked an ear. "Rumours?"

Llewellyn smiled. He had been the 1st Division's intelligence officer. "Rumours."

"Well, I did hear the explosion they set off there a couple of weeks ago."

"Some say they heard it as far as Folkestone," replied Llewellyn. When Ryan raised an eyebrow Llewellyn said, "That was not a rumour."

"If you say so. Well, it was good working with you," said Lieutenant Ryan as he shook Major Llewellyn's hand.

"Keep your head down," said the major.

"Don't I always," answered Ryan as he continued staring at the barbed wire fence.

APRIL 16, 1916
PRIME MINISTER'S HOME, GLENSMERE, OTTAWA

It was four o'clock when Sir Robert Borden opened his front door to find Sam Hughes, dressed in his khaki overcoat and forage cap, on his doorstep. The temperature was dropping with the evening sun, and he could feel some of the chill through his sweater's thin weave.

"Good afternoon, Prime Minister," Hughes said. His smile was strained.

"Come in, Sam," replied Borden as he let Hughes in. He had been dreading this all day. Now that it had finally arrived, he felt rather calm.

It had been a glorious spring day. By nine, the temperature had risen to 44 degrees. Most of the nine inches of snow that had fallen the previous week had melted, but he had to be careful when he took his walks, since the walkways and the streets were now covered with thick ice. He did notice the elders and the lilacs were starting the bud when he walked down Hemlock Path to the Rideau River. The river was still ice-covered, but he had seen some patches of open water.

In the afternoon, he and Laura had sunned themselves on the second-floor veranda. He had gotten a few hours' respite from his worries. The news from Europe was mixed. The Germans were still attacking the French at Verdun, but at least Canadian casualties were light this week compared with the previous losses of the 2nd Division at St. Eloi. He did receive a telegram from Perley informing him he had been invited to the Economic Conference in Paris. The one that another Hughes, the Australian prime minister, had tried to talk him into going to. He told

Billy Hughes he wouldn't be able to attend, and he had been prescient in his statement.

His government was currently facing three crises: the bilingual question, the railways' financial problems, and the Shell Committee. Any of them could bring down his government if they weren't properly handled. The pressure had gotten so bad, he was seriously considering resigning as prime minister. Foster would be a good choice as his replacement. He would then be able to focus on running the Department of Militia and Defence. He couldn't do any worse than Sam.

"How is Lady Borden faring?" asked Hughes as he settled in a chair in Borden's office. Borden took the one opposite Sam.

"She's improving. We enjoyed a bit of sun on the veranda this afternoon," replied Borden. "How was the voyage back from England?"

"It was rather pleasant, but we had a few days of rough seas," replied Hughes. "Sir Mackenzie was kind enough to meet me when I docked in New York."

Borden acknowledged with a nod. Sir William Mackenzie, the president of the Canadian Northern Railway, had volunteered to meet with Hughes to impress on him the gravity of the situation and the attitude he needed to carry.

There was a moment of awkward silence as Borden considered how he could start his conversation. He finally asked, "Did you have an opportunity to read Kyte's charges that he made in the House?"

"Yes, I did," replied Hughes sourly.

"And?"

"It's all horse manure," replied Hughes hotly.

Borden peered at Hughes over his glasses. "I'm afraid this is quite serious. Feelings in the caucus are running strongly against you."

"I assure you, Prime Minister, that I have no involvement in the fuse contracts, or these so-called commissions."

"You do understand why we had to call an inquiry?"

"Yes, I do," Hughes answered. "I assure you that I will come through it with flying colours," he said confidently. Borden masked his serious doubt that it would be the case.

"What I would like you to consider is taking a hiatus during the inquiry. While you're away, I will be administrating your department," Borden stated.

A surprised look appeared on Hughes's face, then his lips began quivering. "But that would humiliate me!" he exclaimed. Hughes's eyes began to tear at the prospect of losing his cherished department.

"I disagree. I think it would strengthen your position," Borden replied as he tried to reassure Hughes. "In your Tuesday statement to the House, I want you to state you asked me to administer your department until the inquiry has cleared you of any wrongdoing."

Hughes looked away from Borden. Borden could see in Sam's profile that he would be stubborn about his request, order, actually. "What about General Lessard?" Hughes suddenly asked.

"I've decided that he will remain," Borden replied. His statement caused Hughes to give him a sharp look. Borden could see in his eyes that Sam was wondering what machinations were behind Borden's decision.

"So I'm being suspended," he finally said.

"You're not being suspended. I will be administrating the department during the inquiry. It's important that the proprieties be maintained. Once the inquiry has been completed, I will return the department back to you to run."

Hughes had crossed his arms with his chin jutted.

"I cannot emphasize enough that you need to do this. Do I make myself clear?"

"Yes, Prime Minister," Hughes replied curtly as he looked away from Borden's eyes.

Borden nearly sighed. He still had doubts whether Hughes would see sense and comply. This solution was in Sam's and the party's best interest. He would have to wait until Tuesday to find out.

APRIL 26, 1916
WOODS BUILDING, OTTAWA

"What's the bloody matter with the Lewis machine guns?" demanded an irate Sir Robert Borden. This was the last thing he wanted to hear, especially after all the problems with the Ross rifle.

The senior officers who were sitting in the fourth-floor conference room of the Woods Building tried not to shift uncomfortably in their chairs. At the table with him were Major-General Fiset, in his capacity as the department's deputy-minister, not as the surgeon-general; Major-General Gwatkin, the chief of the general staff; Brigadier-General V.A.S Williams, the adjutant-general; Major-General D.A. Macdonald, the quartermaster-general; Brigadier-General H.M. Elliot, the master-general of ordnance; his brother John Borden, the department's accountant; and E.F. Jarvis, the assistant deputy-minister and the Militia Council's secretary.

Fiset was chairing the Militia Council meeting today. The council had been set up when the Department of Militia and Defence was reformed in 1905 to provide the minister advice on various topics impacting the department. Hughes never made much use of the council, since he felt they couldn't keep up with him, and he didn't particularly like the man running ordnance or the quartermaster. While Hughes was on hiatus, he was still complaining he was being suspended, but Borden decided to restart the weekly meetings.

Brigadier-General Elliot coughed when Gwatkin and Fiset gave him a glance. "If I may explain, Prime Minister. Colonel White's men…" When he saw the prime minister's confusion, he explained, "Colonel White is our chief ordnance officer in Kent at Ashford.

"His men have been examining and testing the Savage Lewis automatic guns when they received them in England. They discovered the gun's parts were not interchangeable, and some of them were not properly hardened. The unhardened parts could fail, rendering the gun unsafe for the men to operate."

"Is this the same problems as the Ross?" Borden asked Gwatkin. He hadn't forgotten that his chief of the general staff had assured him last December that the rifles were fine.

"The Lewis machine gun is a very good weapon. It will be a fine addition to our men's combat power. It's light, only twenty-eight pounds. A single man can operate it. The BSA models have proven themselves when they came into service last year in France. Last December, our small arms committee in Quebec City thoroughly vetted them. They performed very well during the endurance testing, with very few blockages. Repairs are simple and easy to do," Gwatkin replied.

"What's wrong with the ones that they got in England?"

"What Colonel White indicated," Elliot continued, "was the parts they had received didn't meet tolerances. Each part's tolerance is important for the weapon's proper functioning. They found when they fitted the block in one gun, it was too loose, and when they tried it in another Lewis, it was too tight. If we can't exchange parts, we lose the use of the gun.

"The Chief Inspector of Arms and Ammunition examined the two Lewis machine guns the Savage Company provided to us here in Canada.

He found that there were very minor problems. He says Savage was provided with the technical drawings for the Lewis machine gun and three BSA examples. They, however, were not given the tolerance specifications. When Savage took the BSA models apart, they found the parts were not interchangeable either.

"As you're undoubtedly aware, in the middle of a battle, they need to function properly. If they break down, parts are needed to get the Lewises back into working order. We also have to consider the safety of our men. We can't have machine guns exploding in their hands."

"Of course not," replied Borden. "Can they be repaired?"

"Yes," replied Elliott, nodding. "The ones in England will be sent to Enfield for repairs. The Savage Company has been informed, and modifications will be made at their end."

"I see," replied Borden. He was not entirely satisfied, but he had to rely on his senior officers' judgement. "I would like to be kept informed of the process of the Lewis automatic guns."

"Yes, Prime Minister."

"The next item on the agenda is the 66th and 68th Battalions," said Major-General Fiset, the council's president. "I'm pleased to inform you they have arrived at Quebec City and will be shortly embarking the transports for England."

"I'm happy to hear that," Borden said. "They were a good-looking group of men." He had reviewed them two days ago before they had left Ottawa. The 66th Battalion was from Edmonton, while the 68th was from Regina. He had been impressed by the physiques of the Edmonton soldiers.

Borden then said, "I sent a message to General Alderson informing him that the entire country will be raising the flag to honour the anniversary of last year's battle at Ypres." The raising of the flag was one of the many events being held across the country to honour the men who had successfully held the line against the Germans. Laura had attended such an event at the Russell Hotel last Sunday. There had been discussions about lowering the flag to half-mast, but he and the governor general had agreed it would have sent the wrong message.

He ran his hand through his hair as he thought of the problems between Lieutenant-General Alderson and Sam Hughes. He had heard through George Perley that the two men refused to meet to discuss the administrative problems in England that were impacting the Corps in France. Each man demanded that the other make the first move. He was surprised when Hughes showed him a telegram from Sir Max Aitken with a proposal to smooth relations between Alderson and Major-General Turner. He had agreed with Aitken's approach and hoped that it would solve some of the problems.

"I'm sure the men will be pleased," replied Fiset with a satisfied nod. "Now, next on the agenda, we want to talk briefly about the Irish rebellion…"

APRIL 26, 1916
CHÂTEAU DE BEAUREPAIRE, MONTREUIL-SUR-MER

When Sir Max Aitken's car had stopped in front of the Château de Beaurepaire, a colonel was already waiting for him on the front steps. "Good afternoon, Sir Aitken, would you please follow me? General Haig is expecting you."

"Of course, Colonel," Sir Aitken replied as he followed the colonel into the chateau. The building appeared to be a modest but a comfortable one. The three rectangular windows on both sides of the entrance were framed in red brick with a grey stone trim. Above the second floor, there were three dormer windows that provided light to the attic. To his left there was a one-storey extension that he assumed was General Haig's office. It appeared that there was a patio on top of the extension because of the stone railing running around the top.

Aitken knew General Sir Douglas Haig had moved into his new quarters less than a month ago. Previously, Haig's GHQ had been at St. Omer, but it had been relocated to Montreuil-sur-Mer because the village was better suited to accommodate the British Army's expansion. The École Militaire in the village had become the army's administrative centre for the western front. Since Montreuil-sur-Mer was located halfway between Paris and London, it made travelling between the two capitals for meetings with political and military officials more convenient. In his case, he doubted General Haig would have come to him to discuss the topic of the meeting he had requested.

He found General Haig at his desk, signing papers with a gold fountain pen. Haig was immaculately dressed in a khaki uniform. His Sam Brown circled his waist and chest. On his left breast he wore his ribbon bar. Haig was in his mid-fifties, of medium height and weight. His grey hair and his moustache were streaked with dark strands. He had replaced Field Marshal French last December as the commander-in-chief of the British Empire's forces in France.

He looked up when Aiken entered his office. He rose to his feet and came around the desk to shake Aitken's hand. "Ah, Sir Aitken," General Haig said. "Welcome, please have a seat. I hope that your trip wasn't to tiring. Would you like some tea?"

"Tea would be excellent, General Haig," replied Aitken. "As for my trip, it was comfortable, but I had some moments when I took the ferry across the channel."

Haig smiled. "It was quite crowded during the Easter weekend when I made the trip across. Most of our men wanted to spend the weekend at their homes, but we had to restrict their leave. The rail companies requested it. Easter always taxes their capacity. They needed transport for the civilians so they could enjoy the Easter holidays with their families."

Aitken returned Haig's wry smile. Once the colonel left to get their tea, he could see the general focus his attention on him. Haig was well aware of his roles both as a representative of the Canadian government and his position as a Member of Parliament in the British government. Aitken was also fairly certain Haig had read or at least had been informed about his book, *Canada in Flanders*.

"I've been informed General Plumer has requested generals Turner and Ketchen be relieved of their commands," Sir Aitken stated.

Haig didn't seem to be surprised by his statement. "I did. General Plumer is of the opinion both men performed poorly at St. Eloi. General Alderson has similar sentiments."

Sir Aitken knew he was treading on delicate ground between the British desire to have competent senior officers and the Canadian political desire to have Canadian officers running their Corps. "The Canadian prime minister has expressed his concern with the suggestion to replace Turner and Ketchen, especially if their commands are given to British officers."

Haig gave him a pensive look. Aitken had noticed the slight tension when he mentioned Borden's name. He had heard Haig was somewhat irritated he was to treat the Canadians as if they were an allied country instead of a colony of the Empire.

"I've given the matter some thought," Haig replied. "While it appears that both Turner and Ketchen didn't perform well, they were not totally to blame. They did encounter some extremely difficult circumstances. Also, it is my understanding that it has been a challenge finding Canadian officers with suitable experience." Aitken noticed Haig hadn't entirely absolved them of blame for the St. Eloi defeat. "I therefore would like to minimize any friction between us and the Canadian government. I have decided the two officers will remain in their current posts."

"Thank you," Aitken said. "The Canadian government will be quite pleased with your decision once I have informed them." He paused then said, "You mentioned your concern about friction. I'm afraid there has been a considerable amount between the Canadian government and General Alderson."

"Is the Canadian government requesting that General Alderson be relieved?" Haig asked bluntly. When Aitken acknowledged with a nod, Haig said with a touch of reluctance, "I would have some concerns replacing General Alderson. He has been performing satisfactorily."

"He has lost the confidence of Prime Minister Borden and Minister Hughes," Aitken pointed out.

"Still…"

"What if he were offered the position of inspector-general of the Canadian forces here in England?" suggested Aitken.

"It would preserve his dignity. Give me a day or to consider it," Haig replied thoughtfully.

"Of course," replied Sir Aitken, quite satisfied that his plan was set in motion.

"Ah, here is the tea," Haig said as an orderly wheeled a tea trolley into the office.

CHAPTER 11

"Acknowledged," Paul Ryan snapped into the phone's mouthpiece as he wrote the coordinates down. He was in a foul mood. He wished he could blame getting out of bed on the wrong side, except his bed had only one side.

He rose to his feet and exited the sandbagged bunker. He found Commandant-Captain Benoit Peeters talking with a sous-lieutenant. They were inspecting one of the 75s being worked on by one of the 7th Belgian Field Artillery's gun crews. The commandant-captain was in his early forties, thin framed with a small paunch. He was immaculately dressed in a British khaki uniform with a scarlet mandarin-style collar. Under his steel khaki Adrian helmet, his auburn hair was cut short.

"The Boche are hitting the 2nd Brigade with seventy-sevens, four point ones, and five nine shells," he informed the Commandant-Captain in French. "They would like you to discourage them at these coordinates," he continued as he handed him his note.

Paul didn't need to explain to Peeters that the seventy-sevens were the 77-mm *Feldkanone* 96 gun, which fired a fifteen-pound shell. It was roughly equivalent to the French 75s and the British 18-pounders. The German gun was slightly shorter-ranged than the Allies, but it was highly effective. The 4.1 was the 105-mm *Feldhaubitze* howitzer that could fire a thirty-pound shell nearly seven thousand yards. The 5.9 was the 150-mm *Feldhaubitze*. It was a heavy field piece capable of firing a ninety-three-pound shell nearly ten thousand yards. All of them were within range of the Commandant-Captain's French 75s, or as they were commonly called, the '*soxiante-quinze*.' The gun could send a twelve-pound shell twelve thousand yards, although its effective range was only seventy-five hundred yards.

Peeters took the note and then started issuing orders to the sous-lieutenant. The commandant-captain had been rather formal with Ryan. Ryan suspected that the quality of some of the previous liaison officers had been uneven. It probably accounted for the Belgian CO's stiffness. While he didn't particularly want to be here, at least he did his level best at the job they had given him. When he was recalled back to the 65th Artillery, he thought he would be returned to his original battery. Instead, he had been given to the Belgians. The Belgian 7th, after providing tactical support to the British 3rd Division during their attack on St. Eloi, had been reassigned to the 1st Canadian Division's artillery right group.

He had been here only for two days, so Ryan wasn't certain where he fell in Peeters's estimation. He was a difficult man to read, and the Belgians were a close-knit group. Not surprising, since they had a small army. They manned only twenty-six miles of trenches from Nieuwpoort to Ypres. He did wonder how the Belgian Army was coping with rein-forcements, since most of their country was under German occupation. It was unlikely the Germans would allow young Belgian volunteers to cross their trenches. It also explained the mixture of their equipment. They were fitted with British uniforms, French helmets and artillery, and carried the Mauser 1889 carbines. He had initially thought the carbines were German, but he had been firmly corrected. They were the Belgian version, manufactured by Fabrique Nationale, and they fired a 7.65-mm round.

The Belgian gunners were quick. They made adjustments to the gun, rammed a shell into the breach, and were now waiting for the fire order. Commandant-Captain Peeters nodded with satisfaction. When Ryan first arrived, Peeters had proudly shown off the 75s to him. Ryan didn't need to be told that the soixante-quinze had revolutionized the field artillery. Based on a German engineer's concept of an oil and compressed air recoil system, the French had managed to build an artillery piece where the gun didn't have to be relaid after each shot. The models the Belgians were using had been built by the French arms manufacturer, Schneider.

Paul had to admit the 75s had a cleaner look than his 18-pounder. The 75's gun barrel sat on top of the recoil system, while it was the reverse on the 18-pounder. The 75's shell was a half-inch smaller and weighed nearly five to six pounds less. Not much, but after an hour of lifting shells, it made a difference, especially when they fired forty rounds a minute, which they rarely did. The normal rate was a more sedate four rounds per minute to minimize barrel heat and wear.

"Fire!" shouted Peeters.

Paul watched as all six guns started their fire sequence. When the first shells were on their way, Peeters turned to Paul, raising an eyebrow.

Embarrassed, Paul turned, then hurried back to the bunker to receive the FOs reports on the Belgian's barrage.

APRIL 30, 1916
1ST CANADIAN DIVISION HEADQUARTERS, HOOGRAAF

"So, what do you think?" Tennison asked when he and Major Llewellyn exited Major-General Currie's Headquarters. The building was a large, three-chambered concrete bunker with sandbags protecting the roof. It had been built by the Second Army near a crossroad just outside the Flemish village of Hoograaf. Nearby, they could see men unloading food to waiting motorized trunks and horse-drawn wagons from a train parked on a siding.

Llewellyn glanced at Major-General Currie, who was chatting with Brigadier-General Lipsett. Currie had called a conference of his senior commanders to discuss the report on the 2nd Canadian Division's operations at St. Eloi. "It sounded like they had a rough time," he replied as he watched Currie laughing at some remark Lipsett had made.

"You can say that, since they suffered about fourteen hundred casualties," Tennison said as he cranked his neck, looking for their driver.

"Sure," replied Llewellyn. "They made some mistakes, but it wasn't entirely their fault. They had to relieve the 3rd Division earlier than they had planned. They didn't have time to do an adequate reconnaissance of the line they were supposed to man. But they made problems worse by not getting adequate intelligence on what they had to deal with. It's not fun having a trench on a downslope exposed on three sides to German artillery. Yes, they had it tough. They had the shit pounded out of them."

Tennison remarked tersely, "You need to trust your people to do their jobs and to report the correct information up the line."

"I agree," replied Llewellyn. "But you're telling me you wouldn't have started asking questions about what the hell the men were reporting? Especially when they said the landmarks aren't matching up with the maps. We went through this crap last May at Festubert. You remember how shitty the maps were there. Remember how much it cost us."

"I know," replied Tennison. He had been at the Festubert battle, since he was on Currie's staff at the time.

"Which is a fucking shame. The 2nd Division has some fine hot-corner men, and they did a hell of a job. It leaves a sour taste that we have to learn the same bloody lessons all over again."

"You have a valid point," replied Tennison. "I think they'll be taking it to heart."

"I hope so," replied Llewellyn. He caught something in Tennison's face. "What did you hear?"

Tennison gave him a look.

"Come on," Llewellyn demanded. "You and Colonel Hastings had your head together. And I know he always has the latest gossip."

"It was a disaster. Who do you think they're going to blame? The 3rd Division who lost a thousand men winning ground or the 2nd Division who gave it up with severe losses?" asked Tennison.

"So it started already, the finger-pointing," said Llewellyn. "Why am I not surprised?"

"General Plumer is out for blood. He wants Ketchen's head. The 6th Brigade is the one he thinks screwed up."

"Shit!" Llewellyn replied. "Is Turner going to give him up?"

"Turner?" Tennison gave a so-so hand wave. "He's pretty loyal to his men. If he feels that Ketchen didn't screw up, he'll probably refuse."

Llewellyn grimaced. "That may give Alderson an excuse to get rid of both of them. He and Turner haven't actually been getting along since Ypres."

"Alderson never wanted Turner as the GOC of the 2nd," Tennison replied with a shrug. "He might feel it's a good time to do it."

"Hughes will have a say. Turner's his golden boy," Llewellyn pointed out.

"True, and he has a VC. If they want to get rid of him, they'll likely promote him and transfer him to a new job."

"Yeah, but what I heard is Alderson is in hot water with Hughes and Borden about his report leaked to the *Ottawa Citizen* on the Ross rifle."

"It's complicated," Tennison said.

"Tell me about it," replied Llewellyn when their driver finally showed up.

CHAPTER 12

"Miss Lonsdale?" the matron asked with a questioning eyebrow. She was about Samantha's height and had a few strands of grey in her chestnut hair tied up in a bun. There were wrinkles around her penetrating hazel eyes.

"Yes, ma'am," Samantha replied as she stiffened to attention.

"Matron Macdonald asked that I take care of you during your first day with us. If you would follow me," she stated as she led Samantha pass the sentry who was guarding the building's entrance. "I'm Matron Roberts, by the way."

Samantha had received orders the day after James left for the front to report to CAMC HQ in London. She didn't know when she would see him again. It was doubtful he would be given another pass anytime soon. Their brief reunion hadn't been what she would have called romantic, but all they could do now was to write each other letters to keep in touch. Samantha had been lonely after James left, since it was another week before she was cleared for duty. She had been surprised by the orders, since she had expected to return to her regular duties after her scarlet fever bout at the Duchess of Connaught Canadian Red Cross hospital. Orders were orders.

She had arrived in London the previous night and spent it at the Thackeray Hotel. The Thackeray regularly housed Canadian nurses when they were in London. The staff was quite accommodating and was starting to pick up the Canadian lingo. She had a pleasant breakfast with a half-dozen nurses who had just arrived from Canada and were waiting for their orders. Most of it was spent answering questions about what to expect when they were assigned to a field hospital. She did feel like a veteran when she warned them where they should exchange their Canadian dollars for British pounds. Some places were quite disreputable.

The hotel was only about four miles from CAMC HQ, so she had taken a hack, which hadn't cost her much. She had managed to draw some funds from the paymaster before taking the train. The hack had dropped her off in front of the Victoria Chambers with the street number 13, beside the entrance.

At this hour of the morning, the broad avenue was busy with horse-drawn carts, wagons, and lorries bringing goods to the shops occupying the ground floors of the nearby buildings. On the cab's route, she had also seen parishioners entering Westminster Abbey, about five or six hundred yards up the street. There was another office building next to the Victoria Chambers. The sign read "Westminster Chambers." When she glanced across the street, expensively dressed patrons were entering the Westminster Palace Hotel for their morning meal.

While she had been waiting for the matron, she glanced at the building's directory. Most of the names were those of barristers, societies, and associations. She had noticed, besides the CAMC, there were listings for Inland Revenue and the War Office. She had wondered where on the street the Canadian High Commission offices were.

Roberts led her to the lift, where a uniformed, wizened old man sat on a stool. As they stepped in, the matron told him their floor number. Once Samantha had cleared the doors, he closed them then pulled on a lever to start the lift. It was so pathetically slow that she could have walked up the stairs faster. She was nervous as the elevator crawled up to the next floor. She wondered why she had been ordered to HQ. She guessed she would find out when the lift finally stopped.

"Is this your first time in London?" asked Matron Roberts.

Samantha glanced at her then said with a touch of fondness, "I was here last in October about two years ago. We stayed at St. Thomas Hospital across the river." She didn't feel the need to mention she had been in London last fall with James. That was a memory she wasn't about to share.

"I came over last summer," Roberts said, giving Samantha a glance. She saw a hint of respect in Roberts's eyes. Samantha knew it came because she was one of the originals. It just didn't feel that long ago.

"Have you seen service in France?" asked Samantha.

"I'm afraid not yet," the matron replied with a hint of defensiveness. Samantha chose to keep silent for a moment.

"I understand that you suffered an illness?" Roberts asked diplomatically as they stepped out of the lift when it stopped.

"Yes, but I'm feeling much better," replied Samantha. In truth, her stamina was not quite what it had been, but she intended to remedy it by walking the streets as much as possible.

"I'm glad to hear that," the matron said as she led Samantha down a corridor with dark oak wainscoting with the plaster above it painted white. The doors were the same colour as the wainscoting. Samantha could hear faint sounds of phones ringing and someone banging on a typewriter. They passed the office with a plaque that read "Director CAMC." On the opposite office, there was a similar one that read "Director of Nursing Service."

The matron continued down the hall and opened one of the dark oak doors, motioning Samantha in. Once inside, she saw that the room was occupied by three light oak roll-top desks set against the walls. One of the desks was near the window that opened to a courtyard. The room was painted in grey, with the floor covered by a green paisley carpet.

Two of the desks were already occupied by two young women. "Miss Lonsdale, I would like to introduce you to nursing sisters Leslie Andrews and Carmen Landry."

"Pleased to meet you," Samantha said as she shook the two women's hands. Leslie was petite, with white skin and coal-black hair. Carmen was stout. She had a dark complexion and chocolate hair. Both women had their hair up in buns.

"Hi," the two women said cheerfully.

"Joining us in the salt mines?" asked Leslie with a friendly smile.

"Miss Andrews, that wasn't called for," chided Matron Roberts.

"Sorry, ma'am," she replied with fleeting chagrin. "You see, I'm responsible for our nurses' travel vouchers."

"And I'm responsible for the pay accounts," replied Carmen, just as amiable.

Samantha began to feel a sense of dread. It was confirmed when the matron pointed at the empty desk with stacked folders and said, "Matron Macdonald would like you to start working on the incoming nurses' personnel reports. When the matron-in-chief has a few minutes, she would like to speak with you about your duties and expectations."

"I'm looking forward to it," replied Samantha, keeping any apprehension out of her voice.

MAY 8, 1916
MACHINE GUN RANGE, ST. OMER

"Son-of-a-bitch … son-of-a-bitch," murmured Major Llewellyn softly. He squeezed the trigger of his Lewis machine gun each time he voiced the phrase. He was smiling as he peered over the tangent sights. His bullets were stitching the paper targets down-range. Brass shells rattled as they were spat out of the breech. The bolt locked open when the last round was spent.

"Not bad, sir. Not bad at all," said the instructor, who was watching the targets that had been set up fifty yards away.

"I'm in love," said the major as he grinned at Sergeant Mackay, who grinned back. The major wasn't the first soldier who had fallen in love with the Lewis machine gun. The British called it an automatic rifle, but that was just splitting hairs.

"We only have two of them so far," the sergeant replied.

"I know," the major replied with a sigh of disappointment as he gave the Lewis a friendly pat. The gun was fresh from ordnance. There wasn't a scratch on it. For the last several months, they had been anxiously waiting for them. So had the sergeant. He had sent Mackay, the thirty-year-old balding Calgarian with a reddish-brown walrus moustache on the Lewis training course last month. The Canadian Corps was finally getting them in sufficient numbers to assign four Lewis machine guns to each battalion. The Fusiliers were finally getting their allotment.

"Any problems with them we should know about?" Llewellyn asked as he rose from his prone position. He rubbed his right shoulder where the butt had rested. He glanced at the section waiting for their turn. About twenty-five yards farther west he saw another section being trained on a captured German MG08 machine gun. The gun was resting on four legs, and there were boxes of belted Mauser ammunition next to it. The men were getting a feel for the weapon as they learned how to load, fire, and clear stoppages.

It was a Canadian Corps practice if they captured a German machine gun in the heat of battle, they would turn the gun around and use it against its former owners. Ammunition wasn't much of a problem, since there was usually plenty stacked in the machine gun's emplacement. Sometimes it was impossible because the MG08 was too badly damaged. The problem was the damn things needed nearly five soldiers to man them.

The Lewis instead only needed two men, a gunner and an ammunition hauler.

"The usual ones, I'm afraid. She can't handle sustained fire like the Colts and the Vickers. At about 800 rounds, the barrel gets too hot and it stops firing. We could swap barrels, but that's a pain in the ass," replied Mackay. "That's why we're training the teams to fire in short bursts."

Llewellyn nodded. That was why the phrase son-of-a-bitch was so useful. It helped in squeezing the trigger in three- to four-round bursts. The pause between each burst also helped bring the sights back onto the target. "I assume the usual problems with mud?"

"How did you guess, sir?" replied the sergeant with a chuckle. He pressed a lever on the top of the pan magazine to unlock it. He then pulled it away and turned the pan over to display it to the major. In the pan, he saw slots designed to hold the cartridges. The .303 rounds were dropped in each slot with the nose pointing to the centre. The pan would rotate and drop the slugs into the breech. "If dirt gets into the pan or on the cartridge, the bolt won't close. If there isn't enough gas pressure, the bolt won't open either."

After examining the magazine, Llewellyn asked, "How long does it take to load a magazine?"

"With training and practice, less than two minutes," replied the sergeant. "The second man can carry at least four to five ammo pans. He can refill them from the ammo boxes."

"That means we'll have to requisition more loose .303 rounds," replied the major. Most of their ammo came from the factory in five-round chargers and web bandoliers.

"Yes, sir, and we're going to use a lot of it."

"I kind of figured that. I'll look into it," Llewellyn replied. "Now we have to figure out how we're going to use them effectively."

The sergeant nodded.

Llewellyn dropped his head slightly in thought. The current doctrine concerning the Lewis machine gun was in flux. Some insisted it was an automatic rifle and could not be substituted for a real machine gun. But others saw that its light weight, half that of the Vickers, and its attached bipod would give the Lewis a mobility in the attack and in the defence the Colts and Vickers couldn't match.

That means, Llewellyn thought as he glanced at the waiting men, *we're going to have to experiment to figure out what works and what doesn't work. As usual, we're going to have to learn our lessons the hard way.*

MAY 10, 1916
BILLETS, SAINT-JANS-CAPPEL

Dear Sam,

I guess you're feeling better now. Well enough that you're being posted to HQ in London. At least you'll get some respite from the daily routine of dealing with the wounded. I know paperwork can be a bit of a chore, but this war does seem to run on it. Write when you've settled in to let me know how things are going.

As for me, I'm back to my real duties. My trip back was rather unremarkable. I caught my ferries and trains on time, if you can believe it. When I finally reached my unit, I didn't know what to expect. When you go on leave, the paperwork seems to pile up and it takes several days to catch up, if you're lucky. I was pleasantly surprised that my staff actually had most of it done. I don't know what got over them. All I needed to do was give them a quick review then sign off. I was so pleased I gave them a half-day's leave. Sure, I could have given them a full day, but I didn't want to puff their heads up too much.

The colonel was glad to see me. The first things he said was, "It's about bloody time you're back. Now get your lazy butt back to work. There's a war on."

I wouldn't have guessed. I did an inspection of the men. Morale is pretty good. We got a crop of replacements in that we are currently working up. The men are currently in comfortable billets. But there are rumours we will be moving again. Some of the men are grousing about all the work they had done to fix things up, and now they can't enjoy it. They feel that it was a waste of time. You'd think that by now they would be used to it. We move every couple of months.

There was a funny incident at the YMCA the other evening. It seemed a rather loud discussion broke out among the men when the YMCA ran out of envelopes and writing paper. A general, who will remain nameless, had made remarks in a newspaper about how good the quality of the men's iron rations were. Yes, I know you've eaten them. The men took exception to the general's remarks and decided to tell the so-called general what they thought about his statement. I had to read some of these letters. Such language! Didn't know that the men could be so creative, especially about where the general can stuff it. The postal corps wasn't too pleased. It doubled their normal letter volume.

If my letter was delayed in reaching you, that was probably the cause. Love, James.

P.S. The colonel sends his best regards and hopes you have a full recovery.

P.P.S. If you visit the Army and Navy store in London, can you buy a couple of items for me that I can't get through our quartermaster? I've attached a list. Let me know how much, and I will send you the money.

P.P.P.S. I hope to see you soon.

CHAPTER 13

"You're sure that this is the house they are coming from?" asked Major Llewellyn as he studied the small cottage nestled among a small copse. It was just after dawn, and smoke was starting to rise from the cottage's chimney. When a rooster crowed, Llewellyn turned his binoculars on the chicken coop. The coop was more there to protect the fowl from some of the more enterprising soldiers who liked to forge for something other than iron rations.

A couple of dogs were stirring. One was loping toward the water for a drink. Llewellyn and Corporal Dack were downwind, so the dogs hadn't caught their scents. The dogs worried him because they appeared to be Belgian Malinois. The tan, black-masked dogs were a sheepdog breed, which meant they made excellent watchdogs.

"I'm pretty sure that's the house they are coming from," replied Corporal Dack. The burly corporal was actually an American who had joined the CEF because he wanted to have some adventure. The major and the corporal had set up a camouflaged position about two hundred yards south of the house.

"Hmm," grunted the major. He glanced at the corporal and the shotgun he was carrying. The shotgun was a Belgian-made 12-gauge with Damascus blue steel side-by-side twenty-six-inch barrels. The shotgun couldn't handle the modern shells, but there were plenty of shotgun shells from local sources. The shotgun was not standard CEF equipment, but it was more suitable for the type of game they were hunting than the Ross or the Lee-Enfield.

For the last several weeks they had been trying to track the source of messenger pigeons that had been intercepted flying toward the German lines. They knew that there was a spy within a ten-mile radius of the Canadian lines. Pigeons could fly a lot farther than that, but any information on the location of the Canadian artillery, billets, ammo dumps, and HQs was invaluable to the German intelligence officers.

In fact, the Corps used messenger pigeons to send messages from their trenches back to their headquarters, and, especially, to the artillery. It supplemented their runners and their communication lines, especially if the Germans knocked them out. It was easy enough to train the pigeons for the work. They had to be kept at a home coop, such as CFA HQ, for several weeks, to imprint them with their home location. Then they were transferred to the trenches, where the signallers would feed them and take care of them. It was a rather simple matter to write a message on a small piece of paper, attached it to pigeon's leg, and release it. It wasn't speedy but was effective, especially since it was unlikely the Germans would intercept their birds.

He wondered how the agent obtained their imprinted pigeons. He guessed one of the dogs was being used to sneak them across No Man's Land. From what he understood, in this region it was a national sport to avoid custom duties. Light items such as silk and tobacco were placed on the back of dogs using saddlebags to slink across the border. The customs folks had their own specially trained dogs to give chase. One of the solutions the CEF had to capture them was to attach a bitch in heat near the front trenches. It assumed that most of the smugglers' dogs were male.

The front door of the cottage opened, and woman in her forties with dark hair emerged holding something in her hands. She tossed her hand, and a pigeon fluttered its wings and then buzzed the cottage for a minute than headed straight toward them.

"Corporal Dack, if you please."

"Yes, sir," he replied just before the blast from his shotgun knocked the bird down.

The woman's head snapped sharply in their direction. Even from this distance, he could see hate in her face. There were a lot of reasons why she would be helping the Germans. She could have family on the other side, a lover, or simply for the money. At the moment, he didn't have much sympathy for her. He had the evidence she needed.

"Let's go arrest the woman," he said as he rose. He took out the .45 on his hip. The dogs were barking and heading toward him. He hated the idea of putting them down. "Pick up the pigeon, we'll need it for evidence."

"Yes, sir," he replied as he broke the shotgun and replaced a spent shell. "It's too bad. I'm getting to like roasted pigeon."

"Pellets and all?"

"I nearly broke a tooth last time," replied Dack with a shrug. "I guess that's what dentists are for."

MAY 17, 1916
HOUSE OF COMMONS, VICTORIA MEMORIAL MUSEUM, OTTAWA

Borden was tense as he sat in the House. He could feel his blood pressure rising. He knew the question was coming, he just didn't know when. It was just too juicy for the opposition to pass up. He had only partial answers, which made his tension worst. Major-Generals Gwatkin and Fiset said, after he had demanded a full report on the *Ottawa Citizen's* story, they wouldn't have answers for him until eight this evening, two hours from now.

He had been in the House of Commons since two o'clock, with an occasional break. He had presented a memo from the Estates Branch of the Department of Militia and Defence. There had been complaints about how long it was taking to settle the estates of men who had been killed in action. The memo explained the procedures being followed after a soldier was declared dead. When a man had become deceased, his effects were packed, sent to London, then shipped to Ottawa. The soldier's pay account was closed. The amounts in his account verified to be correct and all fines, debts, and obligations had been paid in full. What remained was then distributed to the estate. If the will in the back of the soldier's paybook was completed, the funds would be distributed as per the man's will. It normally took four to six months to close an estate. When a soldier was reported missing, the family had to wait thirty weeks before he could officially be declared dead. Once he was, the settling of the estate could begin.

He did take breaks to get out of the House and ease some of his tension. During one of them, he had gone to Room 1 to see the plans and models for the new Centre Block on display. The architects from Montreal, John Persons and Jean Omer Marchand, were there to discuss them with the MPs and senators and to answer any questions. And the MPs had plenty, especially when the architects suggested adding an additional floor to give them more space. The MPs already knew that the costs for the new building were rocketing. Initially, they had hoped to save money by stripping everything to the walls. The engineers had said no. It was their opinion that the old building was unstable and unsafe. It needed to be torn down and a new one raised in its place.

Every day, he couldn't help seeing the burned-out shell when he entered the East Block to go to his office. He was glad they were finally pulling it down. Their plan was to salvage as much as they could from the old Centre Block to be recycled into the new building.

Borden was listening with half an ear to the Honourable Frank Oliver, the MP for the Edmonton riding and Laurier's former minister of the interior. Oliver's large walrus moustache quivered as he attacked his government's Patriotic Fund policy. He was demanding Borden's government take over some of the fund's functions. He was arguing that Canadian cities were contributing money to the Patriotic Fund. The only way they could be was by taxing their ratepayers for their largesse. He also expressed concern with the increasing demands on the fund, as he believed current subscriptions would not be enough. Borden watched as both White and Hazen rose from their chairs with sharp questions on Oliver's position.

His ears perked up when Oliver said, "There is another matter that I feel to be so very important and so very serious that I cannot allow it to go by without noticing."

Here, it comes, thought Borden. Oliver was finally going to bring up the *Ottawa Citizen* story. It wasn't difficult to miss, since the headline was, "Gen Alderson very candid criticizing Ross Rifle." The story was right beside the photo of Liberty Hall, the rebel headquarters in Dublin that was lying in ruins. Aitken had warned him, via gram, that the situation in Ireland was serious. He was so annoyed with the Alderson story, he nearly missed the one about the prisoner of war riot in Kapuskasing that had resulted in one dead and eight seriously wounded. He was waiting for a report from the military investigation of the camp that housed twelve hundred German and Austrian prisoners.

Borden finally had enough. He needed to put a stop to Oliver, especially since he was now running the Militia and Defence department during Hughes's hiatus. When he got the speaker's attention, he could feel all the Liberal MPs in the House fix their eyes on him. "As far as I'm aware, no such letter, which appeared in the *Ottawa Citizen* this morning, has come to the government's attention. However, I shall make further enquiries before eight o'clock to ascertain the facts.

"Even if such a letter had been written, it is my judgement that its publication without communicating with the government, without enquiry as to the existing situation, is not a patriotic action for the country at this time."

Oliver rose from his chair and asked the speaker, "Eight o'clock?"

"Yes, eight o'clock," Borden replied.

★ ★ ★

"If I find out who gave that damn letter to the *Ottawa Citizen*," groused Rogers. He was sitting across from Sir Robert Borden. They were in the prime minister's office on the second floor of the Victoria Memorial Museum. "I'll strangle him."

Major-Generals Gwatkin and Fiset, who were seated near him, kept their silence. They had finally arrived to brief Borden on what they discovered regarding the *Ottawa Citizen* broadside.

"I've spoken with Sam Hughes," Borden stated. "He indicated to me he doesn't recall receiving a letter from General Alderson on this topic."

"He didn't?" blurted Rogers in disbelief. Since Borden was looking at Rogers, he missed the surprised look that appeared briefly on the two major-generals' faces.

"Yes, he did," Borden then glanced at the wall clock. "I have less than an hour and a half before I need to return to the House." Normally, it would have been Sam answering the questions in the House concerning the Ross. It was, after all, his personal pet project, and he had been with it ever since it was first proposed by Laurier's government. With the ongoing Shell Committee inquiry, Hughes was, for the past week, on administrative leave. Borden had given up explaining to the stubborn man that he wasn't suspended. He had to admit Hughes was being cooperative of late. Borden snorted to himself. He might have heard he was seriously considering firing him.

"The *Citizen* story indicates there are serious problems with the rifle and that it's putting the lives of our soldiers at risk," Borden stated.

"I'm afraid that's what the story says," stated Rogers. "I think that we should take legal action against the paper."

Borden frowned. As a lawyer he was tempted, but as a politician he knew suing a newspaper was fraught politically. "Let's table that for another time. The solicitor-general is looking into the matter. More important is what I'm going to provide the House this evening to blunt the Liberals' attack."

"Yes, Prime Minister," Rogers acknowledged, chagrined. Gwatkin and Fiset nodded in agreement.

"Prime Minister," Gwatkin interrupted as he pulled out a file from the black briefcase at his feet. "Here are the reports from General Steele on the rapid-fire testing that was conducted last April. It compares the

Ross and the Lee-Enfield. If you read the conclusions on the last page, you'll see both rifles performed equally well. When defective ammunition is used, the Ross performed better than the Lee-Enfield." Borden grunted when he read the summary. As he flipped the pages, he paused at a chart that detailed the testing.

"We also have testimonials from officers and other ranks expressing their confidence in the Ross rifle," Fiset said as he handed over a report as well.

Rogers's brow wrinkled in doubt. "We can put it into the record, but the Liberals will have similar stories saying the rifle jammed at inopportune times."

Borden leaned back in his chair and demanded, "Is the rifle good or not?"

Gwatkin stated, "It comes down to a man's confidence in his weapons. Lack of confidence has a detrimental effect on an army's morale."

"I see," replied Borden. He noticed Gwatkin had not committed himself one way or another.

"Also, I just want to make one correction, Prime Minister. The telegram that we sent to General Haig was sent only three days ago," said Gwatkin.

Borden grimaced. "I'll make the correction in the House." He had mentioned to the Green Chamber that his government had left the decision to replace the Ross with the Lee-Enfield in General Haig's hands. Borden was fairly certain General Haig wasn't going to be pleased at being put on the spot. It did give his government cover, since the decision would be in British hands, not his. Also, it played well with the narrative that the Imperials had a habit of replacing perfectly good Canadian equipment with British-manufactured ones.

Borden suddenly felt tired. He recalled the note he wrote in his diary yesterday when he was in Montreal. In it, he had said he was glad he didn't have to attend the House of Commons. He now wished he could have stayed in Montreal.

MAY 22, 1916
CANADIAN CORPS HEADQUARTERS, ABEELE

"Hi, Malcolm, how are you doing?" Major-General Currie said when he was shown into the small dining room by Lieutenant-General Alderson's batman. Major-General Mercer was seated at the table that had been set for lunch. Through the window behind Mercer, he could see a flight of aeroplanes with Royal Air Corps markings making their way eastward below the grey clouds. They came from the nearby aerodrome.

"I'm doing fine, Arthur. And you?" Mercer replied. His thick walrus moustache hid most of his smile.

"Busy," replied Currie as he took a seat across from Mercer. He had known Mercer since Valcartier, and he had commanded his 1st Brigade until he was given command of the 3rd Division last December. Before the war, he had been a wealthy lawyer in Toronto with a passion for the arts. On leave, Mercer would frequent the local art galleries and museums. "How are things in your sector?"

"It was quiet this morning when I left," replied Mercer. He had driven in from his 3rd Division Headquarters, located in Reningelst about six miles east of Abeele. Alderson had moved into Lieutenant-General Plumer's offices in the village of Abeele, which straddled the French and Belgian border, when the Canadian Corps relieved the V Corps. Currie had to come from his HQ in Hoograaf, which was located nearly halfway between Abeele and Reningelst. "The Germans were quite active yesterday. They shelled Sanctuary Woods, Zillebeke Bund, Maple Copse, and Gordon House for most of yesterday."

"Casualties?"

"They were light," replied Mercer. "We retaliated strongly at Birdcage with our 18-pounders, our heavies, and then with our mortars. They quieted down after that.

"What about 1st Division?"

"Like I said, busy. Some of my observers spotted a long line of supply transports near Hollebeke. I had my artillery shell them and Hill 60," he answered. "By the way, have you seen Richard?" Usually, all three division commanders were called in for meetings with Alderson.

"Not yet," replied Mercer just as Alderson entered the room.

"Gentlemen," he said as he took his usual seat at the head of the table. Currie saw Mercer raise an eyebrow. Currie returned it with a slight shrug. It was obvious Alderson was upset about something. Currie wondered what it was. The Corps staff hadn't shown any sign there was a crisis when he was led to the dining room.

Alderson stared at his plate for a moment then raised his eyes to look at Currie and Mercer. He then cleared his throat and said, "I just received some distressing news." He paused then continued. "I'm being transferred to England to take up a new post as inspector-general for the Canadian Overseas Force."

Currie glanced at Mercer then back to Alderson. He wasn't really surprised by Alderson's announcement. He had gotten along reasonably well with Alderson, and he had learned a lot from his mentoring. But the real problem was that Alderson and Hughes didn't see eye to eye. There had been no doubt the ongoing public friction couldn't continue. He suspected the fallout from the defeat and losses at St. Eloi was the final straw. He was also sure it didn't help when Alderson had tried to have Major-General Turner relieved of his command.

But one thing was certain: Alderson had developed a deep fondness for his Canadians. He had been their leader since they arrived in England. Alderson confirmed it when he said, "I do wish I could see the Corps through to the end. But orders are orders." That was one thing that he had been pounding into them since they first arrived at Salisbury Plain. It was unlikely he would question orders now, even if he disliked them.

Mercer asked, "Do you know who our new commander will be?"

A slight wince of loss crossed Alderson's face. "Yes, it will be Lieutenant-General Byng."

"I'm not familiar with him," Mercer stated then gave Currie a questioning glance. Currie shrugged, showing he had never met him either.

"I think he'll do a good job," Alderson said without enthusiasm. "He commanded the 3rd Cavalry Division before he was sent to Gallipoli to lead the IX Corps. When they had retired from Gallipoli, he and the IX Corps returned to France. Since January, he's been in command of the 17th Corps in Arras."

Currie and Mercer glanced at each other. They weren't surprised that another British officer was being foisted on them. Obviously, the War Office didn't feel there was a Canadian officer seasoned enough to be given command of the Canadian Corps. When he glanced at Mercer, he could see the same thing in his eyes. What kind of officer was Byng? And would he get along with the Canadians?

"I'm sure that you'll give him the same support you both have given me," Alderson stated.

Currie nearly grimaced. The real question was how would Byng and Sam Hughes get along?

"Yes, sir," replied Lieutenant Ryan gloomily.

"I'm afraid the order came down from Division HQ. You're not the only one affected," Lieutenant-Colonel Masterley said as he watched a German Albatros flying above them. Ryan recognized it as the C.V. type reconnaissance biplane that had recently come into service. It continued to circle about a thousand yards south of them above their billets. Movement to the north caught his eye. He glanced at it and saw it was a Lewis machine gun hidden under camouflage netting that was tracking the aeroplane. Farther north, under another camouflage net, his work party was taking a break. They were sitting on boxes of 60-pounder shells, having a smoke and eating breakfast.

Ryan glanced at Masterley. When he was finally transferred back to the 65th, he had been pleased to find the major had been promoted to temporary lieutenant-colonel when their former CO, Colonel Marshfield, was promoted to acting brigadier-general.

Paul shrugged. "No great loss, sir. My leave for the dental work was more enjoyable than the time I spent in the hoosegow." It was rather true. His teeth had been bothering him, so he had taken two days leave to go to Boulogne to see a dentist to have a cavity filled. The dentist had done a pretty good job, he thought, as he ran his tongue over the filling. The dentist had also wanted to pull his wisdom teeth. He balked at that. They were in the back of his mouth pretty firmly. He still had leave owed to him, but Masterley had just informed him of the new policy from Division HQ. Since Ryan had taken leave for a dental appointment, Masterley couldn't approve any of his personal leave requests for the next six months.

"By the way, your friend is in Italy," said Masterley.

"Friend, sir?"

"Sir Conan Doyle is visiting Italy. He's writing stories on the war," he answered. The lieutenant-colonel knew Paul was a great fan of Sherlock Holmes. "The 65th's newsletter hasn't been the same since you left. I want you to start writing for it again. The men's morale needs a boost."

"I'll do my best," replied Ryan. He had a few ideas that the men would like.

"In the meantime, how are we doing with the new gun pit?" Masterley asked as he looked at the work party who were still taking a break.

Ryan grimaced. He was put in charge of preparing the gun pit for the new 60-pounders that the brigade would be receiving any day now. The Corps was adding a heavy battery to each of the brigades' artillery units. The 60-pounder was considerably bigger than the 18-pounder. Not surprising, since the 60-pounder's recoil system had two pistons to handle the weight and forces on its 5-inch barrel. From the orders he had been given, the total length of the gun was slightly over thirteen feet. It meant he had to triple the size of the gun pits he had to dig.

"We haven't gotten as far as we liked. There have been delays in getting materials. Especially for the horse stables. The quartermaster has been complaining about the short notice."

"Quartermasters are always complaining," Masterley replied, implying it was normal.

"And the Germans have been pretty active for the last couple of days. We haven't lost any men as yet," Ryan stated. "Do you think they're up to something?"

"Probably," Masterley said with a sigh. "Staff from the 2nd Division HQ called me this morning. He expressed concerns about the fifty horses that you have here. He feels the horse lines are attracting the Hun's attention."

Ryan looked up at the Albatros still circling above them, then at the horse lines along the nearby stand of trees. Netting was strung above them, but there were some mounds of hay out in the open. While Ouderdom was the 65th's rest area and was four miles behind the front lines, it was still considered part of the 2nd Canadian Division's tactical area. "We've been trying to keep them under cover, but there are only so many places we can put them until we get the gun pits done. I'm told the new 60s need twelve horses each to move the damn things." With the 60-pounders weighing nearly five tons, Ryan wasn't surprised that they needed all the horsepower they could find to move them.

"Yeah, I've just been informed they've arrived last night at Abeele. The trucks will be delivering them here tomorrow."

"Are the men coming with the guns?" asked Ryan.

"Not exactly," replied Masterley with a touch of frustration. "The senior officers have been assigned, and they have been trained on the 60-pounders. But they need a core of experienced men to man them.

We had a meeting about it early this morning with General Loomis and the other senior commanders. The decision was made that one section from each of our four batteries will be transferred to the heavies. Each 60 needs twelve men plus a few spares."

"What about our 18s?" asked Ryan.

"Reinforcements are coming in, so we should be fine. We'll have to train them up to backfill." Ryan winced, but it made sense. There wasn't much difference between the 18-pounder and 60-pounder, just everything was bigger and heavier. The rate of fire was a bit slower, about two rounds per minute. That was partly because of the heavy workload the 60s demanded of its crew. Hauling and loading the 60-pound shells exhausted the gun crews faster than the 18-pounders.

"Are we getting the latest model?" asked Ryan.

"Yeah, from what I hear, the gun doesn't slide back in the cradle for transport. It's going to be a bitch to move it, because it weighs a ton more," Masterley answered.

"So, am I being transferred to the heavies?" Ryan asked. For the last several months, he had been bouncing around a lot. Usually, officers stayed with the same unit for their entire service.

"Nope, you're staying put for now. You're getting your own section," Masterley replied.

"Thanks, I appreciate it," replied Ryan with some relief.

CHAPTER 14

Major-General Malcolm Mercer and his aide-de-camp, Captain Lynam Gooderham, were waiting for Byng in front of a two-storey beige brick building with boarded-up windows. He had been driven to the headquarters of the 3rd Canadian Division located in the small Belgian village of Reningelst, about four miles south of Ypres. Before the war, it had been a small farming community with a thousand or so residents. Across the street, Byng could see workmen making repairs to St. Vedastuskerk, a local Catholic church that had suffered battle damage.

He had spent the last few days at Corps HQ being briefed by his new staff on the Corps' state of readiness and its dispositions. When he got the call to take command of the Canadians, he had been surprised, since he didn't know any Canadians, and had never dealt with them before. He had learned the Canadian Corps was responsible for nearly five and half miles of trenches from St. Eloi to Hooge. The centre was being held by the 1st Division's 2nd Brigade. The 2nd Division was on the right as far as Ypres-Comines Canal and Hill 60. The 3rd Division was on the left, with two battalions in the lines. Also, he had gone through the latest operational orders and intelligence summaries to glean what the German activities and intentions were in his new sector.

He had noticed Mercer's blue eyes flicked to his worn boots and puttees. He liked going out in the field to get a first-hand look at his commanders, their units, and the terrain that they had to defend or attack. Hence, his highly polished boots with worn heels. The 3rd Division was among the many headquarters that he would be visiting in the next few days as he got a grip on his command.

"Welcome to the 3rd Division, General Byng," said Major-General Mercer after giving him a sharp salute. "My aide-de-camp, Captain Gooderham."

"Captain," Byng acknowledged as he eyed both men. They were tall. Mercer was in his mid-fifties, with a bronzed complexion and dark hair. Gooderham's eyes were grey, and the thirty-year-old's complexion was fair, as was his hair.

"I'll give you the grand tour," said Mercer with a brief smile under his moustache as the private guarding the entrance held the door open.

The main room held the usual compliment of men busy performing tasks. With a nod, he released the men who had stood at attention when he had entered. What interested him most was the map tacked to the wall showing the current dispositions of the 3rd Division. He could see fresh pencil marks on trenches 47 to 51. They identified the units that had just relieved those of the 1st Division. The 3rd was now responsible for nearly 2,000 yards of trenches from Hooge in the south to Sanctuary Woods.

"I've read your intelligence summaries. The Germans have been rather active of late," Byng remarked as he indicated with his jaw the German trenches on the map.

Mercer clasped his hands behind his back then said, "Yes, sir, they have. I have some concerns about Tor Top and Mount Sorrel." Tor Top, also known as Hill 60, and Mount Sorrel were key positions in the Ypres Salient that overlooked the German trenches. The Germans didn't particularly like that one bit. "Enemy artillery has been very active in the past week. Last Friday, they shelled us at Hooge, the Appendix, Gourook Road, and Warrington. They've been hitting our support trenches with 7.5-, 10.5-, and 15-cm shells.

"On Monday, they fired 200 rounds of various sizes at Blauwepoort Farm," Mercer said as he pointed to it on the map. "We've retaliated with our field guns, but they continued to fire on us. I've had to call on the Right Group's guns and the Corps' heavies to retaliate. Our OPs reported Germans being taken out on stretchers after our barrage.

"Yesterday, they were pretty quiet. Last night, they hit trench 55 with twenty to thirty rounds from their *minenwerfers*. They did some damage, but our men were able to make repairs."

"Just their artillery?" asked Byng as he looked thoughtfully at the map.

"No," Mercer replied, "three days ago, they had observation balloons up. In the afternoon, their aeroplanes spent a considerable amount of time above our trenches in the right sector." The 3rd Division had divided their trenches into two sectors. The right sector was defended by the 9th Infantry Brigade, with its headquarters at Maple Copse. The left sector was manned by the 7th Brigade with its HQ at Zillebeke Dugouts. He was planning to visit both of them in the next day or so.

"Our men reported last night Germans were connecting the T saps they had been working on for the past week opposite trenches 60 and 61. It looks like they are going to connect their advance trench in front of Clonmel Copse. The aeroplane photos taken on Monday confirm they have extended and joined five saps between here and here," he said as Mercer pointed to them on the map. A T sap was when a trench started to branch left and right to form a T. The T would eventually be connected to create a new trench. "The advance trench is within 200 yards of our front.

"They have put up a screen to block our view of what they are up to in their Hooge trenches. We know they have created emplacement for their machine guns and *minenwerfers*. Unfortunately, the weather hasn't been helpful. We've been having a lot of mist that has been obscuring our view. We think they have been digging a gun emplacement about a mile from St. Peter Street. We haven't been able to confirm yet because there's a hedge in front of it. Aerial photos also show a series of trenches in the rear that look remarkably similar to ours."

"Have your patrols been out to take a look?" asked Byng.

Mercer nodded. "They have. The patrols said the German work parties have been quite active. They've been hearing hammering, movement of lumber, and corrugated iron. They've reported fresh concertina wire and trip wires in front of the Hun trenches."

"It does appear that the Germans are up to something," Byng replied thoughtfully.

"It seems so," answered Mercer.

"What I would suggest is to go and take a look at the Germans' new works. Then prepare a plan to push them back to their original lines."

Mercer stared at Mount Sorrel and Tor Top that were marked on the map. "That sounds like a good idea."

JUNE 2, 1916
4TH CANADIAN MOUNTED RIFLES HEADQUARTERS, ZILLEBEKE
DUGOUTS

Lieutenant-Colonel Ussher was waiting for him when the guide finally led Major-General Mercer to the 4th CMR's HQ. The Zillebeke Dugout was a concrete bunker covered with stacked sandbags that had recent rips and tears from German shrapnel. The usual cables and wires ran out the side into the communication trench, which led to the tunnel that the 2nd Tunnelling Company had dug into the slope of Mount Sorrel.

After the guide saluted Ussher, he rapidly disappeared. It was obvious he wanted to get as far as he could from the red hats as possible. Accompanying him on his reconnaissance mission was Brigadier-General Williams, the GOC of the 8th Brigade, and his brigade orderly, Captain Fraser. Mercer's aide, Captain Gooderham, was also on his heels.

"General, General," said Ussher as he welcomed him and Williams.

"Colonel," replied Mercer. "How are you and your men settling in?"

"Pretty well," replied the lieutenant-colonel. "I completed an inspection shortly before your arrival. The 52th Battalion left the trenches in pretty good shape for us. They're clean and dry. We have good fire bays and elephant shelters." Mercer nodded an acknowledgement. The 4th CMR had completed their relief of the trenches just two days prior. The elephant shelters Ussher mentioned were corrugated iron tubes cut into semi-circles then buried into the trench sides. They provided strong splinter-proof shelters during artillery attacks. "We have A Company on the right, D Company in the centre, and C Company of the left. B Company is in support at the Lille Gate. We also have the 1st Division's 2nd Brigade guarding our right and the 1st CMR Battalion on our left."

"Sounds good," replied Mercer. Mercer knew Ussher was a former Toronto broker before he signed up as a captain in December of 1914. He became the 4th CMR's CO in March when Lieutenant-Colonel Smith was promoted to head of his divisional cavalry. The Mounted Rifles had given him some grief when they were first assigned to his division. They hadn't been pleased when they learned they had to give up their horses to become gravel crushers, the pejorative term the cavalry used for the infantry. Unlike some of the British cavalry units, which fought on their horses, the Canadian cavalry was all mounted infantry. This meant they used their horses to get to the battlefield. Once they arrived, they would dismount then attack on foot. The latest reports indicated the CMR was shaping up nicely.

He was pleased Brigadier-General Williams appeared to be happy with Ussher. "If you'll take us up the hill, we'll take a look at what the Germans are up to."

"Yes, sir, if I may, is General Byng joining us?" Ussher asked.

"I'm afraid not," answered Brigadier-General Williams. "He has other matters to attend to."

"Yes, sir," replied Ussher with a hint of disappointment. Obviously, word had gone out about Lieutenant-General Byng's visits.

When he arrived at Zillebeke Bund that morning, he had been surprised to find General Byng meeting with Brigadier-General Williams. The 8th Brigade's HQ was located in the earth embankment on the western end of Zillebeke Lake, a man-made lake now drained by shell fire. "General Byng, I wasn't expecting to see you so soon," he had said.

"Neither was I," Byng had replied with a raised eyebrow. "I assume you're here concerning my suggestion?"

"Yes, sir, I am. I spoke with General Williams about your concerns by telephone, and we agreed to do a personal reconnaissance of our lines. Once we get a better picture of the situation, we'll create a plan for your approval."

"Like I mentioned earlier, General Mercer and I discussed starting with the 4th CMR at Mount Sorrel, as that is of immediate concern," Williams had informed Byng.

"That sounds like a start of a good plan," Byng had stated.

"Would you like to come with us? Your insights would be invaluable," Mercer said, with Williams nodding in agreement.

Byng had paused to consider his invitation then shaken his head. "I'm afraid that I have other matters I'm required to attend to. I'll be eagerly awaiting your proposals once you've completed your assessment."

It hadn't taken long to climb the nearly hundred-foot slope to the top of Mount Sorrel. It was quiet as the sun beat down on the flattened knoll. To his left, if he raised his head above the trenches, he could see Tor Top and the other two promontories that allowed the 3rd Division to keep an eye on the Hun trenches directly in front of them.

Floating several thousand feet above were two German balloons. The small dirigibles, with fins under their tails, held steadily in the slight breeze. He couldn't see it, but he knew there was a basket hanging underneath with a Boche spotter relaying targeting information to the German artillery.

"They've been pretty quiet today, haven't they?" asked Major-General Mercer as he peered through a set of binoculars at the new works the Huns had energetically been building.

"Yes, sir, they have," admitted Ussher.

Suddenly, they heard the train sound of a German artillery shell. Everyone in the trench ducked as the shells started to land.

"What the hell?" someone tried to shout, but no one heard it. The incoming sounds were loud and numerous as Mount Sorrel disappeared in a fierce, overwhelming cloud of dirt and dust.

4TH CANADIAN MOUNTED RIFLES, MOUNT SORREL

"Shit!" said Trooper Erickson as he finally managed to raise his head above the sandbags, or at least what was left of them. He glanced at his watch with its cracked crystal. It was nearly one o'clock, and he couldn't believe that the German artillery had been pounding his position for nearly four hours. His ears ached. He could barely hear the sounds of the wounded in his trench groaning in pain. The shelling they endured was the worst they'd seen since they'd been dismounted and put into the trenches. It was times like this that he missed his horse, Chester. It had been comforting to know, when they were mounted, that they could have gotten out of trouble as fast as they got into it.

"We need to get Gary and Vic out of here," said Trooper Morse.

Erickson tore his eyes away from the clouds of dirt from the 3rd Division's guns and the British aircraft that were retaliating. Morse, a heavy-set Vancouverite in his late teens, was wrapping a field dressing around Trooper Gary Henry's nasty thigh wound. At least the shrapnel hadn't nicked the artery. He had some concerns about Trooper Victor Adams. A bandage could be seen below his helmet. When Erickson glanced farther down the trench, he grimaced then pointed at it with his steel helmet. Morse turned his head and swore. The section that led to the nearest communication trench had collapsed. Erickson wondered briefly what happened to Major-General Mercer and Brigadier-General Williams since he had last them seen them heading that way toward Armagh Woods.

He heard, then felt, the earth rumbling beneath him. He managed to raise his arms to cover his head just as four mines in front of his trench exploded. Morse tried to cover Gary to protect him from the cascading debris. He finally raised his head to peer over his trench and down the slope. There were four new craters from the mines that the German saps had dug under his barbed wire. What was left was torn and mangled.

His eyes focused on the German lines. He watched as a wave of grey-uniformed men clamber out of their trenches. Sunlight flashed off their bayonets as they formed a line, then they started marching toward him at a leisurely pace. A few minutes later, a second line came out of the trench. It was difficult to tell from this distance, but it looked like some of them were armed with flamethrowers. Then a third and fourth line formed up, all of them heading his way.

"They're coming!" Erickson yelled as he found his rifle. He checked it by opening and closing the breech.

When Morse peaked over the trench he said, "We let the CP know."

"How?" Erikson said, pointing to the collapsed communication trench. Cut cables were visible. "We're cut off."

"Shit! We're going to be reamed!"

"Yeah, but I'm going to take as many of the bastards as I can," replied Erickson grimly as he readied his Lee-Enfield.

RICHMOND FUSILIERS HEADQUARTERS, SWAN CHÂTEAU

"Where the hell have you been?" Lieutenant-Colonel Tennison demanded when Major Llewellyn entered his office.

"I was over at the estaminet getting something to eat, and then I fed the swan," replied Llewellyn as he stood in front of the lieutenant-colonel's desk.

Since the Richmond Fusiliers had been assigned to the 1st Division's reserve, they had taken over the Swan Château as their battalion head-quarters. They were housed in the two-storey white-plastered A-frame barn next to the circular tower. The chateau took its name from the white swan living in the nearby artificial lake. He had seen the swan through the shattered trees that lined the lane to the chateau and had stopped to feed it some stale bread. The swan seemed to have an injured wing, which explained, besides being fed by whomever occupied the chateau, why he stuck around.

The major knew something was up before he entered the barn. On the way in, he had nearly collided with a runner. He had seen that the staff was busy working the phones and preparing move orders as he made his way up to the second floor. *This is what happens when you took a half-day's leave to get something to eat better than army rations,* he thought. The meal had been quite tasty. He was developing a taste for a Belgian delicacy the local Flemish called "frieten," essentially deep-fried potato strips. He did leave a note with the Tennison's batman of where he would be, but he wasn't going to bring it up now. "So? What happened?"

"It seems that the Germans have taken Mount Sorrel and Tor Top," answered Tennison as he signed an order and passed it on to the waiting messenger. The messenger glanced at the header and then headed for the exit.

"When the hell did that happen?"

"This morning. We just got orders to prepare for a counterattack," answered the lieutenant-colonel. "Hold on." He turned his head and yelled, "Were you able to find buses?"

"Not yet, sir," replied one of the clerks with a telephone stuck to his ear.

"Keep trying."

"Yes, sir."

"What's the 3rd Division doing?" asked Llewellyn.

Tennison grimaced. "They got badly chewed up. The 1st and the 4th CMR are gone, as well as half the PPCLIs. What's left managed to stall the Germans. They're in bad shape, and half their trenches have been levelled by the German artillery."

"What's General Mercer doing about it?"

"He's missing, and so is General Williams. They were on Mount Sorrel this morning conducting an inspection, and they haven't been heard from since. General Hoare Nairne has been given command of the 3rd. Colonel Bott has taken over the 8th Brigade," he answered. Llewellyn grimaced at the news. He knew who Brigadier-General Edward Spence Hoare Nairne was. He was the GOC of the Lahore Division Artillery that was providing the 3rd Division with artillery support until the 3rd could create its own. He didn't know Colonel Bott.

"They moved the 8th Brigade into position, but they're too weak to take on the Germans. They've been digging defensive line using the switch and the communications trenches to block the Huns' advance."

"At four thirty, General Byng ordered the 3rd to counterattack. It's set for two o'clock tomorrow morning. We don't want to give the Boche time to consolidate their positions. We got word around six thirty that the 2nd and the 3rd Brigades will be under the 3rd Division's orders for the duration. They will lead the counterattack."

"Jesus!" exclaimed Llewellyn. He looked at the wall clock with Tennison's steel helmet hanging below it on a nail. It read eight o'clock. "There's no way in hell we can make the timetable."

Tennison's face coloured a bit. "I said the same when I got the orders. What I was told was Currie had said the same thing to General Byng. Byng wants a counterattack, and that's what we're going to do."

Shit! thought Llewellyn. First couple of days into Byng's new job, and this crap happens. It was not a good omen. The major's main concern was time. They had less than six hours to move a thousand men into position in the dark under German artillery fire. While it sounded simple, in war simple is never easy. It took time to prepare and transmit orders. The company COs had to receive them, digest them, and start issuing their own. The men needed to be gathered at their assembly points with their rifles, ammo loads, gas masks, water, and rations. Then they have to be transported or marched to their start-lines. If the roads were congested, there would be delays. Once they were in positions, confirmations were needed that units had arrived and were ready. Each unit was then informed as to their objectives and that everyone was clear on what they needed to do. Only then would they be ready to launch their assault.

"Okay," replied Llewellyn. "I guess you want me to go ahead with an advance party?"

"Yeah, get me as much information as you can on the Germans. We're going to need it."

"Yes, sir," replied Llewellyn. At least he got a hot meal. It was going to be a long night.

JUNE 3, 1916
RICHMOND FUSILIERS, MOUNT SORREL

Major Llewellyn hated being right as he watched the Germans prepare for another assault on his position. The bodies of dead Richmond Fusiliers that lay scattered on the slope behind him was a testament to his men's courage and determination. Intermingled among his dead and wounded Fusiliers were Germans wearing the shoulder flashes of the German 125th Infantry Regiment. Captain Wentworth's A Company was gone, while B and C Companies were at half-strength. He was defending what was, until yesterday morning, the 4th CMR's trench. It had now been flattened by the German artillery into a ditch. The Boche had already tried, unsuccessfully, to breech the blockage his men had placed at both ends.

A crouching runner stumbled across one of the bodies near Sergeant Duval just as a German machine gun opened up, probably saving his life. Llewellyn steadied him with his hands as the runner's steel helmet slipped off and fell at his feet. "Better keep your head down," the major said as bullets whistled over his head.

"Colonel Tennison said it was time to go," the runner blurted as he bent to pick up his helmet.

Llewellyn's face became bleak. He hated giving up the ditch, but there wasn't much of a choice. They had no protection on the flanks. Everyone was exhausted, and their supply of grenades, and ammo was nearly gone. And it didn't look as if they were going to get any reinforcements soon.

As he had predicted, they didn't meet the two o'clock timetable. They tried! God, they tried! But they couldn't get a break. There were delays in assembling the men, vehicles breaking down, and the clogged roads didn't help. They weren't the only ones. The 3rd Brigade coming from Poperinge, nearly ten miles away, didn't arrive at the Railway Dugouts until the two o'clock start time. They weren't able to launch their assault on Mount Sorrel until seven o'clock. Any additional time they had to sort themselves out had been negated by their assaulting in daylight, across bare ground, and on an upslope with the sun at the Germans' backs.

Their bad luck continued. The start signal for the assault was six simultaneous green rockets fired from Zillebeke Lake. Some rockets were seen, but not six green ones. The first thing he knew was the assault was on when he saw the 7th Battalion on his right launch their attack against Tor Top. Then the 14th, 15th, and the Richmond Fusiliers climbed out of their newly dug lines to try to recapture Mount Sorrel. He knew the 49th were supposed to take on the Germans between Tor Top, and the Appendix on his left.

Most of the men didn't get far. He had to watch as the lack of coordination and timing between the units proved to be deadly. The Germans were able to concentrate their artillery and machine gun fire as each unit came into their kill zones. As they knocked out one unit, they would move to the next Canadian unit as it came into view. The units that did manage to get to their objective, like the Richmond Fusiliers, had to hang on by the skin of their teeth as they ran out of grenades, ammunition, and men. It was impossible for supplies and reinforcement to run the gauntlet.

"Okay, tell him I agree," Llewellyn said reluctantly. It was either stay here to get killed or captured. "Tell him to start in fifteen, and we will cover him. My section will be the last out. Make sure we get the wounded out first."

"Yes, sir," replied the runner as he started back down the ditch.

He turned his head to Sergeant Duval. "Start getting the men ready."

"Yes, sir," replied Duval as he flicked his eyes at the dead Fusiliers.

Llewellyn hated leaving them behind, but he didn't have enough men for both the wounded and the dead. He asked, "How many grenades do we have left?"

CHAPTER 15

"Stop it," demanded Sir Robert Borden. "Stop creating new regiments, Sam."

Borden wasn't in any mood to bicker with Sam Hughes, who was sitting across from him at the round table in the East Block's Privy Council Chamber. Borden wasn't going to tell Sam how he had found out and why he had insisted it be one of the items on today's agenda for the Militia Council. He could see Major-General Gwatkin was avoiding looking at Hughes, indicating that he agreed with the prime minister. Borden was sure no matter what he said, Hughes would have strong suspicions of who had told him. Hughes was being his stubborn self about creating an army group in France. What the overseas force didn't need were new units complete with senior officers. What they really needed were reinforcements, especially after the last three days of horrendous losses. So far, nearly seven thousand names were on the casualty lists that came into the Woods Building, and more names were being added daily.

He knew some of the names on the list. One of them was George Harold Baker, his MP for the constituency of Brome. He had volunteered at the start of the war after raising the 5th Mounted Rifles from volunteers in Quebec's Eastern Townships. He had been the Mounted Rifles' lieutenant-colonel when he was killed during the German assault on Mount Sorrel. Harry's father had been a senator until his passing in 1910. Harry, who everyone called Baker Harry, had been only thirty-nine. His promising career in politics had been snuffed out. He felt sorry for Harry's two sisters, since they had just sailed to England to see him. They were currently in the mid-Atlantic. They wouldn't find out that their brother had been killed until their arrival in England.

The other name on the list was the Princess Patricia's CO, Lieutenant-Colonel Buller, who had taken over command of the PPCLI when Lieutenant-Colonel Farquhar was killed last March. Borden didn't know all the details yet, but he wouldn't be surprised if Buller had died in the trenches leading his men. He had already visited the governor general to offer his condolences. Buller had been on the duke's staff before he volunteered.

It was that damn Ypres Salient, Borden thought sourly. He had to admit that Hughes had a point about getting the Canadian Corps out of there. When he had sent a gram to George in London on the topic, George's reply was that Lord Kitchener had indicated the Ypres Salient was too important to give up.

Now that Lloyd George was the new secretary of state for war, that could change. Borden had been shocked when he received the news that Lord Kitchener had been killed. Kitchener had been on a diplomatic mission to Russia to keep them in the war when his ship, the cruiser HMS *Hampshire*, struck a German mine near Scotland's Orkney Islands. He was well aware, based on his meetings last summer and George Perley's reports, that the cabinet was losing confidence in Kitchener, especially after the Gallipoli fiasco. He knew there had been speculation that Sir William Robertson, the British chief of staff, would be getting the job. But the cabinet had decided otherwise. He hoped Hughes would have a better relationship with Lloyd George than he had with the late Lord Kitchener. He would have to wait see what Lloyd George's new policies would be. He hoped the new secretary of state for war would see fit to pull the Corps out of the Salient.

"We need them for the 4th Division," replied Sam.

"That may be. How can we reinforce the 4th Division if we can't even replace the losses that we suffered in the last five days?" Borden demanded.

"Like I have previously said, recruiting on a straight voluntary basis is the best system for reinforcements. I have a thousand officers and NCOs working hard across the country recruiting new volunteers." Hughes glanced at Gwatkin, daring the chief of staff to contradict him.

"In the first three months of the year, we recruited an average of twenty-seven thousand men per month. In April, the numbers declined to twenty-three thousand. All the May figures aren't in yet, but it looks as if we only recruited about fifteen thousand," Borden stated.

"It's only a temporary respite," Hughes said, brushing Borden's statement away.

"How are the men recruited?" asked Borden.

"Basically, recruiting is done on a unit basis in that the units are recruited locally. When a unit reaches its authorized strength, it's sent to the nearest training camp, and when a transport becomes available, the entire unit sails for England. There, the units may be broken up to supply men to the divisions in France."

Borden nodded. It explained why there were so many officers sitting idle in England. The Corps' desperate need was for lower ranks, privates, and NCOs. They had plenty of senior officers.

"We've been informed that our rural units are having difficulties. They have already recruited all the available single men in their area. For some of the units we have to transfer men from one district to another so they can reach their authorized strength. Also, when the unit moves, we have to appoint new recruiters, since the previous recruiters move with their regiments," Hughes explained.

"I see," replied Borden. One of the complaints he had received was that some of the recruiters were going into the neighbouring districts to meet their quotas, putting the local commanders' noses out of joint.

"Is there a better way to organize the recruiting?" asked Borden.

"Another way is to establish generic recruiting centres. After training, and when an allotment has been reached, we would assign them to units that needed them the most," replied Gwatkin.

Hughes was shaking his head. "The unit method is better. All the men come from the same town. They know each other, and it helps build *esprit de corps*," he said emphatically. The fact that it was based on the current militia structure didn't enter into it at all.

Gwatkin surprised Borden when he said, "I agree with the minister. While the draft system has some advantages, it will take some time to set up and organize. If we could improve the current system, it would help improve efficiency."

Borden paused to consider the issue then made a decision. "It seems that everyone is in agreement, so we'll continue unit-based recruiting for now.

"Now we have the problem of equipping them. I have been discussing the Ross rifle issue with various ministers of my cabinet. I've sent telegrams to Colonel Aitken and Minister Perley in London informing them we will be leaving the whole question of the Ross in the War Office's hands."

Hughes's jaw clenched in disgust.

"I have been discussing the railway situation with my ministers, and it doesn't appear to be improving. I want to discuss with both of you how we can mitigate any impact on the transport of essential war supplies and troops," Borden said as he continued the meeting.

JUNE 12, 1916
RICHMOND FUSILIERS COMMAND POST, MOUNT SORREL

"Do you have the list?" asked Lieutenant-Colonel Tennison.

Major Llewellyn flipped through the papers on his desk in the command post. The CP was located deep in a shaft that the tunnelling company had dug. It was deep enough to withstand a direct hit from a German heavy. Their office was cramped with the two plank desks. Light was provided by a single incandescent bulb hanging from the ceiling. When he finally found the list, he handed it to his CO and said, "These are the twenty men for the wiring party that HQ requested."

Tennison ran his index finger down it then grunted. "It looks good. Send it to the Division."

"Yes, sir. A runner will be going out in a half-hour with our other status reports." While they had a Fullerphone in the clerk's section of the dugout, for reasons of security it was not currently being used. They were certain the Germans were tapping into their telephone and telegraph lines in the Canadian trenches they had captured. There had been miles of cables, and they weren't a hundred percent sure that all the lines had been cut on the Canadian side. The 1st Canadian Division would be launching an attack along a 1,500-yard front to recapture the trenches they had lost ten days earlier.

"How are the preparations coming?" the lieutenant-colonel asked.

"All the men have been issued iron rations, and their water bottles have been filled. I've ordered them to drink from the water jugs while they are in the trenches. I don't want them going over the top with empty canteens. The sandbags have come in this afternoon, and three have been given to each man. And we finally got enough Mills bombs to issue two to everyone."

"Sounds good," Tennison acknowledged.

"Yeah, if we need more, we can draw on the dump at junction of X and the MG trench. They're supposed to be stocked with a thousand Mills, five boxes of S.A.A., and ten thousand sandbags," Llewellyn informed him. He didn't need to mention that the dumps also had a hundred picks, five hundred shovels, one hundred coils of French wire, four coils of barbed wire, and five hundred feet of wooden planks. It

144

was also sobering that there were fifty stretchers there ready to carry the wounded to the designated casualty stations."

"Let's hope we do better the second time around," replied Tennison tersely.

Major-General Currie had planned this attack very carefully compared with the effort the 3rd Division had done on the 2nd of June when they attempted to retake Mount Sorrel and Tor Top. One couldn't fault the 3rd. They had lost their commanding officer, Major-General Mercer, and Colonel Williams had been captured. Still, they had been ordered to take their lost trenches back with less than a day's planning, and they tried. To help them, Currie had provided Brigadier-General Nairne with the 2nd and the 7th Bridges. The 3rd Division had suffered severe casualties and didn't have sufficient strength to launch an attack with good chances of success. This time Currie was determined to avoid the delays that resulted in the 4th, 14th, 15th, and 49th Battalions attacking in daylight across open terrain. The 7th Battalion alone suffered over a thousand casualties in four days. Now it was the Richmond Fusiliers' turn.

"What do you think of the attack plan?"

Llewellyn paused to think for a moment. "It seems well thought-out. I'm worried about the weather conditions. If it's too windy, the artillery …"

Tennison nodded. "In that case, we'll delay the attack for twenty-four hours. We'll be needing General Burstall's guns for this."

"I always did say you can't have too much artillery!" replied Llewellyn.

Tennison chuckled. "He has nearly two hundred guns. Over half of them are 18-pounders. He's going to do to the Huns what they did to the 3rd Division. We'll be launching three simultaneous attacks. General Lipsett's brigade will be on the right, while General Tuxford will be handling the centre and the left. General Hughes will be in support.

"General Burstall's plan is to bombard their strong point on Mount Sorrel and Tor Top tomorrow. They're going to concentrate on their trenches and support links."

"Well, they had ten days to work on them. And I hope the damn rockets work this time," Llewellyn said bitterly. The attack signal was to be six green rockets sent up from Zillebeke Bund. There had been sharp words exchanged when it was discovered the rockets were defective. In order to get six to fly, they had to go through fourteen of them. It wasn't clear if they were defective from the factory or if they had gotten wet.

The outer skin of the rockets was made from cardboard that was susceptible to humidity. If they had been carelessly stored, it would explain the misfires. The signal rockets weighed nearly a pound and were a foot long. A five-foot stick was attached to give it stability during flight. They normally flew to about eight hundred to a thousand feet before the payload in the nose detonated. On the rocket's outer shell, there was a painted colour band to indicate its colour. The standard colours used were green, red, white, and gold.

Tennison nodded, equally grim. "At 12:30 a.m. for a half hour before the assault they are going to shell the hell out of the Germans before we go in after them. The motor machine gun brigade will use their guns to hit their communications trenches with indirect fire."

"I saw that in the plan."

"Let's gather the senior officers. I want to make sure that everyone knows what our jobs will be tomorrow."

Llewellyn nodded. The Fusiliers were to provide support for the assault companies. One of their companies would garrison the front lines once they were vacated by the main assault groups as they went over the top. They had selected emplacements on Knoll Road for their machine guns to prevent the Huns attacking over the open ground from their old trenches. Their Stokes mortars would be putting a smoke barrage on the Snout to hinder the Boche's visibility. They were also to cover the tunnellers following the main assault groups as they dealt with the mine tunnels on Mount Sorrel.

"I'll order them to get as much rest as they can. They're going to need it over the next few days."

"True, sadly true," Tennison replied.

JUNE 12, 1916
65TH FIELD ARTILLERY REST AREA, OUDERDOM

"Cease fire! Cease fire!" shouted Lieutenant Ryan when his wrist-watch read eleven o'clock.

The men who were feeding the 18-pounders gave him a look of relief as they straightened and stretched their backs. They had been at it since seven this morning. The bending and twisting movements as they lifted shells put a strain on their backs. He already had a couple of men on sick parade due to back strain. This was their first break. They would get a second one at three. Not only would the breaks give his gun crews time to take a rest, get something to eat, and reregister the guns in case they no longer were on target, but more important, it was part of their tactics to wear down the Germans. Each time the barrage stopped, they hoped the Germans would come out of their protective dugouts to defend themselves from the Canadian assault. They knew one was coming, they just didn't know when. It was standard practice to stop the barrage just before the infantry went over the top.

The actual assault by the 1st Division was scheduled for one o'clock in the morning. The plan was to conduct intense bombardments at eight thirty for forty-five minutes then again at fifteen minutes after midnight for forty-five minutes before the assault.

"How are the men holding up?" asked Lieutenant-Colonel Masterley. He had arrived a few minutes to check on his men.

"We're okay. I was about to check the guns, and then I was going to get on the phone to check with the FOs if we're still on target."

Masterley gave him a satisfied nod. "How are the new men doing?" He was referring to the replacements for the experienced men who had been transferred to the heavies.

"A couple of them are very good. We got one who's a real character," replied Ryan.

"Oh?"

"Yeah, a Private Fellows seems to have an endless supply of jokes. I'm going to put some of the clean ones in the newsletter."

Masterley chuckled. "I'm going to read your next one with interest. What's your supply like?" he asked as he glanced at the shells that were stockpiled in the gun pits. For this operation, they had orders to have four hundred rounds on hand.

"We're doing okay. The ammunition column has been keeping us supplied," Ryan replied. At a normal rate of fire, four rounds per minute, they had already fired nearly a thousand rounds per gun. By the end of the day, all four guns would have launched 14,000. "Are we still on for one o'clock?"

"As far as I know," replied Masterley.

"I hope the Huns fall for it," he said as a bombardier ran a long-handled brush down the 18-pounder's "A" tube to clear out propellant residue. He followed with a cloth-covered brush dipped in gun oil. The barrel was still hot as wisps of smoke came out of the both ends.

"It will," said Masterley confidently.

"I wish there was something else we could do," said Ryan.

"I know. Better minds than ours have been pondering. I did have a talk with General Morrison," the lieutenant-colonel stated. Major-General Morrison was the GOC commanding the 2nd Division's artillery. "He mentioned something about creeping barrages he wants to try."

"Creeping barrages?" asked Ryan.

"Yeah, the idea is to have two- or three-minute lifts, with the infantry following close behind."

"I don't know if the infantry would want to do that. Off the top of my head, I can think of a lot of things that can go wrong," replied Ryan. Timing was going to be critical. Too slow or too fast, and men would get hurt.

"That's what we need to work out after today's event."

"Like you said, better heads than mine," replied Ryan. "I better get back to work giving the Germans hell."

"Don't let me stop you," said Masterley with a shooing motion.

CHAPTER 16

"I just got off the telephone with the Brigade," stated Lieutenant-Colonel Hadow tersely to his company commanders. Captains Ayers, Ledingham, Nunns, and Rowsell had just arrived after his runners had found them. Nearby, men were checking their equipment and a few were cracking jokes, while others sat in quiet contemplation. The nearly eight hundred men and officers of the Newfoundland Regiment were positioned in the reserve trench near St. John's Road about two hundred and fifty yards from the front lines. Behind the German trenches, a mere four hundred and fifty yards away, was the tiny French village of Beaumont-Hamel, which once had a population of five hundred. "We've been ordered to advance as soon as possible."

Their faces became grimmer. He had gotten to know his senior commanders well ever since he was transferred from the Norfolk Regiment to take command of the Newfoundland Regiment when they were stationed in Egypt. They had been rebuilding and resting after the Gallipoli campaign. Captain James Allan Ledingham, the A company commander, was in his mid-twenties. He was an unassuming but efficient officer. Prior to the war, he had been an executive with the transportation firm Furness Withy Ltd. in St. John's. Beside him was Captain Joe Nunns, the CO of B company, a short man with a paunch. He was one of the oldest men in the regiment. Scottish-born, he had worked with one of the department stores in St. John's before volunteering. The C Company commander was twenty-six-year-old Captain Reginald Rowsell, a former teacher at the Bishop Field College in St. John's. Captain Eric Ayers led D company. He had worked at the family firm Ayers & Sons, a department store chain in St. John's, before he signed up with his brother and two cousins, 2nd lieutenants Gerald and Wilfred Ayers. Eric's brother was with Hadow's former regiment, the Norfolk. The Newfoundland Regiment had served with distinction at Suvla Bay during the Gallipoli campaign with the 29th Division's 88th Brigade. They had suffered over fifty per cent casualties and had to be reinforced. In March, they had been ordered to France. For the last several months, they had been stationed in the Beaumont-Hamel area of the Somme.

"Have they captured the German trenches?" asked Captain Ledingham. According to the plan, the 1st Battalion Newfoundland Regiment and the 1st Essex Regiment were in the reserve. They were to follow the second wave as they went over the top. The first wave was being led by the 2nd South Wales Borderers and the 1st Royal Inniskilling Fusiliers. The 1st King's Own Scottish Borderers and the 1st Borderers, the second wave, would follow to clear the German first-line trenches as the first wave continued forward to the second-line trenches.

Hadow pressed his lips together then said, "I asked. Brigade said the situation has not been cleared up."

The zero hour for the assault had been set for seven thirty. Ten minutes prior, 40,000 pounds of ammonal had been detonated to destroy the German positions at Hawthorne Ridge, while at the same time the artillery had stopped their barrage to allow the infantry to move forward. They all had heard and felt the massive explosion, and if everything were going according to plan, they were to cross No Man's Land at ten.

Things didn't appear to be going as well as they had hoped. The crater at Hawthorne Ridge was to be occupied by the Lannister Fusiliers. The German artillery and their dugouts should have been suppressed and the wire cut since the artillery had been pounding them for the past week. The Newfoundlanders had sent out two raids several days earlier to confirm the state of the Boche wire. Both came back to report that the Huns were on high alert, well prepared, and the wire was intact.

"Are we going to attack in conjunction with the 1st Essex?" asked Captain Nunns.

"Orders are to go as soon as possible, independently of the 1st Essex," Hadow replied. Nunns acknowledged with a nod.

"We can't use the communication trenches. They're congested with troops moving forward and with the wounded being evacuated. We'll have to go over the top from here then proceed to our first trench line. When we get there, we'll have to cross our own barbed wire. We'll need to do that as quickly as possible. I don't want the men to bunch up. After we've cleared the wire, we'll have to dress our lines for our assault," the lieutenant-colonel said.

Headquarters had insisted on the men attacking in waves. If the first and second waves were not successful, they believed the addition of a third and fourth would carry the attack. Hadow knew his men had to cross two hundred yards from their reserve trench to the front trench in daylight. Planking had been placed across the trenches to allow the men to cross without having to drop in then climb out. The other problem he was worried about was that they would be attacking on a downslope with the skyline at their backs, silhouetting them to the Germans.

"Let the men know the changes in plans. I know that we didn't practice this, but the men will know what they need to do. We'll be going over the top at 9:15."

"Yes, sir," they replied as they turned to go back to their units.

At 9:15, the A and B company climbed up the embankment when they heard their officers' whistles. The second wave C and D company waited until the lead companies travelled twenty-five yards before they climbed out of their trenches to follow. As they stood up, the German artillery and machine guns opened up on them. None of the Newfoundlanders flinched at the onslaught. As they marched toward the German trenches, some tucked their chins into their jackets as if they were fighting a winter blizzard.

HAWTHORN RIDGE, BEAUMONT-HAMEL

Lieutenant-Colonel Matthew Aylward's face was bleak as he watched the 1st Essex emerge from their trenches into withering machine gunfire. In seconds, the 1st Essex had suffered the same fate the Newfoundlanders had two hours before. Aylward had been assigned by Lieutenant-General Hunter-Weston, the GOC of the VIII Corps, to observe the 29th Division's assault from Hawthorn Ridge and send back reports to the corps' headquarters located eleven miles back at Marieux.

He had felt the aftershocks from the mine explosion that had destroyed the German redoubt across from his position. He had arrived at his OP in time to see through a slit in the sandbags that the Newfoundlanders had reached the British barbed wire fencing they had to pass through for their assault. By then the Germans had consolidated and had reinforced the front lip of the mine's crater. They had easily spotted the Newfoundlanders and opened fire with machine guns and artillery. The Huns had caught the colonials out in the open, bunched up at the lanes cut in the wire to give them passage through the entanglements.

At least the 1st Essex's assault had taken some of the pressure off the Newfoundlanders. He could see men emerging from the protection of the trenches in desperate attempts to rescue friends and comrades who were hanging on the barbed wire. He knew those who somehow managed to clear the wire had taken cover in shell holes, but they were too far for the rescuers. There was a clump of men sprawled around Danger Tree, a cut-off denuded tree trunk with a couple of branches still attached despite the bullets and shrapnel that flew around it. There was no way to reach them until nightfall.

Through his glasses, he followed one man as he tried to crawl back to safety. When sunlight glinted off the metal triangle attached to the man's back, the lieutenant-colonel saw the man spasm and reach back with his hands. He saw him jerk a second time then lie still. *A sniper must have gotten him*, Aylward thought as he lowered his binoculars.

"Sir," yelled the telephone operator who was squatting beside him.

"Yes?" Aylward demanded tersely.

"The Newfoundlanders have been ordered to reorganize and launch another assault," he replied as he pressed the receiver to his ear.

With what? he wondered. In less than two hours, he had witnessed two battalions, nearly 1,600 men, being wiped out.

"Did Colonel Hadow acknowledge the order?"

"He did."

Aylward took another look at the Newfoundlanders that were still hanging on the barbed wire. "Send a message to the 29th and to Corps HQ to halt all attacks immediately. Make it clear to them that the Newfoundlanders have been effectively wiped out. And so have the 1st Essex. They are in no condition to launch another assault."

"Yes, sir! Right away, sir!" the telephonist replied as he quickly relayed the message.

TRENCH 52, MOUNT SORREL

"Oh, shit! The brigade-major is coming this way! You better look busy," whispered the recently promoted Corporal Huff urgently. He was proud of his new stripes, and he wanted to keep them.

"How the hell are we supposed to look busy?" Private Esterhouse pushed back. The twenty-two-year-old from Simcoe was sitting on the firing step with a cigarette dangling from the corner of his mouth. His khaki undershirt was stained with sweat from repairing the recent damage caused by the Germans. No one was in a particularly happy mood, since their work party had suffered two killed and six wounded. Not a great start to Dominion Day.

The corporal had seen Major Llewellyn make the traverse and was now examining the men's work. Picks, shovels, sheets of corrugated steel, and sandbags were lying in the trench as the men took a break. One of the walls had collapsed when the Huns had fired about a hundred and fifty rifle grenades at them around three o'clock in the morning. Huff guessed the grenades had been their 1914 model that had a two-hundred-yard range and the punch of an 18-pounder shrapnel shell. The *Karabingranate* were similar to their Hale rifle grenades. The Hale grenade had an eighteen-inch steel rod that was slid down the rifle barrel then launched by firing a blank cartridge. Accidents were known to happen when a real bullet was used instead of a blank.

"The repairs are looking good," the major informed them as he examined the fresh sandbags that were supporting the trench wall. The dirt that had filled the trench was being used to fill the sandbags. The recent rains hadn't helped. It was sunny today, so the work should go faster.

"How are the men holding up?" asked Llewellyn. "I came to give you the word from the medics. Your wounded will make it."

"Thank you, sir. They'll appreciate that. They are doing fine otherwise, sir. We could use some relief," he answered.

"We're being relieved on Monday," the major acknowledged with a hint of a smile. "I know the men have been looking forward to the sporting events they were holding at brigade today, but it couldn't be helped." To celebrate Dominion Day, a half-day of sporting events had been arranged at 2nd Brigade HQ.

"No baseball then," Huff replied with a smile. Everyone remembered last year's game.

"No baseball," the major confirmed.

"Which camp will we be assigned?"

"Dickenbush," replied Llewellyn as he turned his head toward the sound of artillery fire. "They knocked out our communications lines last night. The engineers are working on them. It seems six feet is not enough. If you need support, send a runner or one of your pigeons." The corporal acknowledged with a nod.

"Inform your men that the artillery will be firing three salvoes at the Huns at noon."

"Why, sir?"

"It's Dominion Day; of course. We've been ordered to celebrate it."

65TH ARTILLERY GUN PIT, MOUNT SORREL

Lieutenant Paul Ryan was preparing a return on the number of shells they had fired overnight in retaliation to the German shelling of the 1st Division the previous night. Their battery had spent the morning registering their guns on Château Hollebeke. It was a suspected to be the headquarters of either a German division or brigade. Based on the number of gun flashes they had recorded, there were a considerable number of them protecting the chateau.

"Lieutenant," said Bombardier Oats. "We've finished storing the ammunition we received last night."

Ryan glanced up from his paperwork at the tall and wiry thirty-year-old from West Vancouver. He was then interrupted by the sound of aircraft engines. He and Oats looked through the camouflage netting to see an Albatros two-seater reconnaissance plane flying overhead. "Are the ammunition wagon and the horses under cover?" he asked.

"Yes, sir," Oats replied. The ammunition wagon had arrived late last night, and it was stuck here. Orders restricted daylight movement. The ammunition wagon's horses were being accommodated in the stalls they had built for their own animals. The stalls had sandbags overtop to protect them from flying shrapnel.

"Good. We received orders we're to fire three salvos at the Boche at twelve, 12:02, and 12:04."

"What for?" the bombardier asked.

"To celebrate Dominion Day."

"Couldn't we get a half-day leave like the rest of the brigade to play sports?"

"Baseball, you mean." Oats was a good hitter.

"Yeah," replied Oats.

"I remember last July's game with the Richmond Fusiliers. Do you?"

"Not much," Oats admitted. "I was told after the game that the brawl was a good one."

"You could say that."

Oats shrugged. "What can you expect when the dirty cheating pitcher beaned me?"

FOLKESTONE CRICKET GROUNDS, FOLKESTONE

Over the yelling, screaming, and clapping of the spectators, Samantha could barely hear the booms of artillery coming across the channel. She took her eyes off the pillow fight and gave the nearby bookies a glance of disapproval. They were taking bets on the contest. She returned her gaze to the two bare-chested men in short pants whacking each other with pillows. Both were sitting astride a log suspended above a water-filled pit. The sandy-haired man took a hit to the face, knocking him off balance. He yelped as he slid off the beam and splashed into the pit. The winner raised both hands in triumph. He held his pose for just a few seconds before he too lost his balance then fell, to howls of glee, into the muddy water.

"What do you want to see next?" she asked Sadie Rann, who was standing beside her. Both of them were dressed in their working uniforms: blue dresses, white aprons, and white nurses' veils.

"I think I would like to stay here for a while," Sadie replied. Samantha couldn't help noticing the redhead had her green eyes fixed on the slick, dripping men who were climbing out of the pit.

"I'll see you later," Samantha said. She shook her head as she moved through the crowd. From what she was told, nearly seven thousand tickets had been sold for the Dominion Day sporting events being held at the Folkestone cricket grounds. The thirty-acre site was nearly a mile from Folkestone, near the foot of the North Downs hills. Besides the pillow fights, there were footraces, wrestling, and even a sword-swinging demonstration. One of the fields had also been taken over for a baseball game.

She headed toward the red-brick pavilion with white fencing to get something to quench her thirst. She finally had Dominion Day off, yeh! She had a choice of going to the sporting event here or the review of the Canadian 4th Division at Aldershot. A fair number of people from London were going to see the review, since the king and queen would be attending. Samantha wasn't particularly interested. If you've seen one review, you've seen them all.

As she walked, she could still hear the booming of artillery above the buzzing of voices. It had started at seven thirty this morning. She had no clue who was firing at whom, but she suspected they were Allied guns. The hospitals had received an alert to be ready for casualties. She sighed. She knew they had prepared the best they could. She only hoped the projections were off.

PRIME MINISTER'S HOME GLENSMERE, OTTAWA

Sir Robert leaned on his hoe as he watched a hovering hummingbird gather nectar from the sunflower he and Laura had planted in their wild garden. When the bird fluttered away, he arched his back and knuckled it to remove the kink he was starting to feel.

"Is your back bothering you?" Laura asked with concern. She was standing near the tall rosebush. The basket at her feet was full of cuttings, but the bush was still a riot of vivid colour.

"I'm fine," he replied.

"We should've hired someone to clear the bush and the branches from along the river. I don't want you to strain your back again."

"On Dominion Day?" he said with a raised eyebrow. Laura responded with a shake of her head.

Along the Rideau River side of their home, there had been a tangle of brush and broken branches that he had cleared earlier. Now he was weeding. He didn't mind the physical labour. He needed the exercise after spending most of the morning clearing up correspondence that had accumulated when he was away for four days in New York. He had left on his birthday, June 26, and had returned yesterday. He had gone there to discuss the CNR situation with some of the New York financiers and the presidents of some of the American railway companies. The CNR was in bad financial shape, and it had reached the point where his government was no longer willing to support the company. That was the message he wanted to deliver to the New York men. His feeling was they didn't believe him. At least he had discussed several options with them on how to save the company.

As he gently weeded between the flowers, he asked Laura, "Where would you like to go for vacation this year?"

"I don't know," she replied as she snipped a few more roses. She was planning to make floral arrangements for their home. What she couldn't use, she would gift to her friends. "I haven't given it much thought. With the new governor general coming in, we will have to work around that."

"Hmm," Borden murmured. It was true. Just last week, they had announced the governor general would be leaving in October, and the

Duke and Duchess of Devonshire would be replacing the royals. He had, however, noticed that her enthusiasm for travel had diminished somewhat since their last Christmas vacation.

"I'll give it some more thought, and if I get any ideas, I'll let you know."

"That sounds good," replied Borden as he continued to hoe.

What did sound good was the news from the front. The British offensive at the Somme seemed to be going quite well, from the reports he had read early this morning in his office. There was now some hope that the war would be over by the end of the year. As far as he was aware, the Canadian Corps was not directly involved in the latest operations. The casualties for the month of June were bad enough.

The image of Hughes popped into his head. Hughes was still his old self, giving interviews that offended not only his enemies, but his friends — especially his friends.

He banished Hughes from his thoughts as he glanced around the blooming flower gardens and paths that meandered through the trees on his property. The various birds that made his home their home were chirping quietly. It was turning out to be a beautiful summer's day.

CHAPTER 17

"Ah, Miss Lonsdale, I see you're back. I hoped you enjoyed the Dominion Day festivities," said Matron Macdonald as she looked up from the report she was reading on her desk. Samantha noticed the matron's tired eyes, which suggested she had worked late the previous night.

"Yes, ma'am, but I'm glad to be back," replied Samantha with a slight touch of guilt. She had indeed enjoyed the Dominion Day activities, but it was overshadowed by what she knew was coming. She had come in with her uniform freshly pressed. She had polished her tunic's twin rows of brass buttons and the insignia on her shoulder boards and collar until they gleamed. Her long blond hair was pinned up neatly.

"No doubt, no doubt," Macdonald replied as she opened a manila folder and gave it a quick glance. "I've afraid we're going to have quite a bit of work coming our way."

"The Somme offensive?" Samantha asked as she glanced at the map of Northern Europe that was pinned on the wall above Macdonald's left shoulder.

"Yes."

"How bad is it?"

"Initial reports indicate sixty thousand," Macdonald said grimly as Samantha took a sharp breath.

Samantha felt a knot in her stomach as she acknowledged the number. "Do we have any figures on how many of our boys are hurt?"

Macdonald gave her a smile of sympathy. She was aware of her relationship with Major Llewellyn. "The Corps isn't directly involved in this engagement. As far as I'm aware, they are still in the Ypres Salient."

Some of the tension left Samantha when she heard that bit of news. She hadn't received any mail from James for several days.

"I've been on the phone with Dame Becher, and she has agreed we need to call back all our nurses currently on leave."

Samantha nodded. While she hadn't met Dame Becher, the Queen Alexandria's Imperial Military Nursing Service's matron-in-chief, she knew who she was. From the other nurses, she had learned that Margaret Macdonald, Becher, and Dame Maud McCarthy, who led the QAIMNAS in France, had served together in the Boer War. She wasn't sure if Macdonald liked Becher, but as far as Samantha could tell, they seemed to have a good working relationship.

"General Jones had sent warnings to our hospitals in June about the upcoming offensive. They should be ready to receive them, but I don't expect anyone could have planned for something of this magnitude. The first trains from the ports should be on their way."

Samantha glanced back at the map again. The main disembarkation ports for the casualties were Dover and Southampton, while the secondary ports such as Folkestone, where most of the Canadian hospitals were clustered, did receive their fair share. Normally, a patient would arrive to the appropriate hospital within twenty-four hours of the battlefield, if everything went smoothly. Once they arrived in port, the distribution centres would assign the wounded man to the nearest hospital that had beds available.

"With most of the male nurses and orderlies being transferred to the medical units in France, we had to do some rearranging of the nurses' duties," Samantha pointed out. The orders had been issued in mid-June, resulting in VADs taking over some of the basic tasks of the orderlies. A rule of thumb was that a trained nurse was assigned the responsibility for fifty to seventy beds, depending on the available nursing staff. They were required to supervise two VADs, two women cleaners, and one male orderly. Two VADs were needed to replace the orderlies simply because of lack of training and experience. While the matron didn't like using VADs, they were needed until the crisis was over.

"I know. That's what I wanted to talk to you about. We need the recent arrivals at the Thackeray Hotel assigned to one of our hospitals as soon as possible."

"They were to start preliminary instruction at the Queen Alexandra Military Hospital before we assign them to one of our units," replied Samantha. Thirty nurses had arrived several days earlier and were staying at the Thackeray Hotel. The Nursing Service regularly booked rooms at the Thackeray for nurses in transit.

Macdonald paused to consider the ramifications. "From what I recall, they have significant civilian experience, and they have received instructions on military procedures and protocols. It will be a rough introduction for them, but unfortunately, it can't be helped. We need warm bodies. Go over their qualifications then start matching them up with the appropriate units. I would like to cut orders for them tonight," Macdonald said crisply.

"Yes, ma'am," Samantha replied. She had tickets for a show in the West End. It couldn't be helped; she would have to give them up.

"Send word to the hotel they are to remain on the premises until they receive further orders."

"Understood," replied Samantha. "What about the staff currently being transferred?" There were always nurses being transferred from one unit to another for a variety of reasons.

"If they are already in transit, there is very little we can do," Macdonald replied. "If they are still with the unit, their transfer can be put on hold until the crisis is over."

Samantha met Macdonald's eyes, signalling she understood. Sensing she was dismissed, she turned to leave. At the door, she paused and turned to Macdonald when she said with a tired sigh, "Before I forget, a Colonel Bruce has been asked by the minister to report on our efficiency and to make suggestions for improvements. He and his staff will be interviewing various members of the CAMC."

"Will he be interviewing the nurses?" Samantha asked.

"It's a strong possibility," replied Macdonald. "Just let the nursing staff know, and if they are requested to attend an interview, I would like to be informed."

"Of course," Samantha replied as she headed to her office. *All we need is an efficiency expert,* she thought.

JULY 17, 1916
PRIME MINISTER'S OFFICE, EAST BLOCK, PARLIAMENT HILL,
OTTAWA

Borden gave the letter a quick glance before signing it. He didn't need to spend a lot of time on it, since it was a form letter. The contents weren't particularly earth-shattering. It simply stated that requests for contracts should go to the War Purchasing Committee. It was the standard reply to the usual patronage attempt to bypass the low-bidder contracting system. It didn't even get a rise from him, although it had come from a Conservative Party stalwart. Mentally, though, he was preparing for the meeting that was scheduled to start in a few minutes.

"Prime Minister, shall I show ministers Perley and Hughes in?" asked Blount, his private secretary, from his office doorway.

"Please do," he replied as he capped his pen and closed the red leather-bound folio that held the correspondence requiring his signature. He could already tell the meeting wasn't going to go well. Hughes was visibly irritated when Perley entered before him.

"George, Sam," Borden greeted them. "Have a seat. We have much to discuss."

Hughes glanced at Borden and Perley. Borden could tell Hughes was wondering if he were being ambushed. It wasn't far from the truth. He and George had met earlier to discuss the problems with the military administration in England.

Borden had been pleased to see George. His hair and beard were greyer, and his sixty-year-old face had a few more lines on it since he had seen him last. When George arrived from England last Saturday, he had sent a railroad car to Quebec City for him.

As for Hughes, he seemed to be back to his restless self, despite the events of the past week at Camp Borden. No, it was not named after him, although the general public had that impression. It was named to honour his first cousin, Sir Frederick Borden, who had been the minister of militia and defence under the Laurier government. While it had been unusual that a Conservative would honour a Liberal, much of the current success of the Canadians in Europe was the result of the fundamental reforms his cousin had laid down when he was the minister.

Most of the men, according to Laura — who had attended in his stead — Camp Borden had not been pleased with Sam. He, Laura, and the other dignitaries were attending the official opening of the new camp on July 12th when three thousand men there rioted. They had been disgruntled with the poor conditions at the camp for some time. The tipping point was being forced to drill in the heat and humidity in preparation for Hughes's arrival and inspection of the thirty-two thousand men assembled at the camp for training.

Hughes had built the camp, about fifty miles north of Toronto near Barrie, in the same manner he had done at Camp Valcartier. It was the oppressive heat that had brought the men's tempers to a boil. If it had been anything like it was in Ottawa, Borden wasn't surprised. He didn't find playing golf in this weather very enjoyable. Laura told him it had gotten so bad that thirty-five men had collapsed from heat exhaustion, and heat stroke had killed one of them. The military police had to be called out to restore order, and some of the men had resorted to using bayonets to protect their sleeping tents and belongings.

Hughes had pooh-poohed the riot, stating it was started by a small group of undisciplined soldiers from London. While Hughes didn't show it, he had been disturbed by a group of soldiers who had given him the silent treatment when he boarded his train to return home.

Borden was glad that Laura was safe, but she did mention that the camp was nothing but a sandy plain, and you could smell the fires that were being used to clear the scrubland. What bothered him was that the riot had to happen at Camp Borden.

"I have some concerns about our military administration in England," stated Borden, which was an understatement.

"I'm aware that some of the problems there are impacting the efficiency of our boys," replied Hughes defensively.

Perley glanced at Borden and then Hughes, then said, "One of the problems is that there is a great deal of confusion on the powers and line of authorities of our generals in England. The War Office is of the opinion that General MacDougall has been placed in charge of all the Canadians in the United Kingdom. When General Steele arrived in England, he was given command of all troops in Shorncliffe, except for the training depot. General MacDougall is still responsible for that. General Watson commands the 4th Division, and all of the troops at the Bramshott depot. Then we have General Carson, who is responsible for general administration and correspondence, but he is not in direct command of any troops.

"From what I have seen and been informed, the War Office's view of who is in charge is not the same as ours. My impression is that General Carson acts in the fashion as if he is the supreme authority over our military affairs in England. He has been exercising considerably more power than your order-in-council authorizes."

"He is not," replied Hughes tersely. "I made it quite clear to General Carson that General MacDougall is in charge of all our troops except those under General Steele's command. Carson is only my personal representative in England."

"Well, he's taken upon himself a much greater role. He is insisting that he be consulted on my discussions with the War Office and on our senior officers' appointments."

Hughes glared at Perley and turned to Borden. "I assure you that the problems are relatively minor now since we replaced General Alderson. What I proposed is forming in London a council that will set policy on how we manage our overseas troops."

Borden watched as Perley considered Hughes for a moment. "That is all fine, but I have stated before and continued to state that we need a strong hand in England with the appropriate authority."

Borden could see Hughes tense up at Perley's statement. Borden knew Hughes had been chafing since the beginning of the year as his authority was steadily whittled away, first with the War Purchasing Committee then with the Shell Committee. The decision by the War Office concerning his precious Ross rifle was undoubtedly a blow to his ego. Borden knew Hughes hated delegating and preferred to maintain control.

"I would like to set up a committee similar to what I proposed several months ago," Hughes said.

"But that committee only met twice then never met again," Perley protested. "What I'm proposing is to have a new ministry created and a minister appointed who will be responsible for the overseas force. The minister would coordinate with the Department of Militia and Defence minister."

Hughes looked at Borden in alarm. He didn't like where this was going. Borden knew he was giving Hughes too many chances, but he impulsively said, "What I really want you to do is to go to England and try to rectify the situation and impose the efficiency."

It was Perley's turn to be alarmed that Borden was seriously considering Hughes's request. Borden blinked in surprise when Hughes said, "I would be glad to put a request for an order-in-council approval for me to go to England." It was the first time that Hughes had put in such a request.

Perley had a look of disbelief on his face. Borden knew Hughes was sensing he was treading on thin ice with him. He hoped that he wouldn't regret allowing Hughes to go back to England.

JULY 19, 1916
CANADIAN CORPS HORSE SHOW, RENINGELST

Paul Ryan grimaced when a heavy draught horse nearly stepped on the rider that had just fallen off him. The soldier managed to roll away in time to escape the horse's hooves. He got up very little worse for wear except for the dirt that clung to his sweating, naked back.

"Hoist me up," Ryan ordered Sergeant Reggie, "we're up next."

Ryan put his left foot into his friend's cupped hands and swung a leg over his horse's bare back. He positioned himself slightly farther forward than he would normally have, if he were using a saddle. He had to remember to keep his heels down so that he wouldn't use his knees if he lost his balance. The knees were used to tell the animal to pick up the pace. Having his mount move faster while trying to recover his balance was not a good thing, although he had selected a horse that was calm and steady.

While he had waited for his teammate to get onto his horse, he glanced around the field being used for the Canadian Corps Horse Show. The field had been set up with three rings. The A ring, near the road that was lined on both sides with a single row of trees, was where the turnout competitions were taking place. The winners of the turnouts were the ones who had their horses and mules impeccably groomed with clean tack, the leather supple and well oiled, and the metal bits polished to a high gleam. The immaculate wagons and limbers the draughts were pulling sparkled in the afternoon sun. In the B ring he could see a set of obstacles positioned for the horse-jumping competition. There were brush fences where tree branches obscured the top of a wooden barrier and log fences created by placing planks on pegged two-by-fours. The planks would fall off if the horse's hooves nicked them.

The horse lines were located behind him. Grooms were brushing animals and leading them to drink from the water troughs. A couple of farrier tents had been erected to provide care for the animals' hooves. A veterinary tent had been set up nearby for any sick or injured animals.

The crowd of men, mostly Canadian with a sprinkling of Imperial, Australian, New Zealand, French, and Belgian troops, were being held back by rope lines. Some of them took advantage of a neat pile of lumber nearby to get a better view. Ryan watched as a photographer set up his tripod to take photographs of them for posterity.

He couldn't help looking into the clear blue sky when he felt a slight warm breeze caress his skin. As far as he could see, it was empty of German aircraft. They were only six and a half miles from Ypres, while Mount Sorrel was ten miles northeast of them.

He spotted Brigadier-General Edward Morrison, Dinky to his friends (Ryan was not one of them), escorting a British artillery officer he presumed to be Brigadier-General John Hotham from the 20th Division. Morrison was the GOC of the 2nd Division's Divisional Artillery. A colonel he didn't recognize was accompanying them as they examined the horses in the lines, since they were judging the turnout competitions.

He, however, had been entered in the bareback wrestling event, which didn't need a judge; the last one still sitting on his steed at the end won. There were no real rules in the wrestling match except for no hair-pulling. That wasn't much of a problem, because all the men's hair had been shorn short. All the competitors had to fight bare-chested; their units' designations were sewn into the sides of their slacks.

When his teammate, Lieutenant Ferris, finally gave him the thumbs up, he nudged his horse to the edge of the ring. He saw a soldier with straw-coloured hair fall to the ground to groans and cheers from the watching crowd. He decided not to notice the exchange of money between the winners and losers of the side bets. The final man sitting made a victory lap round the ring before sliding off his horse into the waiting arms of his unit.

The referee, a captain astride a black stallion, blew a whistle to get the crowd's attention and then yelled, "The next competition is between the 65th Artillery and the Richmond Fusiliers." He motioned Ryan and Ferris then motioned to the Fusiliers. Ryan spotted Major Llewellyn give one of his riders some instructions. When the major locked eyes on him, he smiled and nodded at him. Ryan acknowledged the major with a tilt of his head.

"Gentlemen," the captain said when all four riders met in the centre ring. It was then he noticed both men had a shimmering sheen coating their skin. He knew what it was; both he and Ferris had done the same thing. They had oiled their upper bodies, making getting a hold difficult. *Oh well*, Ryan thought, *I'm getting as bad as the Fusiliers; if you ain't cheating, you ain't trying.*

CHAPTER 18

As Sergeant Duval stepped off the subway train onto the Marble Arch Underground Station's platform, he lifted his kit bag over his left shoulder. He then slung his Ross rifle over his right as he headed to the lifts that would take him to the street above.

"Do you know where you're going?" demanded Private Danny Weber, who was close on his heels. The young Bolton, Ontario native was his spotter, so when Duval went on leave so did he. Weber had been born in Liverpool, but his family had immigrated to Canada when he was three. They had been through a lot together over the last few months. Duval sighed. It had been six months since his last ten-day leave, and he wanted a good time. He had hoped once he arrived in London he could ditch Weber for a few days.

"Nope," replied Duval. He glanced at the other three men who had somehow attached themselves to him and Weber. He felt rather responsible for them, although they didn't belong to his company. He was the senior noncommissioned officer of the group. They belonged to the 2nd and 3rd Companies of the Fusiliers. It was standard policy that only one or two men per platoon were sent on leave to make sure the units remained at their authorized combat strength.

"Have you stayed at the club before?" asked Corporal George Taylor. The corporal was from the 4th Platoon, 3rd Company. Taylor was in his late twenties, with black hair, and had a scar running along his neck where he got hit by shrapnel. He was considered a veteran; he had been with the Fusiliers for about a year now. Duval didn't know much about the Halifax native, since he wasn't very talkative.

Duval shook his head. "I got the phone number off a poster. Some of the boys have been to the Charles Street Club. They said they really liked it. There's a library and a pool room. The food is supposed to be pretty good. Not the army slop. The main thing is that they have real beds with clean sheets. They even give you pyjamas and a bathrobe."

"A real bed?" Private Henry Johnston said in a wistful tone. He was a bomber in the 2nd Company's 1st Platoon. He was young, barely eighteen. He was thin, of medium height, and from Rimouski, Quebec. It was obvious it was his first time in London, since he kept swivelling his head to take in all the sights.

"How much is this going to cost?" demanded Private John Vincent, who was from Richmond. He was in his early thirties, with a thick chest and arms. Duval didn't like him. He was a penny-pincher with a sour disposition. "I got a paycheque burning a hole in my pocket. I'd rather spend it on getting drunk and getting my ashes hauled."

Duval did agree with the man's sentiment. He wanted to do the same thing. Of course, if he didn't get a piece of ass, he could always spend a few days with his former wife in Shorncliffe. He had been sending her money regularly until he found out she had been sharing her bed with her other husbands. He was sure she wouldn't mind if he dropped by with some cash in his pocket. "From what I have been told, they charge a shilling a day for accommodations and eight pence for breakfast and lunch. Supper is a shilling."

"Hmm, about 3.6 shillings a day," said Private Vincent. He looked as if he could find something cheaper in London. He possibly could, but Duval wouldn't trust the cheap hotels from stealing his boots while he slept. Besides, the privates were paid a dollar a day with a ten-cent field allowance. The exchange rate converted the British pound to about four dollars and sixty cents Canadian. This meant it would cost them about eighty cents a day. Most of the men didn't spend much money in the field, and all of them had drawn cheques before they left on leave, so eight dollars for ten days meant they would have plenty for other amusements.

Duval stiffened when he saw a couple of red caps standing in front of the lifts. His natural inclination was to go up to them and spit in their faces. He hated the red caps. But he sure as hell didn't want them to ruin his leave on his first day, especially since he hadn't had any fun yet. Still, he would have enjoyed getting into a punch-up with the military police.

The beefier of the two red caps had spotted him and his small group, since they stood out among the late-night crowd who were trying to make their way home. Maybe they should have taken a bus instead of the underground at Waterloo Station. According to the posted schedule, buses ran to the club from Waterloo, Liverpool, Charing Cross, and Victoria Stations, but he had been talked into taking the tube, since they had never been on an underground train before.

He straightened his shoulders then headed straight for the two red caps. Both of them wore the standard British military uniforms, red forge caps, black armbands with red embroidered MP letters, and wooden batons dangled from their wrists. The best defence was a good offense. The four men behind him were startled. It took them a couple of steps to catch up to him.

"Hey, Constable, can you tell me how to get to the Maple Leaf Club?" Duval asked the beefy red cap.

"Canadian?" the man asked.

"Yeah," replied Duval, trying to be respectful.

"Can I see your passes?" the red cap demanded as he presented an open hand.

"Sure," Duval replied as he retrieved his pass from his inner breast pocket and handed it over. The rest of the squad did the same.

"Everything looks in order," the man replied with a touch of disappointment that he wouldn't get any business tonight. "There's no blackout tonight, so it's easy to find. Head west towards the end of Oxford Street as you pass the Marble Arch on the left. Once Bayswater starts, just go up one street to Connaught Place. You should find it easily enough."

"Thanks," Duval said.

"Sure. No problem. See that you don't make any trouble for us," the red cap said as Duval led the men to the elevators. Duval waved back an acknowledgement.

When they stepped onto Oxford Street, Private Johnston said, "Well, what do you know, they have a street named after Quebec here."

"Where?" asked Waters as he turned his head. He finally spotted the street sign that Private Johnston was pointing at. It read "Old Quebec Street."

"Let's head this way," Duval said as he headed westward. He found the Marble Arch easy enough on his left. He couldn't miss the large three-arch edifice. What Duval didn't know or particularly care about was that the arch had been built to commemorate British victories during the Napoleonic Wars. Once they passed the arches, they found the intersection where Oxford, Bayswater, and Watling Streets met. Connaught Place was just one street up. Number 5 was easy enough to find, since there were only two dozen or so buildings on the short street. The building itself was five storeys high, and most of the windows were still lit.

Once they had passed through the front door, they found themselves in a simple plain foyer with a male clerk standing behind a concierge desk. He was dressed in a Canadian military uniform with 1st Division insignia. Duval noted the man's right sleeve had been pinned above the elbow. On one of the walls near the desk, there was a coat of arms with a crown on top. Inscribed in a circle that enclosed a maple leaf was "The King George and Queen Mary 1915." Gold lettering on the maple leaf read, "Maple Leaf Club." Below it hung the coat of arms of the Imperial Order of the Daughters of the Empire. Duval guessed they were the ones responsible for running and supporting this location.

"Good evening, lads," said the clerk as he eyed the five men. He raised an eyebrow at Duval's Ross rifle, since the other four men carried Lee-Enfields. "How can I help you?"

"I'm Sergeant Duval. I called earlier to arrange beds for me and my buddies."

"I see," the clerk said with a frown as he checked the register.

"Is there a problem?" Duval demanded sharply.

The clerk grimaced. "I'm afraid we had an influx of the lads today."

"You gave away our beds!" Duval said as his voice started to rise.

"Fuck!" someone behind him muttered. He was sure that it was Private Vincent.

The clerk didn't seem to be fazed by the sudden hostility. It seemed it wasn't the first time that armed men were upset with him. "We only have one hundred twenty-six beds here. In a pinch, we can add another fourteen men. We're booked solid, I'm afraid."

"Where are we going to find another place to sleep at this late hour?" Corporal Taylor blurted out.

The clerk shook his head. "No, no. You can stay the night. We'll find you lads a place, don't worry. We don't turn men away. We'll put some blankets on the floor. We have some men returning to the front in the morning. When they go, we'll move you into their rooms."

"Are you still going to charge us for the night?" demanded Duval.

"It'll be free until you get moved into the room," the clerk assured them.

"Fuck! I was looking forward to sleeping in a warm bed," muttered Corporal Taylor. "Least the floor is free."

"Good. While you're here, you need to abide by the rules," the clerk said as he pointed to the posted sign behind him with "Rules" printed in large red letters. "The first is no alcohol or women are allowed on the premises. Second, your weapons must be checked in. We will store them safely while you stay with us. Breakfast is between the hours of seven thirty and nine thirty, lunch starts at eleven thirty, and supper at seven. During your stay, you can take tours of the city." The clerk pointed to Thomas Cook pamphlets on the desk. "We can deposit your cheques with us, and we'll give you some cash. We suggest drawing small amounts during your first day's stay with us." From the man's tone, Duval suspected it was an attempt to prevent the men blowing their entire wad on their first day in town.

"Now, that we covered the basics, I'll show you to the bathrooms, where you can get a hot bath. We'll be issuing you clean pyjamas. We have a laundry service, so we'll get your uniforms cleaned for the morning. Now follow me, I'll take you to where you will be spending the night."

★ ★ ★

Duval whistled softly when he finally padded into the reading room. The tables and chairs had been pushed against the wall to make room for him and his four companions. They weren't the only ones. There were another eight blankets on the floor, a couple of which were snoring up a storm.

One of the paintings on the wall caught his eye. It depicted a scene of the Old City of Quebec from the river. He was familiar with it, since it was from the same dock that his ship sailed from nearly two years ago. He guessed the people running the place wanted the men to feel nostalgic for home.

His hair was still slightly damp from the hot bath he had taken. He had nearly forgotten the pleasure of having a bath and slipping into freshly washed pyjamas. He was pleasantly surprised to find clean sheets, another luxury, when he slid under the blanket. Despite the snoring of the dozen or so men in the room, he fell quietly into a deep sleep in which he dreamed of soft, big-breasted women.

JULY 30, 1916
CAMC HEADQUARTERS, 13 VICTORIA STREET, LONDON

"I'm sorry, Miss Barnes, until you have completed your contract with the QAIMNS, a transfer to the CAMC will not be entertained," stated Samantha. "When will your contract end?"

"In about four months," replied Miss Barnes, who was sitting across the table from her in the interview room. The only disappointment she displayed was the thinning of her lips.

Samantha had read the nurse's file before the scheduled meeting. Miss Barnes was from Galway, Ontario. She was twenty-nine years and ten months old, five-foot-six, and weighed one hundred and twenty-six pounds. Her complexion was fair, her eyes blue, and her hair brown. What was not included in the file was the lime-green flowery dress she was wearing and the feather cap that covered the neatly tied small bun.

Miss Barnes was one of the nurses the matron-in-chief would have loved to take on board, since she was professionally trained and experienced. However, the Nursing Service had agreed with the QAIMN, which had been eyeing the supply of Canadian nurses, not to raid each other or to recruit in each other's territories. The NS recruited their nursing sisters in Canada, where they were given preliminary indoctrination before being shipped to England. Some in their eagerness to serve had sailed to England to volunteer in the QAIMNS under the mistaken belief that once in England they could transfer to the Canadian NS. Matron Macdonald's policy was that nurses requesting a transfer had to complete their contacts before they would be considered. The better pay and the military rank were a draw for many. Earlier that morning, Samantha had to turn down an American nurse because her contract hadn't expired.

"If you come back in four months, your request for a transfer might be seen in a more favourable light," said Samantha. When a glimmer of hope appeared in Miss Barnes's eyes, she added, "Of course, there cannot be any promises. Exigencies of the service."

"Of course," replied Miss Barnes as she rose to her feet. Samantha rose as well to escort her out. In the hallway, Miss Barnes shook Samantha's hand and said, "Thank you. I really appreciated your consideration."

"It was my pleasure," Samantha replied as she watched the nurse head to the lifts. Her smile dimmed slightly when she turned to the woman sitting in one of the hallway's guest chairs. "Mrs. Fraser?"

"Yes," the woman said as she rose to her feet. Mrs. Fraser appeared to be in her mid-thirties. Samantha raised an eyebrow at the plain, tailored suit that would have cost her six months' pay. The jacket had simple lines with a row of black buttons. Underneath, she wore a cream Chinese collared blouse. Her ankle-length skirt, with a single pleat, also had a single row of buttons. The ensemble was crowned with a small sailor-style hat.

"If you would follow me," Samantha said with a wave of her arm. Once they were seated, "How can I help you, Mrs. Fraser?"

"I was hoping that I would be able to speak with Matron Macdonald," Mrs. Fraser said.

Samantha replied briskly, "I'm afraid that Matron Macdonald has been called away on important business. She asked me to speak with you."

"That is most inconvenient," Mrs. Fraser answered with a hint of displeasure. "Very well," she continued, "I would like to volunteer as a VAD."

"I see," replied Samantha as she stiffened slightly. "Do you have any nursing training or first aid?"

From the look on Mrs. Fraser's face, she didn't like the question. "No, but I'm raising three children. Nursing a wounded man couldn't be any more difficult than nursing sick children." Samantha raised an eyebrow at the woman's statement. Mrs. Fraser, taking it as an agreement, continued, "Do you know Lady Beatrice?" Samantha shook her head. "No, well, she's a good friend of mine. She has informed me many of her acquaintances are VADs in the British hospitals. Now, if one can be found near my house, I would prefer that. I have time to spare, since I have a governess now taking care of my children."

One of Samantha's less pleasant tasks was to redirect women who wanted to do their bit by volunteering as a nursing aide at a Canadian hospital or a convalescent home. Most were, like Mrs. Fraser, the wives and the sweethearts who had followed their men to England. With plenty of spare time on their hands, they felt the need to find something to do. The problem was, while the QAIMN encouraged the use of VADs as nurses at their facilities, Matron Macdonald was dead set against the practice. Samantha tended to agree with the matron-in-chief as she had seen some of the volunteers at work in England and in France. She hadn't been impressed with most of them. A few did want to do a good job and were ready to learn. All they needed was some classroom time and training. As she had suspected, Mrs. Fraser did not fall in the latter group.

"I understand," Samantha said. "But you have been misinformed. The Nursing Service currently does not use VADs in our facilities."

"You don't?" Mrs. Fraser replied, surprised. "But I just assumed…"

"Well, yes, many have that distinct impression. If you wish, I can supply you with the name and the address of the VAD office at the QAIMNS. I'm quite sure that they would appreciate your willingness to volunteer."

"Well, I never!" replied Mrs. Fraser "I want to talk with Matron Macdonald immediately!"

"I'm afraid that is not possible at the present time," replied Samantha. "As I mentioned earlier, she has been called away. I can pass on a message to her, if you wish. I will ensure she reads it when she returns."

Mrs. Fraser rose abruptly from the table when she realized she was wasting her time. "We will see about that!" she said as she stormed out of the office.

Samantha's mouth formed a small "o" before she pursed her lips. She didn't look forward to informing Matron Macdonald about the result of her interview with Mrs. Fraser. She didn't seem the type to let things go.

AUGUST 1, 1916
COURT OF INQUIRY, BILLETS, RENINGELST

"Please be seated, gentlemen," said Lieutenant-Colonel Roberts as he took his seat in front of the assembled Richmond Fusiliers' senior officers.

Major Llewellyn was quite familiar with the staff officer since he, as well as Lieutenant-Colonel Tennison, had worked with him at Major-General Currie's HQ before they were assigned to the Fusiliers. While he had a decent relationship with the man, it was not the kind where they were drinking buddies. Even if he had such a relationship, he doubted it would have been of much help in this situation. Luckily, the man usually didn't have an axe to grind.

"I've spoken with your men to ascertain the facts of the German raid on trenches 57 to 60 on the night last. The raid resulted in the deaths of Lieutenant Cranston and four other ranks, as well as twenty wounded and three missing," he stated as he glanced at the corporal sitting beside him taking notes.

He then looked at Lieutenant-Colonel Tennison and Major Llewellyn, who were sitting in the front row. "One of the missing men was a cook?"

Llewellyn glanced at Tennison, who gave him a tired nod. Everyone was exhausted, since they hadn't gotten any sleep for two nights now. They weren't going to get much until the inquiry was over. HQ liked getting the facts when they were fresh. "Yes, Colonel, Private Henry Forbes."

"Was he a good cook?"

"I don't understand?" asked Llewellyn. Behind him, he heard someone snort. What did it matter if he were a good cook or not?

"What I meant is would you like him back, or do you want the Boche to keep him?"

"I guess he was a decent enough cook. As far as I'm aware, he hadn't poisoned anyone. With his cooking, I mean."

"What was he doing in the trenches?"

Llewellyn replied, "The Boche have been annoying us of late by firing gas shells at our ration patrols as they bring food forward to the men. The men were complaining they can smell and taste the gas in their meals, even after it was allowed to sit to dissipate as much of the gas as possible. We have alternated our routes and schedules. It only lasts for a day or so before they figure it out and start firing the gas shells at us again.

"We've been experimenting having cooks prepare hot meals in the trenches. We found the men were happier, and there have been fewer complaints. Besides, Colonel Tennison and I feel every man in the Richmond Fusiliers should be able to muster their rifles when they are called upon."

The lieutenant-colonel simply arched an eyebrow as he made a note in the yellow pad in front of him. "It is my understanding the Germans opened up with heavy bombardments on trenches 57 to 60?"

"Yes, Colonel, they started around nine last night, or is it now ten o'clock?" Llewellyn replied, chagrined. "Sorry, sir, this daylight saving thing takes getting used to." Orders had been sent that all timepieces in England and France were to be moved one hour forward as of August 1 to save on fuel.

Llewellyn continued, "They were dropping mortar bombs at a rate of six to eight per minute. We notified the 65th Artillery to retaliate, and we sent an alert to Divisional HQ. It took about ten minutes before the 65th started pounding the Boche mortars. Our Stokes started up as well, working the forward Hun trenches."

"When did you suspect it might be a raid?"

"When we started receiving reports that there was a German observation balloon in the air around nine thirty. Colonel Tennison and I were in the reporting centre getting a handle on the situation. Shortly after, a runner informed us that the Stokes were receiving artillery fire, and one of them got knocked out. The others were still in action. We contacted our FOO and informed him we need the 65th to continue their support. He assured us as long as the ammunition lasted, they would.

"That's when we got reports from A Company that their forward trench had received direct hits, and it had collapsed pulling the wire down with it. They had also suffered three wounded, so they pulled their men out into the communication trench."

"Was it at this time you called up your reserve company, Company B?"

Tennison spoke up, "It's part of my standard policy that the reserve is called out at the same time we inform Divisional HQ. We've conducted raids on the Boche, and we kind of thought they would return the favour."

Roberts made a note then asked, looking at Llewellyn, "You were in agreement?"

Llewellyn nodded. "B Company managed to capture one of their wounded officers and four ORs. Two were severely wounded. One has since died, and the other doesn't look as if he will make it, despite Dr. Moore's ministrations. They didn't have any identification. They took the same precautions we do when we mount a raid. From our preliminary interrogations, they appear to be one of the *Jäger* Battalions. Someone over there has put a lot of thought and planning in this."

Roberts frowned at the news. The *Jäger* Battalions were the German Imperial Army's elite. They were designated light infantry that specialized in woodcraft, skirmishing, and sharpshooting. Many of their skills had not been of much use in trench warfare, except for the snipers. However, if they were starting to copy how the Canadians raided and were developing their own countertactics, it was not good news.

"Did you put out sentries and OPs?" Roberts asked.

Llewellyn acknowledged with a shrug. "We found the sentry at the apex of trench 57 with his throat cut. That was the key entry point they used. Unfortunately, that particular post was isolated. We had plans to make improvements there, and the work parties were to start work on it tomorrow."

"It was also in that section we caught Germans attaching amplifiers to the wire so they could eavesdrop on our men talking. We've issued orders no one was to speak about any raids, attacks, and such while in the trenches."

"You have?" the colonel asked sharply.

"Yes, Colonel," Llewellyn stated firmly. "We've made several reports to HQ about them. We've sent patrols out to remove them and to discourage further attempts to attach them to our barbed wire."

"And when the raid finally took place?"

"It went fairly well, all things considered. We did lose communications temporarily with one section because the lines were cut. The runners proved adequate to keep us informed. Our Lewis machine guns proved quite effective in preventing them from penetrating deeper. We estimated it was a company-size assault, but only two platoons managed to get into trench 57 and part of 58.

"We did notice some of our dead and wounded had their pockets turned out. It seems they took the men's pay books and their personal papers with them."

"Did they get any other documents?"

Lieutenant-Colonel Tennison and Major Llewellyn knew what he was asking. Did they leave, despite instructions to the contrary, orders or reports in the trenches that would be of interest to the Germans?

Tennison replied confidently, "We've been quite diligent in ensuring that no confidential material is carried into the trenches."

"I certainly hope so," the colonel replied sharply. "Now, where were we?"

"B Company made quick work out of them and pushed the Boche out of the trenches. We didn't give them any time to consolidate. They did attempt to assault our Vickers strong point, but they were driven off with heavy losses with minimal damage."

"I see," said Colonel Roberts. He examined his notes then looked up. "I think I have sufficient information to make my initial report. If I have any further questions, I'll be in touch," he said as he closed his leather folio and rose to his feet. The assembled men rose to attention as he made his way out of the room.

Major Llewellyn couldn't tell from the colonel's demeanour if he would write a favourable report or not. Just because Major-General

Currie liked them didn't mean he wouldn't rake them over the coals if they had screwed up. The one thing about Currie was he hated losing.

CHAPTER 19

"Let's get the camouflage net overtop," ordered Lieutenant Paul Ryan. "We need to hurry, the sun will be up soon, and the Boche will have their planes and balloons in the air."

"Yes, Lieutenant, we're getting the spare netting from stores," replied Sergeant Ellis as he studied the edge of the orange glow rising in the east. "I guess we have about an hour or so."

"Yeah," Ryan replied sourly as he made room for stretcher-bearers carrying what remained of the 4th gun's crew.

There wasn't much left after a 5.9" shell landed near it, blasting a large hole that tossed the 18-pounder over onto its back. One of the spare gun crews was working on turning the gun upright so they could pull it out of the hole. Thank God the blast hadn't detonated the shells stored in the gun's pit. They were putting up netting above the swearing men to protect them from the Huns and to deceive the enemy into thinking they hadn't knocked it out. At least, that was their hope.

Ryan saw Lieutenant-Colonel Masterley check with the stretcher-bearers before heading his way.

"How bad is it?" he asked.

"The 4th gun crew is gone," replied Ryan.

"Shit!" said Masterley. "What about the gun?"

Ryan indicated the men working in the shell hole. "They're digging it out now. I've taken a look at it. The barrel's been dented near the mouth. We'll have to send it to the maintenance shop for them to take a look at it. It's risky firing it until we know it's safe."

"Shit, we'll be a gun short until we get it back," replied the lieutenant-colonel sourly.

"I know. And the maintenance people are backlogged with repairs," replied Ryan.

"Can we still cover the Fusiliers as they get relieved?" asked Masterley.

Ryan glanced at his watch. "They should be out of the trenches and on the road by now. We were waiting for the all-clear before we retaliated."

"Good," replied Masterley. "We have orders to provide a barrage at five this evening at Ruin Farm. Intelligence suspects the Boche are digging a mineshaft and tunnel there. We're going to give the Boche the notion we know about it, and to keep their heads down."

"Sounds good to me," replied Ryan grimly. He was looking forward to paying the Huns back for what they had done to the 4th gun crew.

STEENVOORDE ROAD, STEENVOORDE

"I'm looking forward to a hot shower," said Sergeant Duval as his company drew up for an eight-mile forced march to their billets.

"No offence, Sarge, but you do smell a bit," Private Mackenzie piped up. The private was tall and brawny. His rifle was slung over his right shoulder, and the straps of his backpack stretched across his chest.

"A bit?" Corporal Dack snorted in agreement then pointed a finger. "The second platoon complained they can smell him back there. And he's only been in the trenches for what, five days, since he came back from leave?"

"Keep it up, and I'll get the brigade-major to reassign you and your company to the rear guard," the sergeant warned the corporal.

"Now, now, there ain't any reason to be hasty," the corporal protested. The American knew how tight the major and the sergeant were. He had seen the marching orders for the brigade. Two companies of the Richmond Fusiliers would form the advance guard, and they would step off at five o'clock. The Brigade's HQ and signal section would follow ten minutes later. After them, at ten-minute intervals, a battalion would start. At 6:10, the rear guard would step off to cover their rear. Their starting point was a mile and a half east of the Steenvoorde-Poperinge road and just north of the U in "Chau." From there they would march about a quarter mile to Cross Roads near the Belgian border, where they would turn to bypass Godewaersvelde. They would have to cross the railway line twice before they headed to Eeche then back north again toward Steenvoorde. Halfway there, they would turn right to their billets and the waiting hot showers.

"We're all set?" asked the major as he trotted up to them.

"We're all set," replied Dack, quickly trying to forestall Duval getting him and his company reassigned. It would have meant eating dust kicked up from the road. His company had won the fierce competition to get assigned to the front guard, and he didn't want to lose it.

"Good to hear," said Major Llewellyn with a touch of a smile. He had caught the tail end of the conversation. "By the way, happy anniversary."

"Anniversary, sir?" asked Sergeant Duval.

"Yeah, you know, the start of the war," prompted the major.

"Hey, I joined six months ago," blurted Private Mackenzie.

"Are we getting cake with candles?" asked Sergeant Duval.

"I'm afraid not," chuckled the major.

"Just another day, sir." Corporal Dack shrugged. "Just another day at the office."

The major nodded. "It's time; you better get the men started."

"Yes, sir," replied Duval. He started bellowing orders to get the men's feet moving.

QUEEN'S HALL, LONDON

Samantha Lonsdale rose to her feet with the rest of the audience to give Prime Minister Asquith a standing ovation when he asserted Britain's and the Empire's determination to see the war to a victorious end.

It was the first time she'd seen the British prime minister in the flesh. Asquith appeared to be in his sixties, with thinning white hair. Samantha wondered if the whiteness were the result of the great pressure he was under.

At least Asquith's speech was more interesting and entertaining than Lord Darby's reading of the telegrams of support from the colonies. He even read those sent by Sir Robert Borden and the provincial premiers. Asquith had touched on what he believed Germany's intentions were, the growth and quality of the new army, the tragic loss of Lord Kitchener, and the recent successes at the Somme.

Samantha was glad she was sitting in a box on the second balcony. She couldn't refrain from grimacing. She had seen the returns from the Canadian hospitals, tabulating the wounded from the Somme offensive. It deepened when Asquith mentioned that tomorrow would be the start of the war's third year. Earlier that morning, Samantha had attended one of the intercession masses they held throughout London to commemorate it before she started work.

She gave a sideways glance to Matron Macdonald. She was bending over to whisper something to Matron Campbell, who nodded in agreement. Samantha would have liked to be elsewhere, like her office. She had a ton of paperwork to do, but duty called. The Nursing Service had to put in an appearance, as did other representatives of the Canadian contingent at the anniversary rally being held at Queen's Hall. The concert hall on Langham Street was about a forty-five-minute forced march from their offices on Victoria Street. Matron Macdonald had decided they should have an early supper at one of the restaurants along the route before they attended the rally. Samantha was glad they had eaten. It looked like the rally would be a long one.

As far as she could see, the 2,500-seat theatre was full. She didn't particularly like Queen's Hall. The theatre was rather drab, and there wasn't much legroom. She had been dragged to one of the Hall's Prom Concerts they held during the summer months, even though she preferred toe-tapping music.

She missed the name of the French government official who had replaced the prime minister at the podium. Asquith retook his seat on the stage beside Lady Asquith. Her purple hat with a sprig of grapes as decoration didn't quite suit the occasion, she thought. Next to Lady Asquith, she recognized Bonar Law, the secretary of state for the colonies, who would be following the French government speaker.

She sighed. Well, at least she was having a boring evening.

MCGILL UNIVERSITY LOWER FIELD, MONTREAL

"Aye!" the crowd roared when Sir Robert Borden demanded an answer.

The crowd had risen to its feet. As the roars echoing off the surrounding buildings diminished, he couldn't help but glance at the group of reporters scribbling notes at the foot of the stage. Between them and the crowd the 199th Battalion, wearing the insignia of the Irish Canadian Rangers, stood as an honour guard. An estimated eight thousand had come to hear him speak at McGill University's Lower Field. The field was a natural amphitheatre; it was where the university usually held its convocations.

The answer that he had demanded was to the resolution declaring that the war was a righteous one and that the citizens of Montreal had the unbending determination to see the war to a victorious end to maintain the principles of liberty and justice. The same declaration was being read at all the rallies being held across Canada and the British Empire to commemorate the second-year anniversary of the war. For a variety of political reasons, he had decided the Montreal rally was an appropriate place for him to give his speech. George Perley was handling the one being held on Parliament Hill. The crowds there were expected to be larger than the Dominion Day celebrations.

He and Laura had taken the train and arrived in plenty of time for the eight o'clock meeting. He had some concerns about the weather, but it turned out to be a fine day with comfortable temperatures for his two-hour speech. He was grateful for that. Last week, the weather had been unbearable. It had been a hundred in the shade. He didn't get much of it, since for most of the week he had been sitting in a canoe with George on 31 Mile Lake, three hours north of Ottawa, fishing for bass. He had caught a nice three-and-a-half pounder. When he had returned to Ottawa on Monday, he found Laura had been sweltering. At least her hand, which had been badly stung by a wasp while gardening, had healed nicely. Sadly, the heat contributed to a devastating forest fire in Northern Ontario, which had destroyed several towns and caused the deaths of over two hundred and fifty citizens.

He was the last of the three speakers on the bill. The rally had been led off by Albert Holt, the president of the Montreal Canadian Club. Holt's speech was followed by the Honourable Rodolphe Lemieux, the Liberal member for Rouville and former minister in the Laurier government. Borden and Lemieux had crossed swords in the House, but Lemieux was here to show his and the Liberal Party's support for the war.

It was fortunate the anniversary fell on a Friday. For the crowd, it was a diverting night out. And they were enthusiastic. As he waited for the clapping and cheering to die down, he remembered last year's reception at the London Opera House. He had been in England at the time and had given a speech there commemorating the war's first anniversary.

His speech was basically a review of Canada's war effort over the past two years. When he had written the speech, he had been amazed how much was accomplished and how much the country had changed. There were now two hundred thousand workers producing artillery shells, and Canadian industry was producing a million dollars of war materials a day. What was equally impressive was the fact that there were three hundred and sixty thousand men under arms. He emphasized that, since he had seen the recruitment figures for July. They were not good, especially those from Quebec. The recruiting officers had assured him the figures would improve once the harvest was in. He didn't look at Lemieux sitting behind him; he knew the Liberal would be against conscription.

One of his worries was the explosion at Black Tom Island in New Jersey, which destroyed Allied munitions waiting there to be shipped to Europe. German sabotage was suspected. But his immediate concern was the sailing of the German submarine, the *Deutschland*, from Baltimore. Her sister sub, the *Bremen*, was somewhere in the North Atlantic, heading for the States. The Germans claimed they were unarmed cargo vessels. How long will it be before they were equipped with torpedoes and became a menace to Canadian shipping and troop transports sailing from Halifax? He worried about the men he was going to review at Valcartier tomorrow. They might never reach the front. Until now, submarines were short-ranged and stayed near their bases. The new German subs' capability to sail across the Atlantic and reach North America was terrifying.

He also warned the crowd that just as Canada was suddenly plunged into war, just as swiftly she could be plunged into peace. The country needed to prepare for the impact peace would have on Canadian industry and the impact her soldiers returning home would have.

As he took his seat beside Laura, he was pleased that his speech had been well received. The resolution to which he had demanded a reply was needed to shore up public support. Everyone was reading the casualty lists from the Somme battles that were being published.

CHAPTER 20

"It's official then?" asked Major Llewellyn.

"I'm afraid so," replied Lieutenant-Colonel Tennison. He was reading the orders he had received from Corps HQ. "The Lee-Enfield is now in and the Ross is out."

"Not many will be crying any tears," stated Llewellyn. Tennison snorted. He was well aware Llewellyn had run a series of tests on the Ross rifle last year after the Ypres and Givenchy battles.

"We'll have to prepare returns on how many of them are still in our inventory, and we'll have to start shipping them back to England for disposal," Tennison said.

"That shouldn't be a problem. Our quartermasters have been complaining about the space that the crates are taking up." The Fusiliers had converted to the Lee-Enfield last fall. They couldn't get rid of their Rosses, since technically it was, until now, the Canadian army's official firearm. If the brilliant minds in the Woods Building had made an issue of it, they would have been required to convert back to the Ross. "What about our sniper teams?"

"We're allowed to keep a certain number for them. For that role, the Ross is much superior to the Lee-Enfield."

"Good," replied the major with a bit of relief.

"Now," he said. "Along with that bit of news, we're going to receive orders to move to the Somme."

"Are things that bad?" replied Llewellyn.

"I haven't seen the official numbers, but it doesn't look good."

"When are we moving?"

"In a couple of weeks. The entire Corps is moving in stages."

Llewellyn was somewhat surprised Haig was moving the Canadian Corps. The British high command preferred to move divisions around. The British Corps HQs stayed relatively static since they were mainly administrative units for the divisions under their command. It also meant they were moving from Lieutenant-General Plumer's Second Army to Lieutenant-General Rawlinson's First Army in the Somme.

"That gives us a few weeks to train the latest replacements," said the major.

"Well, at least we're getting some," Tennison said.

"They came in last night. I'm going over their jackets to see what training they've received. We'll put them through their paces. I'll have private chats with each one before deciding which platoon we'll assign them to."

Tennison nodded. "After you're done with them, I'll give them a pep talk."

"They'll love that," Llewellyn said with a smile.

"Get out of here," Tennison said with a shooing motion.

"Yes, sir," Llewellyn acknowledged with a chuckle.

★ ★ ★

Major Llewellyn examined the latest draft of replacements dropped off by the regular bus run between the base depots and the billets. In the nearby grassy field, B Company was going through their morning calisthenics. The instructor, standing on a stool, was taking them through the exercises designed to perfect their bomb-throwing techniques. The head count confirmed they got thirty new drafts. He was hoping they could have gotten an extra twenty or thirty. They needed to get to full strength, but they had to make do with what they could get. He had a good look at them as the NCOs lined them up. He was impressed by their physiques and their turnouts. The last group they received looked rather seedy. This lot had formed their review lines rather promptly. He hoped their attitudes matched their appearance. Once the NCOs got to know them, he would be deciding where to send them. Assigning the wrong men to a platoon could cause problems. A disruptive personality could make or break a unit's morale. It was part of his job to make sure that didn't happen. He already had to deal with several men who weren't pulling their weight and who the captains wanted gone.

At least, according to the latest rumours, Lieutenant-General Byng was getting fed up with the quality of the reinforcements from England. He had decided to form a Corps Training School to solve the problem. They were to start sending men through it sometime in September.

The recently promoted senior NCO, Sergeant Taylor, barked the orders, calling the men to attention for Llewellyn's inspection. As he marched down the three rows, he asked the usual questions: name, where they were from, and how long they were in service. Most were from recent battalions that had been broken up for reinforcements when they arrived in England. Half were from the 77th Battalion that had been stationed in Ottawa during the Parliament Hill fire. Some mentioned what they had done that night. The others were from various other places in Canada. One of the young men, barely eighteen, gave him a strange look when he talked to him. Llewellyn didn't have the time to ask him before he marched to the front of the column to give his welcoming speech.

"At ease," he ordered. "Welcome to the Richmond Fusiliers. You might have heard about us. Since we've been in France, we have developed a very good reputation. That reputation has been earned through hard work, stubborn determination, and sacrifice. You're now part of our family. We expect you to help maintain and even improve our current efficiency. We are all here for the same purpose: to make Canada proud and to win this war. We must work together as a team, and we expect you to play your part on that team.

"It's Colonel Tennison's policy and mine that our doors are open to you if you have a complaint. Now, the NCOs will be assigning you to your billets, after which you will have a half-day's leave to square your things. Tomorrow, bright and early, we will take you through your paces. So get as much rest as you can. You will need it. Dismissed!"

He was starting to walk away when the private that gave him a questioning look approached him. *That was fast*, thought Llewellyn, *the first complaint already.*

"Major, if you have a moment?"

"Of course," replied Llewellyn.

"Were you a recruiting officer in Richmond two years ago?" he asked.

"Why, yes," replied the major startled.

"I don't think you remember me, but I tried to join the Fusiliers back then," replied the private.

"I'm sorry, but I don't," replied Llewellyn honestly.

"I was the kid with the forged birth certificate you turned away," he said with a blushing grin.

"That I remember. That was you?"

"Yes, sir."

"Your mother finally let you sign up?" Llewellyn asked.

"She passed away last year. Consumption," replied the private with a slight shrug. "I just wanted to say I'm glad that I finally joined the Fusiliers."

"We're proud to have you, son," replied the major with a firm nod.

"Thank you, sir, for your time. I better get going to find my billet before Sergeant Taylor makes me a new one," he replied as he saluted the major. The major returned his salute. As he watched him walk away, he thought that a lot of lads who were sixteen years old back then were now eighteen. For some reason, he felt responsible for the lad. When the private had caught up to the sergeant, he decided to assign him to Sergeant Duval's unit to keep an eye on him.

AUGUST 16, 1916
CAMC HEADQUARTERS, 13 VICTORIA STREET, LONDON

The two senior officers at the table looked up expectantly when Samantha entered the familiar meeting room several doors down from Major-General Jones's office. "Matron Samantha Lonsdale reporting as ordered," she said as she stood at attention.

"At ease, Matron," said Lieutenant-Colonel Bruce, pointing to the chair in front of the table.

"Thank you, sir," replied Samantha as she took her seat. Her posture showed some tension as she sat with her back erect, a scant inch from the chair's back. She wasn't sure why acting Lieutenant-Colonel Herbert Bruce had requested her for an interview. She wished she had a choice, but then orders were orders.

"Thank you for coming," the lieutenant-colonel said with a brief smile that appeared on his clean-shaven face. Samantha estimated the doctor was in his late forties or early fifties, of medium height and weight.

When she had been ordered to attend the early-morning meeting, she had asked around about him. He had been born in Blackstone, Ontario, and had attended medical schools in Toronto, Paris, and Vienna. He had been a professor of surgery at the University of Toronto's medical school and the owner of Toronto's Wellesley Hospital before volunteering. She should have remembered that. It had been one of the hospitals she had sent an application to when she found out that Toronto General would not offer her a position after her graduation.

What had piqued Samantha's curiosity was the fact that the good doctor had been assigned to the Duchess of Connaught Red Cross Hospital. He only spent several months there before he resigned his commission, which Major-General Jones had accepted. It wasn't clear why he had resigned, but there had been plenty of speculation. It had surprised many when Major-General Hughes had given him an acting lieutenant-colonelcy in July and then appointed Dr. Bruce as an inspector-general.

"As you might be aware, the minister has requested that I and my colleague, Major Malcolm, conduct an inquiry into the work of the CAMC. We have been asked to report on its efficiency and make recommendations for improvements," explained Dr. Bruce.

"I understand," replied Samantha.

The doctor nodded. "I've been informed you have been a member of the nursing service for the past two years."

"Yes, sir. I was with the first contingent when they sailed to England. I was first posted to Salisbury Plain, then to the No 2 Hospital at La Touquet. After that, I was at the Ypres battle. Subsequently, I was ordered to the Duchess of Connaught Hospital."

"You weren't assigned to the units in Lemnos or to Salonika?" he asked. The Canadian hospital at Lemnos had been transferred to Salonika after the Gallipoli campaign ended. Samantha shook her head. That reminded her she hadn't received any recent letters from Emily, who was stationed in Salonika in northern Greece. A force of two hundred thousand men was being assembled to provide aid to the Serbs after they had suffered crushing defeats at the hands of the Austrian-Hungarian and German armies. "No, but I had some friends and colleagues who were ordered to the Med last year."

"As a nurse, what were your general duties?" asked Major Henry, getting the interview back on track.

"It depends on the unit and the work involved," Samantha replied. "But I've admitted patients, updated medical charts, and done the administrative work tracking patients."

"How many of your patients were Canadians?" asked Dr. Bruce after making a note.

Samantha pursed her lips. "We treated any wounded that were sent to us. Mostly our own men and Imperials. But I've treated French, Belgian, and captured wounded German soldiers as well."

Lieutenant-Colonel Bruce gave her a sharp look. "What percentage do you think it was?"

Samantha paused to think. "Hmm, I really couldn't say."

"Can you make an educated guess?" asked Major Henry.

Samantha frowned. "Off the top of my head, I would guess maybe seventy percent were Imperial. No one expected the current casualty rates. What I have seen is when the Corps is in the rest areas, our free beds are available for casualties from other units. I don't know how many British divisions there are, but there are a lot more of them than us. When men are wounded, they are sent to the nearest hospital. The Imperials do the same for us. If we are overwhelmed, they help if they have the spare beds."

"But once they are transported to England, not all of our men are sent to our own hospitals," said Lieutenant-Colonel Bruce.

"That's true," replied Samantha.

"Don't you think they should be?"

Samantha hesitated. She wasn't sure where the questions were leading. "I must admit I would prefer our men to be treated by our people. However, one of the issues we have is where do we send our men for convalescence? The British can send theirs to their own families and homes once they have recovered sufficiently. Now, some of our soldiers do have families and relatives here, with whom they could stay for short periods until they are returned to their units or sent home. Others don't, and they have to be sent to a VAD facility to free up beds for the incoming."

"Is that the reason you think we discovered some of our men were found in facilities as far away as Scotland?" stated Lieutenant-Colonel Bruce.

Samantha winced at the news. "Yes."

"During our investigation, we also found cases where men have recovered fully but were still occupying a bed in a medical unit. It seems in most of those cases, their medical files had been lost."

Samantha said defensively, "That unfortunately happens. Some units are quite good with the paperwork, while others are not. In the field hospital, when you have a hundred men waiting to be treated, you do the best you can. You eventually hope to get back to it, but there often isn't enough time. They try to send the paperwork with the patients, but sometimes it gets lost as the wounded are transferred from the casualty station to the train, then to the ferry to cross the channel, then to an ambulance train, and finally to a hospital."

"Hmm. But, wouldn't you agree it's the hospital administration's job to notice the men had fully recovered and to return them back to their units?" the major asked.

"You would think so, but these things happen. But with the Imperials, it can be a bit of a challenge, especially when the units are in movement. I've had difficulty locating some of our patients' home units. For most of the British ones, we have to contact the War Office, which then provides us with the info where to send them."

"Don't you think most of these problems could be alleviated if the men were assigned to a Canadian hospital?" asked Colonel Bruce.

"There is some logic in that argument," Samantha reluctantly agreed. "I have worked with many of our English colleagues, and they have provided us with invaluable help, research, and other support services. I just don't want to see an implemented policy that may jeopardize their goodwill."

"Thank you for your opinion," Lieutenant-Colonel Bruce replied curtly. "Now I have a few more questions about the training units."

Samantha was somewhat put off by Dr. Bruce's tone. She had no idea what the enquiry had found to date, but it might not be good. She had caught glimpses of Major-General Jones's and Matron Macdonald's concern when Dr. Bruce's name was mentioned. She knew no organization was perfect, but based on her impressions, people were not going to like Lieutenant-Colonel Bruce's final report.

AUGUST 18, 1916
TRAINING GROUNDS, ÉPERLECQUES

"So what do you think?" asked Lieutenant-Colonel Tennison as he lowered his binoculars.

"It seems to be working," Major Llewellyn replied. He continued to peer through his pair as the Richmond Fusiliers pressed the mock attack. The battalion had been arranged in two waves. The first wave was double the size of the second. They were experimenting whether this was a better approach than forming a thin first wave.

"The Australians said they had to keep up with the barrage, and they had to be ready to spring the moment it lifted," Tennison said.

Both Llewellyn and Tennison had read with interest the 4th Australian Division's report on their attack at Pozières.

"How far back did they say they were from the barrage?"

"They wrote fifty yards."

Llewellyn grimaced. "That's rather close."

"I know."

"It depends on how accurate our artillery will be."

"I know," repeated the lieutenant-colonel.

"The men aren't going to like it."

"I know," Tennison said with sigh. "But they'll obey orders. If it works, we'll lose fewer men to enemy fire."

"Yes, if it works," replied Llewellyn as he watched the second wave drop the shovels and picks they had been carrying when they reached the trench. They stabbed downward with their bayoneted rifles at the mock straw German soldiers before they dropped into the entrenchment.

Today was the first day of drill and instruction before the Canadian Corps was sent to the Somme. It had taken the 2nd Brigade three days to march the forty-plus miles from the Railway Dugouts to the training grounds at Éperlecques, just northwest of St. Omer. For the next week to ten days, it would be their home as they conducted brigade-size drills.

"Well, at least Hughes seemed to be pleased with us this morning," said Llewellyn.

Tennison grinned. "I was rather concerned. Especially after the War Office announced their decision about the Ross."

Major-General Sam Hughes had inspected the Richmond Fusiliers at their billets at Moulle before they marched the five miles to their training area. Ten square miles between the villages of Barlingham, Charno de Tir, Wisques, and Cormette had been set aside for the 2nd Brigade's use. The entire battalion had been arranged into its usual formation for visiting dignitaries. Not much had to be done to make sure the men were appropriately prepared for the minister's review. Prior to their march, they had been warned there was a possibility they would be inspected by His Majesty, King George V, when they passed Oxelaëre. It had been his job to make sure all the men carried their steel helmets, gas masks, a hundred and twenty rounds, and accoutrements in a standardized fashion. Sadly, they never saw the king.

The men had worn their forge caps instead of their steel helmets on the march. They had the summer heat to consider. It had been warm, but it wasn't excessive. The ambulances, following them to pick stragglers and those who had dropped out for medical reasons, had done very little business. The men had weathered the march quite well. Besides, there were a fair number of veterans from Hughes's previous reviews. They had regaled the recently arrived recruits with stories of what to expect from the minister's personal inspections.

"He seemed to be particularly interested in the Lewises," Llewellyn said as he watched the machine gun teams clamber out of the shell holes on the flanks. They had been designated to provide covering fire for the first wave.

"He did ask a lot of questions about them," answered Tennison.

"Are we going to get more of them?" Llewellyn asked.

"General Loomis said to expect another dozen in the next few days." Tennison paused as he watched the third wave consolidate the trenches. "Have you selected the men for the next course? We need to run as many men as we can through it."

"It's been a problem getting the time on the machine gun range," said Llewellyn. The range was near Éperlecques. "The new machine gun companies are hogging them." The newly formed machine guns companies had been created around the Colts and the Vickers. Since they were not as mobile as the Lewis, they had been designated as heavy machine guns.

"The Australians said they found having the men fire them before-hand quite useful."

Llewellyn snorted. "No question! However, it doesn't help if we have well-trained men if we can't figure out how to take full advantage of the Lewis in the attack and the defence."

"I've been giving it some thought," replied Tennison.

"Well, we could ask General Currie tomorrow," Llewellyn suggested. General Currie was scheduled to visit them tomorrow morning.

Tennison grunted again. "I don't have a problem consulting better minds than ours."

AUGUST 20, 1916
BLACKTHORN COUNTRY ESTATE, SHORNCLIFFE

The gunfire startled Samantha as she was filling her plate with scrambled eggs from the chafing dish on the buffet table. Luckily, she spilled the eggs back into the half-empty silver pan. Samantha glanced out of the two open glass-panelled doors to the grey stone terrace that the building was currently shading. The dining room was set on its west side to protect it from the early morning sun. Beyond the terrace, she could see a pea gravel walkway splitting the lawn in half. A Chinese gazebo overlooked a fishpond at the far end. On the lawn's wings, beds of wildflowers were blooming below neatly trimmed trees.

"Ah, they had started," said Lady Beatrice Blackthorn as she took several links of sausages from the dish next to the eggs. Lady Beatrice was her host for the weekend. The British, as did the Canadians, liked to go to the country on the weekends, except the country home that she and the matron had arrived at the previous evening seemed more like a palace than the one-room shacks at the camps she had gone to in Sudbury. Besides the lack of black flies, she never had breakfast on what she suspected was Sterling silver dinnerware. She had been lucky to have burned trout out of a cast iron pan.

"The men will be gone for most of the day," she said as she grabbed some brown toast from a plate. Samantha gave the matronly-looking woman dressed in a brown tweed suit a glance. She appeared to be in her mid-fifties, with deep brown eyes. Her brown hair, with a touch of grey, was tied in a bun. She was rather stout, with full breasts. The volume of gunfire didn't seem to bother her. To Samantha's ear, it was reminiscent to the gunfire she had frequently heard at the front. The only thing missing was the artillery.

"What are they hunting?" Samantha asked as she took her place at the dinner table arranged by the servants for the visiting guests. Most of the chairs were already occupied. She noticed all of the seats were taken by women. Samantha had been among the last to arrive, since she had gotten lost trying to find the room.

"Mainly pheasants," Lady Beatrice replied as she took her place at the head of the table. "Last month he bagged nearly a thousand."

Samantha's eyes widened in surprise. A thousand pheasants in a weekend! Where Samantha grew up, everyone hunted and fished. Yes, there were a few who hunted only for sport, but most she knew hunted to feed the pot with fresh meat. She didn't know what they did with the pheasants they killed, but wasn't sure if it was polite to ask.

"Poppa does so enjoy the hunt," said the young woman seated beside her. Samantha had been introduced to Caroline, the youngest of Lady

Beatrice's daughters, the previous evening after she and Matron Macdonald had driven down by motor car from London.

She glanced at Macdonald, who was sitting beside Lady Beatrice. They had been en route to Shorncliffe when the matron-in-chief decided to take advantage of Lady Beatrice's invitation to spend a long weekend at her country home. The matron was scheduled to inspect several Canadian hospitals near Shorncliffe and had wanted to discuss with the units' COs some of the complaints they had received at HQ. Still, it was a working weekend for the matron. She was intent on developing contacts and building relationships that would benefit the Canadian Nursing Service.

"Poppa does complain that the hunt is not as it once was," Caroline said with a tone of regret.

From the previous evening's introductions, most of the men in attendance wore grey hair and moustaches. She had recognized the looks that some of them had thrown at her. She suspected at these weekends something else was being hunted besides pheasants. But it seemed that the game had become rather thin in the last few years. Samantha wondered how many of Caroline's male friends and acquaintances were now gone, especially with the horrendous losses in the last month and a half.

"I understand like Matron Macdonald, you're a working nursing sister?"

"Yes, I had just graduated from Toronto General's nursing school when the war began. I must admit I have learned a great deal since about taking care of the wounded," she replied. Samantha had never expected when she volunteered that she would be in such exalted company.

"I've been told that you hold a military rank?"

"That is true. I'm a captain. Matron Macdonald is a major," Samantha replied with pride. She thought it would be rather presumptuous to add that the matron was the highest-ranked female officer in the Empire.

"That's quite progressive, isn't it, Mother?" Caroline said to Lady Beatrice, who sniffed. Caroline turned to Samantha with a twinkle in her eye and explained. "Momma still thinks that women shouldn't get the vote."

"Politics is men's work," Lady Beatrice replied stiffly.

"I see," Samantha replied tactfully. She didn't want to get into that political discussion, especially if it might reflect badly on Matron Macdonald. Macdonald's unique status as the highest-ranked female officer in the Empire, and the director of the Canadian Nursing Service, had opened doors for her. She had dined with the king and queen on several occasions. She was also on quite a few of the more prominent members of British high society's invitation lists.

"What's it like being a nurse?" Caroline asked.

Samantha nearly winced. She had noticed Caroline kept a corner of her eye on her mother. She had a pretty good idea where she was heading. She had dealt with the letters that arrived regularly from women who wanted to volunteer. "It's a lot of hard work, with long hours."

To discourage her, Samantha added, "I had to do two years of training before I could graduate. It still didn't prepare me for treating the types of wounds and broken men we, the medical services, see daily."

"Mother thinks that I should be a VAD instead."

Lady Beatrice snorted. "It's my understanding that the Canadians don't use VADs."

Matron Macdonald jumped in. "That's correct, Lady Beatrice. It's been my experience that a well-trained professional nurse provides the wounded with a high level of personal care."

"With the recent casualties, there has been a shortage of qualified nurses," Lady Beatrice pointed out.

Samantha nodded in agreement. One of the things she had to bring to Matron Macdonald's attention was that Dame Maud McCarthy, the QAIMNS's matron-in-chief in France, had transferred nurses from the Canadian hospitals to British ones. The problem was they hadn't consulted with the Canadian Nursing Service before they had ordered the transfers. It meant Samantha had to scramble to find replacements in England to send to France. That was one of the complaints they had gotten from the Shorncliffe COs.

"The QAIMNS have found the VADs to be quite useful," stated Lady Beatrice.

"Yes, they have," replied Macdonald as she took a bite of her food. She didn't bother stating that a fair number of the VADs came from the upper class. Some of them were quite good; others, not so much. Removing those who were not was something of a delicate political issue. That was why Macdonald preferred having nurses directly under her control. Samantha kept her face neutral, since Macdonald had made her position clear. *Well, it is going to be an interesting weekend*, thought Samantha.

CHAPTER 21

Major Llewellyn had to put a hand out when the driver hit the brakes on the Model T.

"Sorry, sir," said Private Horner as he turned his head to Lieutenant-Colonel Tennison, who was sitting beside him, after the car stopped squealing. "It's the new brakes. I'm not used to them. I keep forgetting that I don't have to stomp on them like I used to."

"That's quite all right," replied Tennison with a grimace as he stepped out of the car. "I'm sure the good doctor up front can fix us up."

"I'll have to fix myself first," replied Major Moore grumpily as he rubbed his neck. He had suffered a bit of whiplash, since he had nearly gone through the windshield. "I think my breakfast nearly came up."

"Yeah, it would have been a shame. It's been a long time since we had such a wonderful breakfast," replied Llewellyn as he eyed the tent-covered slope of Tara Hills.

They had stopped at one of the cafes along their route and had an English-style breakfast of eggs and sausages with crunchy French bread washed down with black coffee. Much of what they had driven through had been rolling hills, unlike the flat lands of Flanders. It didn't seem to be touched by the war, except for the high prices.

Major Moore chuckled as he moved his round belly out of the car. "Interesting," he said. When Major Llewellyn turned his head, he saw a sergeant approaching them wearing a khaki slouch hat. The brim on the left was raised, and a Rising Sun badge was pinned to it. On the man's sleeve near the shoulder was a grey-coloured patch with a white centre roundel. If Llewellyn recalled correctly, it indicated that the sergeant was a member of the 4th Australian Division's headquarters staff.

Llewellyn noticed the sergeant start slightly when he saw the fresh patches that he, Major Moore, and Lieutenant-Colonel Tennison had in the same places on their sleeves. About two weeks ago, their HQ had issued orders that all members of the Canadian Corps now had to wear patches on their sleeves to identify the units they belonged to. The patch on his sleeve was a green square above a red rectangle indicating they were with the 2nd Brigade of the 1st Canadian Division. The 2nd

Division's colours were blue, the 3rd white, and the 4th Division's were yellow. He was fairly certain the 4th wasn't keen on the yellow, but they would have to grow into it. From what he had been told, the Australians had their patches ever since they were stationed in Egypt during last year's Gallipoli campaign. He suspected someone in Corps HQ had seen the Australian patches, liked them, and decided they were a good idea. As for the colours, the 1st Canadian Division had spilled plenty of red blood to earn it.

"I'm here to guide you to our HQ," the sergeant said crisply in a thick accent. The sergeant was in his mid-twenties, hard-bodied, with the long-distance stare of a hot-corner man. He raised an eyebrow when he saw the same stare from them. The facial scar Tennison wore indicated he had seen some action.

"Lead on, Sergeant," replied the lieutenant-colonel. "We don't want to be tardy."

"No, sir," replied the sergeant as he did an about-face then led them up the hill to the shaft that led to the Tara Hills' redoubt that would soon be the new headquarters for the 1st Canadian Division. Until the transfer was completed, they would be under temporary command of Major-General Cox, the GOC of the 4th Australian Division. The 1st Anzac Corps HQ at the Vadencourt Château was being handed over to Lieutenant-General Byng as they spoke.

Lieutenant-Colonel Tennison, Major Moore, and Llewellyn were the advance party for the Richmond Fusiliers. They had come to work out the details for a smooth handover. Relieving troops in the forward trenches was tricky, since you were moving into a new house as the tenants were moving out, without the nosey neighbours finding out.

Llewellyn glanced at the tents, and he wasn't surprised to see an empty cot here and there. He had read the 4th Australian Division's reports on the attacks they had launched since July. They had suffered over seven thousand casualties, nearly thirty per cent of their men. That was one of the reasons the Canadian Corps was replacing the Australians and the New Zealanders. The Anzacs were tired and worn out after two months of constant combat. They needed rest and time to rebuild. The Canadian Corps was nearly back to full strength, fully rested, and had been training hard for the past two months since they had recovered from the Mount Sorrel battles.

One of the other reasons was that the British Army preferred moving divisions around. It was much easier moving 30,000 men than 120,000. What Llewellyn had heard through the grapevine was that the Australians and New Zealanders were just as adamant as the Canadians in their desire to fight as a unit. So the British decided it was easier and less of a headache replacing one colonial corps with another colonial corps. Llewellyn had also heard rumblings that the Australian government was starting to insist that British officers in senior posts in the 1st Anzac Corps be replaced by Australians and New Zealanders. He had heard that Major-General Cox was a British officer from the Indian Army.

Llewellyn saw what he thought was a Huntley & Palmers biscuit tin with an embossed Britannia image as they made their way up the hill. He picked it up and saw that a hole had been punched into all three ends of the triangle so a string or cord could be pulled through it.

"What's this for?" asked Llewellyn when he held it up. Major Moore and Lieutenant-Colonel Tennison stopped to take a look.

The sergeant gave it a disgusted glance. "Our lads were ordered to wear it on their backs for the aeroplane and artillery observers."

"I see," replied Llewellyn as he gave Tennison a glance. They had heard the stories of what happened at Beaumont-Hamel. German snipers had easily picked off the wounded Newfoundlanders as they tried to retire off the battlefield because of the sun's reflection from the tin triangles on their backs.

The sergeant's face blanked as he snapped to attention then saluted when three generals exited the shaft. Llewellyn easily recognized the pear-shaped body of Major-General Currie standing beside Brigadier-General Loomis. He assumed the man standing next to them was Major-General Cox. He snapped to attention and snapped a salute.

"Ah." Major-General Currie beamed. "I would like to introduce you to some of my officers. Lieutenant-Colonel Tennison, his brigade-major Major Llewellyn, and Major Moore, their senior medical officer."

As Llewellyn eyed Major-General Cox the general gave them a brief smile under his moustache after returning their salutes then said, "Welcome to the Somme."

SEPTEMBER 6, 1916
PRIME MINISTER'S OFFICE, EAST BLOCK, PARLIAMENT HILL,
OTTAWA

"You're surprised?" George Perley asked as he handed the evening *Ottawa Journal* back to the prime minister. The headline on the page it was open to proclaimed a militia subcouncil had been struck in London to solve problems with the Canadian forces in England.

Perley was sitting across from Borden in the prime minister's East Block office. Through the window, he could hear the morning shift working on the new Centre Block. On September 1st, he had attended the re-laying of the original cornerstone of the building by the governor general. He had been one of the dignitaries among the thousands of spectators, with the 207th and 230th Battalions in attendance. They all had come to watch the large cornerstone being raised from its old location and moved to its new spot.

Before they had lowered the cornerstone, they had removed old documents, coins, and other objects from the time capsule in its centre and replaced them with new ones. It had been and still was a rather odd feeling looking across the open expanse where the Centre Block used to stand and to see the Parliamentary Library. He had watched as the Duke of Connaught smoothed the mortar just before the stone was lowered into the northeast corner. The duke then laid a triangle plum-bob to verify that it was level before ceremoniously striking it with a mallet three times. He then declared it had been well laid.

There had been the usual speeches. The governor general had remarked his late brother, King Edward VII, had laid the original cornerstone fifty-six years before, and he was pleased that this was one of his last tasks before his term as governor general ended. Then, Borden had given an excellent speech thanking the governor general for his service. He declared the men who had built the original Centre Block had been far-sighted, and they would have been pleased how far the Dominion they had created had progressed.

"I did warn him before he went to England that he was to cable suggestions to me and the cabinet. We needed to consider them carefully before we implement them," replied Borden in disgust as he creased the newspaper.

"We all know how well he follows instructions," Perley answered. Borden avoided his eyes when he made his statement. Perley knew

Borden's main concern was that Sam Hughes was still a political force to reckon with. Hughes was extremely popular with the Orange Lodge in Ontario. "Did he say anything in his latest messages?"

Borden gave him a sharp look then reluctantly said, "He sent me a telegram yesterday saying he had been consulting with the War Office and our senior officers in London. They had some ideas for improvements and efficiencies. He said he would send me a full report by the end of the week."

"Robert, I said it before, and I'm saying it again. He has to go!" Perley said, emphasizing his remarks with his hands. "I don't think we can perform a major reorganization in our machine in England with him as minister. I just don't think it's feasible."

George recognized the stubborn look on the prime minister's face. He had been promoting the idea for months that a cabinet ranked minister be appointed as the Canadian High Commissioner in London. Sadly, he had been unable to convince Borden. He knew Borden was leaning in the direction of creating a new ministry and a minister to manage the overseas force in England. Hughes wasn't going to like it one bit, if the prime minister went ahead with his plan.

"So what are you going to do?"

"I'm sending a telegram demanding he explain himself!" Borden replied tersely.

Perley was tempted to scoff, but he decided to bite his tongue. He was fairly certain, whatever Hughes's reply, that it would be accompanied by crocodile tears. Changing the subject, he said, "I'm surprised he didn't squawk about the War Office's decision to replace the Ross with the Lee-Enfield."

Borden shrugged. "I wouldn't be surprised that giving him the honorary rank of lieutenant-general in the Imperial Army wasn't part of their calculations in this regard."

"You're probably right. But what are we going to do with the Ross factory?" Perley asked. The Ross Company main production facilities were located at the Cove Fields, next to the Plains of Abraham, in Quebec City.

"I've spoken with Sir Ross and Nesbitt yesterday concerning his plant and production of new rifles. He said that the .27-calibre Lee-Enfield's future was in question, especially since the .303 version has performed extremely well. He said his plant can manufacture the rifle for the Russians."

"At least it will keep the workers busy," Perley stated, hinting it would be politically advantageous.

Borden nodded. "True, and for now the news from the front seems to be good. However, Hughes indicated our men will be heavily engaged shortly."

Perley could feel his face turn bleak at the news. He knew how badly the Allied forces had suffered in the Somme.

SEPTEMBER 8, 1916
FORWARD TRENCH, ALBERT

"Shit!" said Captain Gavin when he saw what he estimated to be a German company clamber out of the trench three hundred yards distant. He didn't bother continuing to swear; it wouldn't have done any good. It wouldn't better the situation he found himself in. He should have known something was up. The German artillery had been pounding the line being held by the 14th Battalion of the 3rd Brigade. They had been halfway through the relief when the Huns launched their raid. It was the worst possible moment, since the two communication trenches, one being used by the Fusiliers to enter the trenches and the other being used by the 14th Battalion to leave, were being flattened. The Boche had been paying special attention to them. They were now quite shallow and didn't provide much protection for the troops who needed to use them. They had tried to complete the relief before dawn, but they hadn't managed to get it done. Now, they were going to pay for it.

This was to be their first day in the line at Pozières after they had spent the previous day practicing contacting the observers in the aeroplanes stationed above. They had used mirrors, white towels, and Very lights to let the aircraft know they were friendlies.

Major Llewellyn had called him into the Fusiliers HQ with the other company commanders for a briefing after the major's meeting with Brigadier-General Loomis and his staff. The 2nd Brigade's HQ had been setup at X.15 Central, a former German dugout. Major Llewellyn had informed them they were assigned to the right subsection trenches from R34 to R52, along with the 7th Battalion. The left subsection would be taken over by the 8th Battalion. The 5th and 10th Battalions would be in reserve at Chalk Pit and La Boisselle.

When the major ordered the men were to carry two days of iron rations and filled water bottles, he knew it wasn't going to be a picnic. The major had included the usual general order: the men were to carry 120 rounds SAA, two Mills bombs each (the bombers would carry twelve), and two sandbags. He had warned him that the Germans seemed to be touchy here. It was likely they knew the Canadian Corps was here and wanted to give them a warm welcome.

"Shit is right," replied Captain Martin from the 14th Battalion. The captain was from Turo, New Brunswick. He was of medium height, with brown eyes. The helmet he was wearing had more than a few scar marks from shrapnel. "What do you want to do?"

Captain Gavin nearly sighed in relief that the 14th Battalion captain wasn't inclined to argue who was actually in charge. He appeared to be following his lead, especially since the bulk of the men in the trench were Fusiliers.

"I don't have much of a choice," he replied. He turned to the telephone operator beside him. "Is the line still working?"

The signaller, with headphones covering his ears, nodded. "Let HQ know that the Germans are launching a company size attack. And I'm going out to meet them. Give them our trench number and time. And let them know that the relief hasn't been completed."

"Yes, sir."

"And, get me Lieutenants Sean and Morris," Gavin ordered as he scribbled a note on his message pad and gave it to the nearby runner. The runner took it and pushed his way down the trench.

Either by telephone or by runner, he couldn't wait for orders from the Richmond Fusiliers' HQ. He had to act now!

"Can I borrow a platoon?" he asked Captain Martin.

"What do you have in mind?" Martin asked.

"I'm going to put my bombers in the middle, with a rifle platoon on both sides to protect them."

Martin nodded. "I'll give you Lieutenant Marshal. He's a hot-corner man."

"Good, now if I can find my Lewis gunners?" he said just as Lieutenant Harris, one of his Lewis squad leaders, pushed his way up the trench.

"Where's your squad?" he demanded.

"On the other side of the traverse, why?" Harris replied.

"Get them ready. The Huns have launched a raid, and I need you to put enfiladed fire on our right flank."

"Damn! Yes, sir."

"Five minutes?" he demanded.

Lieutenant Harris nodded. "Plenty of time."

"Then why the hell are you still here?"

"Yes, sir," said the lieutenant as he disappeared down the trench.

"Sir, the telephone line just went dead!" the telephone operator exclaimed.

"Yeah, I kind of figured that would happen," he said to the signaller. He then saw lieutenants Sean, Morris, and Marshal hurrying toward him. "Get your men ready in five minutes. We have a German company heading our way. Lieutenant Sean, I want your bombers in the middle, with Morris on the left and Marshal on the right to provide protection. Lieutenant Harris's Lewis gun will provide enfilade fire on your right flank, so watch for that. Once we go over the top, I want you to bomb the shit out of them."

Lieutenant Sean nodded grimly. "Will do."

"Good! Let's get this done!!"

RICHMOND FUSILIERS ADVANCED HEADQUARTERS, ALBERT

"Shit!" said Major Llewellyn when he read the message Corporal Michaels handed to him. "And the line's been cut?"

"Yes, sir," replied the telephone operator.

"What?" asked Lieutenant-Colonel Tennison, who was reading a report on the trench stores they were taking over from the 14th Battalion. He had to decide what needed to be requisitioned to replace what the 14th had consumed.

"We just got a message from Captain Gavin," he answered. "He reported the Germans have launched an assault against him. At least company strength."

"Did he complete the relief?"

"We didn't get the 'Ransom' code," replied Llewellyn. "Ransom" was the code word Gavin was to send indicating the relief had been completed. "The last report we got was that they were halfway through."

"Damn," muttered the lieutenant-colonel.

Llewellyn nodded. Either the Germans had gotten lucky, or they had impeccable timing. He had to consider the timing. It implied the Germans knew their schedule.

Both men cocked an ear as shells started landing nearby. "They're targeting the communications trenches," Llewellyn stated.

"Did Captain Gavin say what he was going to do about the attack?" Tennison asked.

"Yes, he's putting his company out into No Man's Land to take them on."

"Okay, let Brigade HQ know what's going on," Tennison ordered Private Leggatt, who was sitting in front of the Sterling transmitter that allowed them to send Morse code messages to Brigade HQ and to the aeroplanes flying above them. Next to it sat the Tuner Short Wave Mk III receiver for incoming messages. They were still reliant on telephone and runners for messages with their company commanders.

To Llewellyn he said, "Alert the Stokes gunners and the 65th to be prepared to provide support. Get the company commanders to push as many men as they can out of the communications trenches. And put the reserve on alert in case we need them."

"Yes, sir."

"Now, let's go take a look," Tennison said crisply as he rose to his feet. Llewellyn followed suit as the Tennison put on his steel helmet, tightened the strap, then headed out the door.

FORWARD TRENCH, ALBERT

"How bad was it?" asked Major Llewellyn after Captain Gavin stopped swearing.

It had taken Lieutenant-Colonel Tennison and Major Llewellyn about thirty minutes to arrive at the trenches the Germans were attacking to get a better picture of what was happening and to determine if he needed to deploy the reserves that they had put on alert.

"It was touch-and-go there for a while, but we managed to push them back. The bombers did a fantastic job," Captain Gavin said. He grimaced in pain as the first-aid man tightened the bandage around the bullet wound on his arm. "But I lost Lieutenant Collins, Sergeant Mack, Privates Peters, Cruickshank, Laurie, and Keiths."

Tennison removed his gaze from the slit in the sandbags that peered onto No Man's Land. A metal plate dropped into place to cover the view port. He said, "I know. They were good men. But it would have been worse if they had gotten into the trench."

Llewellyn didn't think it helped much with the loss, but it was the truth. If the captain hadn't acted as quickly as he had, they would have suffered considerably more casualties.

"I had no choice. We managed to clear the wire easily enough, especially since the Boche artillery had cut most of it. There were plenty of shell holes for the bombers to use as cover as they bombed the fucking Huns. Both Marshal and Harris did a good job protecting our flank.

"The German officer over there was damn good. When he saw he couldn't get around us, especially when the Lewis opened up on him, he pulled out his men right quick."

"Not quick enough, it looks like fifteen or twenty are out there," Tennison said.

"Yeah, I know," said the captain. "It's going to be hot out there tonight when we go out and try to recover our men." Sometimes, each side allowed the other to retrieve their wounded and their dead; sometimes not.

Llewellyn lifted the metal shield to take a look at No Man's Land. "Colonel, I think you better see this." He moved aside for Tennison to take a look.

"Shit!" was his comment.

FORMER GERMAN TRENCHES, LA BOISSELLE

"Lieutenant! Lieutenant!" the urgent voice dragged Paul Ryan from a deep sleep.

"What?" he muttered as he opened his eyes. In the dim light of the dugout, he saw the ugly face of Sergeant Hopegood. He felt groggy. He had been on his feet for the last twenty-four hours, getting his battery dug in near the village of La Boisselle. It was only a name now, since the village's thirty-five homes were long gone.

"The Richmond Fusiliers have sent up a green rocket," the sergeant explained. That cleared his head.

"When?" he asked as he rolled out of bed. He had been so tired, he didn't bother getting undressed before lying down on the cot.

"The first one was spotted a few minutes ago," the sergeant replied as he held an electric torch in his hand.

"Okay," Ryan said as he grabbed his helmet from the table set in the middle of the captured German dugout he had commandeered for his command post and billet. He had been pleasantly surprised how well the Germans had constructed their dugouts. They were a little bit more comfortable than the British ones, since it was well below ground. He had to pound the twenty feet of wooden steps to reach the sandbagged entrance with the sergeant on his heels. When he had reached the top, he glanced over the fire trench at Glory Hole. In the distance, he could see what remained of the former British trenches. He understood why the 34th Division took six days and eleven thousand casualties to take this Hun defensive position in July. It had been built on the high ground, which also explained why the German trenches were dryer than the British ones; water ran downhill.

The trench itself was slightly over four and a half feet deep, and that made it easier for the riflemen to set up in their firing positions. It was narrow, two feet at the base and three feet wide at the top. There were several entrances built in the trench that meant the rest of his men could shift from one section to another without being seen or exposed to rifle and artillery fire. He finally understood how the Huns managed to survive the 65th's barrages. Behind those entrances, there was a series of deep six-feet high tunnels.

Still, he had some qualms about living in the German dugouts. After all, the Huns knew where they were.

When he had entered the gun pit, he saw a couple more green rockets lighting up the sky. The SOS signal meant the Fusiliers needed immediate artillery support. They were in danger of being overrun.

"Are we set?"

"Yes, Lieutenant."

"Okay," Ryan acknowledged. He hadn't been happy when they had to register their guns. Many of the landmarks on the maps had been obliterated in the past two months by both the British and German artillery. The exploding mines at Lochnagar and the Y Sap also had a significant impact on the nearby landscape. If they were off, shells would land among the Fusiliers. It didn't make him feel any better that it would be Major Llewellyn, calling for artillery support, who would be responsible for the casualties among his men.

"Five minutes rapid fire, ten minutes standard fire, and twenty minutes of slow fire," Ryan ordered.

He glanced at the ammunition stocks and winced. While the 18-pounders had the maximum rate of fire of twenty rounds per minute, they rarely fired at that rate. Not that his men couldn't do it. They drilled at that rate often. However, the main reason they didn't was firing at that sustained rate overheated the gun barrel. This meant there was a higher risk of premature detonation of a shell when it was shoved into the breech. A slower rate of fire allowed the barrel to maintain a relatively stable temperature. The other consideration was the depletion of their ammunition stocks. While they now had plenty of it, it was not infinite. The agreed-upon fire plan was to fire eight rounds per minute at rapid fire. Then reduce it to four at the normal rate of fire and then two rounds per minute at slow fire.

Once the order was repeated back to Ryan, all four guns opened fire. Ryan kept an eagle eye on his men until he heard a noise from the second gun that he didn't want to hear. He rushed over and demanded, "What the hell happened?"

"The fucking recuperating spring broke," Sergeant Walpole blurted in disgust.

"Damn," replied Ryan when he confirmed his suspicions. The recoil system used a steel spring to help the barrel stay on target. No one had any idea the 18-pounders were to be put through such extensive and sustained use. The constant pressures and forces on the steel springs meant that metal fatigue would set in, and the spring would eventually break. It could still fire, but the gun's rate of fire would be greatly reduced, since it had to be rolled back into position after each shot.

"Anyone hurt?" Ryan asked.

"Naw," replied Walpole as he glanced around his gun team.

"Cease firing for now. Once we get word how serious the attack is, we may have to use you."

"Yes, sir," replied the section chief with a grimace.

As the other 18-pounders went through their firing cycles, Ryan wondered how the Fusiliers were doing.

FORWARD TRENCH, ALBERT

Lieutenant-Colonel Tennison and Major Llewellyn could see the shells landing in No Man's Land striking the German trenches. The 65th's barrage had slowed the second German company, who had emerged after Captain Gavin's company had stopped the first one. The Hun's rifle and machine gunfire slackening after each shell sent up clouds of dust.

"Shit!" Tennison swore as an 18-pounder fell short. Half a squad of Fusiliers was struck down, as well as a similar number of Huns. One of the flankers, a Lewis gunner, was kneeling, spraying the shell holes with short bursts to keep the Huns' heads down as a couple of bombers crawled close enough to toss in grenades.

It was Llewellyn who heard the sound of an incoming shell. He knew this one was going to be close. "Down!" he yelled as he pushed Tennison farther down the trench. The shell struck the parados behind him. He didn't think he got hit by shrapnel, but he did hear Tennison yell in pain. He did see a wall of sand and dirt engulf him. There was nothing he could do as the weight hammered him and Tennison to the bottom of the trench.

When Llewellyn woke, he tried to open his eyes, but all he could see was blackness. His breathing was ragged. He could feel enormous pressure on his chest. He tried to move his arms and legs, but he found he couldn't. His mouth filled with dirt when he opened it to yell. He barely was able to spit it out. It was then he knew the shell had buried him in the trench. He tried to remain calm and slow his breathing. But he found it harder and harder to draw a breath as the sand continually pressed its weight on his chest. He heard the faint sound of shovels and picks as he passed out.

RICHMOND FUSILIERS REGIMENTAL AID POST, ALBERT

Lieutenant Ryan was intercepted by an orderly when he approached the entrance to the regimental aid dugout.

"Can I help you?" asked the private with an angry glare when he saw the artillery badges on his sleeves. Several of the nearby wounded gave him similar glares. The 65th wasn't very popular at the moment. Before he could reply, he had to make way for a blanket-covered stretcher. The orderlies gently placed the body beside four other similar draped stretchers. From what Ryan had heard, the Richmond Fusiliers had suffered six dead, one officer and five other ranks. There had been nearly thirty wounded, eight seriously.

"I've come to see Major Llewellyn," he said. He was pleased the trepidation he felt wasn't reflected in his tone. He didn't know how the major would react when he saw him, or even if he were willing to see him.

"Yeah, come this way," the orderly said as he led him deeper into the aid station dug into the side of a trench. He pointed to a man in a corner sitting on a chair. His head was down and his arms resting on his knees. Ryan recognized the look on the major's face. He had seen it after the death of Sergeant Booth at Ypres. A momentary glare crossed the major's face when he spotted him, then it was replaced by a wan smile.

"Major Llewellyn, I just wanted to …"

The major stopped him when he glanced around and noticed the glares the wounded were giving Ryan. "Lieutenant, I ordered the artillery support. I'm the one responsible."

Ryan knew what the major was doing. He was sending a clear message that he wouldn't tolerate discourtesy toward the artillery. It wouldn't prevent the angry feelings against the 65th, but at the very least they would treat each other professionally.

"Yes, sir," Ryan replied. It didn't make him feel any better. "How is the colonel doing?"

"He'll live. I'm afraid that he lost his left leg…" He was then interrupted by the arrival of Brigadier-General Loomis. At the entrance, he was met by the station's doctor, then he spoke briefly with a couple of wounded before he reached the major.

"Lieutenant," he said, acknowledging Ryan's presence. "Major, don't get up. How are you feeling?"

"I've been better," replied Llewellyn.

"Quite. I heard we lost you for a few minutes."

Ryan saw Llewellyn gave the brigadier-general a shrug. "When they finally dug me out, they said I was breathing but unconscious. I didn't come to until they got me here. The doc said I was fine, but he needed to keep an eye on me for twenty-four hours in case I had a concussion. He's releasing me this afternoon. He said I may have headaches for the next few days."

A smile queried at the corners of the general's mouth. "I spoke with Colonel Tennison as he was being loaded into the ambulance. He didn't appear to be happy about it."

"The war is over for him, sir," Llewellyn stated.

"True, in the meantime, I need a replacement for the colonel."

"Yes, sir," replied Llewellyn. Ryan could tell he knew what was coming.

"I'm promoting you to acting lieutenant-colonel and putting you in temporary command of the Richmond Fusiliers until I decide on a permanent replacement."

"Ah, yes sir. Thank you, sir," replied Llewellyn. From his tone, Ryan sensed the major had mixed feelings. He felt satisfaction for being offered the job but felt guilty on how it had come about.

"Tell the men that they did the Red One proud today. And I will be recommending they be mentioned in the dispatches."

"I will, sir. The men will appreciate that," replied Llewellyn.

"Good, and I'm confident you will do a good job," Loomis said as he gave him and the major an encouraging nod before he turned and left the dugout.

CHAPTER 22

Samantha felt her feet dragging as she walked to the entrance to the flat she was sharing with several other nurses. The street was rather busy, despite the blackout regulations imposed by the Zeppelin raids. She frowned when she entered the lobby and saw she had mail. She had to admit she was impressed by the efficiency of the Royal Mail, which, even in wartime, delivered the mail twice a day.

She fished out the key from her jacket pocket and inserted it into her brass mailbox, number 205. She pulled out the only item, a postcard. On the front of it, there was an image of a cathedral. The inscription at the bottom read *The Basilica of N.D. De Brebières, Albert*. Samantha's breath caught for a moment. She turned the card over and tilted it slightly so she could read it in the dim light.

Dear Sam,

I just wanted to let you know that I'm fine. We did have a spot of bother, and I'm afraid that Colonel Tennison has been seriously wounded, again. It's my understanding he is on his way to England. As to where I don't know. His wife and two kids are in England and are staying at the Ritz-Carleton. If you find out where the colonel is hospitalized and let Mrs. Tennison know, I would appreciate it.

Love, James

Samantha stared at the back of the card and flipped it over. She had met the colonel last August when he was treated for wounds at the Moore Barracks Military Hospital. She had liked him. She knew the colonel and the major got along. She wondered how well James was actually doing. It would be like him to play down any wounds not to worry her. She examined the black and white image. It looked to her to be prewar, since the church showed no battle damage and the statue of the Virgin Mary on the dome was pointed skyward.

As she rubbed the card gently with her finger, she at least thought she knew where he was.

"At least we didn't have to march this time," grumbled Sergeant Duval as he sat behind Acting Lieutenant-Colonel Llewellyn.

The lieutenant-colonel glanced over his shoulder. He was still getting used to seeing the new pips on his shoulder boards. The sergeant and two other men were sitting beside him. The sergeant's Ross rifle was carefully laid in a case beside him to protect it from bumps and jolts as their bus made their way to the Brickfields billets just outside Albert.

Llewellyn was sure the sergeant, as well as the rest of the Fusiliers, wondered why, after they had marched the six miles to Warloy, they had been ordered to report back to the Brickfields billets just northwest of Albert. They knew something was up when seventeen grey-painted buses showed up that morning to collect them. The drivers had taken the scenic route to Albert through the bombed out villages of Vadencourt, Warloy, and Senlis.

He could see Albert through the single row of trees flanking the road. The town, at the foot of a hill, was quite pretty with its red brick and grey roofs. The town once had seven thousand inhabitants and was quite prosperous with its iron and steel works, fabricating workshops, sugar factories, and brick kilns. Most citizens had left since it had suffered extensive damage. In the distance, he could see the statue of the Virgin Mary dangling at a ninety-degree angle from the Basilica of Notre Dame de Brebières' roof. The local legend was when the statue fell to the street, the war would be over. Who the victors would be was still a question.

They were halfway through the town when a traffic officer motioned them to stop and then motioned for a vehicle on their left to move forward.

"What the hell are those things?" shouted Sergeant Duval as he stared out of the window.

Llewellyn turned his head and watched as a behemoth of an armoured car made its way slowly through the intersection. The vehicle was rhomboid-shaped and moved on metal tracks that ran the circumference of the hull. It looked to him that it had 6-pounder gun in turrets on each side. In the front there was a Hotchkiss machine gun. When the two small wheels at the back of the car passed, he noticed a second machine gun sticking out of the rear. The ground trembled as it rumbled past him. The hull was painted in camouflage of brown, tan, and two shades of green. He wondered what the V-shaped wire mesh on the top of the vehicle was for. The second car that followed was similar, except instead of 6-pounders it was equipped with two Vickers machine guns in each side turret.

"I have no idea what the hell they are," he shouted above the roar of the armoured car's engines.

"Shit, I would hate to see that thing head toward me," said Duval.

"I think they are on our side," Llewellyn said with a grin.

"I certainly hope so," muttered the sergeant.

Once the last of the vehicles had crossed the intersection, the traffic warden waved them through. It didn't take long for their convoy to reach the Brickfields billets. The billets were near a former brick factory that looked over the Ancre River. The field was dotted with a variety of tents. He could see barbed-wire-fenced ammo and supply dumps nearby. Clouds of dust were whipped up from the chalk-based soil when the wind blew. It turned to mud when it rained.

The buses stopped near the camp commandant's office. It was located in the former brickyard's administrative building. Lieutenant-Colonel Llewellyn spotted Major Humber, who was already waiting for them. He had been sent ahead by Brigadier-General Loomis to arrange the accommodations for them at the camp.

After Llewellyn returned the officer's salute, Humber said, "Colonel, my men will guide your people to where they will be staying. General Loomis requested that you report to Brigade HQ in Albert."

"Understood," replied Llewellyn. He turned to Captain Gavin, whom he had promoted to replace him as brigade-major, and ordered, "Get the men settled. When I come back, I'll want to meet with the senior officers."

"Yes, sir," Gavin replied.

Llewellyn was about to jump into his bus when he spotted a staff car parked on the other side of the building. An officer wearing cavalry boots was leaning against the car, puffing on a pipe. He gave a double take when he recognized Lieutenant-General Byng. He shouldn't have been surprised; he was well aware of the lieutenant-general's habit of appearing unannounced and without any pretentiousness. Llewellyn noticed the men in the buses had spotted Byng as well. They gawked at him through the windows as they nudged each other with their elbows. Byng had a rocky start at Mount Sorrel, but since then the men had taken a shine to him and were starting to call themselves the "Byng Boys." Before Llewellyn climbed aboard his bus, he gave Byng a snappy salute, which the lieutenant-general returned with an approving nod.

★ ★ ★

The meeting room Lieutenant-Colonel Llewellyn had found had been constructed out of empty wooden crates piled up to construct walls. It appeared to be used as a classroom, since there was a piece of black slate tied to a wall with a tin cup attached filled with pieces of chalk. The wind rustled the canvas draped overtop. At least the walls protected them, somewhat, from the cool weather for their meeting. Sadly, the men would have to sleep in tents they pitched and would need wool blankets to keep warm.

The men seated on wooden crates stopped buzzing when lieutenant-colonels Llewellyn and Masterley, followed by Captain Gavin, entered. By the time the men had risen to their feet, Llewellyn said, "At ease, gentlemen. Smoke them if you have them."

"I've just come from General Loomis's HQ, where I have been informed that at five o'clock this morning, our 2nd Division attacked Courcelette, and our 3rd Division assaulted Fabeck Graben." Llewellyn didn't need to explain where Courcelette was, since they were all familiar with the German strong point near Albert.

"Also, I can now inform you about the armoured cars we saw when we drove in this morning. Seven similar ones took part in the attack."

"We saw them," said Captain Gavin. "What the hell are they?"

"They've been code named 'tanks,'" Llewellyn replied. "They are a new armoured vehicle designed to breach the German defences by crawling over the barbed wire and the trenches. Two male tanks and one female tank were assigned to the right sector, while one male and two female tanks had been allocated to the left sector. One was held in reserve. Their job was to take out the Boche machine guns."

"What's the difference between a male and female?" asked Captain Marshal, who was sitting in the back.

"Nine inches!" said one of the men beside him.

"In your dreams!" hooted someone in the back.

Lieutenant-Colonel Llewellyn chuckled then said, "The male tanks are armed with two 6-pounders in the side turrets and three Hotchkiss machine guns. The female ones are armed with four Vickers machine guns and one Hotchkiss."

"How did they do?" asked Captain Gavin.

"All things considered, not that badly. A couple of them broke down because of mechanical failure, but the rest were able to make their objectives. It seems, based on the interrogations of the prisoners we captured, it had a demoralizing effect on the Huns' morale."

"The 'tanks' also provided our men with some protection against the Boche machine guns. They couldn't penetrate the armour," he said. Llewellyn noticed the men looked at him thoughtfully. "As well, the Corps has been experimenting with what's called a creeping barrage."

When questioning looks appeared on the men's faces, he nodded to Lieutenant-Colonel Masterley. "Colonel Masterley of the 65th Artillery has prepared a lecture on this new type of barrage."

"Thank you, Colonel," Masterley said as he rose from his chair. "Most of you're familiar with our artillery barrage. The objectives are straightforward: to cut barbed wire, destroy enemy strong points, and to clear the way for you the infantry.

"I know the Huns have adapted to our techniques as we have to theirs. They have prepared dugouts and splinter-proof shelters to protect themselves. When our barrage lifts, they reoccupy their front trenches ready to repel your attack."

"Damn right," Captain Gavin muttered.

"General Horne believes that he has found a solution, the moving barrage. If I may …" he said as he went to the black slate hanging on the wall and took a chunk of chalk out of the thin cup. He drew an arch on the board and on the right side of it he drew an artillery shell. From the artillery shell, he drew lines like rays from the sun. Behind the shell, he drew a stick man. In front of the shell's rays, he made a "U" to represent a trench.

"Basically, it is really simple. The infantry will follow as close as possible to the barrage. Every three minutes, the barrage will move forward until it reaches the Hun's trenches." He made two additional arches. In front of the stickman, he drew an arrow pointing toward the trench.

There was a stunned silence. Then Captain Gavin spoke, "Just to be clear. You want us to walk directly behind your artillery barrage?"

"Yes, that is what we are proposing. The principle is sound, since the shrapnel will travel toward the enemy trenches when the shells detonate. There will be minimal casualties if you don't follow the barrage to close."

The men continued to stare at him. They'd been on the receiving end of the German artillery and their own too often.

"How close?"

"Fifty yards."

That brought mutters from the officers. "Fifty yards! Jesus!"

"Timing is everything," asserted Masterley. "Once the timetable starts, we can't stop or adjust. You'll have to keep up with the barrage. If you're slow, you will be exposed to German fire. If you go too fast…" The lieutenant-colonel paused to imply that some of the men would get hurt.

"What timing are you looking at?" asked Llewellyn.

The lieutenant-colonel turned to him and said, "Three-minute lifts, we're thinking. An 18-pounder shell covers a frontage of fifteen to twenty-five yards."

A lieutenant in the back raised his hand. "Not that we don't trust you," he said, which meant he didn't. "How accurate will you be?"

"At the ranges we are talking about, twenty-five yards short or long of the target. That's why we said you need to stay fifty yards behind the barrage as it moves toward the German lines. You'll want to be in the Huns' trenches once the barrage lifts then move onto the Boche communication trenches."

"Shit," someone muttered.

"Enough of that," Llewellyn said with a stern glare. "Over the next few days, we're going to practice this moving barrage on the training ground. Is that clear?"

"Yes, sir," replied the senior officers.

"Good. If it works it will save the lives of a lot of our men. Let's see that it does," he said as he dismissed the men.

SEPTEMBER 22, 1916
65TH FIELD ARTILLERY, POZIÈRES

"Your unit looks good," said Colonel Hyward as he surveyed Lieutenant Ryan's gun crew at work. "I understand from Lieutenant-Colonel Masterley you've been doing a good job."

"Yes, sir," replied Ryan. He was somewhat embarrassed by Masterley's compliment. He saw the colonel's grin under his neatly trimmed moustache when he met his grey eyes. Hyward was in his mid-forties, slightly taller than Ryan and stockier. He had blond hair under his steel helmet.

"They're keeping you busy?" the colonel asked.

Paul was about to answer when the phone rang. He turned his gaze to Reggie, who was now a sergeant, who answered the Fullerphone near the map table. They were still friends, but Paul had to be careful to keep a certain distance between them since the brass frowned on officers fraternizing with the NCOs. One of the first things they had done was to run cables to the nearest telephone exchange. Technically, the signallers should have done it. If they had asked them, they would have been waiting for several days. The signallers were busy pulling most of the phones out of the trenches except for the lines from the FOOs to their artillery units. Corps had the usual worry that the Germans were capturing the conversations on the earth phones and using the information to launch their attacks. If Corps HQ found out, he would get a nasty warning about fiddling with the telephone equipment. He wasn't about to mention that to his new CO.

Hyward had just taken over from the previous 65th Artillery CO, Colonel Marshfield, who had finally been permanently promoted to brigadier-general. He had hoped that Lieutenant-Colonel Masterley would have been given the job, but he had been passed over for some reason. Masterley didn't seemed to be too upset about it. From the look of Hyward he was fresh from the reinforcement depot at Shorncliffe. He wondered if Masterly had mentioned it to him that he too was one of the originals.

"E.G.D.A!" shouted Reggie into the phone giving their call sign. The sergeant had to yell in order to be heard over the static. Their connection to Brigade HQ was fine, but there was interference between them and their FOOs. The FOOs had been complaining, but the signallers hadn't been able to find were the fault was.

"C.Z.Z.!" he said. The call sign was for Lieutenant Thomas who was with the current FOOs attached to the Richmond Fusiliers who were defending trenches 40 to 45 in the front lines.

"Machine gun eh! What are the coordinates?" Reggie said as he leaned on the map and marked a location with a pencil. "Repeat!" he demanded as he glanced at Lieutenant Ryan who had raised an eyebrow, then to Colonel Hyward.

Ryan noticed the colonel give a slight nod of approval as the bombardiers started prepping the shells for the upcoming action. One of the bombardiers wiped the shell clean and then screwed the fuse into place. A second bombardier had the fuse clamp out to set the timing.

"What do we have Sergeant?" asked Ryan when he walked over to Reggie. He could feel the colonel looking over his shoulder. He didn't have very much choice since the gun pit was rather crowded. Even though they had only taken out the unessential equipment, the 18-pounder and its two limbers didn't leave very much space. Each limber contained thirty-six shells. One was filled with shrapnel while the other was high explosive. Normally, they would have netting over top to provide some camouflage. However, Divisional Artillery HQ said not to put it up. According to them their aerial photography showed a sniper gun was more difficult to spot from the air if it actually wasn't camouflaged. Ryan was somewhat sceptical of that.

Reggie held the receiver under his chin as he said, "There's a machine gun pestering the Fusiliers. They would like us to teach them some manners." The sergeant took a ruler and measured the distance from a black square, their current position, and the fresh pencil mark on the map. "It's about 2,350 yards out."

"Hmm," Ryan murmured. "What does the baro say and the wind speed?"

"The barometer is reading 29.5," Reggie said, "Wind speed is fifteen miles per hour southwest and the temperature is twenty degrees."

"Hmm," Ryan murmured as he did some calculations in his head

"Is the gun registered?" asked the colonel.

Ryan shook his head. "We didn't want them to know just yet that we were here. They will find out soon enough."

The No. 4 gun had been designated as the sniper gun for the week. They would do most of the firing at targets of opportunity and specific targets the Fusiliers uncovered such as work parties or the annoying Boche machine gun. One of their secondary tasks, and the most dangerous, was to attract the German artillery's attention. Whenever one of the 65th fired the Germans would retaliate. By using a detached gun to do most of the firing, it would relieve the pressure on the rest of the battery. Also, part of the calculation was that it was better to lose one gun rather than an entire battery of 18-pounders if the German heavies found their position and range. Equally important, was once the German guns fired, the observers would mark the location and have the rest of the 65th take them out.

Paul spoke to a bombardier, "Make sure the horses are harnessed in case we have to move."

"Yes, sir," the bombardier said as he scurried away.

When Ryan saw the colonel's frown he explained, "We have a secondary position six hundred yards east of here ready for us."

"I see," the colonel replied.

"Okay, set for five degrees, angle of sight one degree, shrapnel, 85 fuse, 2,350 yards," Paul ordered as the men made the necessary adjustments to the 18-pounder. He added fifty yards to the range since from the map the German machine gun was close to the Richmond Fusiliers' front line. He didn't want the first shell to land short. He couldn't forget what happened to Lieutenant-Colonel Tennison and to the now Lieutenant-Colonel Llewellyn.

He took out a watch and glanced at the time. The crew leader pulled the firing lever. The gun fired and as the barrel smoothly recoiled he turned to Reggie. He found that Reggie was already telling the FOO that the shell was on its way.

"Seventy-five yards long and thirty yards left," he said after an agonizing minute.

"Range 2,250 yards, one degree right," Ryan ordered.

He waited for the FOO's report once the shell was on its way. It came in less than a minute.

"Fifty yards left," stated Reggie.

Once the gun crew had made the adjustment Ryan ordered, a third shell went on its way.

"On target," replied the sergeant.

"Fire five rounds," Ryan ordered.

He glanced at the colonel when the last shell was on its way then at his watch. "We sent them an invitation. Now, we have to wait for their RSVP."

CHAPTER 23

"Goddamn it!" growled Lieutenant-Colonel Llewellyn as he saw half a platoon go down after a shrapnel shell burst just above them.

"Yeah, I saw it," replied Captain Lowry, tight-lipped. His company was the first wave attacking the German trench. The 4th platoon had rushed ahead of the other three by about twenty-five yards, bringing them in range of the 65th Artillery's creeping barrage. Lieutenant-Colonel Masterley was coordinating the twenty 18-pounders that had been assigned to cover the four hundred and fifty yards of frontage the Fusiliers were attacking. Their left flank was being protected by the 34th Brigade of the 11th Division, while on their right was the familiar 3rd Brigade of the Canadian Corps.

"Was that Lieutenant Harris's squad?" Llewellyn asked.

"Yeah, I told him during the rehearsals he needed to slow down. I thought I had it finally pounded into his head," Lowry growled in disgust. The Richmond Fusiliers had spent two days at the Brickfields rehearsing their attack. Lowry was from Richmond, Ontario, in his late twenties, lean with sinewy muscles.

"What can we do?" Lieutenant-Colonel Llewellyn said grimly as a new wave of shrapnel burst in front of the German trenches, kicking up puffs of dirt. So far, the Huns were responding with machine gun fire and artillery. He glanced at his watch. Based on the 65th's schedule, they would be moving their barrage in about a minute's time to the next target.

Llewellyn scanned the barbed wire. He saw some of his men had gotten caught up where the wire hadn't been cut. They were using wire cutters to free themselves. A few more men dropped before they could jump into the Boche trench. The trench hadn't been totally empty. He saw Fusiliers thrusting down with their bayonetted rifles before jumping in. In a couple of spots, he could see the dirt kicked up from Mills bombs as his men cleared that part of the trench.

"Let's go," said Lieutenant-Colonel Llewellyn when he saw the barrage lift. He climbed out of the shell hole he and Captain Lowry had been using to observe the assault. Two signallers followed them. One was carrying a Fullerphone case while the other one had a large reel that was unwinding black telephone cable behind him. Llewellyn glanced across the shell-pocked No Man's Land in the general direction where he thought Major Gavin was. They had split the senior command; they weren't going to make the same mistake twice.

He did spot a Stokes mortar team set up in the crater they had just left. One of the men grunted as he dropped the base plate into the shell hole. The other with the tube set it on the base plate and secured the tube. The rest of the Stokes squad started to unload mortar bombs from the satchels they were carrying. Several of the men cursed their rifles, since they interfered with the job they had to do. They were to keep the Huns' heads down when the Richmond Fusiliers assaulted the Zollern and Hessian trenches, their next objectives. Once they captured those trenches, they would then be in shouting distance of their ultimate objective, the Regina Trench.

When he reached the men who had been decimated by the shrapnel burst, he found most were still alive. The steel helmets had protected them, but he could see where the steel balls had indented the Brodies, and a few had holes punched through. Those men hadn't survived. He briefly paused at each man to give him reassurance that the stretcher bearers would be coming soon. He looked behind him and saw the second wave was climbing out of the trenches. The stretcher bearers had been assigned to the second wave to take care of the casualties from the first wave.

"You take care now," he said as he patted Private Edds, a young Torontonian who had been hit in the leg. From the look of it, he doubted it could be saved. He rose to a crouch and tried to slip through the wire. Some of the barbs snagged at his clothes as he passed through. When he had dropped into the trench, he exclaimed, "Whoa, it's me." Three men were pointing bayonets at him with their points touching his jacket.

"Aw, shucks, it's the CO," said one of the men.

Lieutenant-Colonel Llewellyn grinned. "How are things?"

"Hunky-dory," one replied as they lowered their rifles.

Captain Lowry dropped in beside him with a grunt. He glanced left and right. "What a dump!"

"Well, real estate prices have dropped," replied the third soldier.

Lowry snorted. "Find the lieutenants. I need reports."

"Yes, sir," replied one of the privates as they rushed off.

It didn't take long for the first runners to arrive. "Lieutenant Arrell reports that he has suffered two killed and eleven wounded. He's taken twenty prisoners, and he's starting to send them back to our lines for interrogation."

"Private Markel, sir. Lieutenant Chris reports that he has one killed and five wounded. They captured a machine gun with plenty of ammo," he stated. "He wants to know if we should take it with us?"

"No," replied Captain Lowry. "Leave it as a strong point just turn it around. The third wave will take care of it."

"Yes, sir, he said to inform you that in ten his men will form up for the next assault," said Markel.

"Very good. Just wait a moment," Captain Lowry ordered when a third runner came.

"Oh, shit!" someone said. Lieutenant-Colonel Llewellyn turned his head and saw one of the privates was kneeling and was brushing dirt away from a metal object in the bottom of the trench. Beside the private, he saw one of the new helmets the Germans were now sporting. It seemed that the Huns had finally decided to replace their flimsy leather Pickelhaube spiked helmets with steel ones to protect against flying shrapnel. The new ones looked like one of the coal buckets he used back home to feed his stove.

"What is it?" asked Llewellyn when he returned his gaze to the private.

"I think I found a land mine," he said. He looked up when someone gasped as they all took a step back from him.

"Well, don't play with the damn thing. Remove the nose caps and let the engineers take care of it afterward," ordered Llewellyn.

Llewellyn had read the intelligence reports that indicated that the Germans were planting 6-inch mortar shells in the bottom of the trenches as traps. The best method to disable them was to remove the loose nose caps. In the meantime, he had more important things to do. He needed to get his battalion ready for the next assault.

OCTOBER 6, 1916
CAMC HEADQUARTERS, 13 VICTORIA STREET, LONDON

Samantha closed the face of the gold locket that hung by a slim chain around her neck. The small watch face inside it said she had fifteen minutes to get to her office. She couldn't be late today of all days, even if her legs felt as if she were wearing gum boots instead of black leather ankle boots. Not reporting for duty was not an option, though a couple of excuses did come to mind. When she spotted the entrance to the Victoria Chambers, she knew she didn't have any choice but to check in.

The doorman gave her a brief smile as he held the door open for her but didn't greet her with his usual morning banter. She was certain he had heard about what was happening with the CAMC above and wasn't about to say anything that could be misconstrued. He seemed to hear all the rumours and gossip that floated around the chamber. When she stepped on the lift, she could feel the tension increase in the pit of her stomach. Thankfully, there wasn't anyone in the hallway when she peered through the lift's metal gate. She glanced at the closed doors of the directors' offices of the CAMC and the Nursing Service as she passed them.

When she entered her own office, she was surprised to see Leslie at her desk. She had expected the petite, dark-haired women would have reported sick today to avoid the unpleasantness. Carmen, who was seated opposite her, had turned her chair toward them and asked, "Have you heard anything?"

"No, not yet, have you?" Samantha said as she took off her white Panama hat with the blue band and CAMC badge then placed it on top of the walnut roll-top desk. From her pocket in her blue linen dress she took out a brass key and unlocked it. As the desk top rolled up, neatly stacked files were revealed waiting for her review.

"Matron Macdonald was rather upset when I saw her this morning," Leslie said.

"Not surprising, since she and General Jones have worked together for a long time," said Carmen.

Samantha nodded in agreement. Major-General Jones had been the director of the CAMC years before the war started. "But do you think he'll resign?"

She grimaced before she replied, "It seems Colonel Bruce's report was quite damning." Her concerns of what Colonel Bruce would put in his report had been justified. She just wished she had been more circumspect in her answers to his questions.

"Did anyone actually get a copy of it?" asked Leslie.

"I've been told he submitted it personally to the minister. General Jones had only five days to write a rebuttal, and they didn't give him the report until he had written his defence."

"That doesn't sound good. How can you defend yourself if you don't know what you're being accused of?" demanded Leslie.

"I heard that Colonel Bruce is a close friend of the minister," said Carmen.

"Why am I not surprised," Samantha answered sarcastically.

"What does that have to do with it?" demanded Leslie. "Isn't what he said in his report not true?" Both Samantha and Carmen eyed Leslie.

"Colonel Bruce doesn't have much military experience. He only spent a couple of months last year at Shorncliffe before he resigned. After that the minister, his friend, made him a colonel," Samantha replied. "I've heard what he had written may be valid and correct. Just that military medicine is somewhat different from civilian medicine."

"What did you hear?" asked Carmen. "No one's saying anything."

Samantha's nose crinkled at her slip. She didn't want to say where she had gotten the information. "He complained that to many of the volunteers arriving here from Canada were medically unfit, and they had to be shipped back home."

"Well, he does have a valid point," Carmen pointed out.

"Of course he does, but how do you expect to solve the problem?" Samantha said. "Recruiting is dropping, and the pressure is on to find as many volunteers as they can. As long as the recruiting officers make their quota, no one cares if half get declared medically unfit when they get here."

"But … but…"

Samantha continued, "He also had some comments on the fact that our hospitals have been treating both Canadian and Imperial patients. He wants our hospitals to treat Canadian soldiers only. He also wants Canadian soldiers currently in British hospitals to be transferred to a Canadian hospital, and he wants to get rid of the VAD hospitals."

"He doesn't want much, does he? Well, Matron Macdonald doesn't like the VADs, so that ain't any great loss. But having only our hospitals treat Canadian soldiers…" Carmen said with a dubious tone as she raised an eyebrow.

"It's been my experience when they come off the ship, we send them to the first available hospital. We don't really look at whom they belong to. We just look at what their injuries are and where best we can send them," Samantha said. "If we want to treat our men only, then we'll have to identify him as a Canadian and send the paperwork along with the patient. That has always been a problem. They try to keep the man's chart with him, but if you get a hundred men waiting in line, that stuff sometimes takes a back seat."

"Well, if the good colonel wants to learn about paperwork, he should spend some time with the nurses' pay vouchers," snorted Leslie. The other two nurses chuckled.

"What'll happen if General Jones is relieved?" Carmen asked.

"They'll appoint a new director. Whether or not he will be an improvement on General Jones, I can't say," Samantha said with a shrug.

At that moment, the door opened and Matron Macdonald put her head in. "Ladies, General Jones has an important announcement; he would like everyone in the boardroom in ten minutes."

"Yes, Matron," replied Carmen. She glanced at Samantha and Leslie. Samantha had seen the look on Macdonald's face. It was not good news.

OCTOBER 7, 1916
IODE, CANADIAN HOSPITAL, 1 HYDE PARK, LONDON

It was late evening when Samantha arrived at the 19th century town-house on the corner of Bayswater and Stanhope Place. The evening lights threw shadows on the "1" fastened to the left column of the veranda. The building was a three-storey structure with a white stucco exterior. The ground floor walls had been etched to resemble stone blocks. Flower boxes hung on the spiked wrought iron fence, which was interrupted by the home's four-column veranda. Its exterior pillars were square, while the inside ones were Grecian circular columns. Samantha guessed the balcony above needed the extra support. It was enclosed with a railing similar to the ground floor's but without the spikes.

Samantha had to juggle the parcels and bags she was carrying as she tried to reach the buzzer. She finally managed to jam it with her elbow then heard ringing from inside. A few moments later, the door was opened by a muscular orderly wearing CAMC badges on his collar. "Ah, Matron Lonsdale, do you need a hand with your parcels?" he asked in amusement.

"I'm doing fine," she said as her chin held the packages in place. Her smile disappeared, and she groaned when the top parcel slid off. The orderly's reflexes were good. He caught it before it hit the floor.

"I got it," the orderly said as he lifted the parcel to show her.

"Thanks," replied a grateful Samantha as she entered the Daughters of the Empire Canadian Red Cross Hospital for Officers. That was the official name, but everyone shortened it to the Canadian Hospital for Officers.

"Did you have a quiet day, Gary?" she asked. The orderly was from Victoria and had been among the first who signed up.

"The usual. We had a few discharges and a couple of new patients who came in," he replied.

"Is Colonel Tennison seeing visitors?"

"For you, always. Mrs. Tennison and the kids are with him at the moment," he answered.

"Great! These are for them. I went to the Army and Navy store to pick up some things they needed."

"Why don't I give you a hand with those," said a voice behind her. Samantha turned her head and saw the familiar figure of Dorothy Fitzpatrick. She was in her early thirties, with black hair, and was dressed in a VAD uniform, a grey dress with a red cross that covered the centre of her bosom.

"You're still here?" Samantha asked.

"I'm afraid so. My shift doesn't end till nine," Dorothy replied.

"Thanks, Mrs. Fitzpatrick. I appreciate it," replied Samantha as she handed half the packages to her then followed her up the stairs.

She had gotten to know the VAD during her visits to the convalescent home. Mrs. Fitzpatrick had become a volunteer aid detachment nurse in Halifax. She had taken the two courses, first aid and the nurse's course, twelve weeks total that St. John's Ambulance provided for the Canadian VADs. She then had applied to the Red Cross for a posting and had been accepted for overseas duty. Mrs. Fitzpatrick discovered when she arrived in England that she wouldn't be putting her training to good use with the CAMC because of Matron Macdonald's policies on VADs. Lieutenant-Colonel Bruce, in his report, had expressed the same reservations.

She was still here, though, working. She mainly did the domestic duties such as cleaning, laundry, and delivering meals. The only reason she was here was because the hospital had been converted, with the generous donation by a wealthy Toronto colonel and his wife, into a convalescent home for Canadian officers. The home took care of twenty-five patients. Fifteen were housed in the main ward, while the other ten were assigned to four small wards. The equipment had been supplied by the Imperial Order of the Daughters of the Empire. The Red Cross was responsible for the hospital's maintenance. The hospital's medical staff, the CO, the matron, and six nurses, and the seven orderlies, were military personnel. The rest of the staff needed to run the hospital were VADs from the Red Cross.

Samantha had to admit Mrs. Fitzpatrick was a hard worker, and she worked long hours, twelve- to fourteen-hour shifts. She got the impression that she came from a well-to-do family, since the stipend she was being paid was not really enough to support a person.

Samantha was glad when they finally reached the third floor; she was starting to get used to using the lift at her office. The convalescent home didn't have one. She followed Mrs. Fitzpatrick into Lieutenant-Colonel Tennison's ward and waved to the two British officers who were lying reading in their cots. The hospital wasn't restricted, yet, to Canadian officers.

In the cot, near the window that provided a view of Hyde Park, Tennison was sitting up in his bed. She couldn't help feeling a bit of déjà vu. Last year, she had seen him at Moore's Barracks Military Hospital at Shorncliffe recovering from shrapnel wounds. Unfortunately, the man's luck had run out. This time around, he would be returning home. Samantha's eyes fell on his wife, Helen Tennison, and his two children, Beryle and Alexander, sitting on white chairs near the grey-lavender wall with white rectangle accents.

Mrs. Tennison was a handsome woman in her mid-thirties. Samantha could see the worry lines that creased the corner of her eyes. Beryle had more of her father's features, but she was shy and stayed close to her mom. Not surprising, since she was only eight. Her brother, two years younger, looking bored and was fidgeting. Samantha wasn't surprised at that, either, since she had taken him to Hyde Park on a couple of occasions to give Mrs. Tennison a bit of relief; he couldn't sit still for long.

She smiled at Mrs. Tennison and greeted the kids in a teasing tone. "Did you two stay out of trouble?"

Beryle whispered a quiet reply while Alexander nodded a vigorous agreement.

"Good, I got some presents for you," Samantha said as she handed over the parcels that had Army and Navy store logos on them. When Beryle opened hers, she smiled when she saw she had been given novels. Alexander shouted in glee when he opened his box and found a wooden carved horse with wheels on its hooves. Both his father and mother hushed him, warning him not to disturb the other patients.

"What do you say, kids?" Lieutenant-Colonel Tennison asked.

"Thank you, Miss Lonsdale!" the children said in unison.

"I'll take the kids out and keep them busy," said Mrs. Fitzpatrick.

"We don't want to be a bother," said Mrs. Tennison.

"No bother at all," replied Mrs. Fitzpatrick with a smile. "Come on, kids, let's go to the kitchen. They have ice cream."

Once the kids scampered out for ice cream, Samantha asked, "How are you doing, Colonel?"

"Eh," he said with a shrug.

"The leg is still bothering you?" she asked. Sadly, it was common that the men with missing limbs felt phantom pain, in some cases, despite the doses of morphine they were given. The doctors still hadn't figured out what was causing it and what could be done to relieve the discomfort the men were experiencing.

The colonel said regretfully, "I'm afraid that my war is over."

The flicker of relief that crossed Mrs. Tennison's face indicated she was glad her husband was alive. From what Samantha had seen so far, they seemed to be a pretty good match, unlike some other couples she knew.

"Tell the matron what happened when they tried to fit the new leg," Mrs. Tennison said.

"Now, things like that happen," Tennison said to his wife. He turned to Samantha and continued, "You know how the army works." That brought a snort of disgust from Mrs. Tennison.

"What happened?" Samantha asked.

"When they tried to fit him with his new leg, it was an inch short," Mrs. Tennison said tersely.

"I see," replied Samantha as she bit back a remark. "Did they explain why the new leg didn't fit properly?"

"There was a mix-up, and they sent someone else's leg to my husband. Some poor fellow is an inch taller on his left side."

Samantha had a tough time not smiling, although it was serious. Sadly, the making of artificial arms and legs was a growth business. She had seen enough to know that the measurements for the socket, which connected to the limb, the suspension system that kept it attached, and the pylon, the internal frame, and skeleton that supported the weight had to be exact. If they weren't, the appliance would cause discomfort, chafing, and even outright pain. When the new limb did arrive, further slight adjustments still needed to be made. Often, it took several tries to get it right.

"I felt like taking it and bashing the orderly over the head with it," said Mrs. Tennison

"My wife can be quite formidable," Tennison said. A teasing smile appeared when his wife snorted.

"Well, enough about me. How are things going with you at the office?" he asked.

Samantha gave him a sharp look. She wondered if he knew of the tension in the office with the latest news of Lieutenant-Colonel Bruce.

"Things are going all right," she replied evasively.

Tennison, taking the hint, switched subjects. "Have you heard from James?"

Mrs. Tennison's face brightened, and she looked at her with interest. She had heard them talking about James, but she had never met him. Samantha felt herself blush. "I got a letter from him yesterday. He doesn't say much. Talks mostly about the weather."

Mrs. Tennison chuckled. "Reminds me of our courtship."

"I wasn't that bad," protested the lieutenant-colonel. Mrs. Tennison sniffed in amusement.

Tennison asked Samantha, "He didn't say he was enjoying my job?"

"No, he didn't. And he didn't say where he is at the moment either," Samantha stated. Tennison looked at her sympathetically. There were limits to what James could put in a letter.

"Well, he's safe for the moment," Samantha said. She noticed Mrs. Tennison nod in agreement. She understood how Samantha felt.

"Colonel, the reporting centre will be ready on time," said acting Major Gavin. Llewellyn had promoted Gavin after he had given him the brigade-major slot when he became the Richmond Fusiliers' Acting CO. The transition to command had been rather smooth. It helped a bit that there needed to be some rebuilding and training of the replacements for the men they had lost. Llewellyn hadn't been too pleased with some of the men he had received. There was no use complaining, it was the same old story until they got the reinforcement problem sorted out. Llewellyn had to admit he missed Tennison. He had been somewhat surprised by the extra burden that command placed on his shoulders.

"That's good to hear," he said as he glanced at the Fusiliers' new HQ. It was sandbagged dugout with barbed wire draped overtop. He watched as men walked up the wooden ramp carrying the Fusiliers' paperwork into their offices.

The 2nd Brigade was taking over the positions between Pozières-Baptume and the Practice Road. The objectives were the same as the 1st Brigade's, capturing the Regina trench, just that the Gallwitz and the Below trenches had been added.

At the moment, he needed to get his HQ up and running. His immediate staff was rather small: a brigade-major, an adjutant, a quartermaster, and a medical officer. It was the support staff who added to the numbers as he watched Corporal Smatters lead the ten signallers to set up the communications so he could talk with Brigade HQ and his company commanders. He had seen the cook and the sanitation section discussing the water supply needed to prepare meals for his men. The drivers and the stretcher bearers were being pressed into the usual routine of moving the regiment's records and equipment into place. He had cut his staff to the bone to release men for his front-line companies. He was a hundred men below his authorized strength, and he wasn't going to get them. Still, his HQ totalled nearly fifty.

When he spotted Lieutenant Markham passing by, he motioned him over. "How are we doing with the gas masks?" Llewellyn asked as he patted the haversack hanging from his chest that contained his own.

New gas masks had been issued in July, but only recently did they get sufficient numbers to replace their smoke helmets. The new ones were larger than the tube helmets, so they didn't fit into the helmet pockets sewn in their jackets. The masks had a fabric-covered rubber tube that connected to a small rectangular tin box. In the box there were layers of carbon and lime soda sandwiched between cotton gauze to filter out the poisonous gas as they breathed. According to the medical officers, they were quite effective, but there was only one real way to find out.

"All but two platoons have been reequipped. We should receive the rest tomorrow morning, and they should have them by the afternoon," he replied.

Llewellyn turned to Gavin. "Once all the men have them, I want gas drills conducted."

"Yes, sir," replied the major.

"And tell the company COs I don't want sloppiness by the gas sentries. They are not to sound the alarms when they hear someone else down the line sound theirs. They need to check to see if there is actual gas in their sector first."

"I'll them know," the major said then pointed out, "but you know the men. Better safe than sorry."

"Yes, yes," Llewellyn said with a wave of his hand. "But if we have too many false alarms, the men will get lackadaisical and sloppy. At which point, we'll get hit by a real gas attack. I don't want to write any letters home if I don't have to."

"Understood," replied the major.

Llewellyn turned back to the lieutenant. "How are we with picks and shovels?"

The lieutenant frowned. "I think we should be okay. I can check the list of the supplies that the 3rd Brigade left behind. Why?"

"A runner came from HQ. They need two hundred and fifty men for work parties to improve the assembly areas, the communication trenches, and the advance trenches. No point in sending them all if we don't have picks and shovels for them."

"Has the time been set for the attack?" asked the major.

"Not yet, but it's coming," replied Llewellyn. "The Regina Trench is going to be a bitch to take. Our attack a couple of days ago didn't go well." The 1st and 3rd Brigades had attacked on the 6th of October. They had managed to get into the trench, but they couldn't hold it. The preliminary reports indicated both brigades had lost over a thousand men.

Major Gavin added grimly, "It's on the high ground, with 120 to 130 contours giving them excellent observation of our lines."

Llewellyn knew that the German trench ran due east from the Stump Road to where it joined at the Pys-Le Sars line. "The intelligence people are saying it's similar to the Kenora Trench. It's deep and well traversed. The artillery has been chewing up some of the wire, but it's still pretty strong. They have strong points where the Kenora and Regina trenches connect, and they have some near Courcelette. General Loomis is having patrols sent out tonight to see if they've made any major changes since the last reports."

"Are we going to see the tanks?" asked the lieutenant.

Llewellyn shook his head. "Not that I know of. I got a briefing at Corps HQ after they were used at Courcelette. The German prisoners they captured said they had been terrified by them. Especially when their rifle and machine gunfire bounced off their armour."

"We could use them," said Gavin.

"Yeah, I guess. But they said half of them broke down before they got to the German lines. Besides, with the Regina trench on the high ground, they'll see them coming," Llewellyn pointed out. He changed subjects. "Okay, tell the company commanders that we need to pick out the men for tonight's work parties. And tell them I don't want the men to stack their rifles when they are working. They need to keep them close. It is the German Marine Division that is sitting in those trenches across from us. For seamen, they are proving to be tough bastards."

CHAPTER 24

OCTOBER 11, 1916
OTTAWA CENTRAL TRAIN STATION, OTTAWA

"It's time," Laura said when she entered his office. She was dressed in a black skirt and jacket with a similarly coloured hat with white ostrich feathers. Behind her, Borden's private secretary Blount was carrying his coat.

"It's 11:15 already?" he replied as he put down the letter he was reading. He had come in early to deal with the never-ending mountain of paperwork.

"Are the other's ready?" he asked as he rose. Blount held his overcoat as he slipped into it. Laura then handed him his hat so he could keep his head warm. The weather had changed drastically. Last Sunday, it had been a comfortable seventy-four degrees, but now it was a chilly forty-six. In fact, he had to turn the heat on last night when the temperature had dropped below freezing.

"They're waiting for us downstairs," Blount said.

At the front entrance of the East Block, the bulk of his cabinet was waiting for him. They started following when Sir Robert Borden and Lady Borden headed to the train station. The traffic on Sapper's Bridge had ground to a halt. It didn't take long to see why. A large crowd of spectators had gathered in front of the Grand Trunk Railway Station. A squad of Governor General's Foot Guards opened a corridor through the crowd as Sir Robert and Lady Borden approached the station to allow them and his cabinet ministers to pass through. Already waiting for them in front of the station was an honour guard made up from members of the Governor General's Foot Guards, military cadets dressed in blue uniforms, and a local Boy Scout troop. On the other side, standing in a loose cluster, were the six justices of the Supreme Court, the speakers of the House of Commons and Senate, and senior government and military officials.

Borden glanced at the waiting train with the Royal Insignia flag fluttering in the breeze. He could see the last of the trunks being loaded into the baggage car. He had suggested he accompany the duke on his final leg of his goodbye tour to Halifax. The duke had thanked him for his suggestion, but he doubted that the Admiralty would have approved.

The crowd began to clap when the royal motorcade appeared on Sussex Street. Borden was fairly certain one of the governor general's aides had informed Rideau Hall that all was in readiness. When the car had slid to a stop in front of the train station, a Foot Guard officer opened the car door and saluted as the Duke of Connaught stepped out. He was dressed in his usual khaki field marshal uniform. The officer then helped the Duchess of Connaught and Princess Patricia out of the car. The crowd's cheering increased when the duke, the duchess, and the princess waved to them. Borden could see the royals were touched by the number of spectators that had come to see them off and the affection they displayed.

The duchess and the princess smiled warmly when Laura presented them with flower bouquets from their garden.

Borden offered his hand to the duke, who shook it warmly. Borden had been touched when the duke and the duchess had presented to him a silver inkwell. It had been engraved with both the Royal coat of arms and the duke's and duchess's own coat of arms. Borden watched as the duke made a final inspection of the honour guard, the cadets, and the Boy Scouts. He then took a few minutes to give farewell handshakes to the members of his cabinet, the justices, and the other officials before entering the train station.

Borden waited until the train started to pull out of the station before he shouted, "Three cheers for the governor general!"

"Hurrah! Hurrah! Hurrah!" the crowd shouted as the train began to pick up speed.

OCTOBER 17, 1916
CAMC HEADQUARTERS, 13 VICTORIA STREET, LONDON

"I see," replied Matron Macdonald. Samantha saw a hint of disappointment in her tired blue eyes. She wondered if she were getting enough sleep. It was early morning, and the matron's uniform was crisp as she sat behind her desk. The major's pips on her shoulder boards sparkled as the sunlight hit them.

The entire staff was still tense after the announcement that Major-General Jones was resigning as the director-general. Samantha knew Matron Macdonald wasn't pleased by how Jones was being treated. She felt that he should have been treated with more respect, since he had been the CAMC's director-general ever since it had been officially constituted eleven years ago.

Samantha still hadn't seen the report, and she doubted that she ever would. She was certain that Macdonald had taken the criticism in the report personally. She suspected the rumours that Lieutenant-Colonel Bruce would be appointed the new director-general had upset her as well. With the politics involved, she wouldn't be surprised if that came to pass. It was one of the reasons she was looking to get out while she could. She might have a choice now — later, she might not. The colonel was without a doubt going to make changes, for better or for worse.

"May I inquiry why you requested a transfer?" Macdonald asked as she leaned forward. Samantha had given her question considerable thought, since she needed to provide a rationale in her transfer request.

"Yes, ma'am. I would like to return to where I could actually be in contact with the staff and patients." Samantha felt some relief when she saw Macdonald's nod of approval. "I feel my services would be more useful in a field hospital or casualty station."

"Rather than completing forms and shuffling paperwork?" Macdonald added with an arched eyebrow. There was a slight undertone that indicated she didn't quite believe her. Samantha nearly winced when she realized she might sound as if she was denigrating the administrative work being done here. Which was far from the truth, since she knew how much Macdonald cared about her nurses. She also knew as the matron-in-chief of the Canadian Nursing Service, she had to deal with the politics of the CEF, the war effort, the QAIMNS, and the patronage of some of the most powerful personages in England to ensure her nurses could provide the best medical care.

"It's important work, and it needs to be done," Samantha replied. She kept her hands at her side. One of her concerns was the fact that for the last three months she had been praised for the quality of her work. Her handwriting was legible, her files were always up-to-date and well organized. It sounded like she was trying to talk herself out of the transfer. She had to admit the posting was cushy. Yes, you had to put in long hours, but the social life in London with its dinner parties, concerts, and theatres made working here quite pleasant.

"But you like to be more hands-on, so to speak," said Macdonald.

"Yes, ma'am," replied Samantha.

"I also understand you're seeing a young man?"

"Yes, ma'am, He's a lieutenant-colonel with the Richmond Fusiliers with the 1st Division."

"Ah," said Macdonald with a hint of a smile. She always encouraged her nurses to have a good time, on occasion, as long as it didn't interfere with work.

Samantha wasn't about to give that as a reason for her transfer to the front line. The service wasn't particularly interested in her personal life. While she liked the idea of being closer to James, it would be doubtful their duties would allow them to see much of each other.

"At the moment, I'm afraid we don't have any positions open for an assistant matron or a matron in France," replied Macdonald as she raised her hand to brush a loose, dark brown lock of hair from her face.

"I'm willing to take a nursing sister position," Samantha offered.

"It does you credit, but it wouldn't do for a matron to be reduced in rank. It simply wouldn't do," said Matron Macdonald firmly. "What complicates matters is we've already sent Matron Charleston and nineteen nursing sisters to the 1st Stationary Hospital in Salonica. If I had known, I could have added you. You have a good friend there, I believe, an Emily Creighton?"

"Yes, ma'am. I received a letter from her last week. She's doing well," Samantha replied. She didn't say Emily had written that she missed her husband terribly.

Macdonald pursed her lips then said, "Nurse Cotton is being recalled from the Anglo-Russian hospital in St. Petersburg. I can assign you as her replacement."

"Russia!" Samantha blurted out.

"Yes."

Samantha sputtered then repeated, "Russia!"

"Yes, it's that or remaining at your current post," Macdonald said dryly.

"If it would please you, I would be interested," Samantha said quickly before the matron could withdraw the offer.

"Very well," Macdonald replied. "I'll cut the orders. You'll be leaving on the next available transport. We'll have to check the ship schedules to confirm, but I suspect that it will be in the next week or two."

"Yes, ma'am. Thank you," replied Samantha as she knew that she was being dismissed. As she headed out the door, she thought, *How am I going to explain this to James?*

"I have concerns with your latest proposals regarding the reorganization in England," said Hughes as he sat in front of Sir Robert Borden.

The prime minister had been expecting Hughes to raise objections to his plan when he cautiously broached the topic several days ago. He had been surprised how well Hughes had taken it. Borden played nervously with the black fountain pen he had been using to sign some of the correspondence that had accumulated on his desk. He still had another hour or two's worth of work when he allowed Hughes to interrupt him.

"You know that I have the interest of my men at heart," stated Hughes.

"Of course. That is why we need to place the overseas administration on the proper footing. You know as well as I do that we have over two hundred and eighty thousand men in uniform in England and France."

"I agree," replied Hughes. "I consulted with all the senior officers when I visited our camps in England and the Canadian Corps in France asking for their suggestions when I was there. I created the subcouncil in England on a trial basis, since we had already made significant improvements. I clearly informed all the members of the council and the senior officers to that effect. I wanted to gauge how effective it would be."

Borden tightened the grip on his pen. "Was I not clear when I allowed you to go? Did I not say I expected all suggestions and recommendations for improving efficiency were to be vetted and approved by the cabinet?"

Hughes's face coloured slightly before he replied, "You know my methods. If I had waited for cabinet approval for everything, the 1st Contingent would still be at Valcartier."

"I'm well aware of that," replied Borden. "No one disputes your achievements, and the gallantry our men have shown. I just no longer believe those methods are effective or appropriate. As you're aware, expenditures in England are quite heavy. Per our agreement with the Imperial government, we would pay the costs of the Canadian troops in England. Once they were in the field and under the direction of the British commander, we would pay the average maintenance costs of our men. White is very concerned about the expenditures, as we cannot control them effectively from here. We need someone with the appropriate authority to manage the various contracts arranged for the care and welfare of our men and their equipment."

Hughes snorted. "I know that White has always been against me, and he has been whispering with George."

"Come now, Sam. That isn't true. All that White wants to do is make sure taxpayers' money is well spent. That's all," protested Borden. "I've spoken with George before he left for England, and he is in agreement. We need to set up a more efficient method to manage our forces. We cannot continue as we are doing now with the authority being split between you and George."

"George is a sycophant. He's the one who has been whispering in your ear. You know when our men arrived in England that he wanted to wash our hands of the 1st Contingent," Sam said in disgust. "Now you want to make him the minister responsible for the overseas force?"

Borden stared at Hughes. He knew what the issue was. Who would be in charge! Sam's plan meant the head of the overseas ministry would report to him, and nothing would be done without his authorization. Borden's plan would take it out of his hands and place it in George Perley's as the Minister of the Overseas Force. George would be responsible to him and his cabinet. One thing, the most important actually, he didn't like about Sam's proposals was that when Sam caused friction, his government would still get the blame. It didn't matter that he and the cabinet had no idea what Sam had been up to.

"That's what I intend to do," Borden stated firmly.

"But you can't! That would humiliate me!" Hughes said as his eyes began to tear. "That would leave me with nothing to do!"

"You still would be the Minister of Militia and Defence," Borden retorted. "You'll still have plenty to do. The war hasn't been won yet."

"Yeah, right," replied Hughes as he got up from the chair and marched out of the prime minister's office.

Borden turned his head and watched the raindrops splatter his window for a few moments. He sighed. He would have to tell Kemp, Reid, and White about his conversation with Hughes. He doubted, with Sam's mood, that Sam would attend the cabinet meeting this afternoon.

OCTOBER 25, 1916
DMITRI PALACE, PETROGRAD

"Now, there are some excellent shops farther down Nevsky Prospect at the Gostiny Dvor. I have to warm you," Meriel Buchanan said, "you'll have to haggle hard with them to get a good price."

"That's going to be difficult, since I don't know any Russian," said Samantha as she finished rolling a bandage and placing it with the others in a wooden crate sitting on a stool between them.

"Neither did I until I started volunteering at St. George's Hospital two years ago," admitted Meriel as she brushed a lock of brown hair back under the nurse's veil she was wearing. "The first one is *nyet!*"

Samantha laughed. "That one I already know. It took me less than a day to learn."

"That and rolling bandages on your first day," Meriel replied.

"Yeah," replied Samantha. It was her first day at the Anglo-Russian hospital in Petrograd, which was set up on the second floor of the Dmitri Palace. When she had reported for duty with five other nurses this morning, the first thing that Dr. Andrew Fleming, the hospital's CO, did was to give them an orientation tour of the wards.

The palace's two large concert halls had been subdivided into three main wards. The wards were large with eighteen- to twenty-foot ceilings from which elaborate brass chandeliers hung every ten feet or so. The chandeliers had so many bulbs that Samantha didn't bother counting them. Plain white-painted wainscoting had been installed to cover the lower half to protect the ornate Rococo plasterwork that flowed up to the ceiling. Large, arched windows provided plenty of natural light. In the Mirror Hall, the walls still showed markings where the mirrors had hung before they were moved into storage to protect them from damage. The standard white metal-framed beds filled the wards. Above each bed that lined the walls, brass plaques had been placed listing the names of the patrons who provided subscriptions to the hospital.

After her tour, she had been assigned to roll bandages with a Meriel Buchanan, who appeared to be in her late twenties. They hadn't been formally introduced, so she didn't know much about her.

"You don't seem much impressed by the palace," remarked Meriel.

"Actually, I am. But I must admit that once you have seen one, you have seen them all," replied Samantha, testing the waters. A couple of nurses in grey uniforms with white red cross aprons that matched what Meriel was wearing burst into laughter.

She had to admit this palace was magnificent. She had arrived in the Russian capital the day before. Prior to the war, the city had been called St. Petersburg, but the name had been changed to Petrograd to make it sound more Russian than German. Her party had arrived the previous night at the train station after a sea voyage from the English port of Hull to the Russian port of Archangel. This late in the season, they couldn't sail directly into Petrograd. During the winter, thick ice closed the port. The last thing the ship's owners wanted was to lose money if the steamer sat idle, trapped by ice, for several months. The voyage had been nerve-wracking, since they had to sail the same route as Lord Kitchener's ill-fated ship. Everyone aboard their ship was relieved when four Royal Navy minesweepers appeared to clear a path for them as they entered the White Sea. Even then, the ship had to keep a sharp watch for stray mines that might have escaped their moorings. Once they had reached Archangel, they had to disembark to take the Canadian-built icebreaker, *Mikula Seleaninovitch*, to cross the Dvina River to the train station on the opposite side of the river for their final leg to Petrograd.

"Were you able to find a room?" asked Meriel.

"I did, at the Metropol. I have to share it with six other nurses. It's rather tight, but we'll manage."

"With the refugees flooding the city from the fighting on the Eastern Front, finding a place to stay is difficult," Meriel stated.

"That's true everywhere, I'm afraid. I did meet some Russian counts when I had breakfast in the restaurant."

Meriel pursed her lips for a moment then said, "I would advise caution with the Russian counts. Now, Count Dmitri, who has his apartments on the ground floor, is quite all right. But there are some that are less than respectable."

"I've met a few of that kind in England," replied Samantha.

"Ah," Meriel acknowledged.

"If you don't mind me asking, how long have you lived in Petrograd?"

"Nearly eleven years now," she replied.

"What brought you to Petrograd?" Samantha asked.

A small smile appeared on Meriel's face, then she replied, "My father's the British ambassador."

Embarrassed, Samantha hurriedly said, "Oh sorry, I didn't realize."

"No harm done," Meriel replied.

"Oh, good, then you would know all the best sights and restaurants in the city?" Samantha asked.

"I think I'm going to like you, Miss Lonsdale," replied Meriel.

CHAPTER 25

"The court is now in session," stated Major Caldwell as he took his seat.

The major had just finished swearing in the court officials after he had asked the accused if he had any objections to the three senior officers who comprised the court for his trial. The prisoner had objected, but since he hadn't provided any evidence to support his claims, Major Caldwell had overruled him.

Lieutenant-Colonel Llewellyn had requested the major from Corps HQ to be the judge advocate for the Field General court martial he had been forced to call. Because of the seriousness of the charges, and as the president of the court, he wanted to ensure all the rules, regulations, and correct procedures were being followed.

Llewellyn motioned to the prosecutor, Lieutenant Morley, to start.

"Here are the charge sheets," the lieutenant said as he handed copies to Lieutenant-Colonel Llewellyn, Major Gavin, and Captain Coffey."

Llewellyn glanced at the charge sheet he was becoming quite familiar with of late. It was Army Form B116. It listed the defendant's number and rank, who investigated the case, where it was investigated, and the names and ranks of the members of the court. What caught his eye was the character section. It stated the accused's character was indifferent. At the bottom, in the medical section, Doctor Moore had attested that the defendant was of sound mind.

Lieutenant Morley cleared his throat and read from the chart sheet, "The accused, Private Shea, is charged with desertion. On the night of June 20th, 1916, the defendant left his post as a member of a working party assigned to repair a communication trench. He did not obtain oral or written permission to do so. On July 1st, he was declared absent without leave. On the night of September 30th, the accused was arrested in the city of Boulogne as he attempted to stow away aboard a ship bound for the United States."

"How does the defendant plead?" Llewellyn asked as he stared at Private Shea, who was standing at attention in front of his chair. Shea was nineteen years old, with a white pallor, which made him look emaciated. While he was entitled to a friend of the accused to help prepare his defence, he hadn't availed himself of one.

"Guilty of leave without absence, not desertion," Shea replied. Llewellyn knew why he was pleading guilty to leave without absence only. Desertion carried the death penalty.

"I'm afraid he has been charged with desertion," Caldwell said. He directed his statement to Llewellyn, since he was the president of the court. Caldwell couldn't speak directly to Shea.

"Well, not guilty then," replied Shea sourly.

"He is also charged with wilfully losing his equipment, clothing, and regimental necessaries," Morley said as he lowered the charge sheet and placed it on his table. "If it pleases the court, I would like to call my first witness, Sergeant Ellis."

When he heard his name, the short and wide Sergeant Ellis rose from the bench at the back of the room. He marched to the witness chair placed near the judges. After he was sworn in, he took his seat. "Please describe the events of the night you discovered the accused was found missing from his post?" Morley asked.

"Yes, sir," replied the sergeant in a raspy voice. "We've been ordered to work on the communication trenches. Fritz had chewed them up pretty badly. They even hit the privy. Not a great loss…" several chuckles broke out in the room, "but they needed to be redug. So I assigned Private Shea to start digging. Only needed one man, you know."

"Was Private Shea pleased with the order?"

"No one likes working on the latrines," said the sergeant with a shrug.

"You always gave me the bloody latrine duty," blurted Shea.

"Private Shea, you may question the witness after the lieutenant has finished," Llewellyn reprimanded.

"Yes, sir," replied Shea as he sank lower in his chair.

"When did you discover that Private Shea was missing?"

"Near dawn when I went to collect him," the sergeant answered.

"Were you surprised that he wasn't there?" Morley asked.

"Yes and no," the sergeant said reluctantly. "There've been times he had wandered off and I had to chase him down. At least, that was what I thought, but I couldn't find him. I told Lieutenant Readle, and he sent word to our captain, Hastings. An alert was sent out. We searched the trenches just in case he got lost or wounded, but no sign of him."

"Was there any enemy action during the period in question?" asked Morley.

"Just the usual Heinie hen-pecking," the sergeant replied. "But nothing that worried us as we did our work."

"Thank you, Sergeant," Morley said, indicating he was finished.

Llewellyn asked, "Do you have any questions for Sergeant Ellis here?"

"No, Mr. President," stated Private Shea.

When the sergeant rose and went to his seat at the back of the court, Lieutenant Morley handed new sheets of paper to the judges and to the defendant. "I would like to put into evidence a report from Captain Hastings confirming Sergeant Ellis's testimony. And I would like to read into the record the arrest report by Corporal Mannering, the military police officer who arrested Shea at the port of Boulogne."

Morley paused then continued when Llewellyn nodded his approval. "On the night of September 30th, we had received reports of suspicious activity near a ferry. When we investigated, the suspect was discovered lurking near cargo, waiting to load aboard a ship bound for New York. When we confronted the suspect, requesting his purpose and identification, he attempted to flee. After he had been captured and detained, he still refused to identify himself. He was not in uniform, and when we searched him, we found his identity disks in his boots. We also found seven hundred and eighty-five francs on his person."

Llewellyn raised an eyebrow. The seven hundred and eighty-five francs was the equivalent of six months' pay. "Was he asked where he got the money?"

Lieutenant Morley shook his head. "He refused to answer that question, sir. We checked with the paymaster and his paybooks. He didn't have any savings. In fact, he was in arrears."

"I see," replied Llewellyn as he made a note. "Do you have any further evidence?"

"No, Mr. President. The prosecution rests."

"Very well," said Lieutenant-Colonel Llewellyn as he turned to the defendant. "Would you like to call any witnesses in your defence?"

"No, sir, but I would like to make a statement," said Shea as he rose to his feet.

Major Caldwell interjected, "Mr. President, please inform the defendant that he has the right not to speak in his defence, if he so chooses."

"I want to," Shea insisted. Llewellyn waved to him to take his seat in the witness chair.

"You see, I don't like working the latrines. The sergeant and the lieutenant have it in for me. I told them I don't mind working hard, but I just don't like working the latrines. Well, on that night I did start digging them latrines, like the sarge said. It was hot and disgusting work, and I had forgotten to fill my water bottle. I went looking to see if I could fill it from one of the water stations. It was pretty dark, and I got lost. Somehow, and I don't know how, I was out of the trenches.

"It was there that I ran into a Frenchie on a cart. I asked if he had water, he said he didn't, but he had a bottle of wine. I was thirsty, so I helped him drink it. I guess I drank too much and I fell asleep. When I woke up the next day, I realized that I had overslept, and it was midday. I meant to report back to my platoon. I really did. But I knew my CO would be pissed, so I kind of had some more wine to build up my courage, you see. Before I knew it, I had spent a week with this French man.

"The Frenchie was a sly one. He insisted I pay for all the wine I had drunk. I told him I didn't have any money. He said that I had to work for him for a week, or else he'd report me to the MPs. So for the next week, I worked off the wine by working odd jobs as a farm hand."

"Is that how you managed to have the money found on your person? Working as a farm hand?" asked Llewellyn.

Shea smiled slyly. "Yes, sir, once I had paid off the wine, the Frenchie said he needed a strong back to bring in the harvest. That's how I earned my money."

"Why were you found near Boulogne?"

"That was where his farm was, sir."

"What's the name of this Frenchmen?"

"I don't remember his name exactly. I just called him Henri."

"Where was his farm?"

"That I don't know, sir. All the farms look the same to me."

"Why were you found near the ferry?" asked Llewellyn.

"You see, sir, I had just a bit too much beer at one of the estaminets near the harbour. You see, the next morning I was planning to find the next MP to give myself up, so I was trying to find my courage so to speak. Well, when I left the bar, I guess I was tired, and I fell asleep near the cargo boxes. When they woke me up, I was still drunk. I didn't realize they were MPs, so I ran. I thought they were there to roll me. I'm not a deserter, sir."

"I see," replied Llewellyn as he glanced at his fellow officers. "Would you like to add anything else to your testimony?"

"No, sir."

"You may step down, Private Shea. The court will now be adjourned to consider the evidence and make our decision."

★ ★ ★

"What do you think?" Llewellyn asked as he pushed his plate away that held the remains of his lunch. Even though it had been light, a simple ham sandwich, it still felt heavy in his stomach.

"Based on the evidence presented, there's no doubt that the man intended to desert," said Gavin as he finished the last of his sandwich.

"He's guilty," stated Captain Coffey, who was only having coffee. "Don't tell me that you believed his cock and bull story?"

"No, I didn't," replied Llewellyn with a scowl. "I doubt very much a French farmer would have paid his workers that much, even with the shortage of workers. That's better pay than we pay our own. If they had asked us, we would have helped with the harvest. We need the food too."

"I'm pretty sure that he stole the money," Major Caldwell stated. He had moved his chair so he could face all three judges.

Llewellyn fiddled with his cup of coffee as the major glanced at the other two men and back at Llewellyn. The major must have guessed what bothered him. If Shea had deserted in peacetime, he would only be facing a prison sentence. In wartime, it was the death penalty.

"I know the regulations require us to look for anything to mitigate the charges of desertion," said Caldwell. "Unfortunately, Colonel, I don't see how we can, based on his previous absence without leave and petty theft charges. Add to that, he had emptied his paybook before he left. He had hitched a ride to the city of Boulogne, where he was found dressed in civilian clothing attempting to stow away on a ship. When discovered, he resisted arrest, and then refused to identify himself."

"And don't forget, while he was having his fun, the rest of his platoon were in the trenches being shot at and shelled. They don't like him much. You did notice that no one came forward to talk about his good character," Gavin pointed out.

"He's definitely not a hot-corner man," agreed MacInness. He then turned and eyed Caldwell. "I've been reading the announcements of those who have been shot for desertion in the General Orders. There haven't been a lot of them."

The major nodded. "About eighty to ninety percent of the death sentences are commuted to prison sentences. From what I can tell, the Richmond Fusiliers has a very good record for discipline. The likelihood that the sentence will be commuted would be good."

Llewellyn rubbed his face. For the death sentence to be applied, all three had to agree on the verdict. Once sentencing was done, the trial documents and evidence had to be sent up the line. At each brigade, division, corps, and army headquarters, the court martial would be reviewed. It would eventually find itself on General Haig's desk. The general would be making the final decision.

Llewellyn sighed. He couldn't see any way out of it. "Guilty."

NOVEMBER 10, 1916
DETENTION BILLETS, CHÂTEAU DE LA HAIE

Dawn had risen to reveal it was going to be a dull day, but the clouds weren't threatening rain as Lieutenant-Colonel Llewellyn stood before a single wooden post. His face become bleak when he heard the sound of slapping boots on the dew-covered ground.

The sounds came from the procession behind him. A provost marshal was leading a six-man rifle squad. Behind them, two Richmond Fusiliers escorted the prisoner. Father Stoats and Dr. Moore were taking up the rear. Llewellyn was sure his face mirrored theirs. From the corner of his eye, he spotted a man removing a stretcher from the ambulance wagon. He focused his gaze back onto the prisoner as he was tied to the post to avoid looking at the rifle squad. All six were from the prisoner's unit. Since he had been the one who had loaded their rifles, he knew which one held the blank. While the intent had been to make each man think they weren't the one who had fired the kill shot, it didn't work. Experienced soldiers could tell from their rifle's recoil the difference between a blank and a live round.

Once the prisoner had been tied to the post, Dr. Moore pinned a square white piece of paper on the man's chest. He then made way for Father Stoats, who came to stand beside the condemned man.

Father Stoats, wearing his clerical stole, made a sign of the cross and then intoned, "May God have mercy on your soul." He too moved to stand beside Llewellyn.

The provost marshal offered the prisoner a blindfold. Llewellyn was surprised that the man refused. The provost marshal nodded to Llewellyn once he was clear.

"Private Shea, you have been found guilty of desertion. Do you have any last words?" asked Lieutenant-Colonel Llewellyn.

The prisoner shook his head. Llewellyn avoided looking in the man's eyes. "Ready … aim … fire!"

The six rifle shots nearly sounded as one. Private Shea collapsed and slumped against the post. Dr. Moore then approached the prisoner to check the man's vital signs. He looked at the lieutenant-colonel when he was done and gave him a look that Llewellyn recognized. Llewellyn felt a slight bit of relief. If Shea had still been alive, he would have been required to use the .45 on his hip to administer the *coup de grâce*.

With a nod, he dismissed the firing squad. He had given them the rest of the day as leave. He watched as the MPs released the man from his bonds and as the stretcher bearers gently placed Private Shea's body on the stretcher. They then quickly loaded him into the ambulance.

Lieutenant-Colonel Llewellyn would now have to see to Private Shea's burial and notification of the man's next of kin.

CHAPTER 26

"The gall of the man," exclaimed Foster when Borden finished reading Sam Hughes's letter that was delivered minutes before the two o'clock cabinet meeting in the Privy Council chamber. "Why did he wait until now to send it? And good riddance."

Borden could only shrug; he didn't have a clue. He couldn't help noticing that most of his ministers were more relaxed after he had read Hughes's letter. A few were even beaming. The letter had a few sentences explaining why he wouldn't be attending today's cabinet meeting. Borden really hadn't expected his attendance. After all, he had sent Hughes a missive last Friday demanding his resignation.

He was somewhat startled when Hughes had joined him and the rest of the cabinet to greet the arrival of the new governor general as the special CPR train pulled into the Grand Trunk Railway Station at eleven o'clock sharp. A crowd, smaller than usual, had gathered outside the Ottawa station to see the incoming governor general.

When the train stopped, he and Laura had climbed aboard the vice-regal train car, *Alexandria*, to greet Victor Cavendish, his wife Lady Evelyn, and his two youngest daughters, Lady Maude and Lady Blanche. He hoped that his resentment didn't show. He hadn't been consulted before the Duke of Devonshire had been appointed as Canada's new governor general. Still, he had to admit he found Lady Evelyn and the two young girls quite charming.

When they had disembarked, he had introduced His Excellencies to the members of his cabinet. Sam was among the first in line. He noticed Sam had refused to look him in the eye. He hoped the governor general hadn't notice the tension between the two of them. The mayor and the Ottawa city council were also introduced, after which, the duke and his family were whisked to their car for the short drive down Sussex to Rideau Hall. Before the car had driven away, he had called upon the crowd to give the incoming governor general three cheers. After the reception, Sam had disappeared, and now he knew why.

"He doesn't do things by half, does he?" said Foster.

Borden could only nod in agreement. Sam's letter was full of bile and defiance, with little grace. At least with the new governor general and Hughes's resignation, he hoped that he would have a lot less drama. He also felt a great deal of relief. The final straw had been the letter Sam had sent him the previous week. It had been impertinent, to say the least. When he demanded Hughes's resignation, Borden had informed him he was tired of putting out the fires he created.

"I agree," replied Albert Kemp, his minister responsible for war purchasing. "However, as he's now a backbencher, let's hope he can do us little damage."

Borden glanced at Kemp. He was one of the men he was seriously considering as Hughes's replacement as the minister of militia and defence. He had to do some minor shuffling in the cabinet, however; since Kemp was a minister without portfolio, he didn't have to backfill Kemp's current position if he chose not to.

Borden sighed. "I still have a concern. How it will impact our prospects if we call a general election?"

Foster bobbed his head back and forth. "I don't think it will. Hughes has caused considerable friction and now has fewer friends. His reputation has diminished considerably of late. And if you release the letters you have written to each other, it would bolster your case in demanding his resignation."

Borden stared at the letter before him lying on the polished table. "I'll have to take that in consideration. In meantime, I have to inform the new governor general that the minister of militia and defence he had just met has resigned."

NOVEMBER 14, 1916
TRENCH, CARENCY SECTOR, LA HAIE

"How bad is it?" Lieutenant-Colonel Llewellyn asked as he examined the mess in the Gordon Trench of the right subsector of their front line. A couple of men were shovelling oozing chunks of wet dirt into a small, compact wheelbarrow. They were working with their backs hunched over, since they were perilously close to the top of the trench.

"About twenty feet has collapsed," Major Gavin stated as he watched one of the men pull on a wooden post entangled in the barbed wire. When it wouldn't come out, he took out a pair of pliers and started snipping the steel strands. Some of it ran overtop of the trench. If they pulled too hard on the post, the entire fencing system might collapse on top of them. "It's been raining pretty hard, and the ground is well saturated."

"I've noticed," replied Llewellyn as drops from the slight drizzle dripped from his steel helmet. "Did we lose anyone?"

Gavin indicated the negative with his chin. "Two dugouts got filled in. They were able to get out with their rifles, but they lost their kit."

"Well, they had good timing then. We'll be issuing the winter gear soon," Llewellyn replied. He had come from a meeting with Brigadier-General Loomis at the Château de la Haie to discuss the preparations for the upcoming winter. It would be the second wonderful winter for them in the trenches. "Just make sure they fill in the proper forms for their lost kit. I don't want the quartermaster pissed off at me for not having the correct paperwork done."

"Yes, sir," replied Gavin. "We can't have that."

"Any activities from the Huns?"

"Pretty quiet, with the occasional barrage and sniper. Besides, they're in the same boat as we are. Our OPs heard them bailing water out of their trenches last night. They aren't likely to do anything until they get themselves sorted out."

"Misery loves company."

"That's true," Gavin replied. "I would be more comfortable putting up some French wire so they don't get any ideas." The collapse of the trench had dragged down their first barbed wire fence line. They still had a couple of lines in front of that, but it wasn't a good idea to have visible gaps in their wire.

"I'll see if I can scare up some more men for the work parties. They've been pretty busy shoring up the OPs and the strong points."

"Yeah, General Loomis and that intelligence officer of his said the same thing when they were here yesterday."

Llewellyn nodded in agreement. "I guess I'm going to have to beg, borrow, and steal some."

"Yes, sir."

As Lieutenant-Colonel Llewellyn turned, he bumped into his old friend, Simon Rawlings, who was standing suddenly behind him. When Simon examined the condition of the trench he said, "What a mess."

"Yeah, crap happens," replied Llewellyn. He did notice that Simon now had captain's pips on his shoulders and was in a cheery mood.

"What brings you out here?" Llewellyn asked. Simon was with the Royal Canadian Regiment. It was unusual for him to search Llewellyn out in the trenches.

"I heard some interesting news."

"What news?"

"Old Sam Hughes has been sacked," Rawlings answered with glee.

"You're kidding," interjected Major Gavin.

"I ran into one of the wireless signallers, who gave me the head's up. It's going to come through the regular channels shortly." Rawlings still couldn't keep the glee out of his voice. Llewellyn knew his friend had no love for the minister of militia and defence. That was one of the reasons Simon had transferred to the RCRs when they first joined the Contingent at Valcartier. The RCRs were then shipped out to Bermuda for garrison duty until they were shipped to France last year.

"Who's taking over from Hughes?" asked Llewellyn.

"I have no idea," replied Rawlings. "Anyone would be better than old Sam."

"Well, I would be careful who I gloat to," warned Llewellyn. "Captain Leeds is a Hughes man."

Rawling shook his head. "I don't understand why such an intelligent man would support a stupid idiot."

"Still, I wouldn't gloat too much," Llewellyn suggested.

"Why not?"

Llewellyn gave him a grin. "Since he's no longer the minister of militia and defence, he can finally get his fondest wish."

"What wish is that... No!" Rawlings shouted with a look of horror when he realized what Llewellyn meant.

"Well, Winston Churchill did it," Llewellyn said as his grin got wider. Sir Winston Churchill had resigned as the first lord of the admiralty after the Gallipoli disaster. He became a lieutenant-colonel commanding the Royal Scots Fusiliers near Ploegsteert Wood last spring.

"Dear God, not that!" Rawlings wailed.

NOVEMBER 15, 1916
WOODS BUILDING, OTTAWA

Lieutenant-General Sam Hughes looked tired and exhausted as he stood in his office. It had a forlorn look since he had removed most of his personal mementoes, keepsakes, and papers. They were all packed in boxes and crates stacked near the office door.

It was nearly five years to the day since he had been appointed as the minister of the Department of Militia and Defence. It had been one of his happiest days when he received word from Borden that he would be given his most cherished department to run. He had worked so hard to ensure his party would win the election and that he would be in a position to shape its policies. After Borden's announcement of his cabinet, he had returned to Lindsay, where he had been greeted by his old regiment, the 45th, with an honour guard. The regimental band had led him and the procession of cars and horse-drawn carriages from the CPR station to Victoria Park via Kent Street. He remembered how all the businesses and homes had been festively decorated with bunting for the occasion.

At the park, Mayor Beall had led the series of speakers who had been gathered to celebrate his electoral victory and his appointment. Even Lindsay's Liberal Association had congratulated him. In his speech that day, he had promised he would do his best to serve his country and to further the interest of the people. He also had promised to do all he could in building a prosperous Canada.

He had pushed Borden as hard as he could, and he had paid the price. He had only one regret: he wouldn't be overseeing his department to a glorious victory. He knew he was right in the positions he had taken, and when the letters that he and Borden had exchanged were published, he would derive great satisfaction in his vindication.

"General," Fiset said, interrupting Hughes. "The staff has been assembled for your farewell."

"Of course," replied Hughes. He straightened his tie and smoothed a wrinkle in his dark suit. He decided he would be dressed in mufti on his final day with the department instead of his uniform.

"What are your plans, sir?" asked Fiset.

"After my farewells, I'm going to the Château Laurier to have a nice thick steak," Hughes replied. "Then I'm going to Lindsay to celebrate my daughter Roby's birthday on Friday. She'll be thirty-three." Fiset nodded. Hughes's daughter was married to Lieutenant-Colonel Byron Green. "After that, I'm going to take several days to rest and read."

"You deserve it, sir," replied Fiset. "We're sorry to see you go, sir. But you do need your rest. We know how hard you worked."

"Thank you," Hughes replied as his eyes moistened briefly. "I just wanted to say that if I have ruffled some feelings from time to time, everything I did was devoted to the cause."

"Yes, General," replied Fiset as he gave him a salute.

"Good, now call the staff in so that I can tell them how much I appreciated their hard work."

CHAPTER 27

NOVEMBER 16, 1916
CANADIAN CORPS HEADQUARTERS, LE CHÂTEAU RANCHI-
COURT, REBREUVE-RANCHICOURT

Lieutenant-Colonel Llewellyn was in the second car of the two-car convoy when they had to stop at a crossroad just outside the village of Rebreuve-Ranchicourt. They had to wait for a company to pedal past Brigadier-General Loomis's car. The cyclists were from the Canadian Corps Cyclist Battalion headquartered at Divion, about four miles north of their current position. They rode in a four-column formation on CCM bicycles with bedrolls tied to their front carriers. Lashed on the rear carriers were their kit bags, which he assumed contained the usual rations, spare ammo, and personal items. Lee-Enfields were clipped to the bikes' frames, with the butts under the leather seats and the muzzle pointed skyward through the handlebars. Llewellyn knew a cyclist battalion had been formed several months ago when the various cyclist units were reorganized and amalgamated into a single command assigned to Corps HQ. They were frequently used as messengers, traffic wardens, for burial work parties, and for transporting wounded men.

Once the company had passed, Llewellyn's driver followed Brigadier-General Loomis's car down the gravel laneway to the chateau that was currently the headquarters of the Canadian Corps. Lieutenant-General Byng had called in his senior commanders and officers for briefings and planning sessions for operations being considered for December and for the new year.

When the eighteenth-century chateau had come into view, it was obvious whoever built it preferred living in a space filled with plenty of light; the building was more glass than brick. By Llewellyn's count, there were fifteen large, rectangular windows on the first two floors. They were encased in tan and grey bricks, and several were covered by white shutters. Four dormer windows protruding from the black slate roof provided light into the attic. A clock, which looked to him to be rather small for the building, topped the main entrance. The entrance was a single white-panelled affair, and it projected slightly out from the rest of the building. Llewellyn had been here before, so he knew that there was a large ballroom on the ground floor. The living quarters were on the second floor.

On the lawn, several tents had been pitched where Llewellyn knew they would be holding their planning sessions. As they had come to a stop, a motorcycle came around the corner and headed down the lane they had just driven. Llewellyn couldn't help noticing the large wicker basket tied to its rear carrier. As it passed him, he saw several pigeons fluttering in the cage. They didn't seem to be too happy as the bike bounced on the gravel.

When Brigadier-General Loomis stepped out of the car, he was greeted by one of Byng's aides. They spoke briefly, then Loomis approached Llewellyn and said, "There is going to be an hour's delay before the meeting starts. Might as well take a break, if you wish."

"Thank you, General," Llewellyn replied as he saw a second motor-cycle drive by with a birdcage attached to its rear carrier. "I have several men who are taking the messenger pigeon course that I would like to check on."

"By all means," replied Loomis. "Just don't be late for the meetings."

"Yes, sir," replied Llewellyn.

He then followed the trail that the motorcycles had used to the back of the chateau. He ignored the staff cars and the riding horses stationed in front of the stables. He had eyes only for the London double-decker bus parked nearby. On the other side of the bus, thirty men were sitting on the lawn listening to an instructor.

He saw that the bus had been converted into a pigeon loft for the Canadian Corps Mobile Pigeon Unit. He didn't know how many pigeons there were inside, but a dozen or so were cooing as they sat in the wire enclosure on top of the bus. An exterior staircase led up from the top of the bus to the ground. The lower deck's glass windows had been replaced with plywood.

A messenger pigeon winged over his head and lighted on the bus's wire cage. The bird slid through an opening that he hadn't seen. When it poked at a panel, it popped open, and a buzzer rang. At the sound, a private who had been carrying a bag of seed dropped it near the steps then climbed the stairs to the back of the bus. A few minutes later, he emerged with the bird and carefully removed a capsule that had been attached to its leg. He then gently released the bird back into the bus's upper deck. The private then motioned to a nearby runner, who took the message and hurried to the chateau's back entrance.

Llewellyn was curious about the message but wisely decided it wasn't any of his business. He focused his attention on the men who were listening to the lecture. He spotted the three men he sent to the course on the far end of the second row. The officer who was giving the lecture was a captain with signal patches on his sleeves. He was in his early thirties, slightly balding, with a waspish moustache. He seemed to be speaking quite passionately on what was obviously his favourite topic.

"Now, I have explained the reasons why it takes a fortnight to twenty days for the pigeons to get oriented to their new homes. We release several pigeons to make sure they stay in the vicinity. So if we move the mobile loft, the birds you currently have now in your care will have to be replaced with new ones. If you release the old ones, they will fly to their old loft's location. This will mean there will be no one there to read the messages they're carrying.

"Now, it's time for a ten-minute smoke break. When you return, I'm going to explain the care and upbringing of a carrier pigeon. Why it is important to record the bird's serial number and the number of flights it has flown. Be back in ten."

When the men rose to their feet, most of them stretched then lit cigarettes. The captain had spotted him and headed in his direction. "Colonel, I'm Captain Bateon. Can I help you with anything?"

"I was just checking up on my men. How are they doing?" Llewellyn asked.

"They have proven to be quite adequate pigeoneers," the captain replied.

To Llewellyn's ear, it sounded like high praise, which surprised him, since it was not a job many of his men aspired to. "That's good to hear."

The captain acknowledged with a nod then headed off to check his loft. Llewellyn then cocked a finger at Corporal Bowley. After the corporal had ambled over, the colonel asked. "How are you enjoying the course?"

"Beats fatigue duty, sir," the corporal replied. The corporal was in his mid-twenties, medium height, with a lean frame. He wasn't the sharpest pencil in the box, but he was adequate at his job. "But the course has been instructional, sir."

Llewellyn grinned. The pigeons were quite useful when the telephone lines got cut. In some cases, they'd been faster than using the phone. "Learn anything?"

The corporal shrugged. "Last month, they had six hundred birds out in the field and about four hundred and eighty came back," the corporal said.

"That many?" Llewellyn said with a raised eyebrow. That was nearly fifteen birds per day. It didn't speak well for the quality of the telephone system.

"Yes, sir, that was the poop."

Llewellyn grinned then said, "Carry on, Corporal. I have to go to my meetings."

He returned the corporal's salute then headed back the way he came. As he walked, he mentally went over the agenda for the day's meetings. One of the items he recalled was Vimy Ridge.

NOVEMBER 19, 1916
WINTER PALACE, TSARSKOYE SELO

"No, we're not renting a palace!" Samantha retorted in an exasperated tone.

"Why not?" demanded Christine Steward, a pretty young blonde from East London. Unfortunately, her pout confirmed she was at times airless. Oh, she was a good nursing sister, Samantha had to concede. Her medical notations were written in a fine hand, and the patients at the Anglo-Russian hospital adored her. It caused Samantha some difficulties, because they expected the same behaviour from her, especially since their hair colouring matched. *I wonder if James would like me as a brunette*, she thought. It was vexing that she had to spend considerable time re-educating the patients. Once a man had gotten an idea in his head, it was difficult to remove.

"First, how are we going to afford it on a nurse's salary?" Samantha demanded. "Second, we would have to hire staff. Palaces don't clean themselves, you know."

"Oh," replied Christine, perplexed. "What do you mean, they don't come with staff?"

Before Samantha could reply, Christine turned to Meriel, who was sitting beside Samantha in the back of the *droshky* they had hired to take them to the train station. The *isvostchik* cracked his whip to encourage the three horses pulling the sleigh to maintain their quick trot. There were six of them tightly crammed into the sleigh, with blankets draped over their legs to keep their feet warm. In the back seat, there was

Meriel, Fran Hoban, a raven-haired Irish nurse from Belfast, and her. Sitting opposite them was Christine in the middle, with Hailey Smith, a short, buxom nurse from Southampton on her left, and Alice Mason, a freckle-faced nursing sister from Edinburgh, on her right. Everyone wore wooden jackets, scarves, and mittens. Samantha and Meriel were wearing *Boyer*-style hats while the other women were wearing *Usbanka* fur caps to keep their ears warm. The weather was crisp, and there was enough snow for the sleigh's runners to glide smoothly on the road to the train station.

They had spent the day visiting the Tsarskoye Selo, the Tsar's country residence just outside Petrograd. When they had arrived at the Winter Palace, they had been surprised by the village that had grown around it. They were fortunate that one of Meriel's connections, a Countess Stepanov, had invited the newly arrived nurses to have lunch at the palace and to be taken on a brief tour of its public places. What had impressed them most was the Church of the Resurrection, the Tsar's and Tsarina's private chapel. One of the things Samantha noticed, which she later found out was normal for Russian churches, was that there weren't any pews to mar the view of the Prussian blue walls with Corinthian columns gilded in gold and handsomely carved with garlands and angels. They had to crane their necks to gape at the scene of the resurrection beautifully painted onto the chapel's ceiling.

"Did the countess mention she was considering renting her palace?" Meriel asked.

"She did in passing," Christine admitted. "She said she was going to America with her husband on some war purchasing commission for guns, supplies, and whatnots for the army."

"I've been to her palace in the Nevsky Prospect. It's a couple of blocks away from the train station. But I would be careful. When the British government leased our current embassy, we had to spend a considerable amount of funds making repairs. The plumbing and the sanitation in particular," Meriel said as she wrinkled her nose and gave a theatrical shudder. "Thousands of pounds were spent making the palace livable."

Christine glanced at her companions, looking for support. "With the number of people looking for work, we could hire staff cheap."

It was true that the Petrograd population had doubled since the start of the war with the influx of refugees from the war zones. The guards at the hospital spent most of their day controlling the lines of people who appeared begging for work and food. From what Samantha understood, the Tsar had imposed a head tax on the Russian nobility to help pay for food for the starving refugees. Samantha hadn't yet visited the district where the bulk of the refugees were housed, but she was scheduled for one next week.

"That's one of the reasons that the countess is leaving Russia," Meriel stated. "She doesn't like the mood of the crowd. She remembers what it was like ten years ago during the Russian-Japanese war when the crops failed and food riots erupted in St. Petersburg."

Samantha nodded in understanding. "Some of the hospital staff did mention that bread prices had doubled, even tripled, and the lines were getting longer at the bread shops. But their wages haven't increased; in fact, they have been cut."

"I'm afraid that it will get worse during the winter with the harbour closed. Everything needs to be brought in by train. Last winter, coal was difficult to come by, so we had to use wood."

Samantha didn't like the sound of that. It depended on how efficient and well organized the Russian train system was.

"If there are food riots, will we be safe?" asked Alice.

Meriel replied, "I'm sure that the hospital will be fine, but…"

Samantha finished, "The palaces will be targets for people looking for food or money to buy food."

"That's a possibility," Meriel replied.

"But still, living in a palace," Christine lamented.

NOVEMBER 23, 1916
PRIME MINISTER'S HOME, GLENSMERE, OTTAWA

The late evening's cold rain and wind were on Borden's heels until he quickly shut the door behind him. The warmth of his home enveloped him as he removed his damp hat and overcoat.

"Good evening, Prime Minister," his housekeeper said as she approached him from the kitchen to take his coat. She was in her forties, stocky, dressed in a maid's black dress and white apron. Her brown hair was tied in a bun. By the time she had crossed the hallway, he had already hung his coat and hat on the rack.

"Mrs. Hoswell, the weather has turned rather nasty." Borden shuddered as a sudden chill caused him to shiver.

Hoswell gave him a look of concern. "Would you like me to prepare something warm for you? Soup? Tea?"

"I'm fine. The dampness seems to be getting into my bones of late," he replied to relieve her concerns. "Did Lady Borden have something to eat?"

"Yes, Sir Robert. She managed to have some barley soup for dinner. She seems to be getting better, the poor dear. The doctor came by this afternoon. Said she needed bed rest."

"She's in her room?"

"Yes, Sir Robert."

"I'll go up and see her," Borden said. After she nodded, he took the stairs to their bedroom on the second floor. He felt the heat from the fireplace when he entered their room. He saw Laura sitting in their four-poster bed with a book in her lap, reading under an electric table lamp. He examined her critically as shadows played on her face. He had been concerned when she didn't greet him at Central Station at noon when he arrived back in Ottawa after his weekend trip to New York. It was at the house that he found her with her face swollen, causing her considerable discomfort. He couldn't get a satisfactory answer as to what had caused the swelling. Borden wasn't sure, maybe it was the light, but it seemed to him that some of the swelling had gone down.

When she looked at him, her eyes brightened. She mumbled, "How was … day … at office?"

"Please rest, dear. Don't tire yourself," he replied as he sat on the edge of the bed and gently took her hand. "It was the usual at the office. Albert came to see me this morning." She gave him a questioning look. "The Honourable Kemp said yes. He'll take the Department of Militia and Defence. It's a load off my mind. I'll meet with the cabinet and put the OC order through. Sevigny will issue the writ for the by-election tomorrow."

Laura grimaced when she nodded. She knew, since she had been with him on the stumps, that MPs had to resign their seat in the House of Commons when they were appointed to the cabinet. They had to run again as a minister of the Crown in a by-election. Borden had to do the same thing when he became prime minister. It was a holdover from British Parliamentary practice. The commons were fearful that the Crown would corrupt their members by appointing them to offices of power, money, and prestige. It was a way to remind everyone that the people had a final say in who was appointed. Usually, there was a gentlemen's agreement between the parties that the ministers would run unopposed, allowing them to win their seat by acclamation. In some cases, if there were concerns, the minister would run in a safe riding.

When Borden saw the look in Laura's eyes, he knew her next question. "So far Hughes has been good. There have been rumours he will raise opposition to Albert. You know he doesn't like him because he's been the head of the War Purchasing Commission. Ever since I demanded his resignation, the press and the letters I've been receiving have all been supportive. People have been telling me if we leave Hughes alone, he won't cause us any serious problems."

When she snorted, he replied, "I know. I know. I doubt it myself. I think he's going to be bitter when he finds himself alone and without influence."

"Dinner?" she prodded.

"Dinner at Rideau Hall was quite pleasant after the swearing-in ceremony. Everyone was quite charming. The duchess even asked how you were feeling and if you needed anything." Seeing she was forming another question, he said, "No, their children did not attend."

"The duke did ask me if he should wear his uniform or mufti when reviewing our troops. I recommended he wear mufti. We'll see if he does.

"He also asked about my trip to New York. I told him about last February's delegation from New York that had come to offer me an honorary membership to the Lawyers' Club in New York. You would have loved the club. It's on the Broadway at the U.S. Realty Building. It's very nice. Where was I…?

"Oh, yes. I mentioned I had to go to New York last Saturday to deliver my speech to the club. The reception was everything that I could wish for. Christie told me it was one of my finest. Spring-Rice called me Sunday morning to tell me that the reports he had received afterward were excellent. The *Times* and the *Sun* even published copies of it the next day."

When Laura patted his hand, Borden said, "No, I didn't prattle on … much. I did say I regretted you couldn't come with me. You would have enjoyed the show they put on at the Hippodrome. My box was draped with the Stars and Stripes and Union Jacks. Afterward, I was escorted backstage to see how they transformed it into an ice rink, and I was even introduced to a few of the show's stars."

Laura shrugged to say there was a next time.

Robert rose to his feet and began to loosen his tie. "You remember that I told you I met that woman from Calgary, Mrs. Steward." Laura gave him a single nod. "She said she hadn't heard from her husband in over a year since he volunteered. I told Albert about it. He's looking into it. The poor woman is desperate. Her husband hasn't been sending her any money."

He was pleased she hadn't grimaced in pain when she showed her disgust at the poor woman's husband with a deep frown.

DECEMBER 5, 1916
DMITRI PALACE, PETROGRAD

Samantha watched a sanitor, the Russian equivalent of a British orderly, carefully unwind the cotton gauze covering the wounded young man's head as the two Russian doctors standing beside her looked on with interest. "As you can see, we covered the hernia cerebri with gauze soaked with a formula of two per cent for three or four days," said Dr. Waters.

Samantha glanced at the tall, thin doctor. Waters was clean-shaven, and his eyes matched his auburn hair. He had been attached to the Anglo-Russian hospital since it started at the beginning of the year. Prior to that, he had been a well-respected surgeon in London. The two Russian doctors she had just met. She couldn't remember their last names, but the roly-poly one, called Stephan, was balding, with a fringe of black hair, while the hawk-faced man was called Eric. At least it sounded like Eric to her ear. Both men were in their mid-forties, and both wore neatly trimmed Van Dyke beards. Under their white coats, she had seen their Guards military uniforms.

They were here for instructions from Dr. Waters on new medical techniques. He was here for a week before he returned, with eight British nurses, to the Anglo-Russian field hospital currently somewhere on the Austrian-Hungarian-Romanian border. From what she understood, the two doctors were slated to join him, since the field hospital was currently attached to the Guards Regiment.

When the sanitor removed the last layer, Dr. Waters said, "As you can see, the protrusion is covered with a membrane that is partially sterile."

Dr. Stephen leaned over to get a better look. "You stated to drain the wound for several days after the bone fragments are removed to avoid a septic infection."

"That is correct. If a septic infection sets in, the likelihood that the patient recovers is low," replied Dr. Waters.

"Humph," muttered Eric. "They are peasants, no great loss."

A pained expression crossed Stephen's face. Samantha noticed that Dr. Waters stiffened slightly. She hoped her face didn't reveal too much. The language barrier was a bit of a problem, but one of the significant differences she noticed from the patients' attitude was a distinct lack of enthusiasm for the war.

She had been told there was a series of battles during the Bresilov Offensive from June to September in the Ukraine to support the Romanians. She had heard that the Romanians had entered the war, but she hadn't paid it very much attention. When she had arrived in Petrograd, she had been informed the offensive had been a great success, but the casualties had been horrendous, nearly a million Russians. The rumours were that the Russian army's morale had been broken. She wondered if that was part of the reason for the tension she had noticed in the streets of the city.

Stephen continued, "Naturally, you have to remove the bullet from the man's head."

Waters mouth twitched in obvious agreement. "However, most of the head wounds are from shrapnel."

"Shrapnel?" said Eric.

"Yes," interjected Samantha. She was glad to add to the conversation, since her role so far had been silent observer. "Most of the wounds on the Western Front are from head wounds from artillery shells. What the British and French armies have done is introduce steel helmets to protect the men's heads."

Eric asked with a touch of disdain, "You know this how?"

Dr. Waters smiled. "Matron Lonsdale has served as a nurse on the Western Front and in England."

Samantha nodded. 'The introduction of the steel helmets has reduced such wounds significantly."

Stephen had a considering look on his face, while Dr. Eric was not convinced. "It is not our place to make such recommendations to the *Stavka*."

Samantha looked at the two Russian doctors without understanding. "The *Stavka* is the Russian high command," Dr. Waters informed her.

"Ah," Samantha replied. She shouldn't have been surprised. While she might make suggestions, it was unlikely they would flow up to the heights of the director of the CAMC. She already had plenty of experience with that.

"Since you recently come from the Western Front, is there any other differences?" asked Dr. Stephen.

"There is one thing that struck me when I started reviewing the patients' charts," replied Samantha. She had been pleasantly surprised that they were in English. In most cases, they had a Russian interpreter present to give instructions to the patients. Even if they were in Russian, it wouldn't have mattered, since many of the soldiers couldn't read. "You have very few cases of tetanus."

"Is that common on the Western Front?" asked Stephen.

"Very," replied Samantha. Lockjaw, as most people called it, was an infection caused by bacteria found in the soil. The symptoms usually started with muscle spasms in the jaws and then spread to the rest of body. As a young girl in Sudbury, Samantha had seen people contract the disease. It hadn't been a pretty sight, since the spasms had been so severe, they had broken their bones.

"That is true," said Waters. "While supplies of antitetanus serum have been scarce, we've only seen a handful of cases. We suspect the difference is the uncultivated soil that the Russian troops find themselves in. In France and Belgium, the farmlands are cultivated and are fertilized with manure."

Eric shrugged then turned to his head toward Samantha. "So, you're English?"

"I'm a Canadian," she replied.

"She's from the Great White North," Dr. Waters said with a teasing smile.

Eric snorted in derision. "It is Mother Russia," he pointed out as he eyed Samantha.

"I'm used to the cold," Samantha said. "Ice water runs in my veins."

"Vodka will warm you up," Eric said with a touch of a leer.

"Doctor Waters, you indicated you will be showing us a patient recovering from a German aerial bomb?" Stephen interjected, to Samantha's relief.

Waters glanced between Eric and Samantha. "Yes, it is an interesting case. Not only is the patient suffering from several severe wounds from the bomb fragments, but he is also infected with Bacillus aerogenes capsulate. We believe the bomb's outer casing is causing the infections…" he said as he led the group to the next patient hidden by a folding screen.

Samantha suspected the Russian doctor did not take rejection well. She made sure that the other two doctors were between her and Dr. Eric as they continued their rounds.

CHAPTER 28

"How did it go?" Lieutenant-Colonel Masterley asked when Lieutenant Paul Ryan entered his office. It was more of a cubbyhole in the 65th Artillery's HQ. The headquarters was set up in a two-storey red-brick house on the outskirts of Bruay.

"It went," Paul replied after saluting the lieutenant-colonel. When Masterley indicated, he took a chair. It squeaked and didn't feel very solid when Ryan put his weight on it. He placed his feet underneath him in case the chair collapsed.

"That bad?" the lieutenant-colonel asked.

"It wasn't all bad. The march to and from the calibration range was good for the men and the horses. The horses did quite well. It took only two days to get to Tilques, and none went lame."

"That's not bad," acknowledged Masterley. The travel time it took to move the 18-pounders from one locale to another was to a certain degree variable. It was always dependent on how healthy each horse was and how much endurance it had. The guns could only travel as fast as the slowest horse. "And the men?"

Ryan shrugged. "The usual grumbling. At least they had a change of scenery. They did hit the estaminets rather hard."

Masterley snorted. "Not that hard. I didn't get any reports from the MPs. What was the range like?"

"It was a bit on the short side. It's only twenty-five hundred yards long and two thousand yards wide. Tilques in the east and St. Martin au Laërt in the south are only a couple of miles outside the calibration range."

"I don't think the range safety officer would've liked it if you dropped a couple of shells on them." The lieutenant-colonel chuckled. Ryan smiled in agreement. The 18-pounder had a maximum range of 6,500 yards.

"They had four rows of dummies arranged for us as targets. They had them set up at exactly fifteen hundred yards. I followed procedures. I took the barometer pressure, the temperature, and the wind speed. Then we fired a series of five shells to determine how much the variance was from the range tables. From the shots' placements, we calculated each gun's muzzle velocity and painted it on each barrel."

"And?"

"All the shells fell short. Nearly a hundred to a hundred fifty yards when the range was set to fifteen hundred."

"So we have barrel wear between two to three percent," the lieutenant-colonel said with a touch of concern.

"I'm afraid so," Ryan acknowledged. Paul knew the 18-pounders were made of three layers of high-quality steel. The "A" tube through which the shell passed was wrapped with steel wire to contain the expansion from hot gases and to prevent the tube from bursting. The exterior was a sheath in a steel casing. It wasn't the passing of the shell through the barrel that was causing most of the wear, although the metal on metal reduced the effectiveness of the rifling to some degree. The rifling imparted spin that gave the shell its accuracy and range. It was instead the corrosiveness of the expanding gases from the propellant that was causing most of the damage, since it ate at the "A" tube.

"The worst one was the number three gun."

"But the number three was our most reliable gun!" said the lieutenant-colonel in surprise.

"I was surprised as well. I checked the gun's logbooks. That one had the most usage. It had several days where it fired over four hundred and fifty shells. The other three had been in and out of the workshops to get repairs for one thing or another. Also, the breech on the number two isn't as tight as it should be." When he saw the lieutenant-colonel's face, Ryan quickly added, "Its fine for now, but we'll have to keep an eye on it. At some point, we'll have to replace it."

The lieutenant-colonel shook his head.

"It's rather ironic," Paul said.

"Oh, why?"

"First, we didn't have enough shells to fire at the enemy. Now that we are getting a healthy supply, we may not have enough guns to fire them."

"Yeah, that's funny, all right," replied the lieutenant-colonel. He wasn't laughing. "We're going to have a problem in the new year." He must have seen the surprised look on Ryan's face. He continued, "Keep it under your hat, since it's not official yet, but we are going to be tasked to take Vimy Ridge. We may not have enough left on the barrels to do the job when we get there."

Ryan grimaced. "Shit!" He knew 18-pounders were designed so that when the "A" tube was worn out, the gun barrel could be rebored and a new "A" tube inserted. He wasn't sure if the workshops here were capable of doing the work or whether they had to be sent back to the factory. If it had to go back to the manufacturer, it meant the gun would be out of service for several months, if not longer.

"What do you want to do?" asked Ryan.

"If I thought I could get away with it, I would get them rebored now. Since they haven't reached that level yet, what we need to do is even out the wear between all our 18-pounders."

Ryan nodded. "The muzzle velocities are painted on each barrel. They should be pretty accurate. We used the calibration side rulers Ordnance shipped to us to calculate the numbers."

"Good. We'll use the number three gun for sniping and retaliation work. We'll make sure the others are available if we need them to cut wire and support the infantry."

"Okay," replied Ryan. "Sounds like a plan."

"Now, if we're tasked for Vimy, we'll have to recalibrate the guns when we get there. I hope like hell we have enough left on the barrels to do the job."

"I certainly hope so too," replied Ryan soberly.

DECEMBER 15, 1916
DMITRI PALACE, PETROGRAD

Dear James,

Verelogo rozhdestra i schatlvogo novago goda! That's Russian for Merry Christmas and Happy New Year. I dearly hope you get this letter before Christmas, but sadly, the mail in Russia can be erratic. At least, the foreign mail seems to be, because the major ports here are closed. They're all frozen over like back home.

I do wish we could have been together to celebrate Christmas this year. Since we can't, I hope you are well and that you are spending Christmas more pleasantly than you did last year in the trenches. If you have turkey, have some for me. Here, they prefer having partridge and goose for Christmas. I'm not keen on eating goose. The last time I had it, it had a lot of fat. It was disgusting.

As for me, I have to let you know that I'm celebrating Christmas twice, once on the 25th and the second on the 7th of January. It has something to do with the calendar that the Russian church here uses. The staff decided to celebrate both, one for the English staff and the second one for the patients. We've already started decorating the palace wards.

We discovered a problem with the decorations as we were putting them up. Most of the ones we had had been made in Germany. That didn't go over very well. A pity, really, since they are quite gorgeous. We had to throw them out and make do with what we could find or make. Here, Christmas is mostly for the children, since the grownups don't give each other gifts. There is also a tradition here where the kids from the poorer neighbourhoods go door-to-door in the well-to-do areas, where they are given toys and a few kopeks.

I know the Germans have made a peace proposal. I hope this miserable war ends soon, since this will be our third Christmas away from home. The word we are getting is that the Russians are not very impressed with the terms that the Germans are proposing. We'll have to wait and see what happens.

Otherwise, I'm doing fine. I'm sharing a flat with three other nurses. It's a small apartment, but between working and seeing the sights, we don't spend much time there. All three of my roommates are from England. Brooke is from London, Amelia is from Liverpool, and Carla is from Surrey. We get along pretty well, and they're teasing me about the upcoming skating parties. With the ports and rivers frozen, it's a popular activity here. I must admit that it's pretty cold. It's nearly as cold as Sudbury. I don't think I've mentioned to you the skating parties we had on Ramsey Lake. They were great fun. I even had a dram or two of whiskey back then to keep warm. Here, vodka is popular.

Most of the Russian staff at the hospital are great. To be honest, I've been impressed by how well they are enduring their circumstances. Petrograd is full of refugees, and food prices are quite high.

Well, James, I have to go now. I will be writing another letter soon. Stay safe.

Love, Sam

DECEMBER 16, 1916
RICHMOND FUSILIERS, 1ST DIVISIONAL RESERVES, BRUAY

Dear Samantha,

I hope this letter finds you well. I was thinking about you and Christmas. Obviously, this year we can't be together, but next year, when this miserable war is finally over, we can finally be in the same place to celebrate Christmas. At least, that is my fondest hope.

As for me, I'm pretty busy as the CO of the Richmond Fusiliers. One of the things I'm arranging is a Christmas dinner for the regiment to keep up morale. I'm sure the men will be happier with me this year than they were last year. I'm still riding them hard about trench foot. So far this month, we haven't had a single case. Woe to the officer who brings me one; otherwise, things are as usual.

I do miss Colonel Tennison from time to time. He's still in England at the convalescent home. He wrote to me to say he, his wife, and his kids wish you a Merry Christmas. Beryle and Alexander are missing you terribly. He said they should be returning to Canada in January. He would make a great training officer, but it's unlikely that the army would keep him. I wish I could join him, but sadly, until this war is over... What can I say?

I hope it isn't too cold in St. Petersburg. It can't be any colder than back home. I wish I were there to bundle up with you and to keep you warm at night.

Love, James

"Amen," said Samantha as Father Dempsey made the sign of the cross after he finished saying grace. The amens from the rest of the seated guests were somewhat ragged, since some were in Russian.

She was sitting between two Russian counts with a lieutenant-colonel's gold-fringed epaulets on their shoulders. They were dressed in the forest green and scarlet uniforms of the elite *Preobrazhensky* Lifeguard Regiment. Their eyebrows had risen when she arrived at the British embassy's Christmas dinner dressed in her Canadian nurse's mess uniform. They had risen even higher when they saw her captain's pips after she undid her grey, red-trimmed nursing cape. From the colonels' compliments on how well her uniform fitted her, she had a fairly good idea what their thoughts were. She had to admit when she was invited to the dinner, it had made choosing her outfit rather simple. She did notice some of the women give her askance looks. It bothered her somewhat, but she had seen enough of the Russian nobility to realize that buying a suitable dress for the evening's dinner party would have cost her a year's pay.

The dinner was being held in the large dining room on the second floor of the Soltykoff Palace that the British government had leased for their embassy. It was located on the bank of the Neva River, in the English quarter, directly across from the Imperial Palace. In the corner, there was a large Christmas tree lit with candles. Christmas wreaths and bunting were strategically placed among the painted portraits that hung on the walls. In the background, a Russian was playing a *balalaika* and singing Russian Christmas carols.

At the head of the table, Sir George Buchanan, the British ambassador, thanked the padre then indicated to the waiters to start serving. When the priest glanced down the table, Samantha had caught his eye and given him a brief nod. The stocky sixty-year-old priest had been ministering to the large British community in the city for nearly forty years. Earlier that morning, he had conducted the morning mass in the Dmitri Palace's chapel. It had been a small service attended by the Anglo-Russian hospital's English staff. The Russians celebrated the birth of Jesus on January 7th instead of December 25th, since they followed the Julian calendar rather than the Gregorian calendar.

As a waiter poured red wine in her glass, she saw that Meriel Buchanan, sitting opposite her, was in a deep conversation with a British colonel from the military mission that had been sent to help the Russians. At the far end of the table, Meriel's mother, Lady Georgiana, was talking with an aged duchess dressed in a scooped evening dress. Samantha had been impressed by the support Lady Georgiana was providing the hospital.

Much of the discussion at the table was about the recent decision by the Duma rejecting the latest German peace proposals. She had gotten the impression that the two counts were in agreement with the decision. The news in Petrograd was heavily censored, so she wasn't sure how the Russian army was doing in Romania. Since her Russian was rudimentary at best, she didn't get much from her patients.

"Were you pleased that the Duma rejected the German peace proposals?" the Russian colonel on her right asked.

"Of course," replied the ambassador. "Russia is an important ally in the war against Germany. Premier Trepoff has given me assurances that the Russian people would prosecute the war until victory is achieved."

The duchess raised her head, snorted, then said in perfect English, "I'm surprised that the Tsarina gave her permission. You're well aware of her German sympathies."

Samantha noticed the two colonels beside her didn't object. The rumours she had heard were that the Tsar and Tsarina in private spoke English and German to each other. From what Samantha had seen so far, most of the Russian nobility spoke English better than she did.

The ambassador replied in a measured tone. "The Tsarina has been fully supportive of the war effort."

"I wonder how she finds the time," muttered the colonel sitting on her left.

The duchess had heard his comment and jumped on it. "Exactly, especially when she spends all her time with that disgusting man."

Samantha was confused as to whom she was referring to. When she glanced at Meriel, her friend mouthed, "Rasputin."

Meriel had told her of the rumours that swirled around the relationship between the Tsarina and the monk. The rumours were not flattering, and Meriel had assured her there wasn't truth in any of them.

The colonel on her right fingered his wine glass and said, "The man needs to be dealt with."

There was a finality in his tone that surprised Samantha. She wondered what it implied.

"I think," Father Dempsey interceded, "it would be more appropriate to talk about more festive and hopeful things on this day. The day of our Lord's birth."

"Of course, Father," replied Sir George.

BRUAY THEATRE, BRUAY

When the choir started singing, Lieutenant-Colonel Llewellyn was the first in line for the Eucharist. He knew it would take a while for the rest of his regiment to receive a wafer and a sip of sacramental wine. He hoped Father Stoats had calculated the amount of wine he needed correctly. He would have liked to have ordered wine and beer for their Christmas dinner, but it wasn't in the budget and would not have been politic. He knew he would have to deal with some of his men in the morning, who had a bit too much Christmas cheer from other sources.

In the meantime, his men would be enjoying the turkey dinner he had arranged. He managed to book the Bruay Theatre, which was usually used for concerts for the units billeted in the city and the area. Bruay was a large mining town with nearly 18,000 inhabitants. The nearby coal mines were the town's main employers. Most of the men who worked there now were young boys and old men, since those of military service age had been conscripted into the French army. The mines were operating at full tilt, since a large share of the French coal industry was now in German hands.

His men didn't like the town; it was grimy from coal dust. But the shower and bath facilities were first-rate. It was not surprising, since the miners had used them to remove the grime after a long shift underground. Everyone appreciated that tonight, since the men were crammed into the theatre. Llewellyn and his senior officers were sitting at a table placed near the stage. The rest of the hall was covered with white cloth-covered tables that were set with real china and glassware. The heavy dark oak panels and pillars were decorated with red and white bunting. Christmas decorations were hanging from the ceiling, along with Union Jacks and Tricolours. Near the stage, there was a six-foot Christmas tree with boxes of presents underneath to give a semblance of home.

Llewellyn glanced at the stage when he took his seat. An altar had been set up with two lit candles. Behind it, there was a large wooden cross that had wheeled onto the stage. To the left of the altar, a choir formed from the regiment's best vocalists was singing, "Hark! The Herald Angels Sing." A sergeant playing the grand piano beside them was providing accompaniment. Two lines had been formed to receive the Eucharist. Chaplain Hoary from the 1st Brigade HQ had agreed to assist Father Stoats during the Christmas mass. He stood beside the Fusiliers' chaplain as they gave each man a wafer.

The theatre itself was located a short distance from the Bruay Mining Company's administration building in which Major-General Currie had set up his HQ. The general, along with Brigadier-General Loomis, so Llewellyn had been informed, would be dropping by later that evening to give the men their personal Christmas wishes.

When the last of the men had raised his cupped hands to receive his wafer and had taken a sip of wine, Father Stoats and Chaplain Hoary returned to the altar where Stoats cleaned the wafer and wine cups. Once done, Llewellyn saw Stoats turn pages in a prayer book set on the altar. He saw Stoats frown then shut the book as he raised his head to face the hall.

"Now, I won't keep you long from the Christmas dinner that Colonel Llewellyn has promised us." Llewellyn acknowledged with a half-rise from his chair. "We can all smell the roasted turkey." Stoats had to wait until the din from the clinking glasses and a few hoots and hollers to subside before he could continue. "It does remind us of home. For a number of us, this is the third Christmas away from our neighbours, friends, and loved ones. From many, this is a time of sorrow for the friends and comrades we have lost. Let us rise and bow our heads in silence to commemorate their sacrifice." The sound of a thousand chairs scraping on the wooden floor dominated the hall as the men rose to their feet and bowed their heads. After a minute, Father Stoats cleared his throat, breaking the silence. "Now, let us give thanks to the Lord for the meal that we are about to receive. Let's pray and hope that next Christmas we'll be back home in the bosom of our families, safe and sound."

"Amen!" replied Llewellyn and the Fusiliers.

Paul Ryan crossed his arms when Chaplain Mathews offered him a wafer from the small silver plate he was holding. The crossed arms were the proper way to tell the padre he wasn't baptized in the Church of England, was Roman Catholic, and could not partake in the host being offered to him.

The chaplain raised an eyebrow, but without missing a beat, he continued down the line of kneeling men in the gun pit. It was cold enough to see their breath, but the sun was bringing some warmth. The 65th was attached to the 1st Division Artillery Reserve, but they were close enough to the front lines to be called upon to provide support. That was why the padre had ridden out to their position to conduct a Christmas mass.

The men had eaten their breakfast when the greying padre had arrived on his large black rider around ten. They had also by then opened the Christmas gifts and the care packages the postal men had dropped off. There was a faint hint of a smile in the tired, sad eyes of the major when he saw wrapping paper flutter in the slight breeze. A small, scrawny Christmas tree had been decorated, and it was leaning slightly to one of the walls. One thing they could say about the tree was that it was colourful.

The major had tied up his horse near the protected horse stalls then, from his saddle bag, withdrew a white surplice and slipped it over his khaki uniform. He unlaced a dull wooden box sticking out of the right saddlebag and the large canteen that was hanging from the pommel.

"Where can I set up?" he asked. Ryan pointed to the map table set opposite the Christmas tree. He had to remove the range maps and other papers so that the major could set the case on the table. From the case, he removed a white tablecloth then lifted a cross pedestal, two candlesticks, a metal tube, a chalice, and two silver plates.

"Can you call the men for mass?" the padre requested.

The mass seemed rather quick compared with the usual Sunday church parades, but it also felt rather intimate, since there were only his men from the three gun crews. The fourth gun was in the maintenance shop getting the barrel replaced. For most of the mass, he and his men were down on one knee until the communion started, then everyone shifted to kneeling on both knees. The padre had shaken communion wafers from the metal tube onto one of the silver plates, and he then filled the chalice with sacramental wine from his canteen. After he had completed the communion prayer, he made the sign of the cross to indicate the mass was concluded.

"Thank you, Padre, for coming," Paul said as the priest was repacking his case. "The men appreciated it."

"It's my duty and pleasure," replied Mathews.

"Are we your last stop?" Paul asked.

"I'm afraid not, I have several more units I have to visit before the day is over. One of them is the 5th Brigade."

"I understand. We've been tasked to provide them with fire support," Paul replied. The 5th Brigade was launching a raid on the German lines around midnight this evening. Before a raid, some of the units called for a chaplain to give them a blessing before they went over the top. From the padre's bleakness, it was the aftermath he wasn't looking forward to dealing with.

"How are your men holding up?" Mathews asked. The padre was also the unit's morale officer.

Ryan glanced around the gun pit, checking to see if anyone were in earshot. "Between you and me, Padre, I think the men would prefer to have the entire day as leave. We received orders to fire on the Germans this morning."

"Retaliation?"

Ryan shook his head. "It seemed that some of the Germans were getting too friendly, I'm afraid."

When he saw the look in the major's eyes, all that Ryan could say was, "Orders from HQ. Fraternization. There wasn't anything that I could do."

"I know. I know," replied Mathews tonelessly.

ALL SAINTS CHURCH, OTTAWA

The bells of All Saints were calling the parishioners to the morning mass as Borden's car drove up to the grey-white limestone church on the corner of Laurier Street East and Chapel Street. The short flight of stairs that led to the entrance had been cleared from the evening's snowstorm.

When they stepped out of the car, they received warm Christmas greetings from their fellow parishioners. All were dressed in their Sunday best. He noticed a few of the ladies dressed in black scattered among those making their way up Laurier Street. Some of the men wore black armbands to indicate they had lost a family member in France. Still, the Bordens were regulars and were well regarded by the congregation. The church itself was rather young, only sixteen years old, but the congregation had grown to slightly over three hundred families.

Borden glanced at the black wrought iron circular staircase that led to the belfry before stepping into the main hall on their right. The stained glass windows transmuted the sunlight into shades of green, blue, and gold. It reflected on the thirty-two rows of oak pews as he and Laura made their way to their regular seats. They had arrived early because the Christmas mass was usually so overflowing with worshippers that many had to stand during the service.

The pipe organ started up with a few teasing notes as the organist began playing a hymn to get the congregation into the right frame of mind. A moment later, the choir added their voices to the hymn.

Borden glanced around the hall, giving a familiar face a smile and a nod. He felt his tension lessen somewhat. His train trip from Winnipeg to Vancouver had been tiring. He didn't want to, but after the church service he would drop off Laura at the house and then go into the office. He would rather spend the day enjoying a relaxing Christmas Day, but the usual pile waited for him. And he still had to send off his seasonal greetings to the Empire's leaders. At least things had begun to settle down in England after Prime Minister Herbert Asquith resigned. Lloyd George, who had been the minister of war, had replaced him as prime minister.

He also had to prepare for the meeting with the senior leadership of the Trade and Labour Congress who were in Ottawa. Its president, James Watters, had the usual long list of demands such as reducing the workday from ten hours to nine, time and a half for overtime, and better working conditions in the war industries. But the main problem was that they believed his policy on National Service was a prelude to conscription. He sighed. All he could do was state that it was not his intention that National Service be used for conscription. He wasn't, however, about to take conscription off the table, especially if the recruitment rates continued to drop.

All further thoughts about politics were banished when he saw the altar boys line up before Archdeacon Mackay. It indicated the procession would be starting shortly. He fished for his hymnbook and turned it to the appropriate page so he could join in with the choir when the procession started.

CHAPTER 30

Samantha cocked an eyebrow at Christine, who was sitting in the back seat of the Renault. Misha, their driver, was in an upbeat mood as he drove them to the Anglo-Russian hospital. He normally picked them up in the morning. It saved them the trouble of hailing a horse drawn *droshky*, or, God forbid, the tram. With the number of strikes in the city, it would have been faster to walk to the hospital. Christine hadn't given up on renting a palace, but their current apartment in the English quarter was quite comfortable.

"So there are rumours that Rasputin is dead?" asked Samantha.

Misha peered over his shoulder at her. A smile cracked his grey-streaked beard as he answered, "*Da!*"

"How did he die?" asked Christine. She had heard, as had Samantha, some of the outlandish stories about the relationship between the monk and the Tsarina.

"Noblemen shot bastard," replied Misha as he returned his gaze to the road. He blared his horn to avoid a Cossack riding his horse. The Cossack waved an angry fist at them as they continued to barrel down the cobbled street.

"Where was he shot?" asked Samantha.

"Don't know, body not found," he answered as he pulled up the front of the Dmitri Palace. "People happy him gone."

Samantha noticed Misha's shoulders tense when he spotted the extra set of guards standing beside the Anglo-Russian Hospital's coat of arms set in the wall of the front entrance. The coat of arms displayed a British lion and a Russian Imperial Eagle grasping a Red Cross. Samantha recognized the *Preobrazhensky* Lifeguard Regiment insignia they wore. It was the same insignia of the two Russian counts she had met at the British Embassy's Christmas party. Meriel had warned her that the regiment provided support to the Okhrana, the Russian Secret Service.

The cold stares she and Christine received as they made their way through to the main lobby made them nervous.

"*Vashi dokumenty*," the tall captain standing just inside the doors demanded brusquely.

"What does he want?" asked Christine with some tension in her voice.

"He wants our passports," said Samantha. "I think?"

She felt some relief when she saw Captain Kruschev come hurriedly down the stairs. He spoke rapidly to the Lifeguard captain when he reached them. Samantha's Russian hadn't developed to the point that she could follow the conversation. When the guard captain barked an order, Captain Kruschev stiffened to attention. He then turned to Samantha and Christine and said in a neutral tone, "Your passports, please."

Samantha eyed both captains. What she didn't realize until later was that the Lifeguard captain was a grade or two higher than Captain Kruschev.

"Of course," replied Samantha as she pulled out from the inner pocket of her coat a green Russian internal passport. She had to surrender her Canadian passport to the local authorities when she arrived in Petrograd. The passport had her description and her address. The Russians imposed strict travel restrictions within their borders. Christine handed hers over as well. The officer read the passports then scanned them up and down. He snapped them closed and handed them back. After he had dismissed them with a salute, Captain Kruschev escorted them up the staircase.

Near the top, out of earshot, Samantha asked, "Captain, what's going on?"

Kruschev grimaced as he scanned left and right before saying, "Count Dmitri is under house arrest."

"What for?" whispered Christine in surprise as she stared down the staircase towards the count's apartments.

"The Tsarina thinks Count Dmitri had Rasputin killed," replied Kruschev softly.

"Oh, dear," Samantha murmured. "How is that going to impact the hospital?"

"I don't know," replied the captain in an uncertain tone. "I don't know."

RICHMOND FUSILIERS HEADQUARTERS, BRUAY

"Make sure you make a note in the war diary that I will be accompanying General Currie on his trip to Verdun, starting tomorrow," Lieutenant-Colonel Llewellyn said to Corporal Hicks. Hicks was nodding as he made notes on a scrap of paper beside the field telephone. "When you're finished typing, it I'll take a look at it."

"Yes, sir," replied Corporal Hicks.

Normally, Major Gavin was responsible for updating the Richmond Fusiliers' war diaries daily. Once he had reviewed it and initialled it, they were forwarded to Corps HQ and the Canadian Records Office in London. He recalled a memo about the importance of keeping accurate records for future historians. He wondered for a moment what they would make of the war in twenty or thirty years. It was one of the bureaucratic tasks he had to deal with. He had perused the year's diaries to make sure that there wasn't anything major that had been missed. At the beginning of the year, they had been in Lieutenant-Colonel Tennison's handwriting. Llewellyn had received a letter from him letting him know that he was back in Toronto. When he had taken over preparing them, someone had complained they couldn't read his handwriting. So now they were typed. He had to admit the typed versions were easier to read, though he didn't think his handwriting that bad. As he had read them, they pulled out memories of the men that were no longer here.

He did hope that Samantha was having an easier time of it in Russia. He had enjoyed reading her letter that he received just before Christmas.

At least for the next week or so he wouldn't have to deal with it. He was taking a few days of leave before joining Major-General Currie when he visited Verdun for three days or so next week. Lieutenant-General Byng had asked him to talk with the French on their experiences fending off the massive German assault on that front and to learn as much as he could on how they had managed to do that.

"I need to chat with Major Gavin before I go," said Llewellyn. The major would be the acting CO while he was away.

"He's over at the training ground. He is putting A Company through the company drill."

"Good, they were starting to get sloppy. I noticed some of the men weren't at the church parade this morning."

"I've spoken with the medical officer. Some of the men have come down with the grippe. Nothing serious, but they'll be off duty for a few days."

"Okay. I also want the company commanders to warn the men about saluting. I've gotten complaints from some of the senior officers again," Llewellyn stated.

"Yes, sir," replied the corporal.

"Now, is everything set for this evening?"

"Yes, sir. We've managed to book the YMAC. The men aren't going to like it because it's dry," Hicks said.

"Well, it can't be helped," replied Llewellyn. "At least they'll have plenty of fruit punch to bring in the new year."

65TH FIELD ARTILLERY, 1ST DIVISIONAL RESERVES, BRUAY

When the Fullerphone buzzed, Lieutenant Ryan watched Sergeant Reggie answer it. "Batt 65," he replied, stating their unit designation.

"Yes, SZ 15. What can I do for you?" asked the sergeant. Each trench section had been given a code name to prevent identification of the actual units in the trench in case their communications were intercepted by the Germans. "You spotted a flash. Okay, what are the coordinates?" he asked as he picked up a yellow pencil and began scribbling on a notepad. "Repeat the coordinates. N.36.a.95. Good. Keep your head down."

"What do we have?" asked Lieutenant Ryan as he leaned over the map table.

"The FOO at the 1st Battalion spotted muzzle flashes about here?" he said, pointing to a square on the map.

"Mortars or artillery?" Ryan asked.

"They said mortars."

"Okay," replied Ryan. He glanced at the flag flapping in the wind. It had been a grey, cloudy day, and there was a twenty-five-miles-per-hour cross wind. At least the previous two days of rain had stopped. He then looked back at the map. They were within range — barely.

"Hmm," Ryan said as he rubbed his chin. "What do you think, three rounds of shrapnel?"

The sergeant shrugged. "Should make them dance a bit. Serves them right after we spent all that time preparing for the CO's inspection."

Ryan chuckled. The battery had been inspected by the 65th's CO after the morning church parade. He was suitably pleased that everything was in order, but like every inspection, the CO would zero in on what Ryan had missed during his pre-inspection.

"Okay, let HQ know we're firing a salvo in retaliation," he told the sergeant. "Then get SZ 15 on the line and inform them that we're firing a salvo. And to let us know if we need to make corrections. The wind is going to play havoc with our accuracy."

"Yes, Lieutenant," the sergeant replied as he started speaking in the phone's receiver. Corporal Michaels was shouting at the gun crew to start preparing to fire.

Ryan watched them gloomily for a moment. This was the second New Year that he was spending firing shells at the enemy.

PRIME MINISTER'S HOME GLENSMERE, OTTAWA

"It will be the new year in a couple of hours," said Lady Borden as she sipped her tea. She was sitting in the parlour with a black honey-comb shawl draped over her shoulders. Even with the fire crackling in the fireplace, she felt the chill from the subzero temperature outside."

"I know," Sir Borden said with a sigh. He was sitting comfortably in the wing chair opposite hers. He was happy to take some time to think and relax after the usual busy day of returning New Year's greetings from the various heads of states he had received. He also had meetings with several of his cabinet ministers to discuss the situation in Quebec. "I'm glad that the year is over."

Lady Borden met his eyes. "It's been a difficult and trying year."

'The way it started, I wasn't hopeful I would be able to live through it." He shifted slightly as he recalled the pain that had disabled him at the beginning of the year for a month. He didn't want to remember that, or the disasters that had befallen him in the past year.

"I know," replied Lady Borden. It hadn't been a very good year for her either. They would have loved to be down south enjoying the more temperate climes of the States.

"At least God gave me the strength to survive and to carry on my work."

"I'm glad as well," she replied as she sipped her tea. "I do hope the New Year will bring us some good fortune."

"So do I, so do I," replied Borden.

The story continues in

TEMPERING THE BLADE

By 1917, the Canadians have been honed to a sharp edge, but a brittle blade can break.

In Russia, Nursing Sister Samantha Lonsdale finds herself in the middle of the Bolshevik revolution. She and her patients at the Anglo-Russian Hospital in Petrograd are caught in the crossfire as they dodge machine gun fire. When Russia is knocked out of the war, the hard choice is to leave her patients behind when she is evacuated to England.

In France, infantry officer Lieutenant-Colonel Llewellyn and artillery officer Lieutenant Ryan need to harden their resolve. The Canadian Corps is ordered to capture the formidable Vimy Ridge. The French and the English have tried before, with devastating casualties. Now, it's the Canadian Corps' turn.

In Canada, the 50th anniversary of Confederation is tempered by the Corps' horrendous losses. More is to come at Passchendaele. With more men needed at the sharp end, Borden calls for conscription in the middle of a vicious election campaign that threatens to tear the country apart.

As the year comes to a close, the heat of battle has hardened and tempered the Canadians into a flexible steel blade.

For latest news and updates visit
www.sambiasebooks.ca

Lightning Source UK Ltd.
Milton Keynes UK
UKHW010629050221
378309UK00001B/205